Between

The

Lines

Between

The

Lines

Victoria Mae

The characters and events portrayed in this book are fictitious. Any similarity to real persons, living or dead, is coincidental and not intended by the author.

ISBN: 9798376797808

Cover design by: James Thomsit
Printed in the United Kingdom

For the brides, the dreamers, and the adventure seekers.

Prologue

USA – UK
Los Angeles – London

Wednesday
Depart Los Angeles International Airport at 22:05

Thursday
Arrive London Heathrow at 15:25 (GMT)
Duration: 10 hours and 20 minutes
Time change: London 7 hours ahead

Wiggling my toes further into the sand, and surrendering to the hypnotic soundtrack of the ocean, were usually two things that made my heart and soul sing. But not today. Definitely not today. Numbly, I gaze out at the storm clouds on the horizon, oblivious to the fact that my unusually tamed hair and ivory dress are both soaking wet. I lift my hands to my face; *are these tears or drops of rain*? Meshed together, I can't tell anymore. I hear a distant voice; is it him? Turning, I see only Becky, and I howl in pain, as I always do. But wait, there's another voice? I hear it. *Where? Where are you? Where?*

'Excuse me.' I feel a tap on my arm jolt me awake from my recurring nightmare. Lifting my eye mask to my forehead, I check my face for tears (*all clear*), then adjust my noise cancelling headphones, putting one earpiece to the side. 'This is awkward,' my Flynn Rider looking neighbour purrs in what he assumes is a charming tone, 'but is there any way you could keep to your side of the armrest? This is premium economy; it's not like you've not got enough room!'

'Oh, I'm sorry,' I say, embarrassed, 'Was I on your side, in my sleep?'

'On my side, practically in my lap; whacking me in the face with that mane of hair.'

'Excuse me!?' I say with widening eyes, lifting my arms up and over my large, signature messy bun, to hang my headphones completely around my neck.

'I hate to say, but you might even want to perhaps adjust it.' He lowers his voice and says in a snarky tone, 'Even on top of your head, it's insane.'

'And why the hell should I do that?' I frown at his stupidly handsome face and annoyingly perfect cocoa brown hair. He's probably a model.

'Because it's everywhere; you were literally shoving it up my nose when your head swooshed my way, thrashing about in your dream.'

Heat rockets through me, from my cosy travel-sock clad feet, to my face. *I was thrashing? I don't normally thrash.*

'I'd really appreciate it.' His infuriatingly friendly, yet confused, surfer dude accent softens, but I'm brimming with anger. 'Thanks so much.' He puts his headphone earbuds back in and taps the screen in front of him for his documentary to play once more.

After a moment of shock, I rip the headphone cord out of his armrest. 'How unbelievably rude are you?!'

'I believe the question is,' he shifts his body to face me,

while taking out an ear bud, and lifting his aqua blue eyes around the outline of the make-shift pineapple on top of my head, 'how inconsiderate are *you*? Do you block the view of people in large crowds? I suppose only for the vertically challenged like yourself.' Being a writer, I'm rarely lost for words, but my mouth hangs open, speechless. 'But going back,' he flicks his hair, and it falls effortlessly back into place, 'I'd really appreciate a little,' he gestures around him, 'spatial awareness from my travelling neighbour.' *I am mortified.* 'I nearly said something as you were scoffing down dinner, but didn't have the heart to, so,' he looks me up and down, then he adds, 'you should be grateful; I've been tolerant for five hours.'

'Well, how incredibly restrained you are!' I reply with sarcastic outrage. Wriggling out of my blanket to sit up properly, I turn to completely face him. 'You are possibly the rudest man I—'

'And by the way,' he cuts me off, and my mouth remains open, 'when you were writing earlier, you used a preposition at the end of your article.' He gestures to my laptop, neatly folded away in the pouch in the seat in front of me. 'You might want to fix that. Now, if you excuse me, I'd like to get back to *Blue Planet*.' He slowly pulls at the end of his headphones that are still clutched tightly in my hands.

What an arsehole! My body, now pumping with adrenaline, is most definitely awake. I rub my eyes, in order to calm down rather than wipe away any sleepiness. Taking a deep breath, I annoyingly feel the need to retie my hair. Smiling, I make a real effort to dramatically take the band out in my right hand up, out and over into his space before swinging my head like a girl in a shampoo advert. When I'm sure I've flicked him in the face at least twice, (*nicely done,*

Liv), I fluff it up a little more. My curls spring animatedly into action, as if they've heard the insults and are ready to defend themselves, and I actually laugh out loud before swooping it all up and into as confined a bun as it will go.

Glancing to my right I note he's staring intently at his screen — *do I detect tears in his eyes? No. Can't be.* Must be the dehydration of the plane, the three rums he had, or the length of the flight. Or, he probably hasn't slept for almost five hours, unlike me. Smiling to myself, I feel grateful; I always sleep well on planes. They're like a second home to me. Yawning, I stretch a little, trying this time not to affect my Disney character look-alike neighbour, then my mind goes back to my dream. Why do I keep returning there? It's done. I'm over it, aren't I? Automatically, my lips press together, and I subconsciously start playing with the ring on my right hand as I sigh. *You know you're not over it, Liv.* All the travel in the world hasn't helped me get over it, has it? Leaning forwards, I prize my laptop and open it, deciding to put all my energy and focus into writing. I nod to encourage myself. Writing is my home camp. I get lost in a world of prose and love the fact that my fingers dance across the keys without knowing what steps I even wanted to take, but suddenly, it's happening. Again, I glance at my neighbour, he's still making a huge effort to stare at his screen. While it's booting up — my computer, not his screen — I lift the visor to my left slightly to see outside, and the light dazzles us both.

'Bloody hell!' he snaps, in an angry stage whisper, reaching across me, and slamming it back down. 'They say, "leave it down," for a reason! Have you never flown before? What the hell is wrong with you?'

Well, there's a complex question. 'No need for the

attitude man! Sorry! Just wanted to see where we are.'

'Then look at your on-screen map, you idiot.' Angrily, he taps the screen in front of me and I see we're somewhere over the Labrador Sea.

'And,' I sit up a little taller, and say proudly, 'I'm a frequent flyer, actually.'

'Is that so?' he replies dryly, without an ounce of interest.

'Yeah, I used to be a travel blogger, then I transitioned into writing about weddings,' I find my mouth saying before my brain's in gear, 'but I *um...*' I stutter, 'moved back into travel writing. I'm a travel writer,' I conclude. *Why did I feel the need to share that?*

Narrowing his eyes at me, he almost snarls, 'So, you're a what?' He looks me up and down, 'A 30-something—'

'*Twenty-eight* actually,' I correct him, with a frown.

'Fine, late-twenties, wannabe wanderluster? That's mature.'

I narrow my eyes at him, this time, unable to keep the spite out of my voice, 'Well, you seem to have me all figured out, don't you.' *What is this guy's problem?*

'And anyway, I didn't ask for your backstory, Brave.'

'Brave?' I ask, bemused.

He huffs, 'Princess Merida?'

I frown, 'What? Who's that?'

'You know? Merida.' I shrug as my expression stays blank, so he taps my screen again, goes into "Movies for Kids" and selects the Disney classic, *Brave*. He grins at me, 'I swear you look just like her.'

I frown again, 'My hair isn't red.'

'No,' he agrees, taking in my caramel brown and sun kissed blonde locks, before smirking, 'but the...' he pauses and a little chuckle comes out, '*volume* is the same.'

'Do you always feel the need to insult complete strangers?'

Something resembling apologetic washes over his expression for a mere moment before his face returns to a frown. 'Only when I'm easily provoked.'

Narrowing my eyes once more, I vow to ignore him for the rest of the flight. Somewhere between finishing my latest article, eating (self-consciously slow after his comments), and watching *La La Land*, we touch down, and the air steward announces,

'Ladies and gentlemen, welcome to London Heathrow. The local time is a little before three thirty in the afternoon. We hope you enjoyed your flight with us today from Los Angeles, and we look forward to seeing you again in the very near future. Have a safe trip or welcome home!'

Unbuckling my seat belt, I bend down, whip off my travel socks and slip my trainer-socked feet into my cute little brown ankle boots. Collecting my handbag, I throw the travel socks in, place my laptop in its case, then give myself a little sneaky spritz of my favourite revitalising spray from Barton-Reynolds, and I'm ready to roll.

My neighbour frowns at the product, and then at me, 'You know not everyone on this plane wants to smell like lavender, camomile and orange.'

Hmm. He's got a good nose. 'It's refreshing!' I defend.

'It's unnecessary,' he barks at me, before attempting to gather his things.

Stopping myself from pouting, I look down at the little spray bottle, and take in the label: an ocean wave curl at sunset. *Well, I love it.* Deciding to ignore him, I fiddle with my turquoise braided boho stack of bracelets that decorate my right wrist and sit, waiting patiently for the doors to open, loving the fact that I always travel light. Everybody around me is flustered and in a huge rush to gather everything together as fast as they can, in order to race out of the plane; I always find that ridiculously amusing. Flynn Rider here next to me, is no different, and has belongings all over the place. He's now shoving one item after the other into a backpack that's already full to the brim: screwed up pieces of clothing; a couple of camera lenses; he adds a John Grisham novel that was down the back of the seat in front; a copy of the latest issue of *National Geographic*; water; peanuts saved from our snack earlier; the premium class complimentary pack; his laptop; and batteries that he was charging, along with the charger. Now, he's fishing around in this overstuffed holdall, as people start to file out.

'Anytime today would be great,' I find myself saying, ever so slightly smugly.

'I packed in a hurry, OK?!' he snaps rather defensively. 'I just need to find my passport.' He now buries his whole arm and roots around.

'By all means take your time! It's not like I have anywhere to be!' I smile at the turning tables, then he waves his blue-cased American passport at me.

'Got it.'

Huh, American? He sounded Australian to me.

We finally stand then shuffle down the aisle and out of the aircraft with the others; I thank the air staff as I go while he ignores them completely. He's still silently beside me as we climb the ramp to the terminal, then head towards passport control.

'You know,' I look up at him as I walk fast to keep up with his long-legged strides, through the surprisingly empty terminal, 'packing with less is really the secret to great flying; only pack what you absolutely can get away with. You can always do laundry along the way or buy the odd thing or two. Just need to make sure that it can all fit in the minimal space you have. Also: rolling clothes. Now, that's a great space saver,' I say, in what I think is a helpful manner as we reach immigration.

'Thanks; next time I'll try that,' he replies sarcastically while looking up at the signs for which queue to join. 'Well, have a nice life, Brave. Hope we don't meet again.' Giving me a tight smile, he strides off towards, "Non-UK/EU/EEA."

Charming.

Chapter 1

UK
London

'Hi Bob!' I greet him warmly with a big hug. 'I wasn't expecting you; I was just going to hop on the Tube!' Letting go, I smile at this snowy-haired man, who's always been like a grandad to me rather than the main chauffeur for *Wonder*.

'Couldn't have my favourite girl take public transport now, could I? Here,' he offers me a Costa to-go cup, which I accept gratefully.

'Oh, thanks. What about the budget cuts?' I ask as Bob grabs my case, then gestures for us to walk towards the car park.

'The magazine picked my hours back up, so you might see a bit more of me!' He winks, clearly knowing something I don't, but moves on, 'So how was your trip, Liv? Tell me all about it!'

'Oh, I loved writing this latest piece: hidden and off-the beaten track spots in LA.' I grin, my mind automatically goes back there, 'I think hands-down, one of my favourites was Malibu; it's got these beautiful houses right on Carbon Beach or Billionaire's Beach as it's called, and can you believe that the public can access it? I went first thing in the morning and literally had the entire place to myself.' I shake my head, smiling. 'Crazy.'

'Anyone we've met live there?' He's driven many a

celebrity to and from the airport to our HQ on Kensington High Street, for more years than I've been alive.

'Mainly CEOs, business tycoons, a couple celebs I think; oh, Courtney Cox used to live there!'

'I did like her,' he smiles.

***

As we whisk along the M4, Bob nods his head and makes impressed noises as I tell him about this insanely cool rooftop cinema I went to in downtown LA. 'Get this: you envelop yourself in these huge deckchairs, then the films are projected onto the side of the building. It was right at sunset, and you got two free drinks with your ticket, and unlimited popcorn! I'm telling you; it was absolute bliss!'

He chuckles and signals to move back over to the slow lane, always the cautious driver.

'So, any idea what this meeting is about?' he asks kindly as we travel past Hyde Park.

'None.' I open the bottle of water that's sitting waiting for me in the passenger seat; I could never get used to sitting in the back when being driven.

'Janice has really got her back up about something; her email was short and sharp. You think she would give me the day off for goodness' sake!'

When we pull up in front of *Wonder* HQ, Bob turns to me and smiles kindly, 'Well, good luck, kid. I'll see you very soon.' He gives me a nod, telepathically telling me, no matter what it is, I'll be fine.

Opening the grand, ornamental double doors of the Art Deco building, I grin. I've always loved the fact that I work on Kensington High Street; out of the office and into the shops if need be! Our magazine is for women, and covers not only fashion and beauty, but business and pleasure, with a mix of mindfulness, and spirituality; loving and living your best life, at your pace, with your rules. I love it. But admittedly, it hasn't been the same since Becky left.

Getting into the lift, I yawn, still fuzzy from the flight. I can't wait to get home and have a nice hot bath.

***

The sand is soft, and the sky is dark. *Why am I here? I hate it here. Is this happening again?* The waves crash against the beach and spray me slightly, but I'm soaked anyway: drowning in my own tears. How can the elements compete with that? I lift my hands to my face, and I hear a distant voice as I always do; was it him this time? Had he come back for me? I knew there must have been a misunderstanding! I knew in my heart there had to be an explanation. I turn and see only Becky, and I howl in pain, as I always do. But wait, there's another voice? I hear it. *Where? Where are you? Where?*

'Liv...Olivia...Hello?' A distant, wafty voice calls from somewhere.

What is that?

'I think she's actually out of it.'

Hmm? Why does my face hurt? Was that a flash?

'Ha! Got it.'

'Seriously, Liv you've got to open your eyes.' I feel a nudge in my ribs.

Ugh, my hand's asleep. Wait. Am I asleep? Where am I? The last thing I remember, I was at a meeting. When did I get home? Oh no.

Opening half an eye, I dart it around: sideways conference room; colleagues laughing; one of the barely 20-somethings from the beauty department snaps a photo of me, and my notebook pillow. *Oh shit.* I sit up slowly, feigning dignity to the sound of applause, unsticking my bracelets from my face, before opening the other eye and simultaneously wiping away the drool as I go. *I'm never going to live this down.*

'Nice to have you back in the land of the living, Liv. So pleased I can keep your attention. As I was saying...' Janice winks at me, then returns to her usual stride around the room, gesticulating her tiny hands as she talks. I stiffen and gently try to stretch my back without anyone noticing.

What time is it?

Casually, I turn my left arm and observe the clock-face of my watch: 10:30? AM? PM? Oh, no wait, I haven't changed it to London time; that's, *um,* what? Day-light savings for LA, but not us yet, so, seven hours, not eight, making it five thirty in the evening here. Man, I could murder a coffee. Leaning forward I pick up an empty cafetière; pout and then put it back down.

'...which involves Liv.'

What?

All faces are on me again. *Good Lord, I need to wake up.* I look blankly back at the room. 'I'm sorry, I wasn't listening,' I decide to be honest. 'Jetlag,' I defend.

Janice doesn't smile this time. *Whoops.*

'I said, I've got an important announcement and it heavily involves...you.'

Oh my God, I'm getting the sack for falling asleep.

Everyone watches this exchange, pinging their heads from one side of the table to the other, like following a tennis match.

'Quite the little nap you took there.' Janice stands with her hands on her hips. I sit up straight, making an effort not to lean my back on the chair, or place my head on the table once more, which looks surprisingly comfy in my dazed state. She exhales, and claps her hands together, 'So, here it is, Liv.'

Yup, I'm losing my job.

'It's no secret that we've been having problems here at the magazine.' The tension in the room is so thick, you could cut it with a knife.

'*Um hmm.*' I nervously play with my bracelet.

'Well, a solution has fallen into my hands, and I want to grab it. But it very much involves you.'

'OK.' *Yup, she's letting me go. I'll just clear out my desk now.*

'Financially, we are *not* thriving, to say the least, and for a while it was looking like I was going to have to lose several members of the team.' She takes out a piece of paper from the folder in front of her, walks around to my side of the table, and then pauses before handing it to me. 'What do you know about *Blush*?'

'The wedding magazine?' I scrunch my nose in distaste.

'The very one,' she nods.

'*Um*, not much really.' That's a complete lie. It used to be based in New York, then when Matthew Leon became Editor and Chief, their headquarters moved to Los Angeles. It's fun, fresh, fast-paced, and in another life, I would have given anything to work there; I even emailed them my CV once, in the hope that they'd find a position for me. 'It's a bridal magazine,' I choose to say out loud.

'Not *just* a bridal magazine! It's *the* bridal magazine. Top in the world, actually. And as sheer dumb luck would have it, an opportunity has, very recently, spectacularly presented itself.'

'You're giving me the sack but want me to write for a bridal magazine?' I ask, slowly.

'Not exactly.' Janice gives me the piece of paper and I attempt to take it all in. It's a spreadsheet of dates, locations, a myriad of hotels and flight numbers, and a mysterious column entitled, "Couples" under which has "A" through to "I." Dazed and confused, my eyes lift back up, into hers.

Janice begins her signature stride around the room once more, 'Our top three sponsors have left us. However, Chrissy Von Helm is a big fan. Do you know who she is, Liv?'

'She owns half the world's magazines,' I say with confidence; she's also Becky's boss.

'That's right. I had a call from her lawyers two days ago. The theme of their upcoming issue will be: International Weddings. Apart from various designers and what have you, I know there'll be several wedding shows or fayres, around the world, and a rather important feature; this is where you come in, Liv. It's a competition piece, which will act as a crossover/transition article for us. If it's successful, Ms. Von Helm will add *Wonder* to her umbrella.'

'And if it's not?' I dare to ask.

Her expression changes. 'Then our next issue will be our last.'

I swallow. 'I didn't realise we were in that much trouble.' An occupational hazard of rarely being in the office over the past year, I guess. I look around at my colleagues, who are raising eyebrows at each other. Did the whole room have to be here for this conversation? I feel like a show pony on parade.

'So, the piece of paper in your hands is a detailed breakdown of everything you'll need for the next month.'

'A month!?' I can't help but say, louder than intended.

Janice nods, 'Starting tomorrow.'

'Starting tomorrow?!' I sit up, wide-eyed.

She doesn't respond to my mild hysteria, instead she continues, 'Like I said, they're, or rather, *you're*, doing a long-term competition piece. There are nine hometown or destination weddings; as you can see, they're all over the world.'

'All over the world?' I can't help but parrot her once more, as I look at the paper again, and scan down, 'Around the world in a month? That's not possible, is it?'

'It is. Obviously, it's no problem for the UK ones, but there's time allowed for plane delays, time zones, etc. They've done a lot of planning on this; you're in good hands.'

'I'm sorry,' I wave my hand at her, 'I don't understand. If this is such a big piece, then surely there's a writer already in place?'

'There was. She did all the groundwork, research, interviews, and yesterday, got herself sacked; consequently taking all her notes with her. But, I've been informed that all the couples have been contacted, saying that there's been a change in staffing, and know that you'll interview them as you go along.'

'OK,' I take this in. 'But' I can't help but ask, 'Why me?'

'Due to your background, your CV that they had on file, and the fact that Becky vouched for you.'

'Becky?'

'Yes.' Janice looks at me as though I'm slow. 'Your best friend who used to work here, who moved to Singapore?'

'Wait. She's involved in this?'

Janice nods. 'As Fashion Director of one of Ms. Von Helm's magazines, she's in charge of the Singapore Wedding Show that's being featured in this *Blush* issue.' I don't understand how she managed to wangle this for me, but I'll call her later to find out. I shake my head to take all this in, but Janice keeps talking. 'So, the plan is: you are going to replace the woman who got sacked, do a fantastic job and save all of ours in the meantime, and even be back in time for our Annual Spring Bash, where we'll either be celebrating or parting ways!' Janice grins at me, but it's more threatening than friendly.

No pressure then. I sigh, taking this all in. 'But, I don't do that anymore; I'm a travel writer,' *and I hate weddings*, I add silently, folding my arms.

'Exactly. You are perfect for the piece: a wedding blogger turned travel writer; I couldn't have designed it better myself! And besides, you've been to many of these places before, so, you've got the experience and know-how; your jabs are all up to date, and visas are still in place, apart from Canada, but we've done that for you, and it should be in place by the time you get there. Your tone, your voice, they've requested it. They've requested *you*.'

All my colleagues are staring at me with a mix of envy, fear and joy. I'm so embarrassed. 'Well, that's very flattering Janice, but…'

'Liv, I don't think you quite understand what I'm saying here.' She marches back around to my side of the table and leans in so close I can smell the coffee and afternoon blueberry muffin on her breath, 'I'm not asking you to do this; I'm telling you.'

***

By the time I stumble through my front door, tripping over my unopened mail on the floor, it's super late. Pulling my case along with one hand and cradling the pile of *Blush* magazines Janice gave me for, to quote Hermione: "a little light reading," in the other, I kick my door closed. Janice wanted to go over every possible way to make the article a success, but by the end of our meeting, I was admittedly mostly nodding absent-mindedly. Now, all I want to do is pass out. Instead, I place the magazines on the kitchen counter, then wheel my case over to the washing machine, empty the entire contents into it, all mixed colours and fabrics, and throw in a trusty colour-catcher.

I turn on my year-round fairy lights that are all over my apartment, then sit on one of the bar stools in the kitchen. Unwrapping my six-inch veggie patty from Subway that I bought on the way home, taking a huge, unladylike bite, I start to make a list of everything I need to do tonight to get ready. Rubbing my eyes, and shaking my head, I realise I need something to keep me awake. Looking around the kitchen for some inspiration, I spot two bottles: vanilla vodka and Kahlúa. *Yes.* I stand and make a shot of espresso, take some ice out of the freezer and place it into a shaker, then mix the cocktail. Pouring my espresso martini out into a beautiful cocktail glass, I can't help but put two coffee beans onto the foam, and smile at the presentation. Whipping out my phone, I bend down to get the framing right, and take a picture to send to Becky, even though it's, what? I quickly do the maths in my head, *eight hours ahead, so, six in the morning,* in Singapore. Becky can pick this up when she's awake.

"*Cheers to you. Ring me when you can xx*" I add, as the caption to the WhatsApp message and press send. No sooner have I sat back down on my stool, my phone sings to announce a WhatsApp video call.

'I'm sorry, I didn't wake you, did I?' I balance the phone on the vodka bottle and take in my beautiful, but rather sweaty friend.

'Nope; just finished a *Yoga with Adriene* workout.'

I sigh, 'Man, I miss doing yoga.'

Becky leans into the phone, 'You know, you don't have to miss it, right? You're continuing to *choose* to miss it.'

'I know.'

She reads my expression and knows not to continue, 'So, what's up? What are we toasting?' She adjusts one of her AirPods with a hand that's also holding a water bottle, while walking through her immaculate apartment.

'You've got me on an around the world trip.'

'I have?' She takes a sip of water then puts it down as she passes a table.

'Yeah, you recommended me, so I'm going back to being a wedding reporter,' I say, ever so flatly, before taking a sip of my drink; *damn, that's good.*

'Oh, the *Blush* thing! Great!' She dabs her face with a towel.

'And how did you make that happen?'

'We weren't given any details as to why, but everybody at my magazine got an email, directly from Chrissy Von Helm yesterday, asking if anyone had a connection with an experienced wedding reporter, for a *Blush* competition piece.' She looks at my expression then continues, 'OK, look, two years ago, it would have been your dream job, and I know you're thinking you're truly the worst person to cover a wedding right now, but I couldn't *not* recommend you! Are you mad?' She adds softly.

I smile at my friend; I know she meant well, 'To be honest, I'm not sure how I feel.' Staring into my glass, I push one of the coffee beans into the foam and watch it bob back up again.

Becky opens a door and sits on a chair on her balcony. 'I know the matrimonial twist isn't exactly ideal for you, but an around the world trip? Come on! You'll love it, especially since it means you can continue globe-trotting; this last year, you've spent more time travelling, than in that flat,' she points at the phone.

Stopping myself from denying it, I take this opportunity to take another sip; we both know that's true. Becky and I just look at each other, and I know she's reading my mind: the past year has had nothing to do with travelling and everything to do with running away and avoiding my feelings.

'So, tell me all about it. What's involved?'

I scratch my head and feel my curls getting wilder as I go. 'Well, I get an all-expenses paid, around the world trip, for four.'

'Four? Who are they? Anyone we know?' She used to head up the beauty team at *Wonder,* before she transitioned into Fashion Director status, for Singapore's top fashion magazine.

'Nope. They're all from *Blush.* I'm meeting them tomorrow: a hair and makeup person, an overall stylist, a photographer and me; I'm going around the world with three strangers, writing about weddings.' I pause and suddenly want to burst out crying.

'You'll be fine,' she reassures.

'It's a lot of pressure, Bex. Plus,' I take another sip, 'I'm afraid that I'll sabotage something because of...' I pause and make a face, 'you know, *everything*, and I'll screw up.'

'What's to screw up?' She tilts her head to one side.

'I don't know, there's a lot to catch up on. You know Janice gave me this entire stack of *Blush* magazines to read before I go?' I angle the camera to show her.

'Yikes. Have you read any of them?'

'Of course not.' I pick up the top one to show her, 'But, on the Tube home, I drew a nice pair of horns and a tail on one of them; what do you think?' Bex laughs, as I shake my head, and throw the magazine back onto the pile. 'Man, you should see this spreadsheet she gave me too; it's intense!' I whip it out of my bag and wave it at her. 'This thing has been in the works for a year already, and I found out about it hours ago. People wrote in, described every detail of their wedding and these guys were picked. They get their makeup, hair, styling and photography all for free, to be interviewed and featured in the magazine.'

'Really? How can you do that with someone you've just met? I used to need at least three meetings with someone before their event went ahead.'

'All the couples have been working with the existing team for ages: online meetings, everything consulted and decided already, and anything that needs to be picked up, has been organised with each bridal party.'

'Amazing.'

'So, how many weddings are there?'

'Nine,' I say flatly.

'Nine?' she laughs. 'Oh, Liv, I'm so sorry.'

'Yup. Olivia Bennett: around the world in nine weddings!'

We just sit in comfortable silence for a moment before Bex changes the subject, ‘I miss you; you know. And I miss those. Rory just doesn’t make them like you do.’ She looks enviously at my drink as I take another sip.

‘Well, you know if you hadn’t married that gorgeous husband of yours and moved to your dream destination, you could be sitting here, right now, with me, drinking one of these?’ I take another delicious sip.

She smiles at me. ‘Well, I’m free for cocktails!’ she says with a fake bright smile.

‘You are?’ I say, sadly.

She shrugs, ‘Well, probably. I’m late, but I’m not getting my hopes up.’ She’s been trying to get pregnant for the last year. ‘So, anyway,’ she moves on quickly, clearly not wanting to talk about it. ‘Oh,’ her tone changes, ‘I’m guessing you’ll be coming to my wedding show?’

‘I will?’ I scan my spreadsheet again, clearly I’d only focused on the weddings. ‘For someone who didn’t know anything, you do know something!’

‘Well,’ she shrugs proudly, ‘it’s my event. I booked four seats for *Blush*, I’m assuming you’re now one of them!’

I take another sip, and see we are in fact going to the Singapore Wedding Show, in between India and Thailand. ‘Amazing!’ I practically shout, and she retreats, pulling a headphone out of her right ear.

‘God, speak up, won’t you?’ she laughs.

‘I can’t believe I’ll get to see you soon!’ I start to feel a little brighter.

‘So, when does the trip start?’

‘I’m picking the team up from the airport tomorrow for a meet and greet, then we leave the next day.’ I shake my head.

'You can do it,' she smiles.

'Thank you. It's just a little overwhelming and such a quick turn around after my latest trip; I literally got back today. Alright,' I neck the last of my cocktail, 'thank you for recommending me and for listening. And, keep the faith, hon.'

She shrugs, 'It will happen when it's meant to.'

I smile at her. 'It will. OK, miss you. I'll see you soon. Thank you for being awesome.'

'Can't help it.' She shrugs again, 'Part of my nature; it's a curse really.'

Chapter 2

UK
London

Friday

So, here I am, Americano in one hand, *Blush* sign in the other, at the arrivals gate in Heathrow, just where I met Bob yesterday, (who's now waiting in the drop-off area). Even though we're nearing the end of March, the weather seems extra brisk after being in beautiful California. I jiggle on the spot, to keep warm, in my trusty little brown boots, flared jeans, maroon jumper, complete with my wrap that's practically a blanket.

Despite it being a little before three in the afternoon, my day has well and truly flown by. After sleeping through my alarm, I picked up my antimalarial tablets for India, then whizzed around my apartment, packing everything I'd need for a month, so I can simply pick up my case tomorrow morning, without panicking. The result of that, however, meant appearance-wise, all I had time to do was whoosh my hair up in a high ponytail, curls akimbo, and add a headscarf to contain the front of it, and what little makeup I have on my face was done in the car on the way here, as Bob drove.

Sipping my coffee, I gaze around, thinking to myself that I share the same opinion as Hugh Grant in *Love Actually:* the arrivals gate is a lovely place to be. Loved ones excitedly envelop their nearest and dearest in hugs and kisses; it's a beautiful thing to observe. I smile as a rather tanned young girl, maybe no older than eighteen, hair flowing down her bony shoulders, wearing a pair of harem trousers, (not too dissimilar to the ones I packed), with a baggy orange jumper, is covered in kisses by a couple, whom I assume are her parents.

Admittedly, I was a little grumpy last night, but now I've decided that I'm actually going to focus on the trip, not the weddings, and I'm determined to get excited. Plus, Heathrow is one of my favourite places on the planet. It means I'm going on another adventure and that I am moments away from stepping onto a vessel that is going to bring me food and drink; I can watch films, read a book, or actually get on with some work. It's like being given the gift of time; I love it.

Their plane landed twenty minutes ago, so they should be here any minute. Doing zero research on anything, including my soon-to-be colleagues, and in my haste to remember their names, I scribbled the *Blush* team onto a post-it note, and shoved it in my pocket. Tucking my sign under my arm, I look again at the scrunched up note and scan their names. Sarah McBride — *how ironic* — is in charge of beauty; Hugo Falkner, stylist to the stars; and Dominic Russell, photography. With all the catching up I had to do yesterday, it never occurred to me to look up my travelling companions, so, burying the post-it once more, I whip out my phone to do a swift Google. I type: "Sarah McBride Hair and Makeup." *Wow, she is striking.*

The doors opposite me swing open, and I glance up as a large crowd suddenly stampedes its way out of the arrival gates. Realising I'm a little nervous, I stand up straight, hold the sign up clearly, and take a deep breath. Scanning the crowd, I immediately spot Sarah, and give her a wave. Even after a ten-hour flight, the picture on my phone does not do her justice. Her rockabilly, jet-black hair is gracefully swept up around a red and white handkerchief, made into a bow. Her intensely alluring, liquid eye-lined dark eyes are framed by cat-eye specs and her bright red lips form a smile as she waves back at me.

Next to her is an equally as tall, (if she took off her vintage, red Mary Jane heels, I think he'd be taller than her), cool, bearded, hipster-looking dude with a topknot, who's dressed in a smart casual outfit: a perfect fitting pair of skinny jeans, a white shirt and dark waistcoat, who is either Hugo or Dominic; I wish I'd done more research. The party of two reach me and bring their cases to a stop.

'Well, '*eff* me, that was a long trip.' Sarah's opening line makes me giggle as she pulls me in for a tight hug. God, she smells delicious: somewhere between cherries and hairspray. 'Great to meet you, Liv! We're gonna have a blast!' she tells me in her thick Italian-New York accent. She pulls away but keeps one hand on my arm, 'Liv, meet Hugo.'

'You are a saint to step in like this!' He draws me in, and gently places a kiss on each cheek and his facial hair tickles me a little. 'We thought the whole thing was dead, then we heard you saved the day!' His teeth are so white against his light brown beard and moustache.

'Your hair is fabulous; may I touch it?' Sarah is marvelling at my up-do.

'Sure,' I shrug.

'Like *Brave* meets Sarah Jessica Parker,' she exclaims. I frown, thinking of the rude man on the plane. 'It wasn't intended as an insult honey; it is sassy, and sexy!'

'I'll take that,' I smile at her. 'I do love Sarah Jessica Parker.'

Hugo nods his head, 'Her style is impeccable.'

Smiling politely at them both, I then look around at the crowd once more, 'So, we're just waiting for Dominic? Did he get held up with something to declare?' I look past Hugo trying to guess which passing man he could be.

'Oh, Dom's already here.' Sarah holds up a little mirror and checks her perfect reflection. 'He grabbed an earlier flight, so he's already at the hotel. He's joining us for drinks later.'

'Oh, I wasn't told that.' I smile. *Wanker. Could have told me. I hate him already.*

'It was a last-minute thing. He had to sort through some things with his partner, or ex-partner rather,' Hugo says, making a face.

'More about that later!' Sarah cuts him off. 'I'd kill for one of those,' Sarah gestures at my coffee.

'Is this all the luggage you have?' Looking down at the small cases they each have with them. 'I thought there might be more, for a beauty and styling team.'

'We learn to travel light,' Hugo says, and I smile as they're clearly on the same wavelength as me.

'All brides have everything they need, already with them,' Sarah explains, 'Plus, if we want or need anything else, we can always shop wherever we are around the world.'

'That's what I always say!' I grin as Sarah links arms with me.

'Perfect. Now. Coffee then cocktails.'

'Girl after my own heart.'

***

'Well, cheers!' Sarah sits opposite me and clinks her glass with mine. We're sitting in the hotel's low-lit bar, just opposite Hyde Park, on a low table for four, with huge comfy chairs. 'Here's to our adventure. It's crazy Chrissy's paying for this right? But I don't ask any questions! If you're gonna pay me to play, I'm a happy girl.'

'I know it's crazy, isn't it?! Cheers.' I bring my glass to meet hers, and then to my right for Hugo's. 'It's so lovely to meet you both; I'm excited to meet Dom!' *And a bit nervous actually.* I take a sip and notice Sarah and Hugo give each other a sideways glance. 'What is it?'

'I guess there is something we should tell you,' Hugo leans forward, 'you know, to avoid a "shit show."'

I sit up taller, only mildly offended. *Was he calling me a "shit show?"* 'I was only told about this yesterday, after being on a long flight from my last assignment in LA. I'm still a little jet-lagged actually. Let's walk through everything: how we're each involved, what the tone of the piece will be, what the expectations are of Chrissy—'

'Poppet, relax, it's not to do with you.' Sarah blinks her long, mascara covered lashes at me. 'It's to do with the last writer. She…' Sarah's eyes lift above my chair, 'oh, there you are, we were beginning to think you weren't going to join us. Dom this is Liv, Liv this is Dom.'

I sit up straighter in my seat, ready to meet the final member of our travel group. If he's as nice as the other two, it's going to be a great trip. Slapping on a smile, I turn my body to face him. *Please be nice, please be nice. Please…* 'You? No.' I stand up; not that that helps, I come up to his chest. I tilt my head to the sky. '*You're* Dom? No. No!'

'What is it?' Sarah leaves her seat and comes to my side, towering next to me too, in her bright red, vintage Mary Jane heels; I feel like a child.

'You two know each other?' Hugo comes to my other side, leaning on the top of my chair, and points from me to Dom and back again.

'This arsehole,' I jab him in the chest, accidentally, with my point, 'sat next to me on my flight home yesterday and insulted me the entire time.'

'It wasn't the entire time.' Dom's laid-back charming drawl has no effect on me. 'So, I guess that makes you, Olivia?' He holds out his hand and I don't accept it.

'Liv's fine.' I fold my arms.

'Olivia it is then.' He smirks and cocks his head to one side and glances at our table. 'What are we drinking?'

'Espresso martinis,' I say. Figured it helped me with my jet lag yesterday, it might help them too.

He raises his eyebrows but doesn't say anything at first. *What does that mean?*

'Think I'll just go for a beer. Be right back.' Dom turns and walks to the bar. I watch him go, frowning at his back; I have a bad feeling about this.

'How funny that you've already met; what are the odds of that?' I turn to face Sarah, who takes her seat once more, placing one pale leg over the other.

'Can't blame him for being in a bad mood though,' Hugo says, taking his drink, and rejoining Sarah at the table.

'Bad mood?' My eyebrows raise so high I think they might join my hairline. 'He downright insulted me yesterday, over and over again! I'm a complete stranger to him! Who does that?! That brands him as an arsehole in my book.' I sit back down in a huff.

Hugo leans forwards and lowers his tone, 'Liv, very quickly, as we were saying before, there may be a reason for that. The other writer, who got fired, well, that was his partner. Now, ex-partner.' He makes a face.

'What?' I look from Hugo to Sarah, who's now nodding.

'She dumped him when he said he was still doing this assignment,' Sarah whispers.

'Why did she get fired?' I ask, also in a hushed tone, our heads now all together, leaning over the table.

'No one knows,' Hugo shrugs as he whispers. 'But I'll tell you my theory, she—' Sarah coughs and nods, I guess to motion to Dom's return. 'Anyway,' Hugo says in a normal voice, 'we have a lot of time on the road and in the air to talk shop. Tonight, let's just get to know each other. I was born in Paris but raised in a little town outside Lake Tahoe,' Hugo puts his hand to his heart, then gestures to me. 'What about you, Liv?' Dom sits in the empty seat to my left and sips his beer quietly.

'*Um*, I was born in Bristol. But I grew up pretty much everywhere. My family travelled a lot for my dad's work. He works in oil, so we moved every four years or so; Paris,' I nod at Hugo, 'Venezuela, parts of the US, we were even in the Congo for a time. My parents live in Spain now.'

'Wow, that's quite the upbringing! That's where you get your love for travel, I guess?' Sarah cocks her head in interest.

'*Hmm*, I guess. I never really thought about it, but yeah. I got used to packing up and living out of a suitcase, that's for sure.' I take a sip of my drink to swallow my thoughts about the last year. Dom is looking at me intently with complete hatred in his eyes. How am I going to spend every moment of the next month with this man?

***

The next morning, I awake with the dawn chorus. The sun isn't even up as I haul my carry-on sized case down the stairs, out into the freezing morning, and into a cab to head back to the hotel. Only living about half an hour away, it didn't make sense to stay. As I step out of the car in front of the hotel, I hear a voice,

'Hey, Brave! Wait up!' I turn and see Dom across the road at the mouth of Hyde Park, with a camera case draped over his shoulder; I wait for him to cross the road and meet me.

'Morning,' I say curtly.

'Good morning.' He looks me up and down, goes to say something then changes his mind, so we're just standing there looking at each other.

'What were you doing in Hyde Park?' I ask, deciding to break the awkward silence. 'Doesn't look like you've been exercising?' I note his smart black jeans and Ralph Lauren striped shirt, under his long Crombie coat.

'Couldn't resist taking shots of Kensington Palace.'

'Fan of The Royal Family?' I guess.

'No.' He looks at me pointedly, 'You do know the first bride works there?' he says slowly, as if I'm stupid.

I take a deep breath, 'No, I didn't know that. Apparently, all the notes the, *um,* previous writer had, she took with her.'

He looks positively tormented for a moment then settles his face into a frown. 'Well, anyway, I thought it might be useful in the article to have a shot of it.'

I nod, 'Great thinking.' We stand in silence once more, then I gesture to the hotel, 'Shall we head in? It's freezing.' He nods and we walk silently past reception and into the breakfast room. I join Hugo and Sarah while Dom gets a plateful.

'Good morning!' Hugo greets me in a much more friendly manner than Dom, and gestures to me with a latte.

'Morning!' I take a seat next to Sarah. 'How did you sleep?'

'I think I had a full two hours!' Sarah replies, you'd never know it; her flawless complexion is positively beaming, and her makeup is, once again, picture perfect. 'I '*effing* hate jet lag, good thing we've got a driver, I'll sleep all the way there!'

'Good plan!' I say brightly, 'Although, it's not a particularly long journey.' Eyeing the selection of pastries they have on the table, I feel my stomach rumble; even though I ate porridge at the crack of dawn, you know? It's *right there. Ummm.*

'Take one.' Hugo winks at me, clearly my expression reflects my mind. 'I won't tell anyone.'

'Thanks!' Leaning across the table, I select a *pain au chocolat*, just as Dom joins us. I grin and take a bite; *God that's good.* 'So,' I start to speak with my mouth still a little full, 'while you eat, why don't we go over our itinerary for the day?'

'I think you just answered your own question; we're eating,' Dom rudely points out.

'You don't have to talk,' I snap. *It's better when you keep your mouth shut.* Taking a deep breath, I carry on, in my normal tone, 'As it's the first one, I'd just like to run through everything if you don't mind.' I give a sideways glance to Dom, who rolls his eyes at me. 'So,' I clear my throat, 'firstly, Bob, our driver from yesterday, is the go-to guy for all things *Wonder,* and I guess now, *Blush,* related. He'll be our chauffeur for the first two weddings, while we're here in the UK, and will be arriving at 7:45, so we'll meet back in the lobby a little before then?'

'We know this!' Dom frowns.

'Like I said, you don't have to talk.' I narrow my eyes and resist the urge to stick out my tongue. 'When we get there, Dom,' I take in his sour expression, 'you and I are a team first; I'll interview the bride, followed by the groom, while you snap away. That will give Sarah and Hugo a chance to set up everything they need. Then after the interviews, Dom, you'll do the wedding party "getting ready" shots. The wedding isn't until 1 pm, so we've got ample time. Have I missed anything?'

'Nope. I think you're nailing it,' Hugo smiles kindly at me. 'Have another one.' He gestures once more to the pastries.

'Thanks!' I select a small swirly one this time.

Dom scowls at me now. 'You know they're only supposed to be for *paying* guests right?'

'Oh, pipe down, grumpy!' Sarah hits Dom on the arm. 'You're not paying for this, are you?' She turns to me now. 'You have as much as you want, Poppet.'

'You've given her a pet name?' Dom looks at Sarah with distaste.

Sarah looks at me, 'Yeah, I believe I have.' We grin at each other, and it's weird, it's like we've known each other our whole lives.

'Whatever,' is Dom's reply, before taking a bite of his makeshift sausage sandwich.

'Right, I don't know about you guys,' Sarah dabs around her perfectly ruby-red lipsticked mouth with a napkin, 'but my crap is everywhere; I'm going to get packing. See you back down in a mo.'

Chapter 3

UK
London

Saturday
Drive 30 minutes: Hyde Park – Richmond

Couple A
Pembroke Lodge, Richmond Park, London

There's no on-site accommodation at the wedding venue, so we're meeting the bridal party at their hotel, which is only about a fifteen-minute drive away.

Bob drops us off and we parade quickly into the building, to escape the cold. Sarah has what I can only assume is a *Mary Poppins* bag, that can magically pull out everything you can think of, including a side lamp; Dom with a backpack and a camera around each shoulder; and Hugo carrying a simple leather bag and a clipboard.

'OK, so I think the best way for me to stay focused on who's who, is if you guys tell me as we go along, the names of each couple; does that work?' I ask, as we hold the front door open for each other, and step inside the hotel.

'Absolutely!' Sarah smiles at me. 'If I hadn't spent a year on this, my head would be spinning too.'

'Belinda and Timothy,' Hugo says, helpfully, as we reach

the front desk and are directed to the second floor.

'OK. Belinda and Timothy,' I scribble in my little notebook before climbing the stairs.

'Belinda's a little highly strung,' Hugo informs me in a low voice, 'but what bride isn't, right?' He laughs, stroking his beard. 'Although saying that, she was so keen to make decisions, she picked the very first dress that I suggested for her.'

'Bloody brave of these brides to do this, don't you think? They haven't actually met us,' Sarah quips. 'It's one thing to Facetime and Zoom, but another to consult in person.'

We reach the second floor and follow signs to the bridal suite. The sound of a guitar and accompanying voice wafts around the grand stairwell. 'Oh, that's cute.' I stop to listen.

'I guess she's practising for later,' Sarah says, and when I look at her with a blank expression she continues, 'The maid of honour is singing instead of doing a reading.'

'Well, that's a nice touch,' I say, and scribble another note. 'It's that song from the end of *The Wedding Singer*, isn't it?' We all pause to listen and hear the lyrics.

'Yeah, you're right,' Dom surprisingly answers, and we all turn to face him, 'What? I like Adam Sandler,' he defends himself. Sniggering, and following around several more corridors, we find the room, not by the signs, but by an increased level of giggling.

OK, I can do this. I can watch nine couples get married. I'm here to work. I'm a professional. Reaching my hand up, I tap on the door, but the laughing is too loud. I try again, teamed with a 'Hello!?' More screaming is preceded, by the door opening to reveal a rather tall, regal looking lady, with her hair wrapped up in a towel turban.

'Ah, the *Blush* team, I presume?'

'Yes, *how lovely* to meet you,' I catch myself responding, matching her crisp, over-enunciated English accent perfectly, before clearing my throat. 'I'm Liv Bennett; columnist,' I introduce myself and the others, in my normal voice, and she adds "pleasure" to each, while shaking with a limp hand; *why do I feel the desire to curtsy*?

'Hilary, mother of the bride; won't you come in?' She opens the door a little wider to reveal a gaggle of bridesmaids, each one younger and more beautiful than the next; fresh faces, wearing matching silk flower robes and fluffy white slippers, complete with towel turbans just like Hilary's, all sitting on a four poster bed, and drinking a glass of something orange from a champagne flute. As I scan the room, I spot a bottle of Aperol next to some bubbles and I remind myself to take a deep breath; the only other drink Leo loved apart from a cool G and T with a slice of lime, was an Aperol Spritz. 'Belinda, darling, *Blush* are here!'

Belinda swings her legs round and off the bed, to stand; with her champagne flute in one hand, she waves at us with the other. Wow, even with zero makeup, she certainly sets the standard high for "blushing bride" as she glides gracefully over to meet us.

'Hello.' She outstretches a delicate hand and shakes each of ours in the same limp manner her mother did. 'I am simply honoured, just, *honoured* to be part of this feature.' Her voice is even more well-spoken than her mum's.

'Where do you want us to set up, honey?' Sarah says to her.

'Well, I suppose the vanity mirror makes the most sense for us,' her smile dazzles us with her, *I'm-sure-they're-whitened-for-the-big-day,* teeth. 'Hugo,' she glances over, places her citrus flavoured bubbles down, and commands the attention of everyone in the room, 'such a delight to be in your capable hands.' She takes both of his hands in hers. 'I just loved every single email, connection, and suggestion. Thank you.'

'If you look half as good as you did in our last video chat, he won't be able to wait until the honeymoon!' He winks at her. I jump as the bridesmaids erupt in squeals, and I try hard not to roll my eyes at them.

Belinda leans in playfully, and whispers, 'Here's hoping!' Releasing his hands she then turns her attention back to me.

'Thank you *so* much for choosing my wedding.' I wonder if she realises she's said "*my* wedding" not, "*our* wedding." And I ignore the small detail that *I* had nothing to do with the fact that she's in this article. Deciding to turn the conversation back to her; somehow, I don't think that will be a problem, I ask,

'How are you feeling? Excited?' Flashing what I hope is a convincing smile.

'Oh, you've no idea! I tell you,' She sits down gracefully on the chair by the vanity mirror and looks off into the distance. 'It took him *sooooo* long to propose! I thought this day would never come.'

'Oh really,' I pull up another chair, open my notebook and click my pen. 'How long had you been dating before he proposed?' My pen, poised in the air.

She turns dramatically to me and draws out each word for emphasis. 'A whole four months! Can you believe it!?'

I bite my bottom lip to stop a hoot of laughter escaping from my mouth. Clearing my throat once more, I manage a reply, 'Wow, *uh*, must have been tough waiting that long.'

'You're telling me. I mean, for God's sake, just do it already!'

I nod and consciously tell myself to lower my eyebrows that have shot up, and stop myself from writing something offensive. '*Um hmm,*' I agree, catching eyes with Sarah. 'So, if you're agreeable, let's go over your day!'

'Absolutely! She sits up straight. 'I was *born* ready!' she says theatrically.

Dom reaches for the camera on his left and gets it out of the case; head down, expression, like mine, trying not to smirk.

'Dom will just take a few shots as we're talking.'

'Oh, Dom, fantastic! Yes, I loved your sample shots from your website; you are incredibly talented. I particularly like the album from the Patterson wedding you showed me. Like her, my best side is my left. You took her from the right a few times; bad idea for me. My face is sadly, just not that symmetrical.'

Dom pauses while putting on a different lens, 'Absolutely.'

What is this woman on? She could grace the cover of any magazine and not be out of place with a bunch of models. I want to shake her.

'So, great! Dom will focus on your *left side,* and we'll proceed, shall we?' *I can do this. I can do this.*

'Yes, yes!' Belinda squeals slightly. 'I've been dreaming about this. It's like I'm a celebrity.'

'It's your special day,' I say, amazingly without a trace of sadness on the outside. 'So, after a, shall we say, world-wind romance, is it safe to say it was love at first sight with, *um,*' *Oh my God, what's the groom's name again?* I casually glance at my notes, 'Timothy?' I recover after what I hope wasn't too long of a pause.

Belinda, though, is only focused on what she's saying,

'Oh, absolutely,' she says with all seriousness. 'Timothy and I were at a function for work.'

'Oh, you both work for The Royal Family, yes; what does he do?'

'I really can't say.'

'What do you do?'

'I really can't say.'

'Oh, of course not.'

'I mean I *want* to,' she leans forwards and pats my hand, 'I'm not trying to be difficult, it's just, I'm contractually obligated to remain silent.'

'Right. So, love at first sight, at work; how wonderful…'

As I continue to interview the bride, Dom moves around us, snapping away, Belinda is making a huge effort to not turn and pose, and keeps her eyes steadily on me.

'OK, I think I have everything I need in the interview portion.'

'Oh, really?' Belinda sits up and disappointedly pouts.

'Yes; you were perfect,' I reassure her. A comment she approves of and dazzles me with another smile. 'So, I'll leave you to interview Timothy, now. Dom's going to take a few shots of him—'

'Aren't you going to take pictures of us getting ready?' Belinda demands more than asks.

'It won't take long. By the time you've consulted with Sarah, he'll be back,' I say.

'Oh, good,' she says with relief.

'I promise I won't start until he's back, honey,' Sarah adds to her reassurance.

'OK, good. Good.' She breathes out and her glass is topped up by the guitar-playing maid of honour, who's just joined the room.

'Wow,' Dom says quietly when we're on the other side of the Bridal Suite door. I snigger but don't say anything. Continuing along the corridor, we make our way towards the groom's room, on the other side of the building. This time when I knock, it's met by chortles of laughter, before the door opens to reveal an extremely dashing man.

'Hello. I'm Timothy. You must be Olivia and Dominic?'

'Dom and Liv's just fine,' I say, 'but yes, great to meet you.' I take his strong hand.

'The pleasure is all mine.' He steps aside and guides me in with the strength of his palm on my back, 'Come in, come in.'

Timothy is undeniably handsome, and as I gaze around the room of groomsmen, unlike the bridesmaids, they're all dressed and ready to go. The only similarity? They've started drinking too.

'So,' Timothy sits down in a chestnut wood, curved-back chair, and I can't help but think he wouldn't be out of place on the cover of a magazine either; it's like he's stepped right out of a Tommy Hilfiger ad. 'I knew from the moment I saw Belinda that she was the one. She was unlike no other that I had been with, she—'

I hold my hands up, 'I'm sorry to interrupt,' *your rehearsed speech*, 'let's take a moment, shall we? Oh, thank you.' Another handsome man offers me a seat, and I park my behind. 'Let's just start with a few questions, and go from there; Dom will take a couple of shots—'

'Yes, gents! Shots!' Another man refills the seven glasses lined up on the windowsill. I better get going otherwise he's going to be intoxicated.

***

A few hours later, we leave the mildly tipsy bridal party, to head to the venue. Bob drives us up a long winding path, in Richmond Park. Gazing out the window, I see a herd of deer galloping at the same pace as the car.

'Oh, wow.' Sarah presses her face up against the glass, and cranes her neck to keep them in sight, as we wind further around the path. Finally, we pull up in the designated car park, next to a Georgian mansion. Stepping out of the car, I enjoy the sound of crunching gravel under my trusty brown boots. There's still a real icy nip in the air, but it truly is the most beautiful sunshiny day, with a piercing blue sky, and not a cloud in sight. Finding my sunglasses in my mass of curls atop my head, I place them onto my face, then swing my handbag over my shoulder and look for a sign to indicate the entrance.

'This is just beautiful,' I say, smiling at the skyline, before we wander in and are greeted by a table with a small buffet, and a *Blush* sign next to it. 'Oh, yeah.' Pushing the sunglasses back up, I step up and dive in.

'What is it with you and food?' Dom says with mild disgust.

I shrug, 'What can I say? I'm a foodie.'

'Well, you're certainly not shy to go first.'

Sarah shoves a plate in his hands, I think to shut him up, then starts helping herself. 'Man, this is so good.'

Hugo parades around with an olive. 'I love Mediterranean food.'

I smile and share the knowledge I've just acquired. 'It's the combination of the two families: the groom's grandparents were Greek and French, and the bride's grandparents were Portuguese and Spanish. It's an ode to them really, as they've all passed.'

'Wow, quite the eclectic family mix,' Sarah says.

'OK,' I swallow my mouthful. 'I'm going to have a walk through the building to get a feel for it.' I wipe my hands on a napkin as I go and place it in the nearby bin.

'I'll come with you,' Dom says, to my surprise. 'I'll get a few shots before guests arrive.' We walk through the deserted building, in silence; it's a fun little place with wonky stairs. 'This place is obscene.' Dom takes in the beautiful building as we walk around the bar area.

'I don't know; I think it's charming.' I gaze out at the striking view: manicured gardens with a city skyline backdrop, 'Even if I'm not the biggest fan of weddings, right now.' *Whoops.*

'You're not? Why are you doing this then?'

'I didn't really have a choice,' I say honestly, then turn to face him. 'It was sort of thrown at me. Plus, if I had said no, my magazine would have folded, so...' I'm not sure how to finish that sentence.

'*Hmm.*' Neither of us talk for a time. I scribble notes and he takes a few pictures here and there, as we make our way back outside, to explore the grounds.

'Weddings always make you think about your own situation, don't they?' he says sadly.

I have no desire to have a heart-to-heart with this man. 'I guess so,' I say, admiring the vast patio area with a large stone staircase that leads down onto the ample grassy, tree-lined garden.

As we reach the stairs, he breaks the silence again. 'So, what's your deal then?' I feel Dom staring at me.

'What do you mean?' We walk down towards the grass.

'Your deal. Do you have a boyfriend?'

'Why? Are you interested in filling that position?' I say, sarcastically.

'I'm curious. You said you're not a fan of weddings, so? What's your deal?'

I pause, 'My life is too busy for a partner,' is the lie I decide on, as nonchalantly as I can. Whether he believes me or not, he doesn't respond, and we walk the rest of the stairs in silence.

When we reach the grass, I start to walk and write once more, taking in the decorated lawn adorned with delicately dressed picnic tables. Dom matches my pace and takes a few photos as we go. 'So, when was your last serious relationship?'

'Aren't you full of questions! Sure you don't want to do the interviewing?'

'Come on, tell me.'

I take this man in; if he wasn't so rude to me the first time we met, I might find him attractive. 'I'm, *uh,* not sure.'

'You're not sure?' His voice, laced with disbelief. 'OK, why did it end, then?' He focuses his lens on a glass jar full of rosemary, wrapped together by a red ribbon, on the nearest picnic table.

'Well,' I think for a moment. 'I thought it was serious, and he...I guess...didn't.'

He lowers his camera. 'I know what you mean.' We hold eye contact for a while.

Are we connecting? I don't like it; I start to feel uncomfortable. Thankfully, Sarah appears at the top of the stairs.

'Ah, there you two are!' She shouts. 'It's nearly 12:30, guests are arriving; we need to get in position. You OK?'

Sarah adds, looking at me.

'Yes, absolutely,' I yell back and then smile, walking past Dom with caution. *What was that?*

Dom spends the next half hour taking pictures of friends and family, all laughing and joking with each other, here to celebrate the joining of two people they all, clearly adore. Feeling my heart pang, I promise myself that I will get through this; maybe it will get easier with each wedding.

After chatting with a few of the guests, I take up one of the four reserved seats at the back of the room that are for us and continue making notes for the article. Shortly after, I'm joined by Sarah and Hugo.

'All finishing touches are in place,' Hugo nods, satisfied.

'And I just checked on the bride; she's all ready! A masterpiece if I do say so myself!' Sarah beams with pride.

As the guests start to file in, I find I'm a little nervous. Dom was right, you can't help but think about your own relationship status as you sit in the pinnacle of someone else's love story. *Why do we feel the need to compare our lives to others?*

Turning my head to the side, I see Sarah trying to work me out. Giving her a small smile, I decide to swallow those feelings, like I have done for the last year. A hush falls on the room as a Town Crier, dressed in red, gold and white appears. With a booming voice that makes the whole room jump, he announces, 'LADIES AND GENTLEMEN! PLEASE BE UPSTANDING FOR THE BRIDE!'

The guests stand and all turn to face the doors as the remix of the two songs: "Somewhere Over the Rainbow" and "What a Wonderful World," plays. Gliding in one after the other, the bridesmaids are all in matching, long, strapless deep red silk gowns, with white, short-sleeved, fluffy boleros. Belinda appears and I watch Timothy just completely enraptured by her; she's the only person in the room to him. I recognise that look and feel a small lump forming in my throat. Swallowing, I try to shake it off as the bride reaches the front.

'Ladies and gentlemen, welcome to the marriage of Belinda and Timothy. What a beautiful day to celebrate a union of two souls…'

'It just occurred to me,' Sarah whispers in my ear.

'What has?' I whisper back even quieter than her.

'We have to sit through eight more of these.'

I stifle a giggle as the registrar continues with her introduction. 'Instead of a first reading, I'd like to welcome up to the front, the maid of honour, Flo, who's going to sing a special song.'

Flo is visibly shaking as she picks up her guitar and sits down. Her head is hung, so as not to make eye contact with anyone. She strums the introduction, then stops and puts out her index finger, as if to say, "hang on a minute." Her eyes are filled with tears, and the crowd giggles, but in a supportive way. She tries the intro again, gets to the same place, sniffs and pauses before breaking into "I Wanna Grow Old With You," from *The Wedding Singer.* She stumbles, visibly bites her tongue and blubs through the whole thing.

'This is embarrassing to watch,' Sarah whispers to me.

I look to my left and see Dom with his head buried in the programme of the day's events, his shoulders moving up and down. Hugo hits him. 'Get it together,' he whispers.

'Someone should have told her that,' he whispers back and I stifle another giggle.

As the final line comes to its wobbly end, she locks eyes with the bride and they both burst out crying, full-on, ugly tears, as everybody claps.

'Such emotion; thank you, Flo.' The registrar smiles at the maid of honour as she makes her way back to her seat; her face as red as her dress, she throws her head into her hands. *Poor thing.*

***

The ceremony is short and seamless, then everyone is requested to go outside for canopies, before photos.

I walk with the others and we each take a Pimm's from the tray. 'What is this?' Hugo says, examining the glass.

'It's Pimm's,' I say, 'but, I'm guessing it's the Winter version?' I look at the waiter who nods,

'Yes, with warmed apple juice, a slice of orange peel and a dash of cinnamon.'

'Don't they know Christmas was three months ago?' Dom says, giving it a disgruntled sniff.

'Well, Pimm's is a very...' I pause to consider the word, '*British* drink, often given at BBQs or summer weddings typically; I love the spin on that,' I justify.

'I know what Pimm's is,' Dom directs at me with narrowing eyes. 'My dad's American but my mum is English; I was born in London, actually. Lived here until I was seven or so.'

'Oh, *that's* why you've got a confused accent,' I say, without thinking.

'I don't have a *confused accent*,' Dom defends.

'You literally sound like you're from Australia dude,' Sarah takes my side.

'Fine. American plus English apparently equals Australian,' Dom says before taking a sip. '*Hmm,* not bad.'

I sip too, *umm, damn, that's good.*

'While we have a moment, let's have a girly gossip.' Sarah grabs my arm and spins me away from the boys, who are now examining Ouzo shots, that are passing on another tray.

'OK,' I say, a little apprehensive.

'Poppet, you are my go-to girl for the next month; let's bond!' She clinks my glass, and we take a walk across the beautiful lawn.

'Alright,' I smile. 'I loved watching you work earlier; you really are very talented.'

'Oh, shut up,' she bats my compliment away.

'No, I mean it! I find it fascinating; I've never been the best at doing my own hair or makeup. My mum never really showed me how; she's more of a natural hippie.'

'A hippie? That's fun.'

'Oh, nothing crazy. She's big on meditation, likes crystals, and always reminds me to embrace who I am, and when I forget, to breathe and ask the universe what its message is.'

'She sounds like an interesting person,' Sarah smiles.

'She is. But, anyway, like I was saying, I loved watching you work. And I love your style,' I admire her perfect liquid-lined eyes.

'Well, my look is a little more distinctive than some people are expecting,' she gestures to her tattoo sleeve. 'I think some people fear I'm going to doll them up like me. It makes me giggle every time.' She lowers her voice, 'Belinda was so freaked out when she saw me on Zoom for the first time; it was hilarious.'

'How'd you calm her down?' We stroll to a quieter corner of the grounds and I help myself to a small piece of minted halloumi on a cocktail stick from another passing waiter.

'Showed her my portfolio; contrasting looks and bringing out the personality of each person, is my specialty. But, I'm not the only talented one here. I have to say, I was nosing at what you were scribbling earlier; you seem to have a flair for describing weddings; reading between the lines, as it were.'

'Oh, thanks,' I can feel myself blushing.

'It was so descriptive, it made me notice things around me that I hadn't taken in.' Sarah flatters me. 'Like, the little pots of Mediterranean herbs everywhere instead of flowers? I would have walked right past them.'

'Well, actually,' I sigh. 'I used to solely write about weddings.'

'Really? Where? In *Wonder* magazine?'

'Well, at first it was my personal blog that I had when all of my friends were getting married several years ago. Then my friend Becky, who used to work for *Wonder* — *ooh*, you'll meet her in Singapore,' I add, thinking about it, 'anyway, she introduced me to her boss one day, and I was offered a weekly column in the lifestyle section. But then…' I find my voice has trailed off. '...then I…' *I don't know if I want to share this*, '...then, something happened, and I was allowed to switch my focus to travel, and that's what I've done for the last year.'

Sarah considers me, 'That was a lot of squirming.'

I burst out laughing. Then sigh, 'I'm sorry. I'm not very good at being open about my feelings — or my past.'

'The English stiff-upper-lip, I get it. You don't have to tell me, Poppet. I'd just like you to know, I'm very good at keeping secrets, and I'm here if you'd like to confide in me; I think we could be very good friends.'

I smile at her. *I think I'm going to need a friend to get*

through this. Taking a deep breath, I go for it. 'Well, I suppose it's probably going to come out at some point in the next month, being surrounded constantly by all of this. So, I'll start at the beginning, I guess.' I sigh and go for it. 'I was perfectly happy being single; I've never really, ever, had a problem being by myself; happy result of being an only child, I guess.'

Sarah stays quiet and sits on one of the two white wrought iron chairs away from the crowd, patting the one adjacent to her for me to join. Lowering my body slowly, I sit, and continue, 'So, I was at a friend's wedding, and I locked eyes with this beautiful man across the dance floor. Leo was a strong, strapping type, you know? The kind of man where you just somehow knew that no matter what, you could feel safe in his arms. He was by himself and so was I, and we just,' I shake my head, 'I don't know, the whole world seemed to melt away around us; like we were the only two in the room. I've never believed in love at first sight, but my God, I fell.' I look at her perfect cat eyes, and I feel safe telling her this. 'I fell *hard.* Anyway, we lived in each other's pockets for two years; I simply couldn't get enough of him, he was like a drug. Every time he went away on a job — Leo's a wedding caterer,' I add, 'I'd miss him so much, I could feel my insides ache. But, whenever he had an event here, I could just sit and watch him work. Our lives were literally full of love: he'd work a wedding, I'd write about a wedding. We were surrounded by them so much that, thinking back, maybe we got ahead of ourselves. We had planned the most beautiful day: a beach wedding, in Hawaii, and...he never showed up.' I take a sip of my drink and let my eyes fill with tears, but not spill over onto my cheeks.

'Oh, honey.' She grabs my hand. 'I'm sorry, I didn't think

it was anything that serious. Leo left you at the altar?'

'Leo left me at the altar,' I confirm resolutely. 'While I was getting ready, he was packing up his things and hopping a plane back to London, before anyone realised he'd gone.'

'What? Nobody saw him leave? He didn't tell anybody? What a wanker.'

'Yup, a massive wanker. Apparently, he sent the boys out of the room and onto the beach, to welcome guests, and said he would join them shortly. I was all ready to go and so Becky went down to double-check everything was in place…' I sigh deeply. 'When I close my eyes, I can still see the look she had on her face when she returned to the room. She didn't even have to say anything; I knew. I've never been so humiliated in my entire life. All of our friends, family, everybody I knew, loved and cared about were sitting on that beautiful beach, and it wasn't as if I could hide, we were in a resort and everybody had paid to stay the week. So, I held my head up high, left my room: gown, hair, makeup, the whole works, marched to the front, and told everybody to please enjoy the food, drinks and resort, but there wasn't going to be a wedding.'

'Man, you're a tough cookie.' She shakes her head.

'I don't know, I think it was more adrenaline than anything; I was numb. I'm still numb, really, but, you know what the saddest part was? When everyone was eating, laughing and dancing at what would have been our reception, I just stood on that beach, for hours, looking out at the horizon, desperately wishing for him to come back. I don't know how long I stood there for, but, long after all the guests had gone back to their rooms, it started raining, and I didn't even notice at first. And the worst thing is, I dream about it, every single night. I both love and hate falling asleep because I relive that moment over and over, and yet, I want to keep dreaming about it, just in case he comes back to me.' Sarah stares at me, not knowing what to say. 'Sorry,' I sniff. 'Overshare. That was a little much.'

She shakes her head again, 'No. You are amazing in my book. So, what did he say when you finally spoke to him?'

'I haven't,' I say simply.

'What? What do you mean? Why not?'

'When I got home, he'd already moved out, and I couldn't get hold of him. He wouldn't answer my calls, texts or emails; even his family wouldn't speak to me and our friends said they hadn't heard from him either. He sort of fell off the planet. To this day, I've no idea why he left me.'

'*Woah*, looks a bit serious over here; everything alright ladies?' Hugo joins us and I blink away any remainder of tears.

'Oh, yeah, no problem over here.' Sarah pops a protective arm around me, 'Liv was just telling me she's got crazy hay fever.'

I smile gratefully at her, 'Yeah, I dab underneath my eyes. 'Not the best for a bunch of weddings, *huh*?'

'Sweetie, it's a good thing there are herbs everywhere. Just wait until you see Dom around flowers; he's super allergic. Anyway, I've got every antihistamine under the sun at your disposal, you just let me know OK?' Hugo says, and I smile gratefully at him. Maybe this trip won't be so bad after all.

***

'*Fank yoush s'much forz* coming *tooz* my wedding!!' Belinda slurs then shouts, 'My wedding! Mine!!! *My* wedding…' She dances on the spot and waves her arms in the air triumphantly like a marathon winner.

'You're very welcome; thank you for having us.' I go to shake a very drunk Belinda's hand and she slaps it away and falls forward into me for a hug, hiccuping.

'*Yooz,*' she points a chipped manicured finger at Sarah, Hugo and Dom while still hanging on to me. '*Arez simpleesh th'bestest evers. Hic!*' Then she straightens up and looks at me, swaying slightly as she does, '*Yours* not going *t'put*, *hic,* this in, *hic,* the article *ares* you?' She gestures to herself.

'Course not.' I smile, 'Mums the word.'

'Good. Good. I don't think my *bossssssss* would like that. Well, cheerio and toodle-oo!!' She turns and zigzags her way back into the building, shouting, 'MY WEDDING!'

'Wow!' Sarah laughs. 'Please tell me you'll put that in the article. I got a picture on my phone of her mooning everybody if you want to add that in?'

I laugh, 'Thanks, I'll keep that in mind!'

Chapter 4

UK
London – Ongar

Sunday
Drive 1 hour 30 minutes: Richmond – Ongar

Couple B
Potters Barn, Ongar, Essex

The next morning, I head down to breakfast, following the smell of a Full English, wafting through the corridors. Even if I am a vegetarian, I can still appreciate the smell.

'Morning! Hope you brought your snow boots!' Sarah says, enjoying the toast soldiers before dipping one into her soft-boiled egg.

'What?' I say, confused, and sit down at Sarah's side, 'What d'you mean?'

'Are you kidding?' She waves a fork around. 'Haven't you looked outside yet?'

'My room doesn't have a window,' I justify, buttering a slice of toast from the huge stack in the middle of the table.

'Honey, go next door, and look through the window!'

Grabbing my toast, I head through to the bar area, where Hugo is standing. 'Oh my God!' I take in the view, which literally looks like a Kinkade painting.

'It's a winter wonderland!' Hugo beams.

'You like snow, *huh*?' I smile at him.

He shrugs, 'Of course, I'm from Lake Tahoe.'

'I didn't tell you yesterday, but I loved Lake Tahoe!' I beam. 'I was only there one summer, but I heard it snows like twenty-odd times a year, right?'

'Oh, wow.' Dom interrupts Hugo answering. 'This will make for some pretty spectacular photos.' I hear Dom's voice before I see his face. 'Morning.' He looks me up and down, like I've already offended him by my mere presence.

'Morning,' I nod at him cautiously. 'A beautiful white wedding!' I say, now smiling at the window. 'Who could have predicted that? Well, maybe there's less snow in Essex than there is in Richmond?'

***

I could not have been more wrong, if anything, there's more. We wind our way through field after field, revealing nothing but untouched, heavy blankets of snow.

'Where is this place?' Dom whines from the front seat, with his arms folded, clearly missing the Californian sunshine.

I look at my watch. 'Can't be much further.'

'Nope, just a few minutes,' Bob calls.

'So, it's Nicole and Andrew, right?' I say, looking at my scribbles from our chat over breakfast.

'Yup.' Hugo looks up from a spot of spontaneous sketching of the scenery, on his clipboard. 'The main heads-up on this one is the mother-in-law from hell.'

'Oh, really? What's up with her?'

'Let's see,' Sarah joins in, 'what was my favourite?

Maybe the amount of emails she sent each of us, with all of *her* ideas, saying they were Nicole's.'

'Seriously? Oh, wow.' I shake my head.

'That's nothing,' Hugo says. 'How about the fact that she took it upon herself to secretly hire an outside team, for the first three months of consultations, because she, and I quote: "didn't have faith that we wouldn't screw it up."'

'Nicole and Andrew had to pay for their services and then let them go!' Sarah takes a big sigh.

'That's insane!'

'She's insane,' Sarah laughs. 'Man, she was so rude about the venue too.'

'Why?' I ask.

'Well, to be honest, she had an opinion about everything,' Hugo says.

'And shot down every idea that Nicole came up with,' Sarah continues, 'but she took particular offence that it's a converted barn.'

'But the history of the building is often what makes them so special,' I exclaim. 'You know, my best friend's wedding wasn't too far from here, actually, and one of the buildings used to be a First World War museum.'

'Oh, that's romantic,' Dom says sarcastically.

'No, it really was.' But there's no need to go on; we're here. Thanking Bob, we exit the car and I pull my little jacket around me.

'Alright, so according to our last email,' Sarah says, looking around, 'the bridal cottage is that way,' she points to our left. 'So, we'll head there first.' As we round a corner, we spot a rather plump, flustered woman, talking to, what looks like, one of the groomsmen. 'Mother of the *bride*,' Sarah whispers to me. As we get closer, we can hear parts of their conversation,

'Ask me *anything else*, just not that, or I will cry. No, I'm sorry. This is just ridiculous now!'

'Keep breathing; it'll all be OK.'

'I just can't stand the woman! She's—'

'Mrs Jones?' Sarah calls, and waves as we approach them. They turn and suddenly stand a bit taller and slap on a smile.

Her cheeks turn pink, 'Oh, hello! *Blush*!' Sarah nods and introduces us. The little woman flusters, shakes her head and plays with her short spiky white-blonde hair, 'I hope you didn't hear any of that. That was just nothing, really; happy families, on both sides.' She grins with a mix of panic and disbelief.

'Don't worry, I won't put that in the article,' I say, smiling.

Her shoulders drop with her loud sigh, and she grips my hand. 'Oh, thank you, Liv. Let's take you over to the cottage, shall we?'

We follow the mother of the bride. 'I am really excited, actually.' She tries to convince us. 'It's just...a little...' She searches for the right word, 'tense.'

'How's Nicole reacting to the snow?' Hugo says, cautiously.

'Well,' Mrs Jones raises her eyebrows, but doesn't need to explain.

'I did not order any '*effing* snow!!'

'I'll leave you to it.' Nicole's mum smiles at us and we turn a final corner. In front of the picturesque cottage are two young women, arguing. 'What am I *'effing* gonna do *naa*? My *'air*?! My shoes? What the *'eff* am I going to do?!'

'Wow. That's a lot of "*effs*" for a Sunday morning,' Sarah

whispers to me.

'Alright, let's do this.' I take a deep breath and continue towards them.

'And who the *'eff* are they?' The bride frowns at us.

'Hi there,' I say calmly, approaching her like a wild cat that may pounce on me at any moment. 'I'm Liv,' I smile and tentatively outstretch my hand, 'we're from *Blush.'*

'Oh my *gawwwd*! *Sorryyy*! *Ov* course you are! Ain't got me glasses on, couldn't *'effing* see ya!' Her whole demeanour changes, 'What a privilege.' She shakes my hand. '*Fank* you. *Fank* you so much!'

'Don't mention it. Shall we get in the warm?' I jiggle on the spot; the only jacket I brought with me isn't to any stretch of the imagination, warm enough.

'*Ov* course!! Yeah, *righ'* this way!'

The bridal cottage is ridiculously cute, I think to myself, as I take off my little brown boots. As we walk in, along a corridor, and into the living space, there's the same soundtrack of squealing bridesmaids, but the surroundings are right out of a Hallmark film. I immediately walk over to the roaring fire to thaw out, close my eyes and feel the heat on my face.

'Excuse my language won't you, it's just...it's my wedding day, and I did *not* schedule any snow; it's going to ruin everything.' Her eyes well up, and I suddenly feel very sorry for her.

'Oh, honey, how's it going to ruin everything?' Sarah puts a comforting arm around her.

'Because Sarah, as you know from our meetings, my hair: naturally frizzy. My face: prone to spots or shininess. Grey sky: not in my colour palate for the wedding.'

I stifle a giggle at this point.

'Oh, but just look!' Hugo gestures to the windows and pulls the drapes a little further to open, 'Look, at this beautiful framing! Do you have any idea how many brides actually pray for snow on their big day?'

'No,' Nicole says, still pouting.

'Hundreds, upon, hundreds! *You* are the envy of *hundreds* of women!'

'I am?' Nicole says a little brighter.

'Oh, my darling, yes, yes! Look at you! So beautiful. And, you literally have a white wedding!'

'It's going to look so gorgeous in the magazine,' I join in, meaning it. 'Dom is a fantastic photographer and will capture everything.' OK, I'm improvising at this point, as I've never actually looked at any of his work, but that doesn't seem to matter.

'You're right.' Nicole stands taller and nods, more to herself than to us, then jabs her finger in the air towards us all, 'You are *abso-'effin'-lutley* right! OK, OK! LADIES!?' She turns and screams for her entourage to parade into the room. 'We are going to have a great day! We are better than the snow! Yes, we went several shades too dark on the tanning beds and will contrast wildly with the snow that our heels will sink into, and yes, there may be some touch-ups that need to happen! But, it is going to be a beautiful day! Are you with me?'

They all cheer, and I almost expect them to burst into a song and dance routine. Hugo goes straight to the bride and puts his skinny arm around her dressing gown clad shoulders. 'Right, all things planned for outside, now move inside, apart from the lanterns: so beautiful in the snow, right?! Maid of honour?'

A tiny little waif of a thing holds her hand in the air. I

thought I was small, but the bride's eight year old niece is taller than this woman.

'There you are. It is your job to keep the evil mother-in-law away from the bride.' She nods with all seriousness. 'The bride is not to be bothered. All questions go through you.'

She nods once more, and I can't help but observe what a military operation this seems to be. Was my wedding like this? I thought I was much more relaxed, but maybe I wasn't. Was it me that drove him away? Was I bossy or controlling? I don't even remember any more. But I don't think so.

'Liv?'

'I'm sorry?'

'Your interview first?' Dom pokes me.

'Right, right.' I walk towards the bride. 'Where would you feel most comfortable, Nicole?'

'Let's go upstairs.' She grabs my hand.

'Best invitation I've had in months.'

She giggles at me, 'I *fort* I'd like *yous.*'

***

After I've interviewed Nicole and Andrew, (a couple so clearly in love, it made my insides ache), I put my coat and boots back on, and brave it outside, again. The temperature is starting to heat up a little but there is still a nip in the air. The grounds are truly stunning and I see why it was picked as a winner. There's one beautiful building after another, all converted barns and workhouses. As I walk, the maid of honour and a few others are lining up red lanterns to mark the pathways that some of the groomsmen have just created from shovelling snow. Glancing up at the sky, I see the grey fading away, morphing slowly into baby blue; the sun just behind the last few clouds, waiting to burst forth.

I head towards the open doors of the main barn, where the reception will be. There are beams everywhere and all are wrapped, from every angle, in fairy lights. 'Oh wow,' I can't help but say out loud to myself; I've always found something magical about fairy lights. Excitedly, I wipe my feet on the carpet, and step in. To the left there's a bar, (covered in more fairy lights), and following the room around, there's a sweet cart, and then the most gorgeous cake I've ever seen; a gift from the groom's sister, I've just found out. There are three tiers, each with a silhouette of a couple and a date; on the bottom one, the figures are holding hands, so I guess that's when they got together, the next, the gent is on one knee, and then today's date, complete with the bride and groom figures on the top. Walking around, I see the icing being lifted up by a small Lego character; I love that personal touch.

Continuing around, every table has a glass bowl with a mirror underneath it, and you guessed it, more fairy lights, betwixt deep red roses, the bride's favourite flower.

Suddenly, feeling like I'm being watched, I turn to see a lady, in her late 50s, who looks very much like the groom, so I'm guessing this is the nightmare mother-in-law. 'Hi there! I'm Liv,' I wave and walk over to her. On closer inspection, I see she's been crying. 'Are you OK?'

'NO, I'M NOT!' she howls at me. 'This is my son's wedding too! Everyone is getting their hair and makeup done, and I just feel like I'm not a part of this.'

'Oh, hey, don't worry, I'm sure we can sort something out. I'll go and talk with Sarah now, I'm sure she can fit you in!'

'It's just so unfair. I feel like a loose part. I've been given NOTHING to do!'

'Well, what a blessing! Why don't you give me five minutes, and I'll see what I can do.' I smile kindly, then make my way back to the bride's building, passing Dom taking pictures of the groomsman setting up, as I go. When I'm through the door, I can hear laughter, and I follow that.

'Liv!' Sarah greets me, while putting the bride's hair into rollers. 'Nicole was just telling me about her bachelorette and the mother-in-law-to-be.'

'So, she has the *OR-DAS-A-TEA 'ta* tell me, I'm *drinkin'* too much...on *my 'effing* hen do! She really is a *piece-a-work*.'

'Well, speaking of which,' I take the opportunity to dive right in, 'she was in the barn just now, crying, and said she feels left out by being the only one not having her hair and makeup done,' I say gently. 'Sarah, would you mind squeezing her in?'

Sarah widens her eyes and shakes her head as Nicole stands up, and holds her hands up in the air, 'Are you *'effing* kidding' me? I asked her already! So many times, *d'in* I Shel?' She exasperates to her maid of honour, who nods. 'She's always got *ta* make it *abaat 'er*!'

'Maybe we could give her a job, it would keep her busy?' I suggest, 'She said she hasn't been given anything to do,' I offer, and then wish I hadn't.

'I *'ave* given *'er soddin'* jobs! What she means is, she *'asn't bin* given a job where she can control *every-fing*!' She sits back in her chair. 'No, no. I am not going to get worked up. This is my day, and she is not going to ruin it for me.' She takes a deep breath. 'You can tell her Sarah will do her hair and makeup,' she looks at her, and Sarah nods, 'and,' she throws her hands up in the air, 'I don't know, while she's waiting, she can rearrange the sweets, or something.' Nicole looks at her reflection in the mirror. 'This is my day; not hers.'

***

The maid of honour does a fab job, batting the mother-in-law away at every turn, then finally, after she's had her hair and makeup done, she makes a beeline for the bride and yells a snide, completely unjustified remark, as to her weight. After both me and the maid of honour take an arm each, we steer her away, and she's agreed to sit and stay in her seat.

When it's time for Sarah and I to join the guests, it's quite fun to people-watch, while listening to the string quartet. I glance at my watch, the wedding was meant to have started half an hour ago.

'I wonder what the holdup is,' I say quietly to Sarah.

'I'll see.' Sarah takes out her phone, looks at a message then she smiles and talks at me through gritted teeth, 'Let's go.'

'What's wrong?'

She turns her phone to me. It has a simple message from Hugo: *'SOS.'*

We stand up and walk as casually as we can manage, over to the cottage. Just in front of the door. Dom is the only one to be seen, who's focusing his lens on the flower girls, who are twirling and posing for him in the snow.

'Hey. How are we doing?' Sarah says, as we walk over.

'Inside,' is all he says.

We make our way in and see Hugo first who's cornered all the bridesmaids to one side, and is talking in a low voice to the huddle. We look around and sure enough, there's Nicole, looking beautiful I might add, sitting in one of the comfy chairs by the fire, but she's crying her eyes out. All Sarah's beautiful work, undoing itself with every tear.

'Hey, what happened?' Sarah rushes over.

'I'm not sure I can do it,' Nicole sniffs.

Well, this would make an interesting spin on the article.

'Oh, of course you can!' Sarah says, taking some tissues out of her purse and hands them to the bride.

'She's been sitting in her seat, but sending me messages criticising everything: the colour scheme, flowers, accessories, bridesmaids dresses, *my* dress. Telling me she's cold, the musicians are out of tune and she'll never forgive me for leaving her out of everything. She doesn't even have to be in my face to be in my head.' She sniffs. 'When I marry him, I'm marrying his mum and she hates me; I can't do it. How can I join a family where this is going to be my reality for the rest of my life?' She pauses to sniff again. 'I'm actually a really nice person.' She blows her nose. 'Why do I even want to do this?'

I take a deep breath, bend down to sit on the floor in front of her, and say softly. 'Because you're in love with him, and he's in love with you. And you want to build a life together. It's as simple and beautiful as that.'

Her tears continue to stream down her face, leaving little shiny trails as they go.

'You know,' I clasp my hands together, at first, 'do you mind if I try something?'

'What do you mean?' She looks at me, tears still cascading.

'I've been to and covered a lot of weddings, and I picked up a little trick along the way.' I take my right index finger and start tapping the tip of her nose.

'What are you doing?' she looks cross-eyed down at my finger.

'Apparently, by doing this, it can stop you from crying.' I continue to tap.

'Well, I'll try anything.' She shrugs.

'You know, I have to say, when you have a love that's as strong as I suspect yours is, and bearing in mind, that's just from talking to you both this morning, you can get through anything.'

She meets my eyes as I continue my tapping. 'You think?' she says with doubt.

'Oh, yeah. So, his family's a little crazy, who's isn't?' She laughs at this. 'Just because his mum will have opinions, doesn't mean you have to listen to them. What do you honestly think? Why do you want to do this?'

She wipes away another tear with the tissue that Sarah's given her. 'Well,' she shrugs again, 'he's kind and funny.'

'*Ah huh*; what else?' I ask and continue to tap.

'He's really good with kids; I know he's going to be an amazing dad.'

'That's awesome.' I smile.

'And you know,' Sarah pipes up, 'if you don't marry him today, she wins. You don't want that to happen, do you?'

Tapping or no tapping, that does it. Nicole sits up tall, stops her tears and a huge smile explodes across her face. 'Oh, no.' She shakes her head. ''*Eff* her. I'm going to marry the man I love.'

'That's the spirit.' I tap the side of her chair. 'Now, let's just get Hugo to prep the bridesmaids for showtime; Sarah, why don't you freshen up our beautiful bride, here; when everyone's good, Dom can start snapping away; I'll tell the guests we'll be ready soon, and make sure the officiant skips right past the "does anyone object" part.'

Standing, I turn, and notice Dom standing in the doorway. I can't work his expression out; *is he impressed*? I give him a small smile, shrug, and head out of the cottage.

***

The ceremony took place in the orangery, instead of outside. The sun, quite timely, broke through the clouds, and beamed through the glass, making it warm and snug inside. Hugo did a fantastic job rearranging the accessories and flowers, alongside foliage, draping beautifully overhead. Dom offered to help but was sent out of the room after having a huge sneezing fit. The mother-in-law did her best to disrupt the entire ceremony: clearing her throat and coughing during Nicole's vows, and during Andrew's, laughing far too loudly at a playful joke he made. But really, all it did was make those around her roll their eyes, and her husband nudge her in the ribs to be quiet.

I have to say though, my favourite part was when one of the bridesmaids sang. Unlike the last wedding, with a teary performer, it was the crowd that didn't have a dry eye; the song was a surprise for the bride, made up by the groom, arranged by the bridesmaid, and accompanied by the string quartet. *How gorgeous is that?*

After the "I dos," photos, speeches and possibly one of the most delicious meals I've ever eaten, I sit alone at our table and compile my notes from the day, while the party is going on around me.

'Put that paper down, and let's have a dance!' Hugo takes my pen and notebook out of my hands, throws them on the table, and then pulls me out of the chair.

'I'm supposed to be working!' I laugh, as he leads me towards the overloaded dancefloor.

'You are!' he declares. 'You're testing out the dance floor; getting the vibe of the room; shall I go on?' He grins, playfully.

I shake my head, 'Oh, alright, you've convinced me.'

The band suddenly breaks into, "Love Shack." And Hugo and I cheer with the whole party. We throw our arms in the air, bounce up and down, and sing along at the top of our lungs.

'I'm so glad I like you!' Hugo yells at me, which makes me burst out laughing.

'Me too!'

He dances closer to me but continues to yell, 'Heather would have never done this.'

'You're yelling!' I tell him through chuckles. 'Who's Heather?'

He grins, ever-so-tipsy, clearly enjoying the open bar, 'Dom's ex. She's a right boob.'

'Boob?' I laugh at his choice of word.

'Yup. Boob; I'm going with boob. But, I like you!'

'I'm so glad to hear it!'

As we continue to dance into the night, I can't help but notice the mother-in-law, curled sulkily in a corner, finally admitting defeat, while everybody else, including her husband, are lost in a celebration of love and laughter. That's what life is supposed to be all about, right? Maybe this trip will help me find closure, somehow. I smile at Nicole as her husband spins her around and then scoops her into his arms. I'm sure I can find that again. I'm sure I deserve that kind of happiness. I'm sure.

Chapter 5

UK
Ongar – London – Inverness – Fort William

Monday
Drive 1 hour 30 minutes: Ongar – London Heathrow
Depart London Heathrow at 14:20
Arrive Inverness Airport at 16:05
Duration: 1 hour and 45 minutes
Drive 2 hours: Inverness Airport – Fort William (1 night stay)

UK
Fort William – Mallaig – Isle of Rum

Tuesday
Drive 1 hour: Fort William – Mallaig (Leave rental in car park)
Sail 1 hour 40 minutes: Mallaig – Isle of Rum (2 nights stay)

Couple C
MacMullen Castle, Isle of Rum, Scotland

'So, let me get this straight,' Sarah pulls her case along and talks rapidly to me. 'It's roughly a two-hour drive to Fort William?'

'Yes, that's right,' I confirm, looking around Inverness airport, wondering where the car rental place is.

'But, that's not where the castle is?' I glance sideways at her and her expression is disgruntled.

'No, we'll stay the night in Fort William and then it's like another hour in the car, and the rest of the journey is on the boat.'

'Boat?' she says slowly, grabbing my arm.

'That is correct.' My forehead creases with confusion; surely, she knew that already.

She stops so violently, pulling me back to a stop, that Hugo bumps right into us. 'Well, that's it. I'm out. I can't do this!'

'And this is why we didn't tell her until now,' Hugo says to me in a whisper, while picking his case up off the floor.

'I knew you were keeping something from me!' she aims at Hugo and Dom, then turns back to me. 'I can't do this! I can't!' She's throwing her hands up in the air so dramatically that a passing four-year-old looks at her, wondering what she's doing.

'I don't understand. What's the problem?' I look from Sarah to Hugo.

'Imelda May here, has a fear of sailing,' Dom smirks and folds his arms.

'You know Imelda May?' I ask, surprised.

'Can we please focus!?' Sarah hysterically outbursts. 'How are we going to get me on this thing?'

'It's going to be fine! It's such a short ride!' I try to reassure her.

'How short?' she aggressively barks at me.

'*Um*, I think it's a little under two hours.'

'TWO HOURS!?! Oh my God, that's it; you're going to have to sedate me. I can't. I can't. I won't.'

'Settle down Miss Rockabilly!' Hugo puts a comforting arm around her. 'We're all here for you, and I have some very aggressive sleeping pills that might help knock you out.' He smiles at her and then turns his head to raise his eyebrows at me.

We make it to the Enterprise car rental lot, by a mixture of consoling, and dragging Sarah along.

'There's a couple of unusual cars here today; you can pick whichever you like.' The helpful member of staff waves us towards the selection.

I lead the way, completely in my element, gazing at the row upon row of cars. 'Oh, let's go for this!' I say excitedly in front of a dark green, Land Rover Defender.

'I'm sorry, are we headed to a farm?' Dom laughs.

'No,' I admit.

'Off-road?'

'Well, if need be, we'd have no problem, would we?' I open the boot and throw my bag in. 'So, despite being known for mechanical gremlins, it's a great choice of car.'

'How so?' he challenges, but do I detect a twinkle in his eye?

'We're doing a load of driving, and this model is comfy, and despite its size, it's responsive, quiet on the roads and has loads of leg room for all you giants,' I finish my sales pitch with a grin, and he nods, before saying, simply,

'OK then,' and gets in the passenger seat.

***

I'm pleased to say that my description of the car was accurate, and it's really fun and easy to control. I'm happy to drive everybody to Fort William the entire way, even with the soundtrack of Sarah telling us about where her fear manifested, 'Apparently I hated swimming lessons when I was a baby…'

'So, you're a car fan, *huh*?' I can feel Dom looking at me sideways.

I keep my eyes on the road, '*Um*, yeah, I guess so. My dad would watch every car programme going; now he likes *Jay Leno's Garage* on YouTube. And he used to take me to a bunch of car shows throughout my whole childhood.' I smile, 'I guess his enthusiasm rubbed off on me.'

'What was your first car?'

I grin even wider, 'A Mini.'

'Little different from this monster you're driving.' His tone is curt.

'And then when I was four, I capsized!' Sarah continues, 'I was trapped under the water for days!'

'Days?' Hugo asks, his sympathetic nature wavering.

'Well, it may have been minutes – but…'

I stifle a giggle, then clear my throat to respond to Dom, 'What can I say? I've got an eclectic taste; I appreciate all types of cars.'

'Oh, yeah, like what?' He challenges. *Why do I feel like he's testing me?*

'*Uh*, well let's see. I get excited by a VW van.'

'Really?' His voice is ever so judgmental.

'Yeah. I love the idea of throwing a surfboard on the top of a car.'

'*Can* you surf?'

'Well, no,' I admit, 'But, it's on my list.'

'What do you mean?' He says, shaking his head ever so slightly.

'List.' I shrug. 'As in all the things I want to do and places I want to go.' Glancing sideways, his expression is completely blank. 'Don't you have a list?'

He doesn't answer, and I suddenly feel stupid. *Isn't it normal to have a list like that? Maybe I'll just stick to talking about cars.* 'OK, well, what else? I like a Porsche 911, Aston Martin DB5, or an Armstrong Siddeley Sapphire. I've never driven any of them, but one can dream, right?'

'What about cars you've driven then?'

'Well, I love my uncle's G Wagon! That's pretty cool.'

'Pretty sweet price tag. What does he do for a living?'

'He's into mining too, but instead of oil, like my dad, he's into gold and copper.'

'I see,' he nods in my peripheral.

I wait for him to say something else, and when he doesn't, I suddenly feel uncomfortable, so keep talking. 'My uncle's the CEO of his company; the sweetest man you've ever met though. So humble for someone who's on the *Forbes 100* list.'

'Impressive.' He looks out of the window and mumbles, 'A girl from money; who knew?'

I crease my eyebrows, not sure what that means, 'Well, I don't know about that. I appreciate how much work my dad and uncle put in, and watched them both work their arses off, building their companies from the ground up.'

'From the ground down you mean.' He turns to face me again and laughs at his own mining joke.

Meanwhile, Sarah continues her sob story from the back

of the car, '...and then when I was nine, I was on a friend's boat in the Hamptons, and it sank!'

'So, tell me moneybags,' Dom persists, 'what other cars do you like?'

I scratch a tickle on my nose, ignoring the *moneybags* comment, '*Erm*, let's see,' I cast my mind back, '*Ooh*, I've always wanted a McLaren. On my trip before last, to LA, I was doing a piece on The Beverly Hills Hotel; do you know it?' I glance to my side and see Dom is taking me in.

'Yes; I'm from California, you know.'

'You are? You didn't say.'

'You didn't ask.'

'Oh.' *Good point*. 'Where about?'

'Between Malibu and Laguna.'

'And you're calling *me* moneybags?' He stays silent and I can feel him examining me with his eyes, as we weave around another mountainous corner. 'So, you lived between two places?' I attempt to engage in some other way. 'Your parents aren't together?'

'No, they are,' he pauses, 'but they're not. They like their space. Mum loves the community vibe and lifestyle of Laguna, and dad has a lot of work in Malibu, so...' His voice trails off and I take that to mean he's done talking about it.

'OK. Well, anyway, back to The Beverly Hills Hotel,' I clear my throat uncomfortably, 'there were a bunch of McLaren's lined up — you know the ones, all iridescent.'

'You mean pearlescent,' he says patronisingly.

'I do?'

'You do. Iridescent is like a bug: purple to green.'

'That's exactly what it was!'

'OK; iridescent it is.' I can feel his eyes still on me; *man, he makes me uncomfortable*.

I follow the wiggle of the road and we pass a spectacular waterfall.

'Pull over!' Sarah yells from the back.

'What's wrong?!' I glance in my rear-view mirror.

'I'm gonna hurl!' Sarah yells while groping for the door handle. I swerve into a layby, and as I'm still slowing the car, Sarah jumps out.

'Does she get car sick too?' I ask Hugo.

'Nope, she's just been winding herself up,' Hugo shrugs. 'Be right back.'

'Yikes. Poor thing.' I watch as she bends over, and Hugo holds her hair back.

'Poor thing? She's ridiculous. It's just a boat, man. She needs to chill out. She'll feel better when she's yacked.'

'Yacked? What a ghastly word.'

'OK, what's a better word then?' he challenges.

'Chunder?' I offer.

'That's definitely worse.' He continues to stare at me, and I'm determined not to speak first. 'Tell me something else about yourself,' Dom demands, still looking at me intently.

'What do you want to know?' I ask, out of curiosity.

'Anything. Something you haven't told anyone before.'

'I've known you for less than a week, and you want me to tell you something I've never told anyone?'

'Yeah, why not? Let's call it bonding.' He takes a sip from his coffee cup.

'Well, I'm not into that,' I raise my eyebrows.

He snorts and a little coffee comes out of his mouth. 'Wow, she went right there.' He dabs his mouth with a tissue and places his coffee once more in the cup holder.

'I don't know, let's see.' I have a think. 'I can sing, but I can't whistle,' I offer.

'That's rubbish; try again.'

'I tell you something that genuinely concerns me, and you dismiss it? How rude.' I joke. 'OK…' I think again. 'Alright, how about this: I don't like tea.'

'Even worse than your last one. What kind of confession is that?'

'I'm British! It's like a sin if you don't like tea! Peppermint: sure, anything by Pukka: absolutely, but normal, patriotic, British tea: can't stand the stuff.'

'Well, that was disgusting.' Hugo gets back in the car, followed by a green looking Sarah.

'Better?' I ask her.

'*Ugh*,' is all she can muster as she puts her head down on Hugo's lap.

I look into Dom's aqua blue eyes and wonder what the hell that exchange was about. I shake my head slightly before signalling and driving on.

***

Our hotel in Fort William looks like a haunted house: Gothic, black, creepy and we're even met by a Lurch lookalike.

'Welcome.' He stands so straight, it's a little intimidating.

'Hi, we've got four rooms, the reservation should be under *Blush*.' I smile at him, as he turns to his computer. But, after a few moments of tapping away, his face just turns into a pout.

'*Hmm*, I'm only seeing *two* rooms under that name. Let me just try again.' He taps the keys again, before confirming, 'No, I'm not mistaken; only two rooms were booked.'

'Really? Well, can we please have two more then?' I

venture.

'Oh no, the town festival is on, so we're fully booked. You sure you couldn't just make do with the two rooms?'

I look at everybody, who all shrug in agreement, tired from our trip and ready to collapse.

'Any bed,' is Sarah's reply.

'OK, sure,' I nod at Lurch.

'Right, who will be taking the double and who will have the twin?' He asks, looking at our strange party and trying to figure us out, or pair us up, I'm not sure.

'We'll take the double.' Sarah throws her arm around me, more to lean on than out of affection.

We creek our way round the corridor and when we open the door, our room is so small, it's laughable.

'I can just see Dom and Hugo bumping into each other.' I laugh as I sit on the edge of the rather lumpy bed, placing my suitcase next to me.

'Can't believe we don't have our own rooms; you don't snore do you?' Sarah winks and takes her trademark vintage Mary Jane heels off, before curling up into a ball next to me, on the bed.

'No, but I do have a rather disturbing dream every night,' I reply, unzipping my case.

'Oh, yeah. I'd forgotten about that.' She rolls towards me, and then her lips form into a sneaky smile.

'Why are you looking at me like that?'

'I must say, you were getting all chummy with Dom earlier,' Sarah enquires.

I pause, 'You were either talking, puking or sleeping on that journey; how is it possible that you'd notice anything?'

'It's a skill.' She fluffs the pillow up a little more.

'I was just getting to know him, that's all. Or, he was

getting to know *me*,' I correct, while taking out my pjs and wash bag, before heading into the bathroom. I look at myself in the mirror. *What's she getting at? Was Dom flirting with me? Was I flirting with him? I don't think so*. I get changed and ready for bed. When I open the door Sarah's sitting at the tiny little vanity mirror, taking off her jewellery.

'Do you think he was flirting with me?' I decide to ask her.

She looks at me through the mirror rather than turning around. 'Did you want him to flirt with you?' She gazes over her glasses for a moment before taking them off.

'Absolutely not! I don't even like him.'

She swivels in her seat, 'Honestly, I think you were just talking, but, you know, I think that's probably for the best, just maybe think about being careful.'

'What do you mean?'

'Say, something happens, it doesn't work out, and then you've got to be by each other's sides until the trip is over; that's not something I'd like to sign up for!' Sarah picks up a small violet bag, stands up and walks across the room; even without her heels, she still towers over me. She walks past me and into the bathroom but leaves the door open. I follow her in and sit on the closed loo seat lid.

Carefully she unpacks all manner of potions and lotions. She takes to her beautiful cat eyes first, dabbing a cotton pad with something blue, completely erasing any trace of mascara or liquid eyeliner, with one wipe. 'When was the last time you had sex?'

'Excuse me?' I say, embarrassed; far too English and prudish to answer.

'That long *huh*?' She gasps, and pauses mid-wipe, 'Was your ex-fiancé the last person you slept with?' She pauses for my answer, and I slowly nod my head.

'Oh, honey! We need to get you laid!'

'I'm just fine, thank you.'

'Well, we'll see. I'll keep an eye out for you.'

'Thanks very much.' I look down at my hands; you can still see the slight tan line of where my ring used to be.

A fresh-faced Sarah turns to me now, pointing her toothbrush at me. 'Sweetie, I think you need to move on. You're only hurting yourself — and your punani there.' She points briefly to my lady parts.

I laugh loudly. 'Well, we don't want that, do we?'

'Absolutely not!' She grins at me with her naked mouth. She is still unbelievably striking, even without a trace of makeup. Her nut-brown eyes gaze at me. 'I'm just playing, of course; I didn't mean to intrude.'

I shrug, 'Maybe I need intruding.'

***

'You expect me to get on that?! No. NO!' Sarah stays firmly seat-belted into the passenger seat.

'Hon, if you don't, how are you going to get to the wedding?' I reason, unbuckling my belt and then hers. 'Let's just go and speak to the captain, then go from there.'

When we finally drag her out of the car she's practically crying. 'Is there another way to get there?' she asks the captain hopefully.

'*Nay, frayed* not lassie. But *dunay* worry, *ye*, can sit with me!'

She takes my hand, and whispers to me as we board the boat. 'I don't know what's more terrifying.'

Our vessel is small, transporting us and others, who I'm

guessing are all heading over for the wedding too.

'Everybody! Please pass around this form, and fill in your name, address and in case of emergency contact number,' the first mate calls, waving a clipboard around.

'Why would they need that?' Sarah turns to me; I didn't know a person's eyes could get that wide.

'In case we *drooone*!' the captain says dramatically while passing us.

'Oh my God,' Sarah takes another ginger sweet to calm the nausea.

'It's just standard procedure, Sarah,' Dom says. *Hmm, I wonder how he knows that.*

'*Alreet*! Here we go! The weather is not particularly on our side today, so whale and dolphin sightings might not happen, but keep *ye* eyes peeled, *ye* never know!'

'The weather's not on our side Liv!' Sarah grips my hands even tighter, 'What does that mean?! What the '*eff* does that mean?! Oh my God.' She buries her head in my lap.

The ride is a little on the rough side, but still beautiful. The scenery of surrounding mountains is only ruined by Sarah sobbing in my lap or gripping onto my thighs.

'Everybody!' The captain calls over a tannoy, 'as luck would have it! Take a look at 9 o'clock, there's a pod of *wee* sharks! I think they're…'

The moment he says it, everybody on the ship, bar Sarah and I, who are still sitting, stand up and rush over to the other side of the boat, making it rock violently to the portside.

'*AGHHHHH*!' Sarah screams and digs her red nails into my legs, even more.

'Oh look, they're coming towards us now!' The captain

gleefully announces.

The sharks must have gone under the boat, as everyone now runs back to the starboard side, including Dom and Hugo.

'WE'RE ALL GOING TO DIE!!' Sarah screams so loudly that a small child nearby starts crying.

'Sorry,' I mouth to the mother.

***

The moment we've docked, Sarah is the first person who jumps ship onto land, suitcase and all.

'I think you handled that really well!' Hugo puts an arm around Sarah as soon as we're all standing by her side.

'Tell that to the nail marks on my legs!' I pout and rub each side gently. 'So, Couple C, what are they called?'

'Caitlin and Hamish,' Hugo says over his shoulder to me, and I get out my notebook and write that down.

'You know that you can make notes in things called *phones* nowadays. Or perhaps an iPad?' Dom sniggers at me.

I shrug, embarrassed, 'Yeah, sure. But, there's something about physically writing it out, that calls to me; it helps me feel more connected with whatever I'm doing.'

He doesn't dignify me with a response as we walk along a stoney path, and arrive at the most spectacular castle. If I were ever to write about a Disney princess, I don't think she'd be too upset about living here. Good Lord, this is grand: manicured lawns surround the turreted stone building, decorated with colourful stained glass windows, and a gravel path to greet us. I suddenly feel rather important.

We were told to meet our guide in the building adjacent to the castle, in the entrance hall. So, we walk in and follow the sound of voices.

'I can't do this!' a male voice whimpers.

'Yes, you can!' comes a slightly doubtful reply.

'It's not until tomorrow. We can do this tomorrow, right?'

'Nope. It's to be put together today, and then stored in the walk-in fridge, all ready to go,' a third voice laughs.

'*Why* was I put in charge of this? This is too much pressure.'

We walk in further to see several men, who I assume are groomsmen and a few, I'm guessing, partners, nearby.

'Hi, we're from *Blush.* I say to the room, who hadn't noticed our arrival.

'Hi! I'm Amy.' A pretty bright-eyed and bushy-tailed young thing greets us. 'Come watch Fred put the cake together.'

'I literally have to stab the wedding cake! This is too stressful.' Fred combs his hand through his bright red hair.

'Just count yourself down and do it.' A helpful bystander contributes, while not so supportingly, holding up his phone and filming the whole thing.

Fred takes a deep breath and puts one of the feet down for the second tier; everybody applauds.

'Come,' Amy says, still laughing. 'If you leave your stuff here, Fred will take care of it.'

We smile in thanks, as a relieved Fred comes towards us. The videographer has now taken over cake stabbing duties.

'And I'll take you to the happy couple's room.' Amy guides us all back to where we came in.

'They're not separate?' I ask, surprised, following her.

'Why? Cause it's bad luck to see the bride before the wedding? It's both their second marriage, so I think they've had all the bad luck already!' Amy smiles as we make our way into the actual castle. 'It's such a big place, you'd be wandering the corridors for hours trying to find them.'

'So, how do you know the happy couple?' Hugo asks.

'My partner Fred went to school with Hamish.' She leads us around another corridor, and up some stairs, before somehow going back down another set, and finally, we twist our way right then left, before Amy comes to a standstill, tapping on a large oak door. After a beat, nobody answers. '*Hmm*, I guess I should have called her.' She whips out her iPhone. 'Hey, lovely. *Blush* is here. *Uh huh*. OK, *braw*, see you in a sec.' She hangs up. 'Caitlin's in the kitchen; back this way!'

'It really is a rabbit warren, hey?' Sarah says, perhaps regretting wearing her red, vintage Mary Jane heels.

'Yeah, it's somewhere they both fell in love with immediately, but I tell you, I haven't needed to work out in the mornings since coming here.' Amy smiles once more.

After gliding us around the entire castle, we arrive at the kitchens.

'*Ye canny* have it like that! Are *ye* mad?' a loud voice floats towards us.

'*Mam*. It's a *buffay*. It really doesn't matter,' a second voice answers, even louder.

Amy clears her throat, '*Blush*, Caitlin; Caitlin, *Blush.'*

'Settle this for us will *ye*?' The bride turns to us with a red face. 'My mother here says we need a seating chart! I *donnay* need one! *Aye* had that at my first wedding, and I'll be damned to have that again. Nice to meet you,' she adds at the end, with no need for us to settle anything. 'I love you, but we're done here.' Caitlin kisses her mother on the cheek. 'Thank you for caring, but it's supposed to be relaxed, not stressful. See you at the rehearsal dinner.' She then turns to us. 'Why don't I show you your rooms?' Caitlin nods, and then leads us out of the kitchen. 'So, how was your journey?'

Sarah opens her mouth, I'm sure to launch into a dramatic account, but Hugo stops her, 'Wonderful, thank you.'

'Did you see much wildlife on the way here?' Caitlin turns a corner and we begin our up and down hike of the building.

'A couple of basking sharks!' Dom pipes up excitedly.

'Terrifying, aren't they?' Caitlin smiles, clearly not actually afraid of them.

Dom shakes his head, 'They were beautiful.'

Sarah and I look at each other; not sure "beautiful" is the word to describe a shark. When we eventually wind up along a narrow corridor, with doors on one side, and various paintings on the other, Caitlin comes to a stop. 'Hugo, you're here,' she gestures to the first door on her left, 'then Dom, Sarah and Liv.' She points to the adjacent three doors.

'Did you want to do the interview now?' I ask, thinking if we do this, ahead of schedule, I could, cheekily, squeeze in a short nap before the rehearsal dinner.

'Yeah, absolutely, we can get started and I'll message Hamish to join us.' She whips out her phone and starts typing quickly, before returning it to her back pocket.

The room is intensely floral, complete with a traditional Victorian fireplace and four-poster mahogany bed. I spot my case that's been brought up, and placed neatly next to the *chaise longue*. 'Please,' I gesture for Caitlin to sit down, then take a seat on the arm chair opposite, by the window. I can hear Sarah talking on the phone in the adjacent room, and take in the clearly, not so original, adjoining door.

'The walls are very thin here,' Caitlin laughs in amusement.

I stand and walk over to undo the lock, and open the door, tapping on her side.

When she opens it, she grins away, '*Ooh*, adjoining doors! Fun!' Sarah's face beams, then she takes in my face. 'You can hear me, can't you?'

'*Uh huh.*' I laugh.

'I'm sorry, I'll keep it down.'

I turn back, 'So, where were we?'

***

The bride and groom are my favourites so far, for sure. They're both strong, independent, know what they want individually, yet, together, they somehow compliment and balance each other out. They're great travellers and are very insistent on steering away from tradition for their big day. My favourite detail? The fact that Caitlin's going to wear an orange dress and gold heels, and all the gents, instead of kilts, will be in suits, accompanied with canvas shoes, with different superheroes on them.

After they've left my room to join Sarah and Hugo for last minute preparations, I finish my scribbles and stare out of the window. Watching as the waves crash against the shore, I remind myself to breathe. There was a time when I thought that Leo and I complimented each other, but I guess I was wrong. Heading over to the bed, I grab my phone, and lie down, to reread the last messages from Leo, even though I know exactly what they say. I've reread them time and time again, trying to make sense of everything, expecting an answer or reason to materialise from his last words to me. That's the definition of madness isn't it? Doing the same thing over and over again, expecting a different result. My thumbs hover over the keyboard; I suddenly have an overwhelming urge to talk to him. But, what do I want to say? I start typing a message, like I have so many times, and then delete it; it's not as if he's going to suddenly start responding now, is it? My eyes fill with tears and I set an alarm for half an hour's time, before putting my phone down on the bedside table; I'll ask him in my dreams.

***

After one of the most elaborate, three course dinners I've ever been to, we're sat at the table, getting to know the wedding party. I glance around at the scarlet walls, adorned with the castle's family portraits, and numerous, mounted deer heads.

'They're impressive aren't they?' the father of the groom says, following my line of sight.

'Oh, they're definitely — something,' is all I come out with.

'I noticed you didn't touch your partridge; do you not like the food?' he asks with concern, digging into third helpings of dessert.

I smile, 'Oh, the veggies were delicious, but,' I lower my voice, 'I'm a vegetarian, so.'

'Oh no!' He looks horrified. 'Why didn't you say anything?'

'Well, I did, but then,' I clear my throat and whisper, 'your wife handed me a plate full, and I didn't have the heart to tell her.' He turns to his side and taps his wife on the arm with urgency. 'Oh, no, honestly, it's fine!' I try to stop him.

'Carole, Liv is a vegetarian!' he barks in a very thick Scottish accent.

'What? We need to get you more food!' she answers in a voice that is just as panicked as her husband's, and waves over a groomsman.

'Honestly, you really don't; I'm full. Thank you so much.'

It takes me the next fifteen minutes, and I think I've convinced them I don't need any more food. But then a second helping of *cranachan* is handed to me, by Fred.

Amy is laughing from my right-hand side at this charade. 'You can't say they don't look after their guests.'

'I'm going to have to be carried out of here!' I say in a low voice before forcing in a mouthful of the sweet, and rather alcoholic dessert. 'So, how long have you and Fred been married?' I ask, after swallowing.

'Oh, we're not married.'

'I'm so sorry. When I was interviewing Caitlin about the wedding party, she said: Fred's wife, Amy.'

'Yeah, we're not officially married, but that's what everyone calls us; it's been fifteen years; "boyfriend and girlfriend" seems a little juvenile.'

I'm more embarrassed than her. 'I'm so sorry; I didn't mean to pry.'

Amy shrugs, 'Honestly, it's never bothered either of us; we're good. Never felt the need to bend to social convention; it doesn't mean anything to either of us; we're not religious. We're just happy as we are,' she shrugs again. 'So many people don't understand that. But, ultimately, it's not about them; it's about us. I don't need to prove anything; I know he loves me, he knows I love him, we're committed to each other. What's better than that?'

'A ring?' Sarah says from the other side of me, clearly eavesdropping.

'A piece of jewellery can't compare to the feelings I have for Fred. He's my soulmate,' she says softly. 'Plus, if I want a ring, I'll go get one.'

Wow. I stare at my plate, suddenly feeling lost, and honestly, a little empty — metaphorically speaking of course. I shovel in another mouthful and smile weakly at the groom's parents.

***

Leaving Hugo and Dom talking to the groom, me and Sarah sneak back to my room. After a girly gossip and a good crack at the complimentary spiced rum that's a welcome gift from the couple, Sarah stands to leave, 'I think I'll watch a little *Friends* on my iPad before turning in; want to join?'

I let out a little yawn, as she heads over to the adjoining door. 'Thanks, but I think I'm just going to hop in the shower then climb into bed.'

'No worries.' She smiles at me. 'Well, goodnight neighbour,' Sarah says, then she spins around again, 'and thank you for looking after me on the boat today; I think you're awesome.'

I smile, and yawn again, 'You're welcome.'

'Well, you enjoy, Poppet. I'll see you at breakfast.' She smiles at me and shuts her door. I follow suit, but don't feel the need to lock it.

Sighing, I walk over to the bathroom and turn the shower on to warm up, before heading back into the room to grab my toiletries. The walls really are thin: I can hear what Ross and Rachel are saying on Sarah's iPad.

The bathroom's getting nice and steamy, and stripping off, I pull the shower glass door open, step in and close it behind me. The water feels amazing. Standing there, I try to imagine all my problems, flowing off me and down into the drain. I don't want to live the rest of my life feeling this way, but how do I stop it? If I stop thinking or dreaming about my wedding day, that means I have no connection to Leo; it means we're done. I don't think I'm ready for that. He's a part of me. No. I'm not ready. I scrub my face and let all the makeup smoosh together. Pouring a generous amount of complimentary shower gel over my left palm, I lather my face up. Man, this is nice: lavender, and something else, what is that? Ylang ylang maybe? After shampoo and conditioning, I reluctantly admit it's time to get out. I turn off the water and pull the shower door to open. It doesn't budge. *Hmm. Must be stuck with the heat.* I pull again. Not even a tiny bit of movement.

Oh my God, I'm stuck in the shower! My anxiety starts to rise, and I grab the door now with both hands and pull desperately — still with no luck. '*Eff*!' Now clawing at the handle with increasing panic, and pulling with all my might, still to no avail, thoughts start racing through my head: *Oh my God! I am stuck in the shower, and I'm naked and I'm going to have to call for help. And I'm naked!!* 'SARAH!?' I paw at the side of the cubicle. 'CAN YOU HEAR ME?!' I yell from inside my steamy prison. 'SARAH! PLEASE! I NEED HELP! HELP! SARAH!?!? SAR—AGHHHHHHH!' I throw my hands over my naughty bits. 'What the hell are you doing? GET OUT!'

'Get out?' Dom says, looking away, 'It sounded like you needed help?'

'Well,' I say, desperately crimson from embarrassment, not the temperature of the room. 'Yes, I do, but I'm naked here; get me a towel!'

He folds his arms, chuckles, tilts his head, looks right into my eyes, and thankfully nowhere else, and says with amusement, 'I believe you mean, "please" hand me a towel.' He picks up a fluffy white one from the rack and plays with it in his hands.

'Fine. *Please*, hand me that towel?'

He throws it over the cubicle, then kindly turns around so I can catch it and cover myself up. 'So, what happened? Doesn't look like you've fallen or anything?'

'I'm stuck in here!' I draw the towel around myself quickly, now fully wrapped up. 'OK, you can turn around.' I say, still making sure it's not going anywhere. 'I've been pulling and pulling, but the door won't budge!'

He chuckles, then turns back around, 'I think this finds me in a rather powerful position!' Dom takes a seat on the closed loo seat, and casually folds one leg over the other.

'Ha ha! Come on, just please help me? And where's Sarah? Why were you in her room?'

'Full of questions aren't we, Brave? Well,' he picks up my toiletry bag and examines the pigtailed yellow cartoon character on the front. 'Little Miss Sunshine?'

'I've had it since I was like nine, OK? It was a gift from my childhood friend, Becky, before I moved to Paris; it makes me feel safe.'

'*Huh.*' He puts it back down. 'Sarah and I were given each other's bags by mistake, so I came to return hers. She's gone down to the bar to buy me a drink as a thank you. Good thing I heard you; if not, you'd be in there for ages.'

'I have been in here ages, even with you "helping" me. So, what do you say to *actually* helping me out?'

'Oh, no, no, no, this is too good an opportunity to pass on!' He constructs his face in a thoughtful pose, complete with a finger pressed to the right of his lips. 'What do I want in return for helping you out of the shower? I've got to say, I never thought I'd say that after the way we met.'

'Good God, would you just shut up and help me!?'

'No.' He stands and playfully strides from one side of the bathroom to the other. 'So, let's see.'

'Come on! Seriously, I am naked and locked in a shower here!' I look at him desperately.

'How about an apology for the plane?'

'What?' I fold my arms.

'An apology for your behaviour, the first time we met.' He matches my posture.

I scoff, 'I don't think so, buster. You owe *me* an apology, not the other way round!'

'Oh,' he cocks his head, 'I thought you wanted help? Guess not. Have fun sleeping in the shower.' He turns to leave the bathroom.

'No, wait, wait, please!' I say desperately.

'Yes?' He turns slowly back to face me.

'Alright,' I take a deep breath, 'I am...' I pause, 'sorry that you—'

'No, no. A proper apology, please.' He grins.

I huff, 'I'm sorry that the situation caused you to—'

'Nope. Try again.' He shakes his head.

I take a deep breath, 'Fine. I am sorry for invading your space on the plane, and,' I think back, 'whacking you in the face with my,' I pause again, 'what did you call it?'

'Mane of hair,' he helpfully adds in, and I narrow my eyes at him.

'And for dazzling you with the light when I inconsiderately lifted up the window blind, and for generally pissing you off, by just being myself. Will you help me now?'

'I suppose so.' He smiles and then pulls the door, 'You needed to *push* it from that side, not *pull*. He grins and leaves the room, while I stand, embarrassed, with the shower door ajar.

***

The following morning, over breakfast, Dom takes great delight in telling the entire wedding party about my little mishap. Laughter rang round the dining room, and I spent the entire time digging my fork aggressively into my food, pretending it was his head.

As Sarah and Hugo took to last minute preparations, my morning progressed into avoiding wherever Dom was, and turning quickly on my heel whenever I spotted him. Eventually, I decided to take a walk around the property, with the goal of making notes and shifting my mood. There's a chilly breeze, as I make my way around the castle grounds. Thank goodness the guys aren't wearing kilts, we'd definitely find out what they were wearing under them.

When time comes for guests to take their seats, I can't help but wiggle out of my fury at the fact that I ended up apologising to Dom. Looking around, I must say, I do love the little touches that are everywhere. Even though the couple decided they wanted the ceremony outside, with the castle as a backdrop, they have clearly taken into account the comfort of their guests. There's your typical two-sided guest seated set up, with an aisle down the middle, but to frame everything, there are heaters lined up around all edges, to keep everybody warm. Walking to my seat, I take in a sign next to two wicker baskets, filled with rolled up white, grey and black blankets, that reads: "To have and to hold, in case you get cold." I gratefully take a fluffy grey one, and head to my seat.

Choosing one right next to a heater, and after sitting, I wrap my legs with the blanket, bending down and tuck it all the way around.

'Hot chocolate?' I glance up to see The Hulk on a pair of canvas shoes. Sitting up, I see Fred's smiling face, carrying cups of hot chocolate.

'Wow, they really have thought of everything, haven't they? Thank you!' I gladly take it as he strides off to serve others. Gratefully, I warm my hands on the mug and take a sniff, before blowing on it and taking a sip. *Umm. Absolutely delicious!* Glancing around, I see the guests settling in and enjoying this just as much as I am. Wedding or no wedding, this is lovely. The sky is piercingly blue and now with a heater on one side and the sun on the other, I can close my eyes and pretend I'm on a beach.

'Hugo needs you.' I hear Dom's voice, disturbing my visualisation.

'I'm sorry, I'm on a beach; I can't hear you,' I say with my eyes still closed.

'What is it with you and the constant need to apologise?' Dom says with false flattery, 'It's OK, I forgive you.'

I open my eyes and frown. 'What's up?'

'Hugo said to come and find you; he needs your help.'

'Why didn't he message? Can you hold this, please?' I hand him the mug, so I can dig my phone out of my bag. I look back up and see he's taking a sip.

'*Umm,* not bad.'

'Hey!' I wave my phone at him to stop, then see I've got several missed calls from both Hugo and Sarah, *whoops*. I unwillingly unwrap myself, leaving the blanket on the chair, and stand up. Dom offers the mug back. 'I don't want that now that you've had some!'

'Suit yourself,' he takes a large gulp, and we make our way back up the aisle.

When we're out of range of guests, I give Hugo a call and open my mouth, but his voice comes through first, 'No, we've blooming lost her!'

'She's not answering,' I hear Amy say.

I finally speak, 'What? The bride? Well, that would make for an interesting spin,' I think out loud.

'*Huh*? Oh, no, not Caitlin. We've lost the officiant,' he says with a hurried tone.

'AND MY PHONE CHARGER!' I hear Caitlin scream in the background.

'It's got all the music for today on it,' Hugo whispers to me, then starts handing out orders to the room. 'Who's got the same phone? Right, you: go and get yours. Thanks. OK, Liv.'

'Yup, what do you need me to do?' Dom's waving the mug at me again to either tempt or taunt me, but I shake my head.

'Take a walk around and—'

'Crapping hell,' I hear Caitlin in the background. 'If it doesn't charge up in time, I'll be walking down the aisle in silence!' I then hear Amy's response:

'If the bloody officiant doesn't turn up, you won't be walking down the aisle at all!'

'I'm sure everything will work out,' Hugo tries to reassure her. 'Phones charge up super quickly nowadays. You: make a list with Caitlin of all the songs we need for the ceremony and download them onto yours, just in case. And

I'm sure we'll find her. Liv's on the case, now. Liv?'

'Yes, I'm here,' I say, enjoying the drama, if I'm honest.

'Have a wonder: all the buildings, the grounds, everywhere.'

'See you in about a week, then?' I joke, which is met by silence. 'I'll ring you when I find her.'

'Thank you, chick,' and he hangs up.

'Alright, the officiant has gone missing,' I explain to Dom. 'I'm going to have a walk around and find her.'

'I've taken all my pictures for this part of the day; I'll come.' Dom says.

'What is it with you following me? You hate me,' I frown at him.

'I don't hate you; you hate me,' he corrects.

I make a face; *he's not wrong*. 'Look, we haven't got time for this. You go search the building we walked into first yesterday, then come over to the castle. I'll check the dining hall first, then head to the kitchens. Whoever finds her, rings the other, deal?'

'Great plan,' he says sarcastically. 'I don't have your number,' he smirks at me.

'OK, smartarse. What's yours?' I type it into my phone and then ring it. 'There you go.'

We dash off in opposite directions, and I walk through the castle entrance. It's quiet, with not a soul about. The table is beautifully dressed for the reception with candelabras and a bright selection of mango Nairobi roses, sunset calla lilies, contrasting with the violet lisianthus and blue eryngium. I'm just about to head to the kitchen when Dom rings me.

'I've got her. Ring Hugo,' is all he says and then hangs up.

I dial and Hugo answers after one ring, 'Dom's got her.'

'WE'VE FOUND HER!' Hugo yells at the room. 'Thanks, sweetheart. Tell Dom to whisk her our way.'

'Will do.' I hang up and ring Dom, instruct him to go to the bridal suite, then make my way back to my seat.

Sarah and Hugo finally join me, but the wedding doesn't start for another twenty minutes. Suddenly, Queen's "Fat Bottomed Girls" plays loudly over the PA and then stops abruptly. I can't help but join in with the entire congregation, laughing. Then, as if that wasn't enough, her actual song comes on, which I find equally as funny: Etta James' "At Last." Sarah nudges me in the ribs and I bite my lip as we all turn and watch Caitlin glide down the aisle.

***

The happy couple told me they didn't want anything to be traditional or expected. As far as I'm concerned, *this* is far from expected. Caitlin's a trained dancer, and as their first dance, they're doing the full choreography of Ed Sheeran's "Thinking Out Loud." I watch with amazement as she kicks her legs up in the air, jumps and he catches her; they twirl around the dance floor as if they can read each other's minds. I'm trying to stay focused on them, but as soon as the song came on, I instantly felt my eyes well up. This would have to be the very song that was playing when I met Leo. I shut my eyes to try and block it out, but instead, I go right back there.

He glides towards me smiling. 'You're laughing at the couple?' Leo says.

I shake my head, 'I'm sure I have no idea what you're talking about.' I return my eyes to our friends, attempting to dance, and truly failing. 'I think it's sweet.'

'I think it's hilarious,' Leo says quietly, and we both giggle while the happy couple move into an awkward sort of body shuffle, with their own beat. The bride gestures for everyone to join the dance floor, with an embarrassed facial expression. 'Shall we show them how it's done?' Leo asks me, as the rest of the party join the chequered dance floor.

'Dancing with a stranger? I don't know about that,' I play.

'Promise I'll be gentle,' Leo grins at me, offering his hand, and it was like that moment in *Aladdin* where he asks Jasmine, "Do you trust me?" I did trust him. Taking his hand, he guides me effortlessly to the middle, then starts to sing the chorus. By the end of that dance, I was pretty sure I was in love with him.

Opening my eyes, I bring myself back to the room to the sound of applause. Caitlin and Hamish kiss and I numbly join in the clapping. It's not until then that I notice Dom is looking at me; his eyes are filled with tears too.

Chapter 6

UK – Netherlands – France
Isle of Rum – Mallaig – Edinburgh – Amsterdam – Bordeaux – Saint-Estèphe

Thursday
Sail 1 hour 40 minutes: Isle of Rum – Mallaig
Drive 4 hours: Mallaig – Edinburgh Airport (1 night stay)

Friday
Depart Edinburgh Airport at 06:00
Arrive Amsterdam Schiphol Airport at 08:35
Duration: 1 hour 35 minutes (50-minute layover in Amsterdam)
Time change: Amsterdam 1 hour ahead

Depart Amsterdam Schiphol Airport at 09:25
Arrive Bordeaux Airport 11:05
Duration: 2 hours and 30 minutes
Drive 1 hour to Saint-Estèphe (3 nights stay)

I know I've gone into myself. I can't really remember much of the journey from The Isle of Rum to Edinburgh. As if in a trance, I followed everyone, numbly, and didn't speak a word until we landed in Bordeaux; not even my favourite revitalising spray can spritz me out of it.

'I'm sorry,' I say quietly to Sarah as we exit the plane. 'I think I've blacked out; isn't the next wedding in Malaga?'

Sarah looks at me with quiet concern, 'Yes, Poppet, but we weren't able to get a hotel in Malaga, due to the Easter Week celebrations. Hugo mentioned he had family this side of the globe, and so we're staying with them for the weekend, then we fly on Monday to Spain, meet the groom and best man, then continue from there. Are you OK?' she adds, taking me in.

I nod, 'Oh, yeah. Terrific.' I smile weakly.

We make our way through customs and Sarah suddenly runs forwards, 'What the actual? Quick, take a picture of me!' Sarah rushes over to one of the person-sized bottles of Bordeaux dotted around, which is amazingly, taller than her. It's not my first time here so I knew they were there; it's so funny to watch the reaction of people who are seeing them for the first time.

She puts her arms around the bottle like an old friend and gives a thumbs up with the other hand.

'Beautiful,' I giggle after snapping a few shots — one in which involved her pretending to lick the bottle.

'Is that the mystical methuselah?' asks Hugo, spotting it for the first time after checking his phone.

'A what?' Sarah looks at him. I go to open my mouth and Dom speaks.

'No,' he says flatly. 'It's just a prop.'

'Who invited Mr Pooper to the party?! OK, Philippe is outside, opposite the car rental pick up.' Hugo leads our parade into the early April sunshine, which feels very welcome after the chilly breeze of Scotland. Dom marches along by Hugo's side, and Sarah and I walk behind.

I lower my voice, so only Sarah can hear, 'And Philippe

is?'

'Hugo's uncle,' she confirms.

'OK.' I still feel lost. Sarah somehow reads that and continues.

'Philippe moved from his hometown of gay Paris to Saint-Estèphe. He and his wife Giselle run a B and B there, and bonus: give wine tours too!' She raises her eyebrows at me playfully.

Hugo and Philippe greet each other with kisses and speak in furiously fast French, grinning from ear to ear. 'Everybody,' Hugo turns, and introduces us with a gesture of his left hand, 'Sarah, Liv and Dom, this is my uncle, Philippe.'

He lightly puts a hand on each of Sarah's arms before kissing her on her right then left check, '*Enchanté.*'

'I'm afraid I don't speak a word of French, but *Enchantée* to you too!' She replies with a huge goofy grin, clearly smitten.

He turns to me, smiling and kisses me on both cheeks too, '*Enchanté.*'

'*Et toi aussi. Merci beaucoup pour l'invitation*!'

'*Bien sûr! Il nous fait plaisir.*' He turns his head, 'Hugo, you didn't tell me Liv spoke French!'

He makes a face, 'I didn't realise!'

'Just a little,' I brush it off.

'Nonsense, that was more than a little!' Philippe puts his arm around me.

'Well, I may have lived in Paris for a year. But I was nine so...' I fade off, embarrassed.

'*C'est magnifique!* We must talk all about it,' he beams at me.

Finally, he turns to Dom, who, quite firmly sticks his

hand out at arm's length, attempting to not be greeted in the traditional fashion, '*Bonjour*,' Dom says, but Philippe responds by shaking his hand before pulling him in for the same kisses he graced for Sarah and I. 'Come! The car is this way.'

***

I will never tire of the sheer, simplistic beauty of this place. The rustic houses aren't like anything else, and the fields display row after row of grapevines; I drink in every delicious view on the way to Saint-Estèphe.

'I can't tell you how grateful the magazine is for you to be doing this!' Sarah says in between sticking her face to the window like a dog that wants to get out of the car and explore.

'Hugo is family, so you are family!' Philippe beams, 'Actually, your timing could not have been more perfect. We had guests leave this morning, and no one else will be at the house until two days after you leave, so the whole place is reserved just for you!'

'You've managed to give us a holiday in between what most people would consider a holiday,' I say gratefully, feeling my spirits lift slightly.

'We are supposed to be working though,' Dom says seriously. 'They'll want your first drafts and my shots!'

'I know. But, way to take all the fun out of it!' I poke my tongue out at Dom.

'Oh my God, do that again,' he says a little too loudly.

'What? Poke my tongue out? Why?'

'It's huge!' He's staring incredulously at my face.

'No, it's not!' I defend 'It's a perfectly normal tongue.'

'Normal next to Gene Simmons maybe! Do it again!' Dom is laughing hard.

Everyone is now looking at me in the car. 'Let's see it!' Sarah joins in.

'Whose side are you on?' I widened my eyes at her.

'Whatever side gets me to see your tongue!'

'Fine.' I poke it out, and admittedly, I can touch my chin with it.

'Wow!'

'Incredible!'

They chorus together.

'Shall we stop here for some food?' I suggest as we pass a supermarket, which I do mean, but at the same time attempt to change the subject.

'No need,' Philippe turns into a small, winding lane, 'Giselle has been shopping already today. She is preparing a snack for you now; you are not to buy anything while you are our guests,' his tone is firm but in no way threatening.

'Wow. Thank you,' I say, but fully intend to buy something as a thank you before we leave.

We pull up at the house. It is simply, in one word: charming. There's a small swimming pool to the right, a huge garage behind, that stretches up to meet the house; it clearly isn't used to house cars, as you can see a games room through the open doors. We pull up and park on the driveway and park under a giant olive tree.

'This is beautiful!' I gasp as we take our cases out of the boot.

'It is your home for the weekend!' Philippe says, as Hugo puts a loving arm around him.

A lady in, I would guess, her sixties, but you'd never know it, behind her youthful face, appears at the front door, wearing a pinny and drying her hands on a tea towel. '*Bonjour*! Welcome! *Ça va*?' She greets each of us with a warm hug followed by two kisses.

Just beyond the driveway is a huge garden with several choices of places to sit. Fruit trees mark the edge of the property, and the main house, which is typically French with painted wooden window shutters. I marvel at the mezzanine, complete with pergola, and draped in wisteria.

'*Vous devez être affamés! Venez, venez, s'il vous plaît, mangez*!' Giselle waves us to follow her to the house.

'What did she say?' Sarah whispers to me.

'We must be starving, and she wants us to come eat.'

'No need to ask me twice.' Sarah grins and links my arm.

***

Snack wasn't the right word, and Philippe wasn't kidding when he said she'd been shopping; there's a feast here. I tucked gleefully into the freshly bought, and clearly made today, crusty baguette, with an unhealthy slaver of butter.

Giselle looks lovingly at Philippe, 'My darling, would you care to give them a tour, while I finish preparing more wine and dessert.'

I like that sentence. Not even been here for two seconds and I'm eating like royalty, and about to be served some more delicious local wine; I think I might have just made some life-long friends. Giselle kisses Philippe on the cheek and he stands to give us a tour of the property.

'We are renovating everything ourselves; hardest six months I've ever had! But, I can now plaster walls as good as a professional!' he beams.

We walk up a tight, winding metal staircase and Philippe

shows us each to our bedrooms; I decide to freshen up before dessert. Closing my door, I see there's a little key inside to lock it, so give it a turn. My bed is of sleigh design, and the room, according to our tour, has the original wallpaper. I open my shutters with glee and stick my head out; it's the tiny alley we drove down. To the right, I see a field of vines and to the left, the town; it's so sleepy, it's as if we're the only people around. Back in the room, to the left of where I'm standing, is my own en suite. It's so modern compared to the rest of the room, but I love it. *Ooh*, it's got a monsoon shower, with a bamboo tray; can't wait to try that later. I note with a slight giggle, the sliding door, and reckon I'll be OK with this one.

When I come down the spiral staircase and out onto the veranda to join the others, I'm met with joy and laughter. 'Here,' Philippe hands me a glass, *'Blanc, rosé ou rouge*?'

'*Rosé, s'il vous plaît.'*

Philippe selects the *rosé*, and begins to fill a glass, before handing it to me.

'*Salute*,' I take a sip of the gorgeous wine. I'm wearing my wrap, but honestly, I'm comfortable even without it. 'Is it normally this warm this time of year?'

'It's unusually warm,' Giselle answers. 'Normally we are saying goodbye to a little snow! I don't know what is going on, but I do not question it.' She lifts her glass to me. 'So, welcome, family, and friends; to your health.'

***

The day continues into night, just like this, and hours later, I am completely stuffed, and have no idea how many bottles of wine we've collectively drunk.

'Can we spend the rest of the month here please?' I whine to Sarah, who's just as drunk as I am. We weave our way around the garden, arm in arm. My problems seem to be so far away now.

'Sounds fabulous, Poppet; sign me up!' she goes to take a sip of her glass, with a bit too much force, and spills some of her wine over her top, but doesn't notice.

We mosey our way to the elegantly lit pool and sit on two loungers, facing the house. I watch as swallows dart in and out of the garage; they've been doing this on and off all day, but now at night, they look like little bats.

'It's so special here, isn't it? Why is that, do you think?'

'There's our interviewer.' She turns to me, and tries to focus her eyes, 'Well,' she slurs at me, 'Miss...' she stops and looks at me in horror, 'Oh my God, I don't know your last name! What's your last name?'

'Bennett,' I smile at her.

'Miss Bennett,' she continues in a British accent, 'I believe this establishment is special because it is free: free housing, free food, free wine, free, free freedom. Blah de blah blah. God save the King.'

We both fall about in fits of giggles.

'I feel like I've known you forever,' I come out with giving her a hug/strangle.

'Me too!' She looks at me like a long-lost friend, 'It's like we've got this sisterhood vibe happening. And I must say, she lowers her voice to a stage whisper 'You're *mush* better than Heather.'

'Hugo said that to me!'

'Well, that's because it's true!' She taps the side of the deck chair.

'Well, I'll take it!' I tap my chair in response.

'Honestly, I think Dom likes working with you more than her. And who knows where that might lead. You have a...' she pauses and looks at her hands before threading her fingers together, 'a connection!'

'No, we don't! He can't stand me!'

'Exactly! The best relationships start out of hate.'

'I think that's *friendship*, Sarah.'

'Rubbish! In fact!' She returns to her aristocratic accent. 'I, Sarah Talulah—'

'Talulah?!' I laugh.

'Yes, Talulah McBride, declare a prediction that you, Olivia...' she gestures for me to fill in my full name.

'Bethany Bennett,' I finish.

'Olivia Bethany Bennett, you will take Dom as your prize, by having your wicked way with him, by the end of the trip.'

'And what if I don't?' I laugh.

'Then I will sleep with Hugo,' she says with all seriousness and a face that's trying very hard not to break into a smile. We both fall about laughing again as Hugo appears.

'Did I hear my name?' He comes and joins us at the pool.

'Sarah was just saying she's going to sleep with you by the end of the trip,' I laugh.

'Wouldn't that be interesting,' he answers, looking down shyly. 'More likely that those two will get together.' He gestures at me then Dom, who's now walking towards us too.

'That's the bet!' Sarah says, slapping the arms of her deckchair.

'*Shhhhh!*' I put my hand on her mouth, 'Hello!' I say to Dom, who's now sitting opposite me.

'Why the "*shhing*?"' Dom looks from one drunk woman to the other.

'Oh, nothing!' I hurry to say, as Hugo goes to open his mouth.

Dom's eyebrows twitch together, but he leaves whatever thought he had in his head, 'Philippe was asking if we want to go to a vineyard tomorrow.'

'I don't think that's a question, it's a statement: we want to go to a vineyard tomorrow!' I say with all seriousness.

***

I wake the next morning without an alarm, bright and breezy and I know it's early, but decide to get up anyway. Amazingly, my head doesn't hurt; I've always found that European wine is the most kind to my body. It's like magic wine: it doesn't matter how much I drink, I'm always OK the next day. I whip the covers off, throw on my "*In a world where you can be anything, be kind,"* jumper, grab my laptop, my notebook, and pad my way silently down the stairs.

I've always been one of those mad people, who actually likes getting up early, catching a sunrise while sipping a coffee and planning out my day. I used to be someone who also loved a yoga workout too, but since Leo left my life, I fell out of that habit. It's as if I know what's good for me, but I can't bring myself to do it; like I deserve to be punished or something, and I don't deserve to do anything that brings me joy. It also slows me down, and for the last year, I haven't wanted to slow down. If I do, my feelings might catch up with me.

I prepare a cafetière of ground coffee, then flip the kettle to boil. Instead of waiting there, I turn the large key that's in the door to the patio, and head outside to set up a work space. I haven't actually done any writing since this trip started — that's not true, I've made notes, but my article has yet to leave my brain. Sitting on one of the wiry blue chairs, under the wisteria, I place my laptop on the wooden table, open the lid, and then a new word document. I look blankly at it for a moment before my fingers start gliding over the keys like an elegant dancer — sometimes it genuinely surprises me that my hands know what I'm saying before my brain does. I glance at my notebook, then stare ahead of me, to see the first wedding in my mind's eye, when a deep voice makes me jump.

'Did somebody order a coffee?' Dom's standing there with the full cafetière and two mugs.

Clutching my beating heart, I gasp, 'Oh my God, you scared me.'

'Looked like you were in the zone.' Dom agrees, or states that as some form of an apology, I'm not sure which.

I catch my breath, '*Um*, yeah, I was at the first wedding; I can literally transport my brain there.' He looks at me blankly, so I explain. 'I have a vivid imagination.'

'Is that so?' He places the cafetière and mugs down, and then joins me on the adjacent chair.

I nod, 'Yup, it's a gift. Give me any scenario, and I can just,' I click my fingers, 'immediately be there; I can see every detail.'

'Like a photographic memory?' he offers.

'Not exactly. It's more like hyperthymesia,' I say.

'And what the heck is that?'

'Well, I can remember, and even see past events, in my head, in great detail.'

'With your eyes open?' He gently pushes the plunger of the cafetière down.

'Yup, someone could even be talking, and I go somewhere else; I wonder what I look like as I'm doing that?' I ponder out loud.

'Here.' He hands me a cup.

'How do you know I don't want milk?' I ask, hugging the mug with both hands.

'Because every morning you've taken it black,' he answers reasonably.

'Good answer. Why are you up so early?' I sip the coffee; it's perfect, strong, aromatic, and at a "ready to sip" temperature.

'Couldn't sleep; think I might still be drunk from last night.'

'Really? Lightweight,' I quip.

'I'm not normally a wine drinker; espresso martinis are my favourite.'

'Shut up! They're my favourite! Vodka or rum?'

'Rum,' he says firmly.

I shake my head, 'No, you're wrong. The right answer is vodka.'

'I like beer too,' he says, quickly.

'*I like beer too*,' I imitate his voice — albeit rather badly.

'That was terrible.'

'Yeah, I can't really do impressions,' I admit.

He smiles and then graces me with a look of enquiry.

'What?'

'I can't help but feel that sweatshirt is for me,' he gestures to me with his mug before taking a sip.

'My jumper? Really?'

'Yeah, like you still haven't forgiven me from the plane.'

I turn to him, 'You made me apologise to *you*, while I was naked in a shower. There's nothing *kind* about that.' I sip my drink. 'The way you behaved towards *me* when we first met? You have to admit, that was rather a rude introduction.'

He nods, 'I do.' But he doesn't elaborate into any kind of apology, even though he looks like he's internally having a debate with himself. I just watch him with mild amusement. 'Well, I'll let you get back to writing.' He goes to stand.

'You can sit there; I just might ignore you.'

'Fine by me.'

***

We exit Philippe's car, a little after lunchtime and I'm still full from the elaborate spread. Sarah, looking a little worse for wear, hasn't taken off her sunglasses all morning, despite the fact that it's a little cloudy. 'I'm not sure I can handle any more wine.' She confides in me as we walk into the main cinema room for a brief history on the vineyard.

'Well, maybe shut your eyes and have a little snooze for the next bit?' I suggest, helpfully.

'Good plan.' She wobbles to a seat in the second row after Hugo and curls up.

'Welcome to *Chateau Maucaillou*! It was in 1875 that—'

'You know I was trying to apologise earlier?' Dom leans in from my right.

I clear my throat, and point at the screen, 'Excuse me, I'm trying to watch the film.' With Leo racing around in my head, I simply don't have room for another man's ego.

'You seem extra mad today,' he goes on, ignoring my response.

'And you seem extra annoying.' I *shush* him and then apologise to Philippe, who's looking down the row. 'Whatever you have to say, I'm not interested. As far as I'm concerned, we're here to do a job, and that's it. Now, listen, we're missing it.' I point again at the screen, where ladies are now walking around a large barrel, barefoot, and I can't help but think of Lucille Ball, and smile.

'Kind of like that scene from *Pretty Woman*, right*?'* Dom continues to try and talk to me.

'What?' I snap at him.

'Well, not, originally *Pretty Woman*, of course, it was a scene from, *I Love Lucy*.' I look at him and feel my utter disgust rising. He retreats slightly, apparently my face is saying all I need to, 'Alright, no need to look at me like that; you're missing the film,' he says, pointedly, and motions towards the screen.

After the short film has finished, we're taken around the museum of history and the fermentation room, when Dom leans into me, once more, 'When do we get to the booze part, am I right?' I frown at him, and he takes the hint to move far away from me. Dom didn't need to wait long, though, we're now in a large room, with low lighting, which kind of reminds me of that old wine place along the Southbank that shut down, what was it called? *Ooh*, yeah, Vinopolis; except the air conditioning is insane. I shiver slightly as we wander through hundreds of barrels that are lined up; we walk to the far end, where there's a small table and six small samples of wine.

'That's it?' Dom says, I think, unintentionally out loud.

'Honestly, I don't think I could handle any more; this is perfect,' Sarah says, sniffing, then swirling it, as instructed.

'It is, of course, more about the experience, than the intoxication.' Philippe takes the words out of my mouth, and I can't help but think that there is a true, jack the lad, Londoner in there, as I stare at Dom who downs his wine in one large, ungrateful gulp.

Chapter 7

France – Spain
Saint-Estèphe – Bordeaux – Malaga

Monday
Drive 1 hour: St Estèphe – Bordeaux Airport
Depart Bordeaux Airport at 11:50
Arrive Malaga Airport at 13:40
Duration: 1 hour 50 minutes
Drive 15 minutes (cab ride) to hotel (2 nights stay)

Couple D
Church of Santa Maria, and La Cala Mountain Resort, Malaga, Spain

I spend Saturday night and Sunday with my head in my laptop and having polite conversations with Philippe and Giselle over mealtimes; I feel honestly so blessed to be given this kind of treatment, waited-on hand and foot. When we head to the airport early Monday, I'm sad to be leaving such fabulous company. The only thing keeping my spirits up, is that of all the places on the list, I am particularly excited about this one; Malaga truly is one of my favourite places in the entire world.

After our short flight and cab ride, I left the others at our hotel and had the most wonderful afternoon, enjoying a wander around the city, and sitting with my laptop and several *cafe solos*, in the sunshine. There was even time for a *siesta* before getting ready for the evening.

We're staying at the AC Palacio — one of my favourites — right in the centre of Malaga. The rooftop bar has the most amazing view of the city. I told the others to meet me up there, before we go off and meet the next groom (Pablo), and his best man, (Juan-Antonio).

Looking to my left, I gaze out at the sleepy port, then to my right, towards the brightly lit cathedral. Even though night has fallen, there's still a dusky view of the surrounding mountains that wrap beautifully around the city in a big hug. I smile at the city and wonder if there's time for a swift something before we get going. Looking at my watch, I see it's only 10:15 pm; we're meeting the groom at 11 pm; that's right, 11 pm. The Spanish have always been so fascinating to me. Most people, I would think, might want to get some sleep the night before their wedding, but Pablo said they were going out anyway, invited us along, and what better time for an interview with him!

'Oh, wow!' Sarah totters her way around the edge of the rooftop pool, then joins me at a high table. 'This is incredible!' She gazes out at the beauty around us.

'I bet it's a better view from up there,' I point to her slightly higher than normal, black vintage Mary Janes, with a white trim and small bow. 'Nice shoes.'

'Thanks!' She poses before waving at a waiter. 'What shall we have?'

'Wine?' I suggest. Sarah shakes her head, clearly somewhat traumatised from France. 'Or they have this amazing rum called *Legendario*?' I add, excitedly.

'Perfect!' Sarah leans on the adjacent bar stool and gazes

around again.

'Shall we order that for Hugo and Dom, too? I know Dom will like it, but will Hugo?'

'How do you know that Dom likes rum?' Sarah stands tall, flicks her eyes back to me, and looks me up and down.

'He had rum on the plane when I first met him, and he told me he prefers rum in an espresso martini,' I say, almost defensively.

'Fair enough. But, yeah, anything alcoholic is fine for Hugo.' She takes out her phone and snaps several pictures of the view. 'Here, let's do a selfie.' Sarah walks to my side and bends down to have her head at the same height as mine. 'Say: *Legendario*!'

'*Legendario*!' We both chorus as the waiter smiles at us both,

'*Buenas noches*.'

'Buenas noches, quiero cuatro Legendarios por favor.'

'*¿Con cola*?'

'*Solo con hielo por favor*.'

He nods and walks away as Sarah looks at the photo, 'That's cute; I'll send that to you.' She taps away, then, putting the phone down, looks up at me, 'So you speak Spanish too?' She shakes her head, 'I can barely speak English on a good day. What did you say about cola?'

I look up at her, wishing I'd worn some sort of heel, instead of my little plimsolls. 'Just that we'd like straight rum, with a little ice, baby.'

She clutches her chest, 'Fabulous!' Then she throws her arm around me and takes in the city once again. 'Man! This is so beautiful up here.'

'I know, I can't wait to see the view from the reception tomorrow! It's up there in the mountains!' I point up and slightly to the left of the cathedral.

The waiter brings over our drinks, eyeing us slightly suspiciously; I wonder if he thinks we're having two each.

'Well, here is to...what? What shall we toast to?' Sarah pauses with a tumbler aloft, the ice clinking merrily together.

I think for a moment before saying, '*¡Por nuevas amistades, nuevas aventuras y nuevos amores!*' She stares at me blankly and I laugh, before translating, 'For new friendships, new adventures and new love.' I raise my glass to hers.

'I'll drink to that.' She clinks my glass.

'You've started without us?' Hugo whines slightly, now joining us, with Dom by his side.

'Just a toast,' I reassure him, then put my glass down, so I can hand one to each of them.

'You look very handsome,' Sarah comments to both gents.

'I tend to scrub up well,' Hugo says with a lift of his plaid-clad right shoulder, and simultaneous stroke to his beard, giving us a playful side glance. Dom shifts, almost uncomfortably; he's wearing black jeans and another of his striped shirts.

'So what were you raising a toast to?' Dom asks. *Does he do any other expressions apart from disgruntled?*

'Friendship, adventure and love,' I say, lifting my glass once more.

Dom pauses and a wave of hurt crosses his expression, 'I'll certainly drink to the first two.'

'Oh, come on spoilsport.' Sarah moves from my shoulders to his. 'Maybe it's time for you to let go of the past, too.'

'Too?' he questions, looking at me.

'Too,' I say, nodding ever so slightly. If only I could feel as confident as I sound.

***

Pablo and his best man Juan-Antonio, are at the bottom of the steps to our hotel, casually dressed in light jackets, crisp white shirts, and blue jeans.

'*¡Hola!*' Sarah says in her thick Brooklyn accent.

'¡Hola*! ¿Cómo estás*?' Pablo greets her with two kisses. She pulls away and grimaces.

'I'm sorry, "*¡Hola!*" is all I've got.'

'No problem,' he smiles; his teeth are so white, they almost glow in the dark.

'Lovely to meet you in person, Sarah.'

'You too! You must be Juan-Antonio,' Sarah turns to Pablo's right.

'No,' he says, not in an unfriendly way, but definitely with the voice of a teacher.

'No? You're not the best man?' she glances at him, confused.

'No, you're saying my name wrong. It's *WHOOAHN*, A*n-TO-knee-o*.'

She imitates him, elongating and emphasising just as he did, and I can't help but laugh.

Pablo greets the boys and then turns to me, 'and you must be Liv.' He kisses me on both cheeks. '*¿Cómo estás*?'

'*¡Bien! ¡Bien! ¡Gracias! ¿Y tú*?'

'*¡Bien! ¿Hablas español*?'

'*Hablo un poco de español*,' I correct him.

He smiles broadly at me, '*¿Tienes hambre? ¿Quieres comer algo?*'

'Si! ¡Vamos!'

Dom looks incredulously at our exchange, as Pablo leads the way.

'What did you just say?'

'I said, I'm good, I speak a little Spanish and yes, let's go; we're going to get something to eat.'

He shakes his head, 'You are full of surprises.'

'I am just a girl who loves languages: written, spoken, sung, it doesn't matter; sign me up, I want to learn everything!'

His face changes to an expression that can only be described as: impressed.

We make our way towards the centre of town, walking up the brightly lit road: Larios.

'I just can't believe it,' Sarah exclaims as she looks down at the ground. 'It's *marble*?'

'Yup, beautiful, isn't it?' I smile at her. I remember being completely mesmerised by this too on my first visit, years ago. 'But it's the ground! She says incredulously, throwing her arms down and gesturing to the floor. 'Why is the *ground* made of marble?'

As Pablo and Juan answer Sarah and give a detailed account of the money that was put into refurbing the city, I gaze around and take in the tall buildings, shops, and happy people. The weather's kind of perfect too, warm enough for only a little jacket.

I love Spain. It feels like a completely different world, where time shifts into an alternate reality; if it's night time, it's play time. Every restaurant we pass is completely packed out. Friends and family spill out of doors, windows and even onto the patios of every single place we pass, and beyond, encompassing the entire pavement in some cases. We settle on a venue with huge beer barrels outside that act as tables, and are served straight away.

I watch Pablo as he hugs the waiter; I guess they know each other. You'd never think that this guy was getting married tomorrow; it's as if he has all the time in the world, for any and everybody. After the waiter has taken our drinks order, he offers to bring us a little of everything from the menu. I love tapas. Leaning on my elbows, I face the groom. 'So, tell me about your bride-to-be.'

Pablo's face lights up, he touches his hands to his heart, and a part of me can't help but feel a pang of jealousy. 'To me, she is everything. There has never been more of a pure soul. Gracie is, *how you say*? My soulmate.'

The groom continues gushing over her for about half an hour and I'm jotting down as much as I can, in my little trusty notebook, all the while munching on possibly the most delicious *tortilla*, and *patatas bravas* I've ever eaten.

'And how did you propose?' I ask, before taking a sip of my sangria.

'This story is so beautiful,' Juan says, before picking up some breaded squid.

I smile in anticipation, but at the same time try to ignore the pang of jealousy.

'Have you met Gracie's maid of honour, Mel, yet?'

'No, tomorrow's the first time,' I say.

'Ah, OK, well, last year, it was her and her husband's wedding. We were all at the Greenwich Observatory.'

'Wow, that must have been expensive. I'm sorry,' I add, clearly my filter isn't on today, but it doesn't seem to faze Pablo who shrugs.

'They both had a pretty amazing year; he's an architect. He won a huge contract with, what are they called, the sweetie brothers?'

'The Candy Brothers?' I offer incredulously.

He points at me, '*Si*, that's the one. And have you ever had: "Nanna's Favourites?"

'The delicious cake brand at Sainsburys? Oh my gosh I love the coconut, almond butter Twix-like ones!'

He nods, 'Mel is the founder.'

'What? Oh wow.' I take that in. *What must it feel like to follow a dream? How inspiring.* I shake my head, having floated off, 'I'm sorry, so, you were at their wedding.' I gesture for him to continue.

He smiles at me, 'I knew I was going to propose to Gracie and so I plotted with Mel; she was about to throw the bouquet, and instead, Mel walked over to Gracie, handed it to her, and when Gracie turned, I was on one knee.'

'Oh my God, that's the most romantic thing I've ever heard,' I feel my eyes well-up ever so slightly, so I blink them away.

'It was Mel's idea.' He smiles, 'She's a beautiful soul too.' Our waiter calls Pablo to head inside. 'If you could excuse me.'

'Of course,' I smile, and he stands and bows, before turning away.

'All a bit cheesy if you ask me,' Dom says under his breath before shovelling a couple more prawns in his mouth.

'Well, no one's asked you,' I confirm, my eyes fall onto his stripy shirt, and I stifle a giggle. 'You've got a little something, there,' I gesture down to his entire chest, which is now covered in a light pink juice. He looks down, then back up at me and shrugs.

'Who am I trying to impress?'

'Good point.' I scowl at him.

Suddenly a couple of musicians appear in front of us and start singing and playing guitar. I jiggle my shoulders, and smile at them all; a very welcome distraction.

'*¿Quieres bailar*?' I turn to see Juan holding out his hand to me, and raising his eyebrow, playfully.

'Thank you; I'd love to dance, but I'm not sure I could remember what I'm doing. I had a couple of lessons when I was here before: salsa, bachata, even a bit of tango, can you believe, but—'

That's enough encouragement for him, as Juan grabs my hand and leads me onto the makeshift dance floor, which is the alley we're sitting in. 'All you need is two things,' he says with all seriousness, 'one, to follow my lead and two,' he smiles wide, 'to have a good time.'

Man, he's a good dancer, and I have to admit, I'm following really well; I guess that shows how good *he* is at leading. We twist, turn, Suzie-Q, tangle and untangle our arms, and before I know it, the music has stopped.

He takes my hands in his, bows low and then kisses my right hand before straightening up. Still holding my hand, we walk back to the table. Sarah and Hugo are completely oblivious and deep in conversation with Pablo, who I guess returned to the table at some point during my dance, but I can't help but notice Dom is shifting in his seat, pretending not to watch us return. Catching his eye, he quickly looks away. *What a weirdo.*

***

The next morning, we're in the home of the soon to be: *Señor y Señora.* Sarah is doing the bride's makeup, Dom is taking pictures of the dresses and shoes that Hugo is laying out, and I'm sitting on a beautiful sofa, filled with brightly coloured cushions.

The bride is as visibly bouncy as her blonde curls. She's from Blackheath in London, and the groom is from Malaga. From each of the interviews so far, I've learned that the couple had a long-distance relationship, then split their time equally between here and there, but after the wedding they will officially call Malaga their full-time home.

'Well, I do have my heart set on Rincón de la Victoria!' Gracie beams.

'I'm sorry, I don't know it,' I say.

'Oh, it's about a twenty-minute drive from here,' Gracie sneezes as Sarah lightly brushes her nose with powder, then giggles.

'It's annoyingly perfect for families,' one of her bridesmaids, Jill, says, while smiling at her friend.

'You're just jealous she found the man of her dreams while we were on holiday,' maid of honour, Mel, says, seated comfortably on a rocking chair next to us, with her hands in her lap.

'Yes, tell me about that, Gracie,' I scribble in my notebook.

'Mel here was recovering from a broken heart,' I glance at Mel, who is a glowing vision of happiness; I wonder if I'll ever get there? Gracie continues, 'So, we all booked a last minute trip to Malaga, staying at Dave's cousin's apartment, and Pablo was our guide; he's a friend of Dave's cousin.'

'Right,' I say, scribbling to keep up. I'll ask who Dave is in a minute.

'I don't know, we just hit it off from there!' Gracie grins dreamily.

'It was sickening to watch.'

'It was beautiful to watch,' Mel corrects a jokingly disgruntled Jill.

'It was inspiring to watch!' A smartly dressed man with CK rimmed glasses comes out of the bathroom; I didn't realise anyone was in there.

'Hey man!' Sarah stops powdering Gracie's face, and directs the brush at him, 'this is a girls only room.'

'Dave is one of the girls,' Mel says with a smile to me before going over and adjusting his bowtie.

'He's my third bridesmaid,' Gracie confirms.

'Oh,' I say surprised, 'I love that.' I scribble away in my notebook, then look over at Dave. He smiles at Mel and puts his hands on her stomach.

'Is it obvious? I don't just look like I ate all the pies?' Mel says stroking her tiny bump, proudly but ever so slightly insecurely.

'It is, and it's fabulous.' He kisses Mel on the forehead, 'Right! I'll leave you girlies for a moment; Dermott's downstairs with the bouquets!' He prances off.

***

'Best wedding by far,' Hugo says to me in the cab to the church. 'The bride's friend Mish is an event organiser I've been working with; she's beyond brilliant. Practically did my work for me.'

'I'll leave that out of the article, shall I?' I smile at him.

'I took her number; we're going to see if we can do a collaboration in the future.'

'Wonderful!' I say, as we pull up outside the venue, and I gaze up in awe. The church of Santa Maria is huge. Wide sweeping steps, towering up so tall that you have to completely tilt your head up to see the top of the building. The day could not be more perfect for them: blue skies, sunshine, not too hot. I turn my face to the sun, close my eyes and take a deep breath.

As we climb the steps, I take in the crowd: the majority of guests are beautifully tanned, and the rest are pride of England pasty; it's quite the funny mix. But, regardless of background, every individual is smiling, and loving life; and I must say, it's contagious.

We find our reserved seats and I take in the gorgeous church. An impressive stained-glass window right in front of us, and behind the altar, casts an array of coloured shadows in the church. As the congregation stands, I turn to see Gracie in a high-necked, sleeveless satin gown.

Most of the ceremony is in Spanish; the bride is so fluent, you'd think she was *Malaguena*. I don't catch every word, but enough to laugh at the funny vows that include, 'I promise not to keep count, even if I'm winning.' Mel stands and reads, unusually, a scene from *The Mask of Zorro*. I'll have to ask her later about that.

After the ceremony and group pictures on the steps in front of the church, the guests disembark in different directions, apart from the bridal party, who stand in place, chatting happily.

I walk over, 'So, shall we head to the reception?' I ask Mel.

'Oh, no, there's three hours in between this and the reception.'

'Really? Three hours?' That was left out of the itinerary.

She shrugs, '*Mañana, mañana*!'

***

After a lazy couple of hours, in the sunshine, trying most of the coffee menu in the oldest coffee shop on *Plaza de la Constitución*, Juan-Antonio drives us to the reception. Up and up, and round we wind, until we're at the most picturesque building, with green vines everywhere, amidst red *bougainvilleas*. There's a sense of love and laughter in the air, and I feel a combination of sadness and hope as we make our way through the black metal gates.

Outside on the patio, is where everyone is gathering first, and there's several tables of nibbles that you can help yourself to: a leg of *jamon* is being freshly sliced — I don't personally want to eat that but I can appreciate the culture. Instead, I help myself to some *manchego* and take a glass of wine from the passing waiter.

I gaze around at the little groups of guests laughing, take in the abundantly vine-wrapped pergolas, the striking view of the city below, and enjoy a sip of the undeniably delicious wine. *I'm going to make the most of this. I'm going to focus on the positives, and maybe some of this joy and enthusiasm will rub off on me.* I turn to my colleagues, sigh and nod, 'I've decided our jobs are fantastic.' I beam at Sarah and Hugo, and give an, admittedly smaller, smile to Dom.

'It is rather ridiculous, isn't it?' Sarah sways to the guitarist who's sitting in the corner by the fountain.

'What is?' Hugo says, enjoying her dance.

Sarah grins, 'Being paid to eat, drink and be merry! I can think of worse jobs.'

I glance around again and spot Mel; she's dancing with what can only be described as a beautiful man, with a slightly stubbly, cheeky grin, who I'm assuming is her husband. He spins her around gently and guides her around their tiny patch of patio effortlessly; so clearly in love. He gently brushes a strand of her curled chestnut hair off her face and gazes lovingly into her eyes before leaning in and whispering something in her ear. She laughs and then kisses him as they continue to dance.

I involuntarily shake my head, *Man, I hate that I want that.*

'Do you want to dance?' Dom's voice asks behind me.

I turn to look up at him and make a face. 'No, I'm alright.' I go back to staring at this ridiculously happy couple.

'Nonsense,' he replies. 'Anyone in their right mind can see you are a woman who would like to dance,' he incorrectly assumes, taking my wine glass and giving it to Hugo.

I open my mouth, but before I can protest once more, he takes my hand in his and spins me before drawing me in, close.

The guitarist changes to a Gotan Project, tango.

'Oh, I don't think so.' I shake my head, let go and turn to walk away, but he grabs one of my hands and spins me back, holding me firmly.

'What are you doing?' I frown at him.

'Dancing,' he says simply. 'Come on, you said last night you'd had a lesson in this, and who can resist a little Gotan Project?'

He takes my right hand firmly in his left, swooshes my left arm to grab his side, before placing his right hand on my back and pulling me in tight; I'm very aware that my boobs are pressed against his toned chest.

He guides me around the patio with a combination of ease

and drama; I feel like I should have a rose in my mouth or something.

'I love a good tango; very *Mr and Mrs Smith,* don't you think?' he says, before spinning me out and then back into his arms in one swift motion.

'Since they wanted to kill each other, I'd say that's accurate.' I narrow my eyes at him, only half kidding, as he runs his hand down my arm slowly, making me shiver.

'Harsh.'

'Look, I think I'm done here. I'm so embarrassed. People are starting to watch!' I go to leave again, and he pulls me back.

'Did you know,' he ignores my comment, spinning me as we go, 'that Argentine Tango is all about the desire to listen, understand and converse with the person you're dancing with?' He leads me away at arm's length and guides me round on the spot.

'*You* have a desire to understand *me*?' I say, doubtingly.

He frowns slightly. 'I think I do.'

I shake my head to get my hair out of my face after another spin. 'Shouldn't you be taking photos instead of guiding me around the floor?'

He shrugs, 'I'm on a break.' He extends my right hand out and we step towards Mel and her husband dramatically, who are among the guests, entertainingly watching us, before he swiftly turns me again and we head in the other direction. 'You're very good at following.'

'I'm sorry, was that a compliment?'

'It's been known to happen. Have you done this more than once?'

'I'm a fast learner.'

He grabs my leg to his side and I glide forwards as he

steps backwards.

'You've done this more than once,' he confirms.

'I have.'

He looks at me intently before letting go of my leg and leading me to step back. 'Fine. Don't share, then.' He draws me in. 'Let's do quick fire questions instead: chips or rice.'

'What?'

'Chips or rice? Which do you prefer?'

'OK.' I decide to play since I'm literally stuck in his arms. 'Depends on the meal; you can't pick just one. Egg fried rice? Yum, but rice with say, battered fish? Definitely not, got to be chips.'

We twist and turn. 'That's not necessarily true. If you were in Wales, you could have a half and half.'

'A what?'

'And you call yourself a travel writer?' He throws my arms in the air and then catches them again, around my wrists, pausing there as I frown at him. 'It's both rice *and* chips.' He continues and then his hands travel to mine, and he somehow leads me into another spin before we're off once more.

'*Huh.*'

'You're overthinking this. It's meant to be quick fire questions.'

'Fine. Chips.'

'See? Very British,' he approves.

'Thanks.'

'Favourite word?'

'Mellifluous.'

'Favourite colour?'

'Somewhere between fuchsia and magenta.'

'Best restaurant you've ever eaten at?'

'In the whole world?'

'Why not,' he shrugs before guiding me left.

'The Cheesecake Factory,' I say with confidence.

'You *can't* be serious.'

I have to laugh, 'They have the best salads in there! Plus, if you go to the one in Beverly Hills on the weekend, it's like your very own car show,' I grin. 'And I like the cocktails there.'

He shakes his head. 'You are full of surprises.' He glances to his left, either thinking of his next question, or getting into the Tango character. We now zigzag across the floor, 'Best party trick?'

'I can say the alphabet backwards.' I offer.

'Go on then.'

'I have to sing it,' I warned him.

He chuckles, 'Even better.'

'Z Y X W V U T, S and R and Q and P, O N M L K and J, I H G F E D C B A.'

'Why on earth do you know that?' he chuckles, and I notice for the first time that he has rather chiselled cheekbones.

'My cousin's a singing teacher, and she taught it to me one night over a little too much wine.' I let him dip me and bring me back up with speed, and then we're off again to the right hand side. 'Alright, enough, your turn now: Worst habit?'

'Insulting strangers on planes,' he says without hesitation.

I tilt my head to the side and narrow my eyes at him. 'Longest relationship?'

His expression changes, 'A little over ten years.'

'What happened?' I blurt out without thinking.

'One question per topic.' His tone is sharp as he swooshes

me round, effortlessly.

'That's the rule, is it?' He guides me to walk around him.

'Absolutely. Next.' He then grabs me and we're off.

'OK, favourite TV show.' I offer, trying to get far away from that topic.

'*The Big Bang Theory*.'

'Me too!' I exclaim, excitedly before yet another spin. '*Um*, name of your first pet.'

'Bingo the Beagle.'

'Do you have any life regrets?'

'I have a tattoo I'd rather not discuss, in an interesting place.'

'Where?' I laugh.

'No follow up questions!'

'Spoilsport. Best picture you've ever taken.'

He thinks for a moment, then his eyes slightly glaze over. 'I'd say, probably a seal in Newport Beach. It was just staring right into the lens, like we understood each other or something.'

'Strongest memory,' I continue.

'My grandad dying,' he says without a beat of hesitation.

'Oh my God. I'm sorry.' I can feel my face fall; this no longer feels like a game.

He shrugs, 'Thanks. It was seven years ago, but still.'

'I'm sorry,' I say again, as he dips me and we hold there, just looking at each other. His eyes are ridiculously blue. The music stops and suddenly I hear everybody around us applauding. Still holding my eye contact, he guides me up gently, and then we break apart. I catch Mel's eye and she's grinning from ear to ear and clapping. Smiling back at her, I shrug. I'm suddenly really embarrassed. Touching my hands to my cheeks, I feel they're hot and I walk back over to

Sarah and Hugo.

Sarah's standing there with a shocked expression. 'I'm sorry, but where did that come from, and how can I learn?' She grabs Hugo and dips him. I can't help but laugh.

***

Man, the Spanish know how to party! I have to admit, I was struggling to keep my eyes open at our table as the night fell into the morning; yet family and friends of all ages, from grandmas to toddlers, were having the best time. One thing that I really noticed was that not a single person was drunk. Not one. Happy and tipsy? Sure, but, without a problem or a care in the world, and the only tears I saw were of joy.

There were several toddlers in prams, who would go and have a power nap and then wake up to dance again. It wasn't until five thirty in the morning that Juan drove us back to our hotel. When my alarm goes off, after what feels like only a few hours' sleep, I reluctantly fumble for the switch on the nightstand to raise the blackout blinds, and instantly regret it. '*Aghhh*! My eyes!' I yell in pain as the beautiful spring sunshine fills my room in an instant as I scrunch my eyes shut in pain and search blindly for a pillow to throw over my face.

Somehow, I manage to peel myself out of bed and into Juan's car, who's kindly taking us to the airport. He lingers for longer when saying goodbye to Sarah, and we watch him drive away.

'Well, I'm never going to see the man again, but boy, is he beautiful!' She grins broadly as we walk towards the entrance of the terminal.

'Did you sleep with him?' Hugo says, frowning at her, as

the crisp air conditioning hits me in the face, and tickles my brain.

She shakes her head, 'Oh, no, no! Of course not.' She turns to me and whispers, 'Just a little making out and mild over-the-clothes fondling.' And winks as we make our way towards departures.

I laugh out loud then try to pass it off as a cough as Hugo gives me a dirty look. 'I think that was my favourite wedding so far,' I say, trying to draw the attention away from Sarah, as we bounce our way through the line to security.

'Oh, yeah, how come?' Hugo asks, smiling, looking from me to Dom and back again, raising his eyebrows.

I shake my head and make a face of disgust, as we come to a stop in the queue. 'It was just…' I pause, and wave my passport around, 'it was so full of joy, you could feel it, you know? Kind of makes you feel hopeful.'

'You've got a bigger imagination than me,' is all Dom grunts, clearly hungover, still wearing his sunglasses.

Chapter 8

Spain – Turkey – UAE
Malaga – Istanbul – Dubai

Wednesday
Depart Malaga at 17:50
Arrive Istanbul at 23:15
Duration: 4 hours 25 minutes (1 hour 30-minute layover)
Time change: Istanbul 1 hour ahead

Thursday
Depart Istanbul at 00:45
Arrive Dubai International Airport at 06:00
Duration: 4 hours 15 minutes (17-hour layover. No hotel.)
Time change: Dubai 1 hour ahead

The magazine, despite all its efforts, had to book us on some pretty ghastly flights, so I'm taking every advantage to sleep in between our long layover in Dubai, before heading to India. The first flight from Malaga to Istanbul literally flies by; I suppose it helped that I fell asleep before we'd taken off and didn't wake up until we landed. Just like when we first met, I woke up to Dom frowning at me. I can't seem to work him out. Is he my friend or what?

Now, on our second flight: Istanbul to Dubai, I'm sleepy, but I just want to make a few notes about the Spanish wedding, while they're still fresh in my head. I pause, give myself a little spritz of my revitalising spray to wake up — again Dom frowns at me. As I tap away, I can't help but smile and enjoy an exchange between a sweet little man, across the aisle from us, who has trapped Dom in a conversation, apparently oblivious as to what time it is.

'I grew up in London and found myself in the same pubs as Barbara Windsor and Kenneth Williams! At one point I was playing the piano to entertain them all; my grandad owned a pub you see.'

'Fascinating,' Dom exhales and shifts once more in his seat, picking up his *National Geographic* and starts to flick through. On this occasion, I don't think he's being rude, he's been trying to end a conversation with him for the last forty minutes; it's quite amusing to watch. I tap away at my keys and smile at my computer.

'I tell you a fun game I like to play on planes,' the man continues, jovially.

'What's that then?' Dom says, defeatedly placing his magazine down in his lap once more, audibly getting wiry.

'So, it's a little game I like to play, called: Guess the Couple.'

'OK,' I hear Dom saying, as I type about the beauty of the view from the reception last night.

'Let's see.' The guy leans forwards and looks around his chair, across the aisle and scans the rows opposite him, behind us. I pause in my typed sentence and watch. '*Ah*, here we go,' he points, not very subtly. 'There are two couples there; the ones nearest to us aren't married.'

Dom obediently follows the point, looking round and then back at the man, 'And why is that?'

'They're holding hands,' he says triumphantly. 'And, I'm

guessing, the couple next to them,' he kneels on his seat now and looks over the top of his chair. 'Yup, I'm guessing they're married.'

Dom doesn't turn around but guesses, 'Because they're not holding hands?'

'Exactly!' He nods at Dom, 'Now, let's see if I'm right.' He stands up and walks over to ask them.

Dom turns to me, 'Can you believe this guy?' he asks with wide eyes.

'I personally love a talker on a plane,' I jest, while typing away happily.

'*Ah huh.*' Dom shakes his head, and I can hear the little man tell, I assume, the unmarried couple, that they should be careful not to hold hands while in Dubai, before making his way back to his seat.

'I was right!' he beams at us.

'So, why do you think that is?' I can't help but ask. Dom turns to me sharply and gives me a look as if to say, "Why are you encouraging him?"

'For some people, the magic goes,' he says shrugging. 'When you're dating it's a choice to keep that magic alive.'

Smiling politely, I sit back in my seat, close my laptop, stow it away and shut my eyes; I guess I didn't choose to keep my magic alive.

***

'And where have you just come from?'

'I've absolutely no idea,' Sarah yawns. The immigration officer looks at her incredulously and I nudge her. 'Sorry, it's been a long trip. *Um,*' she scrunches her face up in concentration, 'Malaga via Istanbul. Before that, Scotland

and England; I started in Los Angeles. I'm here on business.' He looks her up and down and she grins, uncertainly, clearly realising that it wasn't a great time for a joke. He finally nods and stamps her passport, then gestures for her to carry on.

When we're all through passport control, we head for the exit. Sarah grabs my arm and links it with hers. '*Gee*, apparently a girl can't make a joke.' We make our way through the airport, passing a huge indoor waterfall. '*Ooh*, it kind of feels like Vegas, doesn't it?'

'But, even more elaborate, somehow, right?' I agree.

'Yeah,' Hugo nods. 'Nothing quite makes sense, though; it's a little space-age meets, well...Vegas.' Everything we pass is big, exaggerated and extremely clean, it's almost clinical.

'So, we've got to keep awake for the day,' Hugo yawns, as we follow signs for taxis.

'Should be easy; lots to do and see! Oh, holy hell!' We step outside of the crisply air-conditioned airport and into the sweltering heat. 'It's like we've just stepped into an oven!' Sarah immediately unwraps herself from me and takes off her cardigan.

'Well, that's the weirdest thing I've ever seen.' Dom is looking at all the cabs that are lined up.

'What do you mean?' I ask, walking over to his side, and following his line of sight.

'The windows have water on the outside.' He looks up at the cloudless sky. 'It's not as if it's been raining,' he ponders, 'But, then why?'

'The combination of the heat outside and the air-con inside; it's condensation,' I confirm.

He frowns at me. 'How do you know that?'

I shrug, 'I asked last time I was here. Strange isn't it.'

He nods, 'Yeah.' He continues to look at me without saying anything.

'Come on guys, I've got one,' Hugo calls, waving us over to a cab that has its windscreen wipers on to clear the condensation.

'Hurry up! I need to get out of this heat!' Sarah yells before diving into the car.

We hire the driver for the day, so we can keep our luggage in the boot, and mosey our way round until our flight this evening. We stop first to pick up water, sugary drinks, and a few snacks. Then we make our way to The Gold Souk. When we arrive, the market is busy and bustling, and shop after shop is, unsurprisingly, selling gold, interspersed with some platinum and diamonds. I'm more of a boho chakra colours kind of jewellery gal, but this is some sight to be seen.

'How many shops are there?' Dom asks no one in particular, but I happen to know the answer.

'Nearly 400,' I say, as we weave into another lane, lined, either side, with jewellery stores. Even though there's an undercover walkway in the middle, it's absolutely sweltering, and we keep going into the stores just for the air conditioning. I sigh in relief as the cool air envelops me, and I gaze around the latest shop.

'You really are a bit of a know-it-all, aren't you?' Dom says to me as we pass a pure gold-plated dress.

'No, I'm not.' I make a face at him. 'I did a piece on Dubai not too long ago, and I've got a good memory.' I fold my arms in defence.

'OK, then, enlighten me,' he challenges. 'Tell me something else about the Souk.'

'*Erm*. Alright, let's see.' I frown, and search my memory for a few more titbits, 'It was established in the 1940s.'

Dom narrows his eyes at me, 'Think you've got that wrong. The UAE only came into existence in the '70s.'

'No, that's right,' I say as we make our way out of the store and continue our walk. 'This market was a place for trade and economy before the country even came into existence; Dubai's nickname used to be: "The City of Gold."' Appropriately at that moment we pass a sign that confirms just that, and I gesture to it. Dom raises his eyebrows and nods, taking it in. I glance at Sarah who's stopped outside the next store.

'Holy, man! Look at this!' Her point is aimed at a display of wedding jewellery.

'A steal at only AED 500,000!' The shopkeeper comes out to greet us. 'Would you like to try it on?'

'Oh, no, not me. My friend Liv would though.' Sarah grins at me.

'Me? No, thank you, I'm fine.' I say politely and try to move on, but Sarah grabs my arm.

'Don't be rude, the nice man asked if you would like to try on an '*eff-ton* of gold!' She ushers me in, and before I know what's happening, Sarah's removing my bracelet, watch and ring, and I'm being decorated like a shop mannequin. My wrist is now emblazoned with a chunky, square bracelet that looks like a jack-in-the-box, and my fingers now have numerous gold rings with rubies.

'Oh my gosh.' I'm now being weighed down with a necklace that reaches below my belly button.

'I know. It is beautiful, is it not?' The shopkeeper misinterprets my cries.

'Yes, it is, but it's so heavy!'

He nods at me, while putting the *pièce de résistance* on my head: a decorative headpiece that comes down my forehead, around the sides and back of my head. 'It is all 2.5 kg.'

'What's that in pounds?' Hugo asks me, and Dom answers.

'About five and a half.'

'Wow.' I catch my reflection in one of the many mirrors around the room and smile at myself. It's definitely a different look from what I had for my wedding.

'Say cheese!' Sarah is laughing and holding her phone out for me to pose. I oblige, then thank the man, before he takes everything off me.

Both Sarah and I come out of the store with a little something: I've opted for a pair of small diamond earrings and she's gone for a gold ring.

We continue walking around and then Hugo's mouth drops open at another spectacular display.

'Now *that's* a ring!' Sarah says gazing upon it too.

I go to open my mouth but stop myself as I see Dom staring at me.

'Go on, miss-know-it-all, tell us about it,' Dom says snarkily.

'No, no.' I shake my head and look at the ring too. 'You can see the sign there with the information.'

'Yes, but we want to hear from you,' Sarah says, clearly oblivious to the tension between me and Dom.

'Well, the Star of Taiba is the largest gold ring in the world. It weighs 64 kg.'

'Which is what?' Hugo asks for a translation again.

'*Erm*, like...' I try to quickly do maths in my head, but Dom gets there first.

'141.'

'Now who's the know-it-all?' I say to Dom, and he gestures for me to carry on.

'OK, *um,* it's 21-carat gold, has around 5 kg, or 11 pounds,' I nod at Hugo, 'of precious stones, and it costs an estimated $3 million.'

Hugo whistles and leans in to get a closer look at the Swarovski crystals emblazoned upon it.

We stand staring at the ring for a while and when we continue our walk, Sarah leans into me. 'I've got to go,' Sarah says quietly.

'What? You don't like it here?'

'No,' she wiggles. 'I've got to *go.* All the water I've been drinking has gone right through me.'

'Oh.' I smile. 'I think I saw a sign this way,' I point, and we head off in that direction.

It does not smell great in here. I open the door to a cubicle and Sarah takes the one next to me.

'What the?!' Sarah howls from next door.

I'm assuming that's in reference to the fact that the loos aren't loos; they're just holes in the ground.

'How the '*eff-ing* hell am I meant to do this?'

'Foot either side, and then you've got to crouch,' I help through the wall.

'In these heels? Oh my! Good thing I do squats every morning, *huh*?'

I'm embarrassed but laughing too. 'You can do it!' I encourage.

When we exit, we get a couple of dirty looks from the ladies in the queue, but Sarah doesn't notice; she strides along without a care in the world, happy to be herself. *Why can't I be like that?*

***

After the market, a trip to see the Burj Khalifa and the Burj Al Arab, we decide to drive to Atlantis and park ourselves in a restaurant. 'And that's where Victoria and David Beckham like to vacation,' our driver tells us, knowingly. 'We are now on The Palm, the three man-made islands that look like a palm tree, but you can't see it from the ground, obviously; it's got to be up high,' he continues.

'Oh, we got to see it from the plane!' Sarah says, excitedly.

When our driver drops us off, we decide on a shady spot outside and order drinks.

'Anyone want to take a walk around the corner and dip their feet in the water with me?' I venture.

Sarah shakes her head viciously at me, 'Oh, no, can you see this face?' She points at her increasingly pink complexion. 'I need some time in the shade, man.'

'What you need is a hat,' I reason, sensibly.

'With this outfit? I hardly think so.' She reties her short-sleeved polka dot, tie top (that I convinced her she needed to put back down to cover her stomach, while we were walking around), and high-waisted jeans. 'A fascinator: absolutely; bandana: don't you know it! But a full-on hat? I hardly think so.'

'Alright then,' I chuckle at my friend's face, which is competing to be the same colour as the polka dots on her top.

'I'll go with you,' Hugo says, jumping to his feet.

'Dom? Want to come? You might get a good picture of Atlantis?'

He scrunches his face at me. 'No, I'm OK.'

I frown at him as he slides further down into his chair,

sunglasses still glued to his face, and he looks down at the food menu.

'Oh, thanks,' I accept Hugo's arm that he's held out for me, and we make our way around the path, towards the water.

'So, I've been wanting to ask you...' Hugo says as we get out of earshot. 'Your dancing was impressive at the Malaga wedding. How did you learn?'

'Oh,' I bat him away. 'I had a few lessons when I was last in Europe, but I was just improvising really.'

He just looks at me, doubtfully. 'I'm not sure I could learn something like that,' he says, scuffing one of his shoes as we continue our walk.

'Oh, it's definitely harder for the man,' I confess. 'If I'm honest, I kind of switch my brain off and let the man lead me.'

'No pressure then,' he mumbles.

'Well, it's more about having fun and just going for it, really. I'm actually really interested in all kinds of dance; I'll have a go at anything. I did an article once on different types of dance around the world, everything from belly dancing to the Vietnamese Waltz, and the Haka of New Zealand, and even a Hopak.'

'What's a Hopak?' he asks as we reach the water. I slip off my flip flops and place my bare feet on the flaming hot sand, before standing on top of my shoes again.

'It's from the Ukraine. Lots of arms stretched out to the sides, running around, and the men have to do lots of jumping and squatting.' I demonstrate, with the hot sand now helping me move my feet quicker, much to Hugo's amusement. 'Anyway, every time I had to dance with a partner, the main feedback I got was not to lead.'

He bursts out laughing. 'Really? That's hilarious.' He takes off his shoes and socks.

I shrug, 'Apparently, I'm strong-willed. Anyway, so, if ever I'm dancing with a partner, I've learnt it's about being aware of where they want to guide you, rather than what moves you want to do.'

'You have to work as a team, hey?'

'Exactly.' We both roll our trousers up; easy for me in loose harem ones, which are instantly above my knees now, but Hugo's in his trademark skinny jeans and they hardly go above his ankles.

'Oh, well; that'll have to do!' We both laugh.

'They'll dry in two seconds if they get wet,' I reason, as we make our way towards the water. 'So, why do you ask about dancing?'

'Oh,' he bashfully looks down, as we step into the water, me a little further in than him, enjoying the water caressing my calves. 'I'd like to impress someone,' he finally comes out with.

'You have somebody back home? I've been meaning to ask,' I say, and he visibly squirms.

'No.' Again, his eyes dart down.

Does he like me? I don't think so. I'm trying to read his face.

'Sarah's a strong-willed woman,' he says quietly.

'You like Sarah?' I practically shout.

'Not so loud!' He waves at me as I splash my legs around happily.

'They can't hear us!' I wave my hand around. 'I could totally see that! You with your new-age hipster thing and her with her vintage style; yeah.' I nod, 'I like it.' I bend down and touch the water with my fingertips and wave them around. *God, I love water.* I stand back up and Hugo looks tortured. 'I didn't mean to offend you!' I gasp.

He shakes his head, 'You didn't.' Then he buries his face in his hands and talks into them so the sound is all muffled.

'What?' I wade a few steps closer to him.

He raises his head but keeps his hands on his bearded cheeks. 'We've worked together for so long; I know her.' He shrugs, 'I know she's the type who likes to have fun, doesn't want to be tied down; she has such a big spirit, I don't ever want to squash that, but, I also don't want to lose our friendship.'

I smile at him, loving the fact that he's felt comfortable enough to share this with me.

'I've tried convincing myself that I don't like her, but,' he looks at me with sad eyes, and shakes his head again, 'I can't change how I feel.'

'Well, why don't you talk to her?' I encourage, kindly.

'Oh, no!' he says, holding his hands out, 'I know she doesn't see me like that,' he says firmly, before sighing. 'You won't say anything will you?'

'Course not.' I reach out and take his hand.

'Thanks.' He squeezes my fingers affectionately.

'Hey, maybe Dom could teach you a few moves or something?'

He makes a face at me, 'I highly doubt that he will do that, but thanks for the suggestion, Liv.'

'You're holding hands?' We turn to see a furrow-browed Sarah, staring right at us, from the sand, with her hands on her hips. Hugo and I break apart, guilty. She takes in the scene, and for a moment no one says anything. 'The drinks are here,' she finally breaks the silence, before turning and walking back to the table.

Chapter 9

UAE – India
Dubai – Goa

Thursday
Depart Dubai International Airport at 23:00

Friday
Arrive Goa International Airport at 03:40
Duration 3 hours 10 minutes
Time change: Goa 1 hour and 30 minutes ahead
Drive 30 minute (cab) to hotel (3 nights stay)

Couple E
Kenilworth Resort, Goa, India

We take a taxi from the airport to the resort where the wedding is taking place. As we pass through several shanty towns, it hits me, just how much I take for granted: not only my ability to hop all over the world whenever I fancy, but everything in my life, really. I live in a comfortable flat, in an area that I love, that's surrounded by beautiful buildings and an abundance of history. I'm passionate about my job, I'm healthy, I have amazing friends; at the end of the day, aren't those the things that really matter? For people who literally have nothing, I really am blessed. Taking a deep breath, I vow there and then to stop acting so privileged, almost to the point of entitled. Each moment is precious, and I'm going to stop feeling sorry for myself, and soak everything up.

It's about five am by the time we pull up outside the hotel. The sun is starting to rise, so everything has a sleepy, warm glow about it. The property is surrounded by coconut palms, and the dawn chorus is alive and singing. I yawn as we walk up the few steps, in between a couple of rather grand pillars.

'Welcome to Kenilworth!' A thin, smiley man, with the name tag, "Jaber" emblazoned upon it, bows to greet us.

'I like to *jabber* too.' Sarah winks at him.

'I'm sorry mam. *I am not understanding your meaning*,' he says politely in broken English.

'Your name.' She points to the name tag.

'Ah. I understand. *You are funny woman*.' He smiles. 'To translate, my name means: to comfort others. So, anything I can do for you, I will do for you. Come.' He gestures. 'We are to go this way.'

'That was a little rude,' Hugo whispers loudly into Sarah's ear.

'It was a joke!' She defends, while yawning. We follow Jaber through a windowless walkway structure, with a wooden peaked roof; I love that it's basically a jetty, and that underneath us is a stunning water feature, with water lilies; a gentle current lazily drifts the flowers from one side to the other. The walkway leads to an open, high ceilinged, air conditioned reception space with numerous sofas and several check-in desks.

Jaber is talking away, but I'm not taking any of it in. Just lead me to a bed, and I'll be happy. We don't have to meet the bride until noon, so that leaves roughly six hours for sleep, and half an hour for a shower and freshen up.

We follow Jaber around the corner and into a lift, down a long corridor, and finally to our rooms. When I close the door, I drop my bag, fall onto the bed, fully clothed and instantly conk out.

***

The sand is soft and the warm breeze delicately brushes the tears on my cheeks. I feel like my heart has been ripped out of my chest. *How could he do this to me?* Even through the pounding rain, lashing loudly on the ocean in front of me, it doesn't drown out the laughter and music behind me. Closing my eyes, I know my makeup is now long gone with the combined help of the storm and my tears. I let out a howl of pain, and then jump at the thunder. *Thunder?*

'Liv? Are you awake, Poppet?'

Sarah. I open my eyes and feel my cheeks — they're wet. I wipe my tears, sit up and away from my dream, and head to the knocking door. When I open it, Sarah's smile falls.

'You alright?' She asks with wide-eyed concern.

I nod. 'Just dreaming.'

She replies with a nod; no need for me to explain. 'We've got half an hour before we meet the bride,' Sarah says softly.

I sigh, 'Great. And they are?'

'Nisha and Harry.'

'OK. Nisha and Harry,' I repeat, while wiping my cheeks once more. 'Alright, shall I meet you down...' I stop talking at the sound of shouting. I step a little further out of the room; both Dom and Hugo open their doors too.

'Who's yelling?' Hugo says, looking up and down our

corridor. Then rounding the corner, we see, marching towards us, a strikingly beautiful woman, (even with a military focused expression), yelling at Jaber, in Gujarati. Jaber is pulling a large empty luggage trolley along with him, his head down as the beautiful woman gesticulates. Power walking ahead of them, is a lady dressed in loose white linen and thick, black-rimmed glasses, who stops at my door,

'Hi there, I'm Marigold, mother-of-the-groom; you can call me Goldie.'

'Hi.'

'Nice to meet you.'

Sarah and I answer in unison. As Dom and Hugo give her a wave. We glance past Goldie and take in the beautiful young woman, who's still yelling. 'What's wrong?' I dare to ask.

'Oh, you've been given the wrong rooms,' Goldie says. She looks over her shoulder and then back to us, impressively. 'Isn't Nisha something?'

Goldie's proud look at her future daughter-in-law throws me for a second; I recognise it. *Why? Oh.* I feel my face frown; Leo's mum used to always look at me like that. I shake my head to get rid of my memories and adjust my expression, just as Nisha finishes verbally bashing Jaber, then turns to us.

'Hi. They should have upgraded you when you checked in. I'm just rectifying that.' Nisha says, with a dazzling smile, in a Liverpudlian accent, which surprises me.

'Oh, there's no need for that! We've—' I start, but she cuts me off.

'It's already organised,' Nisha closes the matter. 'Jaber and Goldie will take care of your luggage, moving them to your proper rooms, so why don't we all go and grab a drink while they sort all of that.'

Luckily I hadn't even opened my case, so I was ready to just hand it to an embarrassed Jaber, but it takes Sarah a good ten minutes to sweep all of her stuff back into her bag. When Dom and Hugo are ready too, the whole *Blush* team follows Nisha downstairs, and to the bar.

We each grab a welcome cocktail and are taken on a tour. The grounds are in a word: stunning. I happily sip my sex on the beach as we pass a gorgeous inside/outside restaurant, manicured grounds lined with more coconut palms, before weaving around a huge chess board, which goes on to the pools, hot tubs and sun loungers, to a large open grassy space, where just beyond, is the beach.

'We're getting married in this spot right here,' Nisha gestures to the grass around her. 'We'll be on the *Mandap*,' she looks at my blank expression, then adds, 'it's a decorated structure with pillars and a cover; kind of like a stage.' I get out my notebook to swiftly scribble that down, as Nisha continues, 'For friends and family, there'll be a cover for shade, over the chairs, and fans that lightly spray water, which will keep everyone cool. Of course my aunts don't like that, they say it messes up their hair, but trust me, it will be welcome! It's supposed to be no less than forty degrees in the next few days.'

Sarah looks at me with a frown, and I go to open my mouth but Dom speaks first.

'100 odd degrees,' Dom says with a smile, as her wide eyes reach a new level of incredulousness.

Nisha turns her back to us and moves her arms, 'We'll be up there with both sets of parents,' she pauses, turns back and takes a deep breath, smiling. 'Anyway, thank you so much for coming all this way; I can't tell you how much I appreciate it. Even before we knew about that article, I was blown away by how many friends and family were willing to make the trip.'

'Are you kidding?' A bouncy, dark-haired beauty comes to her side, 'It's a wedding *and* a group holiday, all meshed into one. Hi, I'm Lilly, soon to be sister-in-law. It's beautiful here, right?'

'Truly is,' I say looking around and sighing in contentment at the sun beaming down on us; my dream feels so far away now.

'I love the sun,' Sarah pants, fanning herself with her hand, 'but it doesn't really love me. Shall we head in for some shade?' Her normally snowy complexion has transformed from pink, to tinges of red, on both her forehead and nose.

We sit and grab another drink in the very welcome air-conditioned bar and soak up the atmosphere. Lilly wasn't kidding; the large group of friends were out in force and loving each moment. I watch with amusement as they all laugh and joke at the swim up bar, some with a book in one hand and an umbrella-clad cocktail in the other.

'This is fun!' I realise I've said out loud, when everyone laughs at me. I smile with embarrassment before taking another sip of my drink; I guess I'm deciding to embrace this moment that life has thrust upon me.

'I'm so glad you approve!' Nisha laughs. 'So, I know this was emailed across to you, but shall we just go over it?'

I like this bride; confident, sassy, and thorough. 'Absolutely; fire away,' I say, happily swinging my legs from the high bar stool I'm sitting on, and getting ready to jot things down.

'So, instead of the traditional two weeks of celebrations, we have crammed everything that we wanted to include into three days, and we've put our own twist on it.'

'Smart, officiant, going against the parents' wishes; I love it.' Sarah licks the stem of the umbrella from her cocktail, and I can't help but notice Hugo longingly gazing at her.

Nisha smiles but doesn't say anything; I'm sure it's been a lot tougher to keep the peace between families and their expectations, than she'll admit. 'So, we've got welcome drinks and High Tea in about an hour.'

'You're so chilled about this,' Hugo says with awe; his focus now clearly on the bride, not his lust. 'Honestly, off the books, the most relaxed bride so far,' he winks and finishes his sentence in a hushed tone, as if the other brides can hear.

Again, Nisha smiles but instead of responding, she continues with her plans. 'There'll be speeches, and a buffet. Then tonight we've got the *Sangeet* function. Tomorrow: *Mahurat*, which is basically prayers and blessing the ground that we are getting married on, asking mother earth to look after us, and we'll combine that with the *Griha Shanti,* asking for the blessing of the solar system, alignment of charts, that kind of thing, so, after I'm ready, tomorrow morning,' she nods at Sarah and Hugo, 'Dom is the only person I need to be there.' She looks down embarrassed, 'It's just going to be my side of the family really,' she adds, as an after-thought, 'but, the rest of you are welcome to come if you want.'

'We'll do whatever you want,' I say, writing as fast as I can, and she smiles appreciatively.

'Then preceding that, the *Pithi* where I'll be covered in *Haldi*,' she makes a face and I make a note to ask her more about this, 'and then a casino themed, *Mehndi* night. As well as the opportunity for guests to have *henna* done, there'll be cocktails, a BBQ buffet, dancing, and musicians. And the following day is the beachfront ceremony, where we've just been, and finally, the evening reception.' Nisha points in the direction of the lawns. 'There'll now be a copy of this in each of your rooms. I've also taken the liberty of providing each of you with an outfit for the concluding day.'

'Oh honestly, there's no need!' I say, pausing from my writing, 'Just think of us as being very much in the background,' I smile, and take another delicious sip of my second helping of sex on the beach, as it were.

'It's already organised,' she waves her engagement hand at us, and I get a flash of her huge diamond. 'The morning of,' she continues, 'we've got several helpers to come and help tie the *saris* for all the guests, so you don't have to worry about doing that yourselves.'

I'm excited. I've always wanted to wear one. 'Well, thank you. You've gone above and beyond.'

She smiles, so poised. 'It's going to be fun.'

***

Now, in my new and very spacious room, I admire my reflection. The dress I've picked out for the welcome drinks and High Tea, is elegant, and has always reminded me of Kate Middleton; not that she'd ever have completed her look with a high messy bun, but hey, back to the dress. It's deep raspberry in colour, with decorative diamonds around the hem of the three-quarter length sleeves and the neck. It's always been a dress that I can only zip up halfway, and then need the assistance of someone else. Only thing is, even in this air-conditioning, three-quarter length sleeves, and a high neck are definitely a no-no. I go to unzip it, but it doesn't budge. I try bringing the zip up a little to help it go back down, but that doesn't seem to work either. *Bugger. I am now trapped in my own clothing. Great.*

I pop my head out of the corridor, and try to remember which room Sarah is in; *was it two down, or three?* 'Sarah?' I call out quietly but hopefully loud enough that she can hear. *Oh, sod it.* I start tapping on door choice number one: two down from me. She answers in just her bra and pants.

'What's up chick?'

'I'm stuck. I can't get the zip up or down, and I need to get out of it,' I say quietly with increasing panic.

She smirks at me. 'Cute though! Why do you want to take it off?'

'It's like a million degrees,' I justify and fan myself.

'Why d'you think I'm in my underwear? Come in.' She pulls the door back to let me pass. I step in and my eyes dart wide.

'How on earth does your room look like this? We literally only arrived about five seconds ago.' The contents of her suitcase has exploded around the room; not a single surface is clear of either clothes, shoes, makeup, or hair accessories.

'What can I say? I'm moving in! So, let's have a look here.' I put my hands on my hips as she attempts the manoeuvre of negotiating the zip up and down. 'Wow. Yup, sorry chick, you're not only going to have to wear it, but live in it.'

My face is starting to match the colour of the dress. 'You've got to help me out of here! Haven't you got, I don't know, hairspray or something that will help?'

'Poppet,' she looks at me with amusement, 'hairspray is

designed to keep things where they are.'

'Well, I don't know!' I flap my arms up and down. 'Please help me!' I say desperately.

She laughs, 'OK, OK, let's see here,' she tries again, to no avail. 'How about you grip the dress above and below the zip, and I try to move it?' I feel the friction, but no movement. Sarah stands back now, and puts a hand to her chin, thinking. 'Can you get it above your head?' Together we try to hoist the dress up, but it gets stuck on my boobs. 'Alright, that's not going to work; nice underwear by the way.' She nods to my turquoise Asda pants.

'Thanks!' I say sarcastically.

'Alright, let's try the other way, if we get your arms out, then maybe we can bring it down?' Willing to try anything, I pull the bottom of my right sleeve, and one arm is free, now the left sleeve. Sarah moves carefully around me. 'OK, let's try this.' I wiggle on the spot as we both try to shimmy the dress down and over my hips. No such luck.

'Great! Now I'm wearing the dress like a belt!' I say with my mis-matching bra and pants now both on show, and my poor dress rolled up around my middle. *This would never happen to Kate Middleton.* 'I can't go out like this! Oh '*eff*!' I throw my arms around myself to cover up, as a knock comes from the other side of the adjoining door. 'We're not decent!' I find myself shouting.

'What do you mean, *we*?' Hugo comes in without invitation and examines the scene: Sarah in her underwear and me in mine, with a dress for a belt. 'Oh my.'

'I'm stuck,' I pout.

He laughs a little too hard before composing himself, 'Hang on.' He turns into his room before returning with a small sewing kit. Sarah dutifully unrolls the bottom half of my dress to cover my arse, then Hugo returns, and gets to work. 'I'm going to unpick it to get you out; who knew I'd be helping a lady out of her dress so soon in the day!' He chuckles to himself.

Fifteen minutes later, I am in another, admittedly much cooler outfit: my aquamarine, strapless, loose-fitting, knee-length dress, matched with a pair of wedges, and we're making our way down.

As we follow the crowd into the dining room, it's clear that Nisha has a lot of family; far more than the groom. Much like Malaga, there's a wonderful mix of cultures: English and Indian. Harry, the groom, and his entire family are from Somerset, and Nisha, even though she grew up in Liverpool, was born in Goa.

I gaze at the seating chart, and see that we've been assigned to the friends' table. When we make our way in, even if I hadn't seen them in the pool earlier, it's quite obvious who the English friends are: a rowdy group, but not enough to disrupt the whole room, just happily keeping to themselves, laughing and drinking away. As we get nearer, I spot who I'm guessing is the leader of the group; he's loud, blonde, and I'm going to go out on a limb here and say, is clearly the biggest troublemaker.

'I really don't think Nisha thought this through; she wants this to be a good article right?' A young woman with a face full of freckles says with a giggle as we take our seats. 'Why would she sit you next to Ollie?'

'Clearly, because I'm the most fun here!' Ollie, the troublemaker says, sitting up tall.

'And he's so modest.' Another friend chips in and the whole table laughs.

***

Both sides of the family made loving and comical speeches and then each table in turn, helped themselves to food; apart from me, that is. I made it to the corner of the room, and was trapped, amusingly, by the father-of-the-bride, who from the smell of his breath, has been taking every moment possible, to celebrate. I'm laughing at his stories, none of which I'm sure Nisha would appreciate me knowing. I particularly enjoy hearing a dramatic and detailed tale, describing how Nisha used to try and drown her brother in the bath.

'Dad!' Nisha comes over with her empty plate, ready for seconds. 'Are you *still* talking to Liv?'

'I am,' he slurs.

'Have you eaten anything yet?' She asks me and I shake my head, grinning. 'Dad, she hasn't even eaten anything yet.'

'Neither have I! We're just having a lovely conversation, all about you, *ladoo*.'

'*Ladoo*?' I question.

Nisha shakes her head slightly and smiles. 'I used to be small, round and sweet.' I open my mouth to ask more but she continues, 'Well, both go and get something to eat.' She orders. 'You'll be telling everyone about the bath story soon.' She turns from her dad to me, and reads my expression. 'You've already heard the bath story, haven't you?' I nod once more. She grabs her dad and steers him away from me, 'Go, now Liv!' She laughs and I head to the buffet table.

There is an abundance of food, and as I grab one oversized ladle after the other, helping myself to the contents of each chafing dish, the next smells even better than the last. At the very end of the table, there is a selection of sweets that I'll definitely come back to. I laugh out loud as I read the label for the small balls that look somewhere between mini scotch eggs and falafel: "*Ladoo.*"

When I've piled my plate high enough to feed my hungry belly, but not enough to look like I'm taking advantage, I return to my designated table, and everyone, including my colleagues, look slightly glazed over.

'Livvy! Where have you been? You've missed a lot,' Sarah says, swaying in her seat.

'Getting to know some family members,' I chuckle and take my seat.

'All work and no play this one,' Sarah gestures to me and then grins.

'Catch me up, then. Hey!' I say, laughing at her helping herself to a savoury lentil cake on my plate.

'The food is insanely good, isn't it?' Hugo leans forward and tries to put on a sober face, but all he's managing is a goofy tipsy grin.

I take a mouthful of *Panchkutiu Saag.* 'Oh, wow!' I say with my mouth still full of the veg curry; the coconut and coriander flavours exploding, 'This is so good!' I swallow, 'Like, I've been to India before, but this is another level. So, tell me what I've missed,' I say before helping myself to a forkful of *Shaak. Umm. Tomatoey!*

'Well, these,' Sarah drunkenly points to every guest at the round table, 'are now our new *breast fiends*,' Sarah says and then bursts out laughing when she realises what she's said.

'Best friends!' Hugo corrects her, laughing hysterically, and I wonder just how long I was actually away from them; they're all hammered. 'They all went to school together,' Hugo drunkenly points to the right side of the table, 'and so did they!' he moves his hand to the left then throws his hands up in the air in celebration, 'and now they're *allllllllll* friends!'

'Fantastic,' I say, slightly wide-eyed and smiling at the craziness. 'Where's Dom?'

'Out for a *fag*,' Hugo enjoys the English word with a fake British accent, 'with Ollie.' He finishes his sentence in his normal voice.

'He doesn't smoke, does he?' I ask. *I don't think he's smoked at all on this trip has he?* I try to think back.

'Ollie's a bad influence,' a jolly guy says with his arm around a blonde beauty.

'He quit smoking about a year ago,' Sarah says, now finger-picking at some potatoes from the *Gujarati Bhandi* from my plate. 'Guess he's decided to take it up again.' She takes a bite of the potato, then makes a series of faces, I can't help but laugh.

'You OK?'

'It's so hot!'

'Well, blow on it!' I say reasonably.

'No.' She points at me, 'Not temperature hot, flavour hot. Delicious, but I now can't taste my taste buds.'

I laugh, 'I'm not sure you can *taste* your taste buds.'

She waves me away, 'You know what I mean.' Then she slides my plate in between us both, clearly no longer planning to discreetly take nibbles; she then picks up her own fork, ready to dig in.

'There's plenty up there you know,' I say to her, almost racing to get a mouthful in before she does.

'Nowhere near as much fun. Always tastes better from someone else's plate; don't you think? Now, what's not too hot?' she says scanning each item that I've picked up.

I scan my plate, too, 'Maybe the *Palak Bhaji*? They're not normally too bad.'

'*Bhaji* it is!' she says and digs in. A moment later, her face hangs open, mid chew. '*Agh*! Not hot; my arse!'

***

The evening is a mixture of pure fun, and pure sweat. If I didn't have my hair up in a bun, it would absolutely resemble Monica from *Friends*: "It's the humidity!" I can almost hear myself saying.

As well as another round of top-notch food, the *Sangeet* function is principally a dance! I quietly sit in a corner of the room and tap my pen on my notebook, to the music, and enjoy all the friends as well as the family, happily joining in on the *Dandiya Raas*. Basically, everybody is given colourful bamboo sticks, and from observing, it's a repetitive dance, where you stand in two lines, each one facing the other. Then to the beat of the music, you tap your sticks together, then tap your right stick with the person opposite you, followed by your left, then turn away to your left and hit your own sticks together, before returning to the partner, hit the right sticks again, and finally, move two places to the next partner, to repeat the whole thing. I think it's rather fabulous.

Ollie has a GoPro on his chest and is dancing around with it like he's carrying a baby. Everyone is smiling and having fun. I watch some of the uncles, jump enthusiastically into the air, and numerous cousins, making up their own, much more complicated moves. Now, Nisha takes Harry's hand and they entangle themselves around the cousins; Harry's a little uneasy but Nisha reassures him with her dazzling smile.

How she's dancing in that outfit, I don't know; it looks heavy! Beautiful, but heavy. The *chaniya choli* has bright, vivid colours and decorative swirls of gold, making her stand out from the colourful flurry of material that's wrapped around each female family member.

Taking a sip of my bottle of water, I stand to get some air. Stepping outside onto the patio, I'm not sure if it's any cooler than the room they were dancing in. Several other family members are enjoying another wonderful buffet that's laid out on the far side of the patio, surrounded by several round tables. I see Sarah sitting at one, and walk over to join her, carefully weaving around a large uncle to avoid the now visibly drunk father-of-the-bride.

'I'm going to need to up my exercise if I keep eating like this,' Sarah says as she stuffs a large fork-full of rice into her mouth.

'I know, I'm grateful I'm wearing this baggy dress.' I tap my feet to the music from inside, then look at my friend. 'I'm sorry, but I have to ask: how are you sober right now?'

Sarah shrugs, 'I think I've sweated the alcohol out!' She dabs her red face with her napkin.

I laugh, 'Well, that's quite the talent! Cheers to you, my friend!' I hold up my bottled water to salute her.

She smirks and then takes a large forkful of her curry. A second later, I swear, steam is coming out of her ears. 'Oh holy '*eff*!' she says with her mouth still full.

'What is it?'

She chews furiously, 'My mouth is on fire.' She swallows, visibly in pain. 'I'm on fire.' She grabs my water from me and downs it in one sitting, before throwing it back at me. 'That didn't help!'

'Well, of course not! You need yoghurt or milk or

something.' I look around to try and help my friend, trying to keep the smile off my face.

'How is this allowed to be served!? Oh, my God!' she waves her arms around frantically, 'I think I'm going to be sick, or pass out, or something. Help me!'

I glance around at a few guests, who are now watching her little show, and they're all laughing.

'What did you put on your plate?' I take it from her and give it a sniff.

'I don't know, a *Kodi* or something.' Sarah's now turning a perfect tomato shade of red.

'The *Solantule Kodi*?' I say putting her plate down slowly.

'Maybe; and the man over there,' she points to an uncle standing next to Nisha's dad, both of whom are laughing, 'told me to put in these fried peppers too.'

'The *chillies* with salt and cumin?' I say wide eyed.

'He said they were tame *peppers*!' She's almost crying now.

'Oh honey, they're both insanely hot.'

'Well, I didn't know that, did I? It looked good.'

Hugo comes over with a bowl of yoghurt. 'Here.'

'What are you superman?' I say to him as Sarah shovels the yoghurt into her mouth.

***

Late the next morning, after I've had a little lie-in, and Sarah has made the bride up for the prayer ceremony, we meet for brunch, where an even more delicious buffet awaits us. Sarah, going in a lot more cautiously, decides on bacon and eggs. I'm happily digging into my *dosa*, filled, admittedly, not very traditionally, with an English vegetarian breakfast, and an accompanying side dish of fresh fruit; I'm sure that will balance it out right?

Dom comes and sits directly opposite me, looking a little worse for wear.

'Morning, sunshine!' Sarah laughs.

'Yikes, what happened to you?' I say, and take another mouthful of *dosa*.

'Ollie and the other best man had me doing shots until about four this morning.' Dom's voice is so gruff, I can just about understand him.

'How are you sitting here right now?' Sarah says, looking at her watch.

'I literally have no idea.' He puts a hand to his forehead and gives it a little massage. 'I must have passed out on one of the sofas in reception. I woke up to the smell of food, so I'm going to eat, then head up to my room, and pass the '*eff* out again.' He scratches his head, 'Honestly, I'm grateful I woke up on a sofa; Ollie was trying to set me up with one of the bridesmaids.'

'Which one?' I laugh.

'The tall one; she's rather frightening, to say the least. That looks good,' Dom observes my choice of breakfast. 'What is it?'

'*Dosa* with hashbrowns, mushrooms, tomato, scrambled eggs and cheddar cheese.' I happily wave my hand over my plate like a quiz show assistant showing off a prize.

'Need some meat with that,' he nods with distaste, and steadies himself to get up again.

'I'm a vegetarian,' I say slowly.

'Really? You sure?' He looks at me like I'm mistaken.

'Pretty darn,' I nod, before narrowing my eyes.

'How have we been around each other for so long, and I've only just noticed that.' Dom creases his eyebrows even more; he almost has a unibrow.

'You're too far up your own arse,' Sarah confirms, bearing all her teeth in a fake smile, before eating a bit of bacon.

He nods, 'Fair enough,' then stands and walks off to get something to eat.

'Oh my God, I couldn't do shots until four in the morning any more, could you?' I ask Sarah before sipping my filter coffee.

'Depends who it's with. But on a job? No.'

'Wait a sec,' a thought occurred to me, 'weren't you at the prayers this morning?' I ask Dom as he comes back to the table with a full plate that's ninety percent meat.

'Oh, shit.' He looks around in panic, and spots the bride. She smiles calmly and comes over. Dom places his plate on the table, 'I'm so sorry,' Dom starts but she puts up her hand, which, I notice, is now covered in *henna*, from her fingertips, all up her arms.

'Ollie can be intense,' she says simply, as if she understands completely.

'But I'm so sorry. What about the prayers?' he says, apologetically.

'My brother was taking photos this morning. He's actually pretty good for an amateur; we can use those for the article. When I walked past you on the sofas in reception—'

'I'm so sorry,' Dom repeats, and she waves him away, once more.

'I asked my brother to take photos, and told my mum that it would help raise his profile if we used some of his shots in the magazine. She thinks that was your idea, so don't act surprised when she comes over to thank you.' I'm so impressed by this woman. 'So we've got a couple of things today that I do need you to be around for.' She smirks. 'Check the schedule, grab some sleep and a shower, then see you in a bit.' She glides off.

'I think I'm in love with this woman,' Dom says, staring after her.

'Me too,' Sarah and I say together.

***

Walking with Sarah, we head over to the grassy, shaded area, where the *Pithi* ceremony will take place. Hugo and Dom are already there; I catch Dom's eye and can't help but smirk; he still looks awful but is clearly determined to act like a professional from now on.

After speaking with Nisha, I learnt what she meant about being covered in *Haldi.* All the guests cover the bride in a paste, made of turmeric, sandalwood, saffron, rosewater and chickpea flour, which, according to my interview with her, is said to bless the bride with a long and strong marriage; purify the heart and soul; ward off evil; ease anxiety, and give the bride a natural glow for her big day. Typically, the groom also takes part in this, but Harry, being just about as pearly as Sarah, didn't want to be bright orange for the ceremony the next day.

We all gather around the bride, who sits in the middle of the circle of family and friends. It's then I notice that the *henna* is also delicately drawn on the tops of Nisha's feet and up her legs too. I'll have to ask her about that; I thought the point of a *Mehndi* night was to do that then. I scribble a note for later.

The first to smear the turmeric mixture over both of Nisha's cheeks, is her mother. Cradling Nisha's cheeks into her own palms, they just pause looking at each other for a while; it's quite touching.

Then one by one, guests take their turn to paint the bride orange. Nisha sits and laughs, as the friend with freckles places a particularly large dollop of it at the end of her nose. When the last of the guests are done, I spot Ollie in the corner of my eye, carefully, and quietly carrying something. I nudge Sarah and a moment later, a water balloon flies past my left ear and hits the bride squarely on the forehead. The bride's brother runs over to Ollie, who puts down a box that's filled with water balloons, then joins in; pelting one balloon after the other at any guest within his aim. The rest of the male bridal party runs over and suddenly the air is filled with colourful broken balloons, laughter and squeals from guests; it's the most hilarious scene I've ever watched. Sarah and I run and take cover behind a tree as Nisha stands and makes a dash for the box, clearly taking no prisoners. She nabs a few and starts aiming with perfection at her attackers. Dom is snapping away, while being careful to keep out of the firing zone. Hugo comes over with a few for us, 'Here. Go for it!'

I can't remember the last time I had a water balloon fight. I giggle with glee as all the girls team up against the boys.

'Dom! Put that camera down and join in!' Ollie cries, mid throw, hitting a flustered aunt in the backside as she goes to grab more balloons. Dom quickly returns his camera to its case, placing it carefully down on a nearby table, away from the madness.

I pick up as many as I can carry, anticipating who he'll be throwing them at, and hop to the side, narrowly avoiding a cousin's aim. Dom scoops up an armful and scans the crowd. He spots me and then points. 'You are going down, Brave!' And he throws with perfection, hitting me right in the boob, celebrating with a small dance. Laughing, I throw several his way, and miss him each time. 'That was terrible!' he yells at me.

'Let's get him,' Sarah's back by my side, hair completely drenched, and makeup running down her cheeks like war paint. She kicks off her heels and I follow suit, flip flops now to the side of me. I nod at her, and we hurtle towards him, balloons flying in every direction as we get a little closer. We start firing away and he runs towards the ocean, throwing a few behind him and hitting us each time. Sarah takes her aim and gets him squarely in the back of the head, he turns, and I go for it, finally making contact with his chest. The balloon explodes and gets him right in the face. He stops running, and wipes his eyes with his free hand for a moment, and we go to town, throwing all of them one after the other until we're empty handed.

'Alright! Alright! You win!' Dom says, with his arm in the air. Then before we know it, he places a balloon in each hand, and simultaneously bursts them on our heads.

***

Between the *Pithi* ceremony and the evening, there was time for a doze on a sun lounger, and a dip in the pool. Now, freshly showered, dressed in my ruby red strappy dress, feeling sun-kissed and rather relaxed, Sarah and I make our way to the *Mehndi* and casino evening. Even at nightfall, it's still deliciously warm and I'm glad I've got bare legs and my flip flops on. Sarah, however, is still in her signature heels; it must be comical to watch us walking together; little and large do Goa.

'I don't think I'm designed for these kinds of temperatures,' Sarah says, fanning herself with her hand, as we walk along the illuminated pathway towards the festivities.

'Stick out your tongue,' I instruct.

'What?' she stops in her tracks, and looks at me as if I've gone mad.

I laugh, 'Trust me, stick out your tongue, like this,' I demonstrate, curling the sides up, so they meet, making a small gap in the middle, like a straw. She imitates me, and I continue, 'then breathe in and out; it's supposed to cool you down.'

'Like this?' she asks, concentrating hard. I nod and we stand there for a minute, both breathing through the small gap in our tongues, before continuing our way around the path.

'Oh, wow! This looks amazing!' I cry, as we get nearer (Sarah's still breathing with her tongue out). A "casino theme" was right. The lawn has been completely transformed into a huge square, around a large dance floor. All to the left, the casino and lounging side, then straight ahead, one lengthy table, which I presume the buffet will sit on, then curling around on the right side, and to where Sarah and I entered, are numerous large round tables with surrounding chairs.

Walking further in, there are enlarged single cards from a deck, hanging like windchimes from white, cube structures, open on all sides; big dice are placed all over; craps, roulette, and blackjack tables are ready, waiting for players.

To add to the party atmosphere, I gaze at the colour-changing lights around various, cushioned seated areas. Sarah and I weave around the large dangling five of hearts. '*Ooh*, I can't wait to get some *henna* done!' I say excitedly, and spot a couple of men setting up. 'Come on, let's do it now before all the guests arrive.' I pull her along and ask the two men if they would be ready to start. The man in front of Sarah nods, and gestures for us both to take a seat. 'Thank you!' I beam, and my young man grins at me.

'Hello.' He smiles politely at me.

'Hi! How are you doing today?' I ask.

'Hello,' he replies, smiling once more; I guess that may be the extent of his English. I extend my left arm into his open palms. Glancing over at Sarah, her young *henna* artist is looking quite apprehensive, wondering where to begin with her already tattooed arm; she offers him her other one. I can't help but smile.

Turning back, I watch with glee as he starts effortlessly drawing swirling patterns from my left index finger, onto the back of my hand, along my wrist, and finally up my forearm. Within no time at all, he's putting in little dots and final flourishes; I absolutely love it. I've always wanted a tattoo, but haven't ever decided what I wanted; kind of an underlying statement for my life really.

When he's finished, I hold up my arm proudly and admire it. 'Thank you so much; it's gorgeous.'

He smiles, nods, and says, 'Hello,' once more.

Standing, I wait for Sarah, who's not quite finished with hers, and take the opportunity to look around once more. A couple of musicians are walking across the lawn, towards us, as are a few guests.

'You wait until it dries,' the man who's with Sarah instructs from behind me. 'The longer you leave, the stronger it is,' I hear him tell her.

'I'm not sure I'll leave it all that long,' Sarah says, now at my side.

'Why not?' I ask, then look down. 'Oh.' It looks nothing like mine. Here and there are huge blobs, instead of delicate dots like mine.

'How did yours turn out?' She grabs my arm, as we walk away from the gents, so as not to offend them. 'Oh, man, yours is beautiful!' Sarah whines.

'So is yours,' I lie. Then taking in her face, 'OK, well, it may look a little like a toddler doodled on your arm, but, as soon as it's dried you can pick it off,' I reassure her.

Guests are coming in fast and merrily now, taking seats at tables, getting *henna* done or heading over to the games tables. I spot Hugo heading over with Nisha and Harry; Dom then appears on their other side.

'They both scrub up quite well, don't they?' Sarah says, voicing my thoughts.

'Yeah,' I nod. 'They do.' Despite the warm evening, Hugo is dressed in a white shirt with the sleeves rolled up, and a grey and blue waistcoat, complete with his standard skinny jeans, hair pulled back into a high topknot. How they are both in jeans, I've no idea. Dom is in another bold, perfectly fitted, striped shirt, also with the sleeves rolled up. I can't help but notice that the shirt highlights his toned shoulders, and slim physique. His sunglasses sit casually on top of his head, despite the fact that it's dark out, sweeping his hair away from his face. His skin, like mine, is sun-kissed, making the aqua blue of his eyes even more prominent somehow.

'Evening ladies!' Hugo greets us with a big grin. I glance behind them, and watch a procession of chefs filing out, carrying large chafing dishes.

'Oh my!' Sarah says, her eyes following the long line of chefs gracing the far table with what is sure to become another delicious buffet. 'You'll have to tell me what to avoid on the spicy scale!' She turns to Nisha and Harry.

'Well, we've got a bit of a mix for this evening,' Harry says. 'Traditional of course — stay away from the pork,' he adds as a precaution, 'but we've also got stonebaked pizzas, burgers, and macaroni and cheese.'

Sarah's too polite to say so, but from her expression, I can see she's grateful.

'*Ooh*,' I remember I had a question for Nisha, and everyone turns to me, 'your *henna*.'

She smiles, 'Yes?'

'Well, I thought this was the *Mehndi* evening; isn't that typically when a bride would get her *henna* done?'

'It is, but it takes like three to four hours, and I wanted to enjoy the casino and everything, so had it done before, in stages.'

'That's amazing,' I grin. 'Can I get a closer look at it?'

'Sure,' she holds out her hands. 'So, there's actually a few hidden things in the design. See here,' Nisha points to the side of her left hand, 'both our initials are worked into the pattern.' If she hadn't told me, I wouldn't have seen it, but sure enough, I spot them, next to an intricate swirl. 'And here,' she flips her right hand over and points to her pinky finger, 'there's a little apple here; we had our first date at a cider festival.' Nisha and Harry grin at each other. Dom takes a picture of both details, clearly still determined to stay in her good books. 'Traditionally, the idea behind it is that when the bride's family comes over to the newly married couple's home, the *henna* is an indication of how well looked after she is.'

'What do you mean?' I ask, taking mental notes for later.

'Well, say it's all faded, that means she's been doing all the cooking, washing her hands often, etc. If it's dark, she's had help; it's like a secret way of communicating with your family.'

'*Huh*, I love that.'

'Anyway, we'll leave you to enjoy the evening,' Nisha grabs Harry's hand and they head off towards a couple of family members.

'So, before the rest of the guests arrive, what do you think? Fancy your chances on one of the tables?' Dom says, rubbing his hands together.

'I have absolutely no idea how to play anything,' I admit.

'Perfect.' He grins.

***

'BLACK 17!'

'Are you actually kidding me?' Dom puts his head in his hands, as Sarah and I have our fifth consecutive win. 'How are you doing this?' He frowns at us, as we gather our mounting chips pile, and he watches the last of his being swept away.

'Pure luck!' I can't help but giggle as I gather our winnings, scooping them into Sarah's handbag.

'I thought you said you were good at this!' Hugo says to Dom, shaking his head.

'I'd say we're done here; what do you think, Poppet?' Sarah says, smugly to me.

'Absolutely! Maybe next time you could play on *our* team,' I nod at them both, before Sarah and I laugh and walk arm in arm, away from the table.

There's a drummer now entertaining the crowd and a few professional dancers, bringing guests up to join them. The entire friend group is going for it, as well as a couple of young cousins. I jiggle my shoulders and catch the eye of one of the dancers. He beckons me forwards, and I shake my head.

'Go go!' Sarah encourages. 'Hey, I'll even come with you!' She turns to Hugo and Dom, 'You don't mind holding our winnings now, do you boys?' Sarah laughs and throws her handbag into Hugo's hands before leading me onto the dancefloor.

***

The next morning, I wake bright and early, and YouTube an instructional video on: "simple wedding guest updos," knowing that I'll need my hair out of the way, but also wanting to be a little more formal than my usual messy bun. I settle on one with lots of little plaits everywhere, then whoosh my hair up with an amazingly strong grippy clip. I admire myself in the mirror; not bad.

Putting on the underskirt of the *sari*, I smile at the colour; Nisha picked out a palate for me that's somewhere between teal and emerald, and I love it. I pop on my trusty flip flops, as my shiny diamante ones were catching the inside of the dress; I couldn't give it back ruined! Apart from that, I'm basically wearing a crop top, which Nisha told me is called a *chorli*. I carefully carry the stunning bejewelled *pallu*, over my arm, which is like a beautiful long scarf. Giggling slightly to myself, I'm so tiny, I'm wondering how many times this will have to be wrapped around me, to not drag along the floor.

With my small clutch purse that only holds my tiny notepad and pen, in case I want to jot anything down, I'm ready to go. I pull my door keycard out of the slot that turns the lights and the ceiling fan on, shut the door and head to Sarah's. She should be back from seeing to Nisha by now. I tap gently and wait for her to open the door, but hear one open behind me.

'Not sure you're fully dressed.' I turn to see Dom's smug face back at me, holding a camera, casually in his hands.

'Well spotted,' I say sarcastically, before turning on my heel, with every intention of ignoring him. Tapping for Sarah again, a little louder this time, I hear a muffled voice and some heavy footsteps, before the door opens.

'Coming, coming!' Her ensemble matches mine, except it's royal blue.

'Love the colour on you!' I say to her very pale back, as she disappears into her makeshift woman cave, to grab her *pallu*. 'OK, I'm ready.' She rushes back to the door, shuts it, and looks down at herself. 'Now, don't get me wrong, I really appreciate it, but it's *way* too bright for me!'

'It's not your typical style, no,' I admit, 'but I think you look super!' I say, and mean it.

'Well, thanks Poppet; I don't know. Also, I can't remember the last time my midriff had a proper outing,' she self-consciously touches her very flat stomach, then looks at mine. 'Oh my God, how are you so tanned?'

Dom snorts a laugh, from behind me. We both turn to face him, 'It's like Snow White and Miss Hawaiian Tropic!' He laughs again, and I ignore the flip in my stomach at the mere association with Hawaii, before turning to Sarah.

'Ignore him; you look beautiful.'

'*We* look beautiful.' She corrects me, then links my arm. 'Alright, let's go.'

'Say cheese,' he snaps a picture of us in our half-dressed ensemble, and we pad our way down the corridor to find the rest of the gaggle of women waiting to be wrapped, as it were.

As we approach the right room, Lilly, the sister of the groom, comes bursting out, hand clenched tightly onto a phone. 'When you get this, please call me.' She hangs up aggressively then frowns at us.

'What's happened?' I ask.

'Bloody people coming to do the *saris* up aren't here and aren't answering! I have no idea what to do! There's fifteen of us in here and not one has a freaking clue!'

'Well, I'm sure we could figure it out together—' I start, but Sarah interrupts me.

'No, we need Hugo,' she says firmly, 'Here, hold this.' She gives me her blue decorative *pallu*.

'Hugo knows how to tie a *sari*?' I say, with disbelief.

'I think so. I'm pretty sure he mentioned doing an Indian wedding in San Francisco, once.' Sarah whips her phone out of her small clutch and dials him at warp speed. 'You're needed with an '*eff-ton* of safety pins. Room 1276; down the corridor from our rooms, across the walkway and on the left,' she barks into the phone without so much of a hello. 'Right.' She hangs up and nods at us all. 'He's on his way.'

Leaving the door ajar, we enter the room to the gaggle of friends, bridesmaids, and English family members. All of them are around one iPad, half dressed, in identical outfits to Sarah and I, in various colours, shapes and sizes, watching someone tie up a *sari*; it's quite comical.

'*Ooh*, I love the way you've done your hair,' Lilly says to me. 'But, I feel you're missing something. I know, try these.' She picks something off the dresser and shows them to me: a gorgeous pair of gold studs, with a decorative swirly line, that must curve their way up the whole of one's earlobes.

'Oh wow, those are beautiful; you sure?'

'Oh yeah, no worries at all.' She puts them back down then takes out a small bottle of hand sanitiser, puts a couple drops on a makeup pad, and cleans the ear-rings. 'I got a little carried away shopping online before I came. I haven't even worn these ones.' When she's finished cleaning, she out-stretches her hand, offering them to me, 'You can have them!'

'Oh, wow. Thank you!'

Hugo steps inside. 'Right! I'm here. Let's do this!'

***

Half an hour later, every woman is ready, thanks to Hugo. As Sarah heads off to check on the bride, I make my way down to the lawn with the gaggle. We're met by Harry, all of his side of the family, and the male side of the English friend group. Each guy is wearing varying degrees of wedding attire, from smart short-sleeved shirts with shorts or linen trousers, to more traditional clothing. I particularly like the *kurta's*, (a knee length tunic shirt with long sleeves). But, I can see just how hot those friends are; not surprising when they're wearing *jodhpur* trousers; the material is loose at the top, but tight fitting from the knee to ankle.

Most spectacularly though, is Harry, Ollie, and the father-of-the-groom, who are all wearing cream knee-length jackets, which, Nisha tells me, is called a *sherwani,* that have intricate gold and red detailing. Upon their heads, both the father-of-the-groom and Ollie are in red cotton *pagri's*, and Harry's — just to be different — is pink.

I smile as little groups of friends are taking pictures, clearly just as excited to be wearing a *sari* as me. Swooshing mine, happily, I gaze around, and spot what I've been most looking forward to: the horse.

As part of the *Jaan*, (where the groom is welcomed by the bride's family), the *Baraat* takes place. Harry and his sister Lilly, have to ride on horseback, over to Nisha's family on the far lawns, among Harry's family and friends, who must dance their way into the ceremony. As Harry mounts the horse, Lilly looks up apprehensively. 'How the hell am I supposed to ride that in a *sari*?'

'Sidesaddle!' A smiley uncle of Nisha says, before putting down a drum and picking Lilly up with ease. She screams but makes it up there, to the sound of cheers of everyone around.

'Good thing I love Nisha,' Lilly says to Harry, 'But *you* owe me one for being up here!' She grips onto the horse's decorative saddle, and then they're off. Both of them look extremely uncomfortable.

'Ever ridden a horse, *me mucker*?' Ollie taunts from below.

'Bugger off, mate,' Harry says to a hysterical Ollie, as the uncle starts to beat his drum.

'OK! Now we dance!' he instructs us all. I grin and wiggle from one foot to the other. It's not until then that I spot Dom, smiling away at me.

I point up to Harry and Lilly on the horse, and mouth, 'Them; not me!' at him. He grins again, and takes shot after shot of brother, sister and the horse, and of us all dancing. Dom's got two cameras with him today; one over each shoulder, and he moves so swiftly, it's almost a dance within itself.

We're greeted by Nisha's family, who are waiting at the entrance of the decorative aisle, with a gift, but Nisha's uncle is shaking his head at Harry, and holding out his hand.

'What happens now?' Sarah whispers to me, suddenly at my side and pulling at the *sari*, so she doesn't trip over it.

'There's several stages of bribing throughout the ceremony, this is the first one; he's got to pay to get off the horse.' We watch as Harry hands over money to the uncle with the drum, then, before Harry knows what's happening, a cousin runs over and steals his shoes, and everyone laughs.

'What's up with that?'

I giggle, and turn back to Sarah, 'It's to stop the groom leaving with the bride, again, it happens all throughout the—what are you doing?' Sarah's bending over, and her hands are now up her skirt.

'The underskirt has made its way up my legs; I have to hitch it back down.' Luckily, everyone is distracted as they watch Lilly, followed by Harry, dismount the horse, while a few young family members of Harry's chase after Nisha's cousins and uncles. Some of the friends chase after the shoe-stealers too.

'Ah, there we go,' Sarah says, now the right way up and gives an appreciative little noise, as we watch Ollie tackle the shoe-stealing cousin; they both land on the floor. Everybody cheers and then starts to take their seats.

'Where shall we sit?' Sarah asks, as we walk down the crimson-carpet aisle, looking for reserved seats, among the now ivory covered chairs, decorated in gold bows, some of which don't make the shelter, and are in the sunshine.

'No offence honey,' Hugo suddenly appears behind us,

'but we need to get you into the shade, or you're going to die.' Hugo grabs Sarah's shoulders and parks her in a shady seat, nearest a fan spraying little bits of water.

Harry's now at the front with his best men, standing in front of the *mandap*, where the pillars are draped gracefully in a beautiful red and gold material. I gaze excitedly around at the guests: it is without a doubt, the most colourful wedding I've ever been to. An outfit pallet of pink, orange, red, green, blue, yellow, you name it, it's here.

The priest gestures to Harry and after removing his shoes once more, he takes to the stage. As soon as his back is turned, I see a cousin steal his shoes once more.

Then Goldie, her husband, Lilly, Nisha's parents and brother, all join Harry on the *mandap*, and take a seat. I catch them all looking up, and smiling down the aisle. Nisha is walking towards us, with her uncles, each holding a corner of a light-weight material, over her head. Everyone stands and takes in the bride: she looks absolutely amazing. Her ribbed bodice (that she secretly told me her mum hates), and long *lehenga* skirt, are both cream, emblazoned with gold, bejewelled swirls, and touches of red with a minuscule amount of green, but *man*, that thing looks heavy!

Upon her head, is a red *dupatta*, (an Indian veil), with matching decorations of gold. Her jewellery reminds me of what was placed on me in Dubai, but way more classy. A choker graces her neck, displaying more gold and red touches, delicately down to each collar bone; her wrists now carry numerous bracelets; chandelier earrings glitter in the sunshine; and a teardrop shaped *tikka*, has been placed on her forehead, from her hair parting.

As Nisha removes her shoes, climbs the steps of the *mandap,* and meets her groom, the Uncle's place the material that was above her head, between her and Harry, like a curtain. A blessing is said by the priest, and then Nisha's uncles lower the material, and they gaze at each other, up close, for the first time; Harry looks like his breath has been taken away.

As the ceremony continues, I try to match what Nisha told me will happen, with what's in front of me, with the help of the priest's commentary. Harry first touches Nisha's mother's feet, as an acceptance for the wedding to go ahead, meanwhile, she, in turn, tries to grab his nose.

'Yes, quite right, you let her take your nose!' The priest says over a microphone, and Nisha's mother grabs it, from him, and speaks to the crowd,

'Remember Harry, Nisha is always mine!' she says, jokingly, handing back the microphone, and she gives Harry a big hug on the stage.

'And next, we have the change of garlands,' the priest continues, 'to welcome in, one family to the other.' I watch as Nisha's mum places one around Harry's neck, and Goldie does the same to Nisha.

After this, I love all of the traditions: Nisha's mum washing Harry's feet and offering him milk and honey: a sweet welcome that ensures he's ready to go, has energy and is ready to be married; and then Nisha's dad gives her hand to Harry, and they are bound together by the end of her *dupatta*. After which, a large necklace is placed around the two of them (to ward off evil, the priest informs us). I giggle during the *Chero Pakaryo*, which is basically a cheeky way of asking for a payment for taking the bride. Nisha's family each went up to give blessings and advice on a happy marriage, and Harry pretends to not want her. He catches the end of Nisha's mum's *sari* and asks for more cash and gifts.

She batts him away, and you know that it's all done in good humour, to honour the tradition.

But, I think this is my favourite bit. The *Saptapadi*, or seven steps, in which the couple, while tied together with the *dupatta*, make seven promises to each other, walking clockwise, around a fire. I watch Harry lead Nisha for the first four, then they switch places and she leads him for the final three.

'They must be cooking!' Hugo leans into me.

'They're not the only ones,' I nod at him, and he's perspiring at a rate of knots.

Sarah looks at us both, looking a little faint, 'I'm sorry, I haven't got the energy to talk to you.'

I make the tongue gesture again at her, in which to help cool her down and she nods, imitating me immediately. Smiling, I continue to watch the ceremony, and observe Dom running around; I can see he's sweating buckets too. I decide to keep to myself that personally, I love this heat. It's intense, but, to me, not unpleasant; much like a sauna. It feels cleansing somehow.

'They have now tied themselves together for seven lifetimes to become one.' The priest says to the perspiring friends and family, as Nisha smiles at Harry. Her smile doesn't drop throughout their vows to each other, or through the ritual of touching seven betel nuts with her toe; she wiggles slightly, but Harry helps her keep her balance.

'And now, we shall see who is to hold the power in the marriage,' the priest announces, and I see Nisha raise a competitive eyebrow at Harry. They both race to sit down first, and Nisha takes her place a mere moment before Harry, to the immense pleasure of everyone around us, who erupts into applause. '*Aw*, bad luck Harry! Perhaps you will have more luck with the *Aeki beki.*' I watch excitedly as a bowl is brought out. 'So, for those who do not know, we are to place the wedding rings into this bowl of milk and red canku — a red powder. Nisha and Harry are to find their own, and the first to do so, will rule the marriage!'

The audience cheer them both on, and each of them are laughing as they fight to be the winner. Nisha's hand emerges first, and as she is declared the winner, they kiss.

'I don't think he was trying very hard,' Hugo says to us.

'I don't think he's supposed to,' I say, while clapping with everyone else.

Soon after, Nisha and Harry walk down the few steps, to leave the stage, not looking back at their families; Nisha told me that they're not allowed to, as it marks the start of their lives together and the end of her parents' responsibility. I glance at Nisha's parents, and they are smiling with tears in their eyes.

Nisha stops to put her shoes on, but Harry realises that his aren't there. A cousin holds up the missing shoes and tauntingly dangles them out in front of Harry. He walks over and pays the cousin for his shoes, before joining his bride once more. They happily walk up the aisle, but it's then blocked by more of Nisha's family members.

'I haven't got any more money!' Harry laughs.

'Well, you cannot leave with the bride!' A young, cheeky cousin says, with his arms folded. Harry looks around and gestures to Ollie, who comes running over with his wallet, the cheeky cousin shakes his head and asks for more. When Ollie has emptied his wallet, the couple are allowed to pass, stepping into their brand new life together.

Chapter 10

India – Singapore
Goa – Mumbai – Kovan

Monday
Depart Goa International Airport at 07:30
Arrive Mumbai International Airport at 08:45
Duration: 1 hour 15 minutes (2-hour 45-minute layover in Mumbai)

Depart Mumbai International Airport at 11:25
Arrive Singapore Changi Airport at 19:25
Duration: 5 hours 30 minutes
Time change: Singapore 2 hours 30 minutes ahead
Drive half an hour to hotel (2 nights stay)

Singapore Wedding Show

'How beautiful were the lanterns last night? Oh, I loved it; it was just like *Tangled.*' I grin and flick through the in-flight magazine in front of me, and quietly sing, "I See the Light," from *Tangled.*

Apart from the fashion show tomorrow, we basically have the evening, a day and a morning to chill out in Singapore; it's a hard life. I can't wait to see Becky.

'I don't know, I've never been one for lanterns,' Dom

brings me out of my thoughts, frowning from the seat to my right. 'Not very environmentally friendly. The last thing the ocean needs is more rubbish for the sea life to get wrapped up in, or choke on.'

'So I'm not the only one who's gone green?' I lift my top slightly to reveal my stomach, which, courtesy of my *sari*, has been dyed green. Dom barely smirks at me and Hugo chips in, from the far left seat of our middle group of four, also, ignoring my joke,

'The ones last night were environmentally friendly, actually. They were biodegradable, made with environmentally friendly materials, and were fireproof.'

'There we are! See!' I turn back to Dom, who's still frowning.

'I still don't like them.' He folds his arms.

'God, you're so grumpy. Loosen up, man! You know what you need?' I put my magazine down in Sarah's empty seat, to my left.

'What?' He looks at me, unimpressed.

'A good song.' And I continue singing, "I See the Light," with passion, waving my arms around in his personal space.

Sarah walks out of the aeroplane loo, steadying herself as she goes on the top of each seat she passes.

I stop singing, and sit up, concerned, resisting the urge to ask if she's still feeling blue, (her stomach also matched her *sari*). 'What's wrong?' I take in her sunburnt complexion that's now tinged with grey. Removing my magazine from her seat, I place it in the pocket in front of me. 'Do you want to use my revitalising spray?'

'For God's sake,' Dom says under his breath, and I ignore him.

Sarah gently shakes her head, gingerly steps in front of

Hugo, and sits back in her seat, 'Well, you know I went to freshen up in the airport during our layover?'

'Yes; I waited outside with your suitcase,' I say, remembering.

'I saw this woman next to me brushing her teeth, so I opened my travel case in my handbag, and thought, "Oh wow, that's a great idea."'

'You used the tap water?' I say, horrified.

She nodded, 'I used the tap water.'

For a moment I just press my lips together and try not to laugh.

'I put the toothbrush in my mouth, and then thought, "Oh shit."'

'And then she did,' Hugo says, and we all burst out laughing.

'Come on!' Sarah hits us all in turn. 'This isn't funny!'

'No; you're wrong;' Dom points at her, 'this is hilarious.'

'You're an arsehole!' she reaches across me to hit him once more.

'And you're about to experience a very sore one,' Dom quips back.

Sarah buries her head in her hands, 'I'm not going to be very well for a while, am I?' She looks at me through her fingers.

I smile, sympathetically and nod, 'You may get the full experience, yes. How do you feel now?'

'Fine, I think. Maybe I'll be fine?' She says as more of a question than a statement.

***

A few hours and several trips to the loo later, I stroke

Sarah's hair, as she curls up in her seat, legs over Hugo, and head in my lap.

'How are you doing hon?'

'*Ugh*,' is her response.

'The sky's really pretty if you want to take a look?' I gaze to my left and peer in awe out of the little cabin window.

'I'm just focusing on not being sick here, OK?' she groans.

'OK.' I go back to stroking her hair. Glancing out the window, it is the most magnificent sight I have ever seen — and that's saying something as a travel writer. The tall, thick, vertical cloud in full view is clearly a storm one; it's moody and dark, but with the sun setting behind it, it's got tinges of pink and purple, among threatening grey; it's beautiful, and I can't help but think, beauty can be found everywhere; you just have to remember to look.

***

After settling into our hotel, we pop into a cab and head over to Becky's apartment. All the buildings are identical: tall and numerous. We're buzzed into the complex, and weave our way around the pool. I've only been here once, so I'm glad I remember which way it is. I knock on the door; a friendly, tanned and rather handsome man answers, 'Hey buddy, how are you?' I give Rory, Becky's husband, a big hug.

'Great to see you, Liv.' He squeezes me back.

'So sorry to break up the reunion, but I've *gotta* use the washroom.' Sarah pushes past him and into my equally tanned, equally beautiful, best friend.

'First door on the right,' Becky points and Sarah groans in appreciation. Becky walks towards me, grinning from ear to ear, 'Hey you!'

I give her a huge hug, 'It's been too long! I've missed you so much.' When I finally let go, I take a step to the side. 'Let me introduce everybody: this is Hugo, Dom, and,' I point inside the apartment, 'that was Sarah.'

'Hi!'

'Great to meet you both,' Becky and Rory answer at the same time and shake hands with them, then Rory puts an arm around his wife and looks at her in the same way Leo used to look at me.

'Well, come in, come in!' Becky takes a step to the side and pulls Rory with her.

'Oh wow, you moved everything around,' I say, taking in their new layout.

'Yeah, it just made more sense this way, you know? OK, so when Sarah's finished,' Rory raises his eyebrows and makes a face, 'what do you say to grabbing some food and a couple drinks?'

'Sounds perfect.' I glance out at their balcony and take in the sky. I forgot just how overcast it can be in Singapore. It's really mild out, but a dull grey hue lingers; kind of like how London is, but with humidity.

'So, is there anything you want to do whilst you're here, in between the fashion show?' Becky says, gesturing for us all to take a seat on her lovely L-shaped couch.

'Sentosa Island? I missed that last time.'

'The event's on Sentosa, so you're sorted!' Becky grins at me and takes a seat on one of the comfy solo chairs opposite the couch.

'Shall we take them to Tower 63?' I say.

'Oh, yeah, definitely!' Becky nods, 'It's called: 1 Altitude, now, and it's got a rooftop bar!'

'*Ooh*, fancy!' I grin from ear to ear; she knows rooftop bars have always been at the top of my travel list.

'So, what's special about this Tower 63 or 1 Altitude?' Dom asks.

I smile. 'You'll see. Hopefully Sarah's stomach can handle the lift!'

***

After a gorgeous dinner at an open air restaurant, and with Sarah (who refused to stay at home), having to excuse herself several times to go to the loo, we walk past Raffles Hotel. I love this building, it's big, old and white and looks like it belongs in Monte Carlo; old money, mixed with true class.

'What's that?' Sarah says, pointing across the harbour at a boat atop two towers.

'It's Marina Bay Sands; a hotel, bar, and it's got an infinity pool!'

When we arrive at our after-dinner drinks venue, I stop in my tracks. 'Are you sure we'll get in?' I say, looking at the crowd.

'Oh, yeah, no problem; we reserved a table!' Becky says, leading us towards the front of the queue. She greets the doorman, we bypass the crowd, and then head into the lift. 'Hang on to your stomachs!' She grins at each of us.

'What?' Sarah says, as the lift jolts and shoots upwards. 'Oh holy '*eff!*' She grabs onto Hugo's arm as the lift climbs at such a speed. I feel my stomach leave me but all it does is make me giggle. When the lift comes to a halt, we make our way out with the other party goers.

There's an air of sophistication. Most people are dressed

in suits, mingling, and chatting happily, but not a single person is loud, obnoxious, or drunk. You can almost feel success in the room; it's a different calibre of clientele from any bar I've known in London. My guess is that the room is filled with mainly successful expats, especially bankers.

'Oh wow.' Hugo gazes out at the floor to ceiling windows, revealing a 360-degree view.

'We're on the 63rd floor; it used to be the tallest bar in Singapore, but more and more are being built, it's hard to keep up,' Rory says, smiling at the room. I take in a set of stairs on the opposite side of the room, I guess they take you to the rooftop.

'You can see my boat from here!' Sarah says, spotting the Marina Bay Sands.

'I think we're over this way,' Rory leads our pack towards a low-lit table, and hands us each a menu, as we take a seat.

Suddenly I have a rush of affection for everyone and feel so lucky to have these great friends — old and new. I smile at Becky and Sarah.

'So how has your trip been so far?' Becky asks the open question to the whole table.

'Really good,' Sarah answers, 'I've either been suffering from heat exhaustion, food poisoning or a dodgy belly.'

'Or sea sickness,' Hugo adds.

'Yeah! Sea sickness, I forgot about that!' I say.

'And, Liv got stuck in a shower, and in a dress,' Sarah fires back, playfully sticking her tongue out at me.

Becky laughs, 'I meant more about the weddings, but, this is good!' She faces the waiter who's come over. 'I'll have a sparkling water with a slice of lemon please,' she aims at him.

'Don't go too crazy,' I say.

'Oh, I've got an early meeting tomorrow, before the fashion show, so, better keep a clear head.' She briefly makes a funny face before smiling, but it was long enough for me to see a sparkle in her eyes; I decide to play along,

'You're not even going to have one drink with us? Man, you've changed,' I tut, and shake my head. 'White chocolate martini for me please,' I say to the waiter, putting the menu down. Becky then catches my eye, and signals that she'd like to tell me something — a secret, telepathic mannerism that we've had since school.

'*Ooh*, that sounds great! I'm feeling better, so I'll have one of those too!' Sarah says with excitement.

'I'm just going to nip to the loo; any idea where it is, Bex?' I stand.

'I thought you'd been here before,' Dom says to me, creasing his eyebrows.

'She has, but it's changed since then,' Bex directs at Dom, upholding the girl code of covering her friend's lie. She stands to join me, 'They're this way,' she points, 'I need to go too, I'll come with.' We zigzag our way, arm in arm, to the ladies and when the doors shut Bex turns to me beaming.

'You don't have an early meeting, do you?' I smile at her.

She shakes her head, 'Nope.'

'How far along are you?' I grin.

'Well, you know I said I was late?'

'*Ah huh*.'

'I didn't say *how* late, as I didn't want to jinx it.' She puts her head down, briefly then glows at me, 'I'm sixteen weeks!' She starts jumping up and down as my jaw hits the floor, 'I can't believe it! It's finally happened!' I grab her hands and join her in a jump, and we squeal like little teenagers.

The last time I was here she was sure she was pregnant and then got her period. We drank a lot that night, here, in this very bar; there's a nice symmetry to it.

Several drinks later, Dom and Hugo are off checking out the view from the rooftop, and I'm staring at my childhood friend, happily whispering in Rory's ear; so in love. Suddenly, I can't help but get the sinking feeling that I'm behind in life. All these weddings, people are starting families or adding to their already existing ones; what am I doing with my life? Gallivanting around with no real aim or purpose, apart from avoiding my feelings and admitting how I really feel, that's what.

'You alright?' Sarah asks from the seat next to me, tilting her head.

'Yeah,' I lie, then after a beat, decide to be honest. 'Do you ever feel like, I don't know, you're behind everybody?'

'What do you mean?' She twirls the remaining contents of her martini glass.

'Like, everyone's above you somehow?'

She stands up, tall, and puts a hand on her hip, 'No one is above me!'

I can't help but laugh, and pull her back down to sit again. 'No, nothing to do with height. I mean, ignoring the fact that we're on this wedding adventure, how many weddings have you been to, of people you actually know?'

She makes a face, '*Um*, I don't know, maybe, like, seven?'

'And how many Christenings, Bar or Bat Mitzvahs or children's birthdays have you attended, as an adult?'

'Too many to mention,' she makes a face that is less than disapproving.

'Exactly. So, me? I have been to thirty weddings.' Sarah opens her mouth to say something, 'and that doesn't include work,' I add, and she shuts her mouth again. 'That's thirty weddings of friends and family, and sometimes, it makes me feel like I have surpassed Katherine Heigl for goodness sake.'

'What?'

'You know, *27 Dresses*? Always a bridesmaid?'

'Oh, yeah, I like that film.' She takes a sip of her drink, then places the glass on the table.

'Anyway, I don't know;' I feel myself sink into my seat a little more, 'it just makes you think, you know? I mean, I live in a flat that I've rented for years, all my friends have houses and mortgages; I'm not with anyone, all my friends are married with kids; I'm nearly thirty, and I don't have kids, and to be honest, I'm not even sure I want kids. I just want to travel, and live, and…' I look at my hands, 'run away from reality.' I pause, sigh again, and then look up at her, 'Everyone in my life is moving on, and I'm sort of stuck in a crappy, shame-filled time warp, where all I'm doing is distracting myself, and denying or numbing how I feel. But, I've no idea how to change.'

She takes me in with her mesmerising cat eyes, 'My darling, Poppet, how many of those thirty people can say they are being paid, for an all-expenses taken care of, trip around the world?'

'Zero,' I admit.

Sarah then gestures around the room, 'And how many of those people are sitting in this fabulous bar right now?' She doesn't let me answer. 'How many of them get to do what they want when they want? Are they getting up and doing a work-out, or lying-in and then going for brunch on the weekends, just because they can and they feel like it? No! They can't! Because of *their* life choices. Yes, all of that is a blessing, and some day, if you decide marriage, kids and the white picket fence with a mortgage is what you want, then you can have all of it, too. But right now, we are on the 63rd floor of a building in Singapore, looking out at a stunning view, part of which has a boat in the sky!' She gestures again, this time to the window, then turns back to me. 'Plus, you know your life choices and decisions don't have to make sense or sound good to anybody else, because they are just that: *Yours*. Come on dude. This is the time to be grateful, to embrace the now, and to let go of all those thoughts that really don't serve you. We…' she pauses to grab my hand, '...are awesome. We are good at what we do, and we get paid to travel the world and eat at other peoples' life events. Now,' she hands me my martini glass, with her other hand, then grabs hers again, 'here's to friendship, and to the fact that we are strong, independent women, who make up their own rules, and write their own stories.' She clinks my glass and I grin from ear to ear.

'I love you.' My eyes have filled with tears, as I bring my glass to hers again.

'I love you too, Poppet.'

***

The fashion show is being held in a hall that reminds me of ExCel in London: deceptively large, and can clearly be transformed into any shape or desire. The room is warmly lit, with what I would describe as a romantic light: flattering and almost dream-like. I'm sitting in the audience, in the last seat of the front row, on the left hand side as you look at the catwalk, happily swinging my left leg over my right, and admiring my trusty brown ankle boots; I do like how versatile they are. Today, I'm sporting a boho red, floral dress that's high at the front and low at the back.

I glance over at Dom, who's alongside all the other photographers, all poised and ready for showtime, in the Press seats, facing the end of the cat-walk.

It's quite exciting; I literally don't have to do anything today, except enjoy myself. I sip on the complimentary prosecco and grin at the room.

Both Sarah and Hugo are backstage with Bex, taking the opportunity to schmooze with as many international potential clients; I mentally applaud them both. Looking around, I take in the room. It's alive with future Mr and Mrs's, and brides with their gaggles of friends. There are various booths lined up alongside each other, continuing around the entirety of the room in one large square, with the catwalk claiming the central feature. Each booth represents a different wedding designer, shop, venue, possible entertainment or honeymoon destination. It's funny, the air isn't so much about competition, but pure respect; I like it.

'Penny for your thoughts?' Dom says from a few paces away, sitting in the far left Press seat.

I lean forwards, and gesture around the room with my glass, 'I was thinking how much I like this environment.'

'What?' He looks at me as though I've lost my mind.

'No, no,' I wave my hand at him, 'I mean, the *business* element of it all. No one's in competition with anyone else; I like that. There's no feeling that anyone is comparing themselves to anybody else.'

He looks at me strangely, and doesn't say anything, so I take the opportunity to take another delicious sip. When he still doesn't reply, I ask, 'Do you feel like you have to compete?'

Dom nods slightly and stays straight-faced, 'Always.' He goes back to his camera, takes a practice shot, then examines it. *Hmm, guess I touched a nerve.*

Having left my watch on the bedside table of the hotel, I whip my phone out of my little, over-the-shoulder, brown bag, and check the time. The seats are starting to fill up; must nearly be showtime! Chucking my phone back in my bag, I finish the last of my prosecco and look around, wondering if I can cheekily grab another one; *where's that guy with the tray?* Instead, I see a mildly white-faced Bex, heading in my direction.

'Morning sickness hasn't come back, has it?' I ask quietly, as she reaches me, looking down.

'I hate to do this,' she starts.

'Nonsense! You love your job. And might I say, you are very good at it! Loving the complimentary bubbles, by the way!' I wave my empty glass at her.

'Oh God! How many have you had?'

'Just the one,' I say, mildly offended. 'Although, admittedly, I was looking for a second,' I grin. 'Any chance you can shimmy that waiter back over here?' I look around again, spot him and wave. Bex grabs my arm and throws it back down, putting her hand up to stop the waiter from moving.

'Will you just *shush* for one second?' she says in a panicked low tone.

'Alright.' I sit up a little straighter.

'I need to borrow you.' She smiles politely as a few people have started to watch our exchange.

'For what?' I ask slowly.

'Like I said,' she talks through a fake smile, 'I hate to do this; I hate to even ask you, but—'

The penny drops. '*Noooo.*' I say, wide-eyed with horror.

'Look, I know getting in a wedding dress is absolutely the last thing that you want to do right now, but I need you.'

'Why? You've got an army of models back there!' I wave my arm.

'Yes, I do, but I'm one down.' She bends down to face me, and lowers her voice even further. 'She was walking in the shoes, tripped, and has twisted or broken something.'

Becky retreats quickly as I stand up. 'I'm sorry,' I keep my tone low, 'you're asking me to not only put on a wedding dress, but to have my picture taken, which is to be printed on a double page spread of the world's most popular wedding magazine, among others, and to do that, walking in a pair of shoes that a *professional* broke her ankle in? Are you freaking kidding me?' My voice is a loud whisper now.

'I know, I know,' she dances her head, side to side, 'it's not ideal.' She scrunches her face, then grabs my hand and starts walking me along the front row of people, towards the backstage area.

'Ideal? What part of this is ideal? Bex, I've no experience in this!'

'Nonsense, we used to watch *America's Next Top Model*!' She picks up our pace, as we leave the catwalk area; it's as if she's dragging her child through the supermarket.

'Watching *other people* walk in high heels, while eating a Chinese take-away, isn't experience, Bex! And have you not noticed? I'm at least a foot shorter than these girls! I saw them parade in; it was a tower of giraffes for God's sake!'

'I know,' she almost cries. 'But, I have to have all the dresses out, at once for the finale, Liv. It's in the contract; I can't not.'

'Well, you wear it then!' I almost yell at her, and she stops in her tracks.

'I can't.' She says in a dignified and ever so slightly smug manner, 'It doesn't fit me.' She smiles.

I narrow my eyes, 'Liar. You're using your pregnancy as an excuse?'

'Yes, I am,' she folds her arms in finality.

'You're barely even showing yet, and we've been the same size since primary school!' I say angrily, placing my hands firmly on my hips.

She tilts her head, 'Look, you know I wouldn't ask you to do this if I really didn't need you too. There's no way I can be in two places at once. You've got the perfect body, all we need to do is,' she pauses, looking at my signature messy bun, 'a little something up there, and on there,' she gestures to my fresh face.

'Oh God, I'm going to be sick.'

She takes my hand again and we walk backstage.

'OK, here we are! I've saved the day!' Becky says to the room. It's the most bizarre scene ever: all the giraffes are wandering around in wedding dresses, of varying styles, from full-on princess puffballs, to elegant, skin tight, silk numbers. Some are sitting, reading magazines, others casually eating carrot sticks, but most notably, there's one sitting in her underwear, with a leg up on another chair, a great big ice pack on her ankle, and a pissed off expression on her face.

'*You're* going to walk down the catwalk in my dress and shoes? Good luck!'

'Ignore her,' Bex directs me towards the mirrors, 'she's just grumpy. And in pain. And a bit of a bitch,' she says in an even lower tone.

'Isn't this exciting!' Sarah bounds over to me. 'Your very first fashion show!'

I snort, 'I, *ah*, *um*, no! It, *phah*!' I can no longer form a sentence.

'She's understandably a little nervous.' Hugo joins the party. 'What do you need us to do?' He directs this at Bex, not me.

'Grab the shoes,' Becky points to Hugo, who races off. 'Face,' is all she directs at Sarah, who nods and suddenly, everything's a blur. Bex throws me down in a chair. 'Right, drink this.' She hands me a bottle of water. 'Wash some of that prosecco out.' I do as instructed, in a kind of numb state, as both Bex and Sarah get to work, simultaneously. 'Alright, let's see. I'm thinking...' They both examine my face, in the mirror, from behind me; I can see their mouths moving but I can't take in what they're saying.

Bex spins my chair 90 degrees, and they work around me, swiftly picking up various bits and pieces, as they go 'OK; yup.' Bex talking to herself. Before I know it, my hair is down, and being tamed with some sort of product and at the same time, Sarah is working on my face so quickly it's as if someone's pressed the fast forward button. I feel Bex twisting sections of my hair, pinning them, and then pulling one small section into a french plait at warp speed, while my face tickles from a brush Sarah's using, before I'm instructed to shut my eyes.

'I'll just put the shoes on for a try, Liv,' I hear Hugo say as my eyes are still closed.

'OK,' I manage to reply, as I feel him take my boots and trainer socks off, and place a shoe on my right foot, and start wrapping something around my ankle. My hair now travels up into a ponytail.

'They're a little big, Bex, what do you think?' Hugo asks. She swears loudly, and I feel Hugo taking them off again.

'OK, I'm done.' Sarah says, after applying something to my lips.

'Great.' Bex exhales and I feel her place something at the top of the ponytail. I open my eyes then she throws my hair over my face and fans it around my head, places one hand to keep it in place, and works quickly to *whoosh* it round, neatly. Sarah holds out a jar of pins for Bex to use, and she works them around what I now see is a doughnut bun, to keep it in place. She then spins me another 90 degrees, facing me away from the mirror, and gently pulls out a few strands here and there, letting them fall around my face.

'Great.' She and Sarah high-five. 'Alright, now for the dress. Oh '*eff*, what's the time?' Bex says loudly to the room.

'One minute *'til* showtime,' I hear someone yell back.

I look down at the discarded shoes that Hugo tried to put on my feet, and thank the Lord they didn't fit me; they must be six inches tall.

Bex pulls me out of the seat, and towards a rack of dresses. 'Why are there so many dresses here, get it together people, we're nearly on!' She yells at the room, before taking a deep breath. 'OK, get naked.'

'Naked?! What the hell are you getting me to wear?'

'No, not, *naked*, naked, you know what I mean, underwear on, everything else off,' she says quickly.

I look around self-consciously. 'Really? Isn't there a changing room or something?'

'This *is* the changing room, sweetie. No one cares. Come on, please. You're on in like thirty seconds.'

She holds up a dress that, admittedly, is not too dissimilar in style, to the high-low that I'm wearing, except it's ivory.

'I'm first?' I say, with horror, reaching for each side of my dress to pull it over my head.

'No, fourth. Mind your hair!' she adds in panic.

'OK, now, I see the rush,' I say, starting to take my little high-low off anxiously.

'Here, let me help you.' Sarah comes over and helps keep my dress away from my hair, and suddenly I'm standing in my underwear.

'Can I see a line please, ladies!' Bex yells at the room again, while taking my wedding dress off the hanger. 'OK, here we are, just step in.' She places the gown on the floor for me, and I take Sarah's hand, so as to not step on it, and rip it or something.

'Are you sure this is going to fit me?' I suddenly fear, as now Sarah and Bex are hitching it up over my body and placing my arms inside delicate lace, three-quarter length sleeves.

'It's bloody perfect,' Bex says, buttoning me up.

'*Um*, I hate to point it out, but I'm not wearing any shoes.' I wiggle my toes. 'I am going down barefoot?'

'Oh, balls!' Bex yells, and looks around for inspiration.

'*Ooh*, I've got an idea,' Sarah races off, and comes back with my little brown boots.

'Really?' I say, scrunching my nose.

Bex thinks for a moment, 'Yeah, I like it.' She nods. 'Boho, country bride; there's a whole market for that; the embroidered fabric, the lace and light sparkle. Honestly, I think I like you in it just as much as I did in your actual wedding dress. Sorry,' she adds, pulling a face.

Sarah now bends down and puts my socks and boots back on my feet.

'At least this is one way you'll be comfy going down the catwalk,' Bex smiles at me.

'What about this?' Hugo holds out a floral headpiece.

'Perfect!' Bex places it on my head, and they all smile at me, admiring their work for a moment, before Bex lightly spins me around to face a mirror, 'What do you think?' She exhales.

I walk slowly to it, 'I think you're all magicians!' My makeup is subtle, and classy, yet, my eyes really pop, and I've never seen my hair so tame. Well, once before, but there's no way I can process that right now. The dress flows out behind me beautifully, as I walk, so I'm not stepping on it with my shoes. You wouldn't think it would work, but, Bex is right, it does. I don't recognise myself.

Becky starts clapping to silence the room, 'OK, show time! Energy! Have a great one everybody!'

Bex grabs my hand and places me in fourth position, in the queue of giraffes; I feel like I'm a primary school kid, visiting secondary, as I look up at them all.

'Cute twist, the giraffe in front of me nods at my boots. 'Good luck.'

All I can manage is a nod. The music starts and my heart beats so loudly, I'm surprised people don't ask me to turn it down.

'Alright, Anna: go!' Bex barks at the giraffe at the front of the line.

'So,' Bex turns to me, 'All you have to do is pose for a moment after you've stepped out, then walk down on the right-hand side; stop at the end; pose; give the photographers a moment to snap you; do a couple of different poses, a twirl if you're feeling it.' All I can do is laugh at that comment. 'Fine, no twirl,' Bex says firmly. 'Then turn and walk back up on your new right-hand side, which is the left as you're looking at it; kind of like a swimming lane; there's a one way system.'

I nod at her, 'I can't remember the last time I went swimming,' I mumble.

She ignores me, 'But the idea is, to show off the dress.' I stare at my friend blankly. 'OK. Do you remember that time we drank so much, we had to eat an entire loaf of bread when we got home?'

'You'll have to be a little more specific.'

She smiles at me, 'We went clubbing, in Sloane Square, and we were dancing up and down those steps and posing, and walking around like we owned the place and were the only two in there?' I nod. 'We were so confident! *That's* the Liv you want to tap into. Is she in there?' She looks at me with all seriousness.

I nod again, 'Sure. Yeah.'

She looks at me doubtfully, 'OK, try this.' She darts her eyes to the front of the line, 'Gemma: go!' Giraffe number two heads out of the curtains.

'Leo is at the end of the catwalk, and you want answers. You get there, and decide he is not worth a single moment of your time. You show him what he's missing, and then march your arse back up stage.'

I stand up tall, watch as giraffe number one enters the room again.

'Leoni: go!' Bex says to giraffe number three in front of me.

'If I didn't think you could do this, I wouldn't have asked you,' Bex looks at me with her steady eyes, and for a moment, I believe I can. I smile at her. 'OK; you ready?'

I nod. She looks out at the runway, as giraffe number two

enters the room, 'Liv: go get *em*!'

I have no idea what takes over my body, but suddenly, I feel taller than any of them. I pose in the mouth of the runway, hand on hip, and I'm blinded by flashes, but I don't let that phase me; out I go. One step in front of the other, I make my way down the catwalk. I see giraffe three posing at the end; she *swooshes*, to the right, *swooshes* to the left. *I can do that.* The lights are so bright that I can't see the audience. *Leo's at the end. Leo's at the end.* That's all I'm thinking, and I can feel my eyes slightly narrow, and my lips pout. I look straight over the flashes of cameras as I pass the nice giraffe, who I feel watches me and gives me a nod of approval.

And suddenly I reach the end: *flash, flash flash!* I place my right hand on my right side, and move my head slightly to the right. I swoosh the dress around, and move my weight to the left-hand side, and pose again, and then my body takes over, and before I know it, I'm twirling, before hitting a final pose. *Bam! Take that Leo!* It's not until that moment that I remember Dom's taking photos, our eyes meet for a moment, he's gazing at me in shock above his camera, still holding it up, but not taking any photos, and I can't help but burst into a huge smile. He quickly snaps, before I turn and stride away, back up the catwalk, passing another giraffe, and I resist the urge to give her a high-five as we pass. When I reach the mouth of the catwalk, I turn, pose once more, and walk out of sight.

***

'That was nothing short of brilliant,' Bex says as we exit the building and head over to Tanjong beach on Sentosa Island.

‘I have to admit, it felt amazing.’

‘You could definitely consider modelling,’ Sarah says, for the fourth time.

‘I keep telling you, I’m too short,’ I say, but admittedly, I am loving the flattery.

‘And I keep telling you, there are such things as petite models,’ Sarah beams.

‘And you my dear,’ Hugo walks to my side, and puts an arm around me, ‘are definitely petite.’ And he gives me a little squeeze. ‘You’re like, pocket-sized.’

I notice Sarah’s face form briefly into a frown, but Hugo appears to be unaware. I then glance over at Dom, who’s completely silent, and seems somewhat lost in thought. He hasn’t said very much at all, since our little chat before the fashion show. Becoming accustomed to his lack of flattery or general niceness, I don’t let his silence faze me.

Sentosa island is really neat. There’s a cool statue everywhere that has the head of a lion and the body of a fish; it doesn’t matter how many pictures I’ve taken, I want to take more. Positioning my phone to take a snap, everyone gets in for a selfie apart from Dom. I glance up at him. ‘Come on grumpy, get in.’ Reluctantly, he does.

‘Nope; in closer,’ Sarah instructs, putting her arms around everyone and squeezing, so Dom’s cheek is pressed up against mine. My stomach does an odd flip, but I force my face into a smile anyway.

‘Say cheese!’ I say, and everyone, apart from Dom, says it, in chorus.

‘It’s a Merlion,’ Bex says to a confused Hugo, looking up at the statue, after we’ve taken our picture.

‘Part lion, part fish?’ Sarah says, taking it in too.

‘Yup! I forgot the meaning if I’m honest,’ Becky says.

'I bet little miss know-it-all can tell us,' Dom says, grumpily.

I smirk at him, then direct at the others, 'The fish represents the fact that Singapore used to be a fishing village; "Mer," as in "Sea," and the lion, represents the city's original name *Singapura,* which translates as "lion city." So, Merlion.' I smile, and gesture to the statue, happy that I remembered that titbit from the piece I did on Singapore, for *Wonder* magazine.

We make it to the man-made beach, and instinctively, I take off my shoes and socks.

'*Ooh*, good idea!' Sarah says, leaning on Hugo to take her vintage navy Mary Jane heels off, without them, she is indeed, just a little shorter than him. Smiling, I sigh contentedly, proud of myself for massively jumping out of my comfort zone. We walk further, and admire the stretch of golden sand. I see a little island of beautiful, luscious, green trees; kind of like how I imagine one of the only meditations I get along with: an oasis in the middle of a desert. I turn to ask if we should find a spot to settle, but see a family of four running past us, to the island.

'What the hell?' Hugo says, watching them go.

'What are they running from?' Sarah asks, taking them in, too.

I follow their gaze, backwards from the direction they're running, 'OH!' I point. The others follow my hand and spot sideways rain, chasing its way towards us.

'RUN!' Becky screams, smiling, and we all race to the green oasis; Dom and Hugo in the lead, followed by Becky, then me and Sarah.

Giggling as we go, I reckon there's no way we can outrun the rain. And true enough, a moment later, it's as if a large shower head in the sky decided to water us all. In a millisecond, *wet* doesn't even begin to accurately describe it: we're completely drenched. We finally make it into the oasis, coming to a halt, everyone is laughing apart from Sarah.

'How bad is it?' Sarah gestures to her face, from our leafy shelter.

'Well…' I can't quite find the words.

She fumbles in her bag and pulls out a mirror, 'Oh, God!' she exclaims at her reflection. Her face looks like Alice Cooper has just run through a car wash.

Hugo comes over, 'Oh, honey! He dips into his man bag and takes to her face with a makeup wipe.

'Why are you carrying these?' she says, looking at him in surprise.

He shrugs, 'Part of my emergency pack for brides. Now, come here,' he smiles kindly, and dabs her face.

Looking over at Dom, he meets my eye with a small smile, which I return. His wet hair hangs over his face; I suddenly feel the urge to sweep it to one side. *Where did that come from?*

'Ever been in a monsoon shower?' I decide to say.

'Nope, first one; I'm a monsoon virgin.'

I find myself start to giggle like a 14-year-old, and immediately berate myself. *It's official: I'm going mad.*

Chapter 11

Singapore – Thailand
Kovan – Bangkok

Wednesday
Depart Singapore Changi Airport at 12:55
Arrive Bangkok International Airport at 14:15
Duration: 2 hours and 20 minutes
Time change: Bangkok 1 hour behind
Drive 20 minutes to hotel (2 nights stay)

Couple F
Bride's Grandma's house, Bangkok – Wedding 1 of 2

We arrive in Bangkok and it's busy, bustling and just as crazy as I remember. The weather is warm but overcast, so the air's a little muggy. I remember the first time I was here, the rain was pelting down, and my soft purple suitcase got completely drenched. By the time I'd arrived at my hotel, and opened my case, not a single thing in there was dry. And not only that, everything had taken on the mix of colour from the case. My blue beach bag and red dress in particular, tie-dyed my white playsuit, which, admittedly, I still kind of love.

After we've thrown our suitcases into the latest hotel, (which, again, I love, with its typical Chinatown charm, complete with hanging lanterns and a koi pond), we taxi our way to the next address on the agenda: the bride's grandmother's house. There's a gathering before the first big day tomorrow.

'OK.' I get out my little notebook as we pull up, 'And this couple are called?'

'Toi and Nong,' Sarah answers me, while checking her flawless makeup in the mirror of the passenger seat.

'They both live in Kent,' Hugo says from my right, 'but have Thai heritage on both sides, so they wanted to honour that.'

'Nice,' I say, scribbling quickly, as Dom pays the taxi.

'Such a shame we don't have any time between the wedding tomorrow and our flight to Phuket; I'd love to tour around,' Hugo says as we exit the cab.

'I agree,' Sarah nods, 'It reminds me of parts of New York: vibrant, colourful, smoky.'

'And this couple get two weddings in the article? How come?' I ask as we walk our way along the pedestrianised streets, to the house, and happen to look up at Dom.

'You think I'd know just because my ex was in charge of this?' He frowns at us all.

'Yes,' Sarah and I chorus together, without flinching.

'Well,' he scratches his head. 'From memory, both weddings are unique, so Toi was allowed both in the article; it was the ultimate, oriental, vs English contrast.'

'*Hmm*. A little like India then maybe?' I say to the group, before stopping to scribble that in my notebook. I then look at my piece of paper and check the address as we go. 'Alright, well, this should be it,' I say as we take a right and turn into a brightly decorated road. We head towards the crowd, and immediately I know who the bride is. Not because she's dressed in a special outfit, but because she is marching over here with determination, and a face like thunder.

'What the actual hell?!' she barks at us.

'I'm sorry?' Unfortunately, that is my go-to response, assuming that I'm in the wrong. 'Are you Toi?'

'Yes, I'm Toi!' the bride snaps at me. 'Why the hell weren't you here earlier?'

'You said to come any time,' Sarah says cautiously, then hands her the piece of paper I'm holding, with our schedule on it.

'This is the old one!' She thrusts the paper back at me, before barking once more. 'I updated Heather!' She hysterically waves her arms around.

I thought *Blush* got in touch with every couple? 'Heather's no longer part of the team,' I decide to say out loud, with a strength that does not resemble how I feel. 'And I'm afraid that message wasn't passed onto us.'

'Are you '*effing* kidding me!? This is my wedding day – well one of my wedding days, and you lot,' Toi waves a finger in our direction, 'missed it!' Her hands rest on her hips as she waits, wide-eyed, for an explanation.

I look shame-faced at the others, before my brain fires into action. 'Alright. We can't go back in time; obviously Heather wanted to sabotage this in some way due to–' I glance at Dom, who's red in the face, '–not being involved any more. First things first: were any pictures taken at all by friends and family?'

'Well, of course but...' Toi softens a little, but the disappointment is still in her eyes.

'Great. Dom – speak to every single person here, give them your details, and we will gather together the best pictures. Let's sit together with you and Nong, and you can walk me through everything that happened; we will make it a beautiful piece.'

Two hours, and several mai tai's later, Toi has finally calmed down. I'm actually really sad that I missed it; not just the ceremony, but afterwards, where a group of drummers led a street parade of family and friends, all dancing to celebrate. Never mind the article, *I* would have loved that.

'You have beautiful skin,' Toi's grandmother has been staring at Sarah since we arrived. 'It is so white!' She strokes it. Sarah smiles politely but I can tell she's embarrassed, not flattered.

'So we're going to the night market to get orchids for the Phuket wedding; you should come along!' Toi smiles now, and I'm thankful that I seem to have diverted her attention away from the disaster.

'Shall we meet you there? Would you like us to organise a car or something for you?' I say, very keen to keep on her good side.

She smiles, 'I'm all set, I'll meet you there. Why don't you get the full Thai experience?'

'What do you mean?' I lean back and hope she isn't thinking what I'm thinking.

'Ever been on a *tuk tuk*?'

***

'Isn't this nuts?' I scream in delight at them all.

'This is insane!' Sarah grips on for dear life as we whizz and weave our way through traffic at high speed. 'This surely isn't legal. Oh my God, I'm going to be sick.'

'What's new?' Dom laughs loudly from the adjacent *tuk*

tuk he's sharing with Hugo, that we've been chasing the whole journey.

'You'll be fine!' Hugo yells reassuringly at her.

Horns beep all around us, we narrowly miss a motorbike, whose rider, I'm pretty sure, is now swearing at us. Suddenly, we're braking hard and letting a series of cars pass. Each driver is waving their arms out of their windows and yelling at anyone nearby. And just as soon as we've come to a halt, we're off again.

When we arrive at the market, Sarah's face has surpassed green and is almost grey.

'*Khob khun ka*,' I say to the driver as we steady ourselves onto the pavement.

'You're telling me, you speak Thai, too?' Dom gets out of their *tuk tuk*, shaking his head, incredulously at me.

'Not at all; "thank you," is all I know.'

'*Khob khun ka,*' he repeats, bowing his head slightly.

'Oh, no.' I put my hand up, 'You're a guy, so you have to say, "*khap*" at the end, so, for you it's: *khob khun khap*.' He looks at me funny. 'OK, *now,* that's the end of my knowledge.'

He smiles and turns to the driver, '*Khob khun khap*,' who nods in approval.

'Well, that was a ride!' Hugo beams then tries to steady Sarah who's visibly wobbling on the spot.

'I've only ever been on one in India before, and I remember the driver said, you need three things for driving a *tuk tuk*: good horn, good brakes, good luck.'

We all laugh as we make our way into the market. The smell absolutely floors me; it is the most beautiful scent. Dom on the other hand, appears to be welling up.

'This is ridiculous, you're allergic; why are you here?'

Sarah laughs at him.

'I'm the sodding photographer, remember?' He rolls his glossy eyes at her. 'Plus, I think it's kind of important that I take a photo of *something* today.'

'Oh my God!' I dart off excitedly in the other direction from the group.

'What is it? Sarah calls after me.

I turn excitedly to them all, still heading in the other direction, 'They have sugar cane here!' I yell back. Everyone looks at me, deadpan. 'It's amazing, I'll get one for each of us.' Gleefully, I purchase four and return to them, all of whom are watching me with amusement. 'Honestly, it's so good; you won't regret it!' I hand them out. Dom looks at his with confusion.

'You have to suck it,' I say, mildly smirking.

'Excuse me?' he smirks back, sniffs and stares at me, red patches now forming under his eyes.

'That's how you get the juices out. You don't actually eat it; you suck it,' I repeat and demonstrate. 'Oh, wow. It's as good as I remember,' I say in between swallowing. '*Ummm*. Hey!' Dom snaps my picture. 'I don't think Toi will want any pictures of me in her article.'

'It's not for the article; that was just too good to miss,' he says, looking at me strangely, and I feel very awkward all of a sudden.

We wander through, stall after stall, of vibrant flowers.

'Roses for 20 baht? What's that in dollars?' Sarah looks at me.

'*Erm*, it's like 40p or so, so, like, 30 cents?'

'What?' Sarah says in astonishment. 'Surely that can't be right. No wonder Toi is getting her flowers from here.'

'I'm confused.' Dom rubs his eyes. 'How are they going

to survive from here to Phuket? The wedding's not for another three days?'

'They're refrigerated!' Hugo says, 'Apparently, they could last for up to somewhere between seven and ten days that way! Incredible *huh*?'

'What's incredible,' I say, as we mosey our way casually around the market, taking in the vast array of colour, 'is that we now have a couple days off.' I grin from ear to ear. 'And, I've double, and triple checked everything with Toi, as to when we are due in Phuket and what she expects from each of us. Everything else is right on our list, so we have tomorrow here, before we head to the airport the following morning, and then the whole day to explore Phuket, or instead, we could grab a boat to Krabi, or somewhere! I'm so excited!'

'Travel nerd,' Dom says, pointing his sugar cane at me.

'Always and forever!' I say proudly. 'So, what do you guys want to do tomorrow?'

'Look around the Grand Palace maybe?' Hugo suggests.

'Oh yeah!' Sarah beams, 'Isn't that where the lying Golden Buddha is?'

'Yup,' I smile, very happy to go back there again. 'And the Emerald Buddha is there too, which is really cool. Or we could go to the largest market in Thailand? It's got like 15,000 stalls.'

'I hardly think so,' Dom says with a face that clearly says, he couldn't think of anything worse.

'Oh, no, wait, what day is it?' I ask.

'I have absolutely no idea,' Hugo laughs. 'Maybe Thursday?'

'No, it's Wednesday,' I say, consulting my phone. 'The market's only open Friday to Sunday,' I shrug, putting my phone back in my bag. 'The Grand Palace it is then!'

'Do you know how to get there from our hotel?' Sarah says, taking in a row of yellow calla lilies.

'Oh yeah, we'd take the *Chao Phraya* Express Boat.'

Sarah makes a face at me, 'Another boat?'

'Honestly, it's hilarious; it's more packed than the underground.'

She makes another face that's a little more pleasing. 'Somehow, people packed in makes the idea of a boat more tolerable; like safety in numbers or something. OK, and what about Phuket?'

'Well,' I take a sniff of, (according to its sign), some Arabic Jasmine, which has been made into garlands. 'If we want to stay on the island, there are these really neat hot springs we can go to, or we could maybe go to *James Bond* Island or the beach where *The Beach* was filmed. It's a little touristy, but so absolutely stunning. Oh, maybe Railay Beach?'

'How long do you think we're here for?' Hugo smirks.

I respond by poking my tongue out.

'I'd love to go to *The Beach* beach,' Sarah says.

'And I'd like Railay,' Dom pipes up. 'Can we do both, do you think?' He looks at me, and for the first time, I feel he respects what I have to say.

'Oh, yeah, absolutely! But, I hate to tell you hon,' I look at Sarah, 'it does involve several boat trips, if you want to do that.'

'Brilliant,' she says with a straight face.

Planning it out in my head, I think back to my previous trip, 'If we transfer our hotel, on Friday, to Ao Nang, instead of Phuket, then, after we land, we could catch an early two hour boat from Phuket to Ao Nang.'

'Two hours?' Sarah's face falls.

'Oh, but it's so worth it,' I try to convince her. 'Then we could casually enjoy a trip to maybe Phi Phi — which is where *The Beach,* beach is, then pop over to Railay, and catch the last longboat back to our hotel. Then Saturday, we grab the first boat back from Ao Nang to Phuket, in time for wedding preparations!'

'I'm exhausted already,' Hugo says, but he's smiling.

'No need to worry, just think of me as your tour guide,' I say, grinning.

'Oh, we do Poppet,' Sarah says, linking arms with me.

***

Thursday

'Oh my God, you weren't kidding.' Sarah and I are face to face, well, boobs to face, and a little further down than Hugo and Dom on the *Chao Phraya* Express Boat. None of us have to hang on, it's so packed, it's as if you've got your very own bumpers on every side, like bowling, except with people as the safety pillars.

Dom, in his element, has somehow managed to dislodge his arms, and is poised with his camera, taking shot after shot.

'I can't wait to get off,' Sarah says, with her eyes shut.

'You know you'd probably feel better with your eyes open,' I say, with my face up, so as not to bury them in her ample bosom.

'Not possible.' She shakes her head. 'I'm focusing on not throwing up.'

'Oh, this is us,' I say, grabbing her hand and attempting to make our way through the crowd. 'Excuse me! Thank you. This is our stop.'

'Why aren't we slowing down?' Sarah says, eyes now open.

'That's how they pull in: at speed, then they tie it up and hit reverse, as people get off. You'd know that if your eyes were open.' I smile, as we squeeze our way to Dom and Hugo. I pick up our pace as one of the sailors jumps out of the boat and onto the deck, to tie up a rope. People are now starting to exit, including Dom and Hugo, but we're not making good progress through the crowd.

'We're not going to make it, Liv!' Sarah says in panic.

'Yes, we are, don't worry,' I grin, but she somehow pushes past me, taking the lead and starts waving an arm around to clear a path for us. 'EXCUSE US! WE HAVE TO GET OFF!' Sarah shouts and shoves people, and we start to run. The little sailor is now back on board with his rope.

'We've got to jump, Sarah; you ready?'

'Why am I always in heels?!'

'I'll take that as a yes. Ready? 3, 2 1!' We leap together and onto the dock. Sarah lands in Hugo's arms, and as I land, I can't help but notice Dom lowering his camera.

'Excellent.' He turns his camera round to show us the picture. Legs akimbo, mid-air, both Sarah and I silently screaming. 'Nothing like an action shot!'

We head away from the water to The Grand Palace, all laughing apart from Sarah, who's still trying to compose herself. Getting my bearings, I look around for the entrance, spotting a small gentleman with a *tuk tuk*.

He grins a toothless smile our way, before speaking in broken English, '*You wanting Grand Palace, yes*?' Before I can reply, Hugo speaks up.

'We are, yes! Thank you! Can you please tell us the way in?'

He hangs his head, 'I am afraid, today it is closed; special holiday. But, I take you to a much better place.'

'We're fine, thank you very much,' I say, and steer the group around in the opposite direction.

'It's not open?' Sarah pouts, her pink complexion slowly returning. 'Oh, that's a shame.'

'It is open,' I say without a shadow of a doubt. 'We just need to get away from here.'

'Why would he say it wasn't open?' Hugo asks.

'He probably wants to take us to his wife's, brother's, upstairs shop full of carpets and gold; all overpriced and designed for gullible tourists.'

'Wow. Good thing we have you, hey!' Dom says, putting his arm around me.

I look at it and then up at him; it feels weird. 'What are you doing?' I can't help but ask.

He looks down, but doesn't move his arm, 'What do you mean?'

'You don't like me; why is your arm around me?'

He makes a face, 'I don't know.' He scans his own thoughts. 'It just felt right, so I went with it.' He lifts his arm back up and continues walking next to me. 'And you're wrong by the way.'

'About what?' I ask.

'I do like you. You've grown on me. Like a fungus,' he bares his teeth at me.

'Charming. Words every girl dreams of hearing,' I say, straight-faced.

We join the small queue at the entrance and after buying

tickets, Sarah is handed a small bundle of clothing; putting it on, she turns to me.

'This is not a flattering look,' Sarah parades around in an over-sized, safari-like shirt, on top of her strapless cherry emblazoned dress.

'I think you look cute,' Hugo reassures her.

'I told you you'd have to cover your shoulders; it's a sacred place.' I smile at her, and wipe a little sweat from the bridge of my nose under my sunglasses.

As we make our way around, I fan myself with my map, even though I know, technically, that won't cool me down, it's just wafting the hot air around.

Dom is snapping away beside me, and I can't help but feel his excitement rubbing off on me. 'Having a good time?' I ask him.

His face is still buried in his camera, 'This is incredible.' He stands poised, lining up the perfect shot. 'The angles, the composition, the colours.' He finally looks up and his face is positively beaming. 'Thank you for bringing us here.'

I smile back at him, taken aback, 'You're very welcome.' Surprised to get so much gratitude from him. 'I remember the first time I came here; I was so excited to see the Emerald Buddha, and it was so much smaller than I'd imagined. It's amazing how you can build something up in your mind.'

'Easily done.' He shakes his head. 'You know, Thailand's been on the top of my travel wish list for years.'

'Why haven't you been before, then?' We walk along and I glance down at the map in my hands to get my bearings.

He looks down at his shoes before answering, 'My ex developed a fear of flying.'

'And she was a *travel* writer?' I say slowly.

'Well, not exactly. She was principally a wedding journalist, and sometimes that involved travel.' He frowns. 'I know it doesn't make sense at face value, but she wasn't always like that; she had a scare on a flight a few years ago, and *uh*,' he sighs and then continues, 'it limited her to only writing about places she could drive to. Honestly, I think that's why she got fired, but she wouldn't tell me that.'

'*Huh*.' We walk along a path lined with square shaped topiary that reminds me of *Alice in Wonderland*. I stay silent for a moment, not quite sure what to add to his confession time. 'Well, I guess that would make sense; but why wouldn't she tell you that?'

'I don't know.' He shakes his head, 'Something was just off the last day I saw her. I've known her for most of my life, but I looked at her that day, and I just couldn't work out what it was, that was wrong.'

'When was all this?' I put my sunglasses on my head as the sun goes behind the clouds.

'The day I met you,' he blinks away what could have been a tear. 'That's why I was so vile to you; my world had come crashing down.' Dom looks me steadily in the eyes, and I suddenly want to give him a huge hug. 'I'm sorry,' he continues, 'Heather and I had been arguing for months in the lead up; she was convinced she could write the article without actually going.'

'How was that going to work?' I ask, before wondering if that was insensitive.

'I don't know. She said she could just look at my photos and that was it. At one point, I thought I'd convinced her to come; after all, they needed a travel writer who could actually *travel* for God's sake. Anyway, turns out, I hadn't, and she asked me not to go.' He stops for a moment, and shakes his head, clearly conflicted with his own feelings, 'But I had to go! This is my livelihood, and like I said, Thailand has been on my wish list forever...' His voice floats off.

I look at his pained face, he clearly still cares for her. 'Do you regret coming?' I can't help but ask.

He shrugs, 'A part of me does. I don't know.'

'It's hard to put yourself first, sometimes,' I try to sympathise. 'But, if I can be so bold to say, a relationship should be about supporting each other's dreams, not making each other feel bad for even having them.' He just looks at me, silently, and I'm pretty sure I've overstepped the line. 'I'm sorry. That was too much.'

'It's fine,' he brushes me away. 'Anyway, she gave me an ultimatum: her or the trip.' He shrugs, 'So, she told me to get the hell out; I threw everything I could think of in my bags and within twenty minutes, I was booking an earlier flight on my way to the airport. She's probably burnt the rest of my stuff by now.'

'Oh my God! No wonder you were in a bad mood when I met you!'

'That doesn't excuse my behaviour though, does it?' He looks remorsefully at me.

'Well, it's all water under the bridge,' I bat him away, and we walk silently for a moment.

'So, I've spilled my baggage, as it were. What about you?'

'What about me?' I ask, as we enter the room with the Emerald Buddha.

'Well,' he lowers his voice, 'is there someone waiting back in London for you?'

I shake my head. 'You asked me that at the first

wedding.'

'Come on, you were a closed book then! I can tell you've been through something too.' He looks at me, and I feel reluctant to share. 'You've got to give me something; I'm all out on a limb, by myself, here!'

I stare at the Emerald Buddha, willing it to give me strength to say this out loud, 'OK, well, about a year ago,' I say quietly, keeping my eyes ahead, 'I, *um*, was standing on a beach in Hawaii, and, let's just say, I didn't get married.' I glance sideways, and he looks at me wide-eyed.

'*Woah*. No wonder you said you're not a fan of weddings.'

'When did I say that?'

'At the first wedding.' We look at each other, and I can't believe he remembered what I said.

'Well,' I decide to continue. 'It was a whirlwind romance,' I try to excuse, justify, or make myself feel better, I'm not sure which.

'How long?'

'Two years.'

He shakes his head, 'That's not a whirlwind.'

'Well, in any case, I was sure he was the one, you know?'

He nods, then takes a couple pictures, before declaring, 'Maybe we have more in common than I thought.'

I don't know what to say. We make our way, silently, out of the building and back out into the sunshine. I place my sunglasses on my face again. 'Anyway,' I continue, 'he left me at the altar; I still don't know why. I dream about it, well, have nightmares about it, like I relive the whole damn thing every time I think I've moved on. That's what I was dreaming about on the plane, by the way, when I met you,' I add, looking up at him, vulnerably.

'His name's Leo, isn't it?'

I widened my eyes, 'Oh my God, I was talking in my sleep?'

He nods, 'Not loudly, but I heard you.'

My face heats up, 'I'm so embarrassed.' I bring my hands up to my cheeks, who knows why; that surely doesn't cool them down.

'Don't be. I'll tell you what.' He puts his arm around my shoulders for the second time today, 'Let's make a deal: neither of us is allowed to feel embarrassed, or sorry for ourselves, OK?'

'OK,' I say, taking in his aqua blue eyes.

'We are going to enjoy the rest of this trip, and to quote Jack Black, we are going to celebrate being young, and being alive!'

'Oh my God,' I laugh, 'you are not quoting *The Holiday* to me.'

'Very square peg, very round hole,' he goes on.

I laugh even louder this time. 'OK, deal. Only because I love *The Holiday*; it's my favourite.'

'I've been to the house you know.'

'Cameron Diaz's in the film?'

'Yeah; how'd you know I wasn't talking about Kate Winslet's?'

'Because that one was built for the film.'

He looks at me impressed, 'Not many people know that.'

I grin, 'Told you, it's my favourite. Anyway, that's amazing; did you go in?'

He smiles, 'Oh, no, people live there! I've just driven past it a bunch of times; I used to live in Pasadena.'

'Pasadena? That is so awesome.' I smile at him even wider. 'Have you been to The Cheesecake Factory there?'

'Yes.' He looks at me, smirking, 'I remember in Spain you said that's your favourite, but you realise that it's not the actual one from *The Big Bang Theory*, right?'

'Oh, yeah, of course,' I say, only mildly embarrassed, 'But still, it's on my list!'

'You're hilarious.'

'Why, thank you!' What is this weird feeling in my stomach? *Hmm,* maybe my breakfast is making my stomach dance.

Chapter 12

Thailand
Bangkok – Phuket – Ao Nang – Phi Phi – Railay Beach – Ao Nang

Friday
Depart Bangkok International Airport at 05:30
Arrive Phuket at 07:10
Duration: 1 hour 40 minutes

Sail 2 hours: Phuket – Phi Phi
Sail 1 hour 30 minutes: Phi Phi – Ao Nang (drop bags at hotel - 1 night stay)
Sail 15 minutes: Ao Nang – Railay Beach
Sail 15 minutes: Railay Beach – Ao Nang

As we sail away from Maya Beach, (*The Beach*, beach), I marvel at the turquoise water. ‘Oh my God! I love it here!’ I giggle, and take in the tall limestone cliffs around us, reaching up to the sky.

‘I’ve never seen anything like this!’ Dom says excitedly next to me.

‘Where has this Dom been hiding? It’s like you’re suddenly a little five-year-old.’ I smirk.

Dom just grins back at me. ‘I told you: I’ve wanted to come here for ages. It’s like a dream.’

I smile at him, 'It's quite something, isn't it?' I shake my head at it. 'How's Sarah doing?'

'Still throwing up,' Dom says, calmly, 'Hugo's looking after her.'

'He always does,' I say, leaning on my elbows, at the starboard side, and looking out to sea.

'He's in love with her, you know?' Dom says from my side.

I stay guarded, not planning on breaking my promise from Dubai, to keep Hugo's secret. 'Is that so?' I volunteer, nonchalantly.

Dom looks at me, unconvinced; I've never been the best liar. 'Oh come on. Don't tell me you can't see it?'

'Oh, I don't know,' I continue to gaze out, enjoying the sun on my face, 'I don't interfere in people's personal lives; I'm simply here on business you see.' I sigh happily and tilt my face to the sun, smiling.

'Oh, yeah, it's all about the work, *huh*?'

'Exactly.' I giggle as Dom takes a few pictures of the lofty cliffs. He then examines his work.

'Man, I think these boats are amazing. They just make the best pictures.' Dom shows me a picture of three wooden longtails, from Maya Beach.

I stand back up and then lean in, to take a closer look at the small screen on his camera, 'You are so good!' I look from him to the camera display scene, and back again. 'The beach was insanely crowded; how on earth have you made it look like nobody else was there?'

'Thanks. It's all about framing.' He blushes slightly, and looks back at his photo.

When we arrive at Railay Beach, I take the lead, thanking our captain as we disembark.

‘This isn’t what I thought it would look like,’ Dom frowns.

I shake my head, ‘We’re on Railay East; it’s more of a port. We need to head over to Railay West,’ I point in front of me at the cave we have to walk through to reach it. ‘It’s not too far, like a ten minute walk, maybe. Can you manage it hon?’ I look at Sarah, who’s wobbly frame is being held up by Hugo.

She nods, and we make our way over.

‘Oh wow!’ Dom exclaims as we exit through the caves and onto Railay West. ‘Now that’s more like it! This is incredible!’

‘Travel nerd,’ I bat back at him, staring out at the limestone cliff jutting out of the turquoise water.

‘And damn proud,’ Dom retorts, before burying his head in his camera once more.

‘Oh, yeah,’ Sarah points, ‘I’ll be over there if you need me.’ She wobbles her way to a nice shady spot, just below the cliffs.

‘And I’ll just make sure she’s OK.’ Hugo follows after her. I can’t help but laugh as she throws herself onto the sand, and by the looks of it, passes right out. Hugo, dutifully, sits by her side, stroking her hair.

‘So,’ I turn to my new found friend. ‘Shall we build a sandcastle?’

‘Sandcastle? *Nah*, that’s for kids,’ Dom says, still with his eye glued to his camera lens.

‘Alright then,’ I say, mildly put-out, then he lowers the camera and looks at me with an excited glint in his eye.

‘How about a sand car?’

‘A sand car?’ I smile. ‘What do you mean?’

‘Make a car, in the sand,’ Dom says, simply. ‘You said in

Scotland you're a car girl; what car shall we make?' He places his camera back in its case and then into his backpack, before falling to his knees, starting to gather a pile of golden sand before him.

'*Um*,' I grin and join him in the sand. 'I don't know, what do you think?'

'I think, something distinctive,' he scoops more sand, with increasing playfulness. 'What would you say to a Duesenberg?'

'I'd say that's a little cliché and you have no imagination,' I tease. 'Hey!' He swipes a little sand at me.

'Alright, Miss Smarty Pants, what would you suggest?' He pauses mid sand-scoop, for my answer.

'How about a Citroën Traction Avant?'

'Very well! Coming right up!'

Several hours later, we have not only a Citroën Traction Avant and a Duesenberg, but a whole fleet of cars, all lined up like a showroom. The heat has been so intense all day, I've kept my cover-up on, over my bikini the whole time, to stop myself from burning, pausing from our creations only to dip into the sea to cool off. Thankfully, the sun's nearing its bedtime.

'Hey Brave!' Dom calls from the shore on my latest dip into the turquoise water.

'What?' I bop up and down, as he mouths something, but I can't hear him, I'm a little too far from the wave crashing shore. 'I can't hear you,' I yell back. 'I'm not moving yet.' I grin from ear to ear, enjoying the coolness surrounding me. I wave at him, 'Come in and join me if you want to say something!'

He takes off his t-shirt, and I can't help but stare as he walks towards the water; he puts Ryan Reynolds' six pack to shame. Realising my mouth has fallen open a little too late, a wave hits me in the face and I swallow a mouthful of salty water. Coughing and spluttering, Dom swims to my side with ease and then pats me on the back. 'You alright?' He looks at me with concern.

'Yeah, surprise wave, that's all.' I smile, guiltily, then attempt to distract him, 'So you were saying?'

'Yeah, I was thinking we should get a group shot of us all with the sun coming down, you know, limestone cliffs, the pink of the sunset reflecting on the turquoise water? Quite the memory, right?'

'Yeah, great idea!' We begin our swim, slowly back to shore. I giggle.

'What?' He turns his face, mid-breaststroke.

'I was just thinking, I can't believe we're being paid to be here; not too shabby, right?'

'Not too shabby,' he repeats. 'You know, I was thinking. Your job must be amazing.'

'How so?' We're now swimming in sync; our fingertips nearly touch as we glide forwards.

'Well, you get paid to just jet set around the world! I'd love that. Being constantly surrounded by different cultures, natural beauty and nature! There's so much to see in the world! I haven't been to half, no, a quarter of the places I want to go. You know, last year, I had this idea to pack a small case, get in the car, and just keep driving along the coast, wherever I fancied, but I just…couldn't.'

'Why, what stopped you?' I take in his side profile and his expression falls somewhat. He doesn't answer as we reach the shore, he just smiles at me. 'You're looking better!' I say to Sarah, who's admiring our sand art with Hugo.

'Yeah, that nap sorted me right out,' she looks around, for what I'm guessing is the first time. 'Pretty here, isn't it?'

I giggle as Dom ushers us all into the right framing. 'OK,' Dom says, extending his collapsible tripod, and placing it into the sand. 'Hugo, Sarah, go stand next to Liv.'

'Man, these colours are insane!' Hugo says, now at my side, but gazing in awe at the pink and purple sky. Sarah stands on Hugo's other side.

'Alright, now,' Dom has positioned his camera on top of the tripod, and is gazing through the lens, 'everyone, take five steps to your left.' We do as instructed, arms around each other, giggling as we go. 'OK, now, take three, back.' We step back. 'And another.' We step back again and all scream and burst out laughing, as we step into the ocean. 'Perfect!' Dom laughs, clearly having taken our picture, 'Right, now, two steps forward.' He presses something on his camera, a little light starts blinking, and then he comes around to join us, standing on my other side. Dom places a warm arm around me and I shyly place mine around the middle of his naked back; my hand reaches his side, and without meaning to, I move my hand slightly over a muscle, sending shivers down my spine. 'And smiling, three, two, one!'

Dom's camera takes our picture then he lets go of me, to check how it's turned out, leaving me feeling sad all of a sudden and I don't know why. Glancing to my right I see a young couple, running for an overcrowded longtail.

'Geez, what's the rush, it's so gorgeous here!' Hugo says, now cross-legged in the sand, enjoying the sunset.

'What's the time?' I casually walk over to my bag, get out my phone and check. 'Oh shit.' I rustle up my things.

'What's up?' Dom looks from his camera to me, with a

sunset glow upon his happy little face.

'We need to get on that longtail guys, or we'll have to swim back!' I say with panic.

'What?!' Sarah grabs my hand, and we make a run for it.

'No more passengers!' A tiny little man yells at me as I stand on the boat, holding Sarah's hand, who's still on the sand.

'What? There's plenty of room!' I say, clearly unconvincingly.

'Is there another boat after this?' Sarah asks.

'No. Last boat,' he points to his vessel.

'What do you mean, no more boats?' Sarah says with a little panic in her ever-cool voice.

'Then you have to take us!' I say, bringing Sarah on board with me and waving frantically to Hugo and Dom; *why is he still taking pictures?!*

'Look, there's clearly room for four more, you have to take us! We're doing a wedding tomorrow!'

'*You off boat*! *You off boat*!' The little man starts yelling at the two of us.

We obediently get off, and wade our way back to the shore, to watch as the longtail sails out with ease; all its passengers wave at us while laughing.

'Oh my God,' I say in disbelief. 'We're going to miss her second frigging wedding!' I'm still watching the boat disappear into the night, as Dom and Hugo meet us.

'What the '*eff* are we going to do!?' Sarah says with increasing volume in her voice. 'This is a disaster!'

'There has to be another boat somewhere, come on,' I say, marching off with determination towards the bar area on Railay East.

'We're on the same island as our hotel, right? Why can't

we walk back?' Hugo says, struggling to keep up with my pace.

'You feel like walking through a pathless jungle?' I ask, looking behind me, as I continue my march.

'Guess not,' he says to Sarah.

'But why can't we just get a boat tomorrow morning from here?' Sarah tries.

'Because, I've no idea what time boats start sailing from here. Unless we get the first boat from the other side of the island tomorrow back to Phuket, we'll be late.' I glance behind Sarah and Hugo and notice we're missing a colleague. 'And where the hell is Dom?'

'Just taking a few more photos, I think,' Hugo says.

'He is unbelievable!' I throw my arms in the air. 'We're all going to get sacked, and he's still taking bloody pictures!'

'Hey! Wait up!' Dom runs from around the corner of the limestone cliff, and within a few powerful strides, he's next to me. 'Who knew those little legs could lead the race!'

I can't help but laugh, 'Come on, this is serious! If we don't find a boat to get on tonight, we can kiss goodbye to our jobs!'

I run, even faster, ahead of everybody, and reach the little strip of bars. Holiday-goers are laughing and drinking, without a care in the world. I dash up to the nearest, brightly lit bar.

'Hi! What can I get you?' The gorgeously tanned barman asks me while cleaning a glass with a tea towel.

'Hello,' I say crisply. 'Oh, I don't want a drink. We need to get to the other side of the island tonight. Please, tell me you know someone who could take us?'

He makes eyes with the only guy sitting at the bar, drinking a beer, and I follow his gaze. The man sitting, shakes his head ever so slightly, then the barman looks back at me. ‘No sorry, love. I don’t know anyone.’

‘What was that about?’ I point my finger accusingly at both of them.

‘What was what, love?’ The barman plays dumb.

‘That!’ I’m even less subtle with my finger pointing. ‘Excuse me. Do you have a boat?’ I ask the man who’s now grinning from ear to ear.

‘I do,’ he nods, but that’s all he has to say.

‘That’s fantastic! Could you please take us back to—’

‘No, no, no,’ he cuts me off. ‘I’m not going anywhere tonight,’ he says in finality.

I slump onto the bar stool next to him as I hear Dom’s voice, ‘May as well have a drink, while we come up with a plan, *huh*?’ He saddles into the seat next to me, filled with what can only be described as pure joy.

‘We’re all going to get fired,’ I say matter-of-factly. ‘How can you be this calm?’

He shrugs, ‘Because, we’re on this island—’

‘*Stranded* on this island,’ I correct him.

‘Fine. *Stranded* on this island that I’ve dreamed of being on for the last decade! I’m not about to cry over the fact that we have to spend a little more time here than we thought. It’s a beautiful night, and there are fire dancers for goodness sake!’ My eyes follow where he’s gesturing; there are indeed three men dancing and spinning fire on the beach.

‘OK; I have to admit, that’s pretty damn cool,’ I say reluctantly.

‘My dear,’ he takes my hand in his; they’re warm and comforting. I look into his eyes, ‘we are here, and we are going to enjoy ourselves. The wedding’s not until four tomorrow, we don’t have to be there until twelve. I promise you, something will work out. We will get back in time, but for now, let's make the most of this ridiculous scenario.'

When did he get so charming? I suddenly feel unnervingly calm in his presence. *Is my heart beating faster? This is ridiculous.*

'So, what are you having? Mai tai?' He lets go of my hands and looks at a menu in front of him.

I laugh, 'Fine. I give in.' I smile.

'Two mai tai's, it is!' He cries triumphantly to the barman, who's been watching us with amusement.

'Is this your first trip together?' The barman asks us while preparing our drinks.

I wave my hand, 'Oh, we're not—'

'Yes, it is,' Dom interrupts me with all seriousness. He raises an eyebrow at the barman, 'She's been a *bloody nightmare* the whole time. All I want to do is take some pictures of a lifetime, and will she just relax and go with the flow? No!' I narrow my eyes at him. 'She's always thinking about tomorrow! She can't just live in the now!'

'You think,' I say to the barman, happy to play along, 'he would appreciate that I'm trying to get us home tonight.'

'What about a little adventure?!' The barman directs at me.

'Can we buy you a drink, good sir?' Dom asks the captain to my right.

'I'm trying to get him to give us a ride back; we don't want a drunken sailor!' The barman laughs at this. 'But he says he won't be sailing tonight,' I explain to Dom.

'That's right,' the captain says, 'unless it's full.'

'Full?' I question. 'OK, now we're getting somewhere, how big is your boat?'

'Take ten *peoples*; are you ten *peoples*?' he takes another sip of his beer.

'We are four *peoples*!' I find myself matching his broken English. 'Would you make an exception?'

'No,' he says flatly, just as the barman places our mai tai's in front of us. Crestfallen, I slump even further into the bar stool.

'Cheer up, Brave,' Dom gives me a nudge before pushing my drink a little closer to me.

The sailor stands and walks away. The barman lowers his voice and leans into us. 'He's just toying with you. Leave it a couple of hours, you might have to pay more than you intended, but you'll get back to your hotel tonight. He does this every night; it's how he makes his money. The later you leave it, the more he'll knock down his price.'

'What? That's awful!' I say after taking a sip of my mai tai. 'Not the drink — that's delicious, thank you — what he's doing is awful.' I confirm, gesturing his way. 'Ripping off tourists like that; that's just diabolical.'

'If you play the game, you'll end up winning,' the barman says, shaking his head. 'Like I said, give it a few hours, no problem.' He smiles at us. 'Relax, enjoy your night, guys; you're not stranded here,' he winks at me before going to serve a bikini-wearing blonde at the other end of the bar.

'See!' Dom clinks his glass with mine, 'No problem.'

'Where are Hugo and Sarah?' I look over his broad, still naked, shoulder to see the already dark beach, now lined with people, all sitting near campfires, and enjoying the poi dancers.

'Watching the show; Hugo's calming Sarah down. Want to join them?'

'Sure.' I stand, and we grab our drinks and head towards the beach.

'So, is the island everything you'd hoped it would be?' I ask as we pad our way along the sand.

'No. It's more. Much more.' I burst out laughing. 'Why on earth are you laughing at me?' He puts his *mai tai*-free hand to his chest, as if I've insulted him.

'You did *not* just quote *27 Dresses*.'

'And so what if I did?' he takes a sip.

'Are you in fact a woman?' I ask, mockingly. 'Why do you know so much about rom-coms?'

He pauses for a moment, 'Well, if you must know. I am one of those men who can appreciate a rom-com.'

'I call bullshit,' I eye him suspiciously.

'And now *you're* quoting, *How to Lose a Guy in 10 Days,*' Dom says reasonably.

I narrow my eyes, waiting for him to give, 'I'm not buying it.' I play with my straw.

'Fine. You got me.' He holds his one free arm in the air. 'I may have grown up with four sisters, who would never let me watch what I wanted. So, I came up with a plan.'

'Oh, yeah, what was that?' God, this drink is strong.

'My plan was to learn as many lines as I could from every sappy film—'

'Sappy film? Oh no, you did not just insult all rom-coms did you?'

'No, of course not. Every, *um*, quality, absolutely truthful, could totally happen in real life moments, film.' He gives me a sideways look, to seek my approval.

'That's better! Please continue,' I feel myself weave slightly as I smirk and sip at the same time; *am I drunk already*?

'So, as I was saying, my plan was to learn as much of the *quality films*,' he gives me another sideways glance and I nod in approval, 'as possible, so I could then use it to woo women.'

'*Woo*?' I laugh at him again. 'Who are you trying to woo? A woman from the 18th century?'

'You are very mean,' he says before sipping his drink.

'There you are!' Sarah laughs, and throws her arm around me, clearly a little more relaxed. 'Oh, that looks yummy. Where's mine?'

'This is yours!' I say handing it to her. I don't think I can drink much more of it. I take a seat in the still-warm sand.

The fire dancers in front of me are really talented. I take a deep breath and listen to the waves crashing against the shore.

'Holy hell, what's in this?' Sarah's voice sounds behind me.

'To be fair, I think it's mainly rum,' Hugo says, drinking from the same glass as Sarah.

'That's too strong for me.' Sarah thrusts it back into my hand. 'Beer?' she says to Hugo.

'Beer,' he agrees, and they head off towards the bar again, leaving just Dom and me.

'So, tell me seriously,' I look up at him, 'how does Thailand meet your expectations? No quotes: just you,' I say, putting the drink down safely in the sand, then wrapping my arms around my slightly chilly legs.

Dom joins me on the sand, his face lit by the warm glow of the fire. 'Honestly, I think it's magical.' He smiles at the dancers, then turns his face to me. 'There is so much beauty everywhere.' He looks deep into my eyes and for a moment I think he's going to kiss me. I think I might let him. 'Oh my God.' He says, shifting his eyes ever so slightly past my right ear.

'What?' I ask, and turn slowly.

'There are fireflies,' he whispers, as not to frighten them away. 'Actual, like Disneyland, *Pirates of The Caribbean,* fireflies!' I turn back to face him and have to smile; Dom is absolutely mesmerised. 'It's like a fairytale.'

I giggle softly, then turn again to the fireflies. 'They are amazing, aren't they? I was actually here the first time I saw them too,' I share my memory, but I don't think he's listening; he's in his backpack unloading his tripod.

'This is incredible.' He grins from ear to ear, before leaning in and placing a soft kiss on my right cheek. 'Thank you for bringing me here.' He disarms me with his gratitude, once more, and I touch my palm to my face.

'You're welcome.' Our eyes lock for a second before he buries himself in his backpack, to find the right lens, but I'm still taking him in.

'So,' I clear my throat, 'what kind of lens do you need for fireflies?' *Am I disappointed that he only kissed me on the cheek?*

'You need something with a bulb lens; it's all about the slow exposure.'

I whip out my iPhone. 'So, something like this won't do?'

'Years ago, I would have said absolutely not, but nowadays, they are producing phones with cameras that are getting better and better. Here,' he grabs my phone. 'What's your password?'

'I don't have one,' I shrug.

'OK, then.' Dom swipes my phone to unlock, then crouches back in the sand and positions himself so his cheek is inches from mine. 'So, you go into your camera, and right here, you see…'

I'm not focusing on the phone; I'm looking at him. *When*

did he get so good looking?

'Are you even listening to me?' I realise he's now looking right back at me, smiling, thankfully.

'Yes, yes, absolutely,' I lie, and move my eyes to focus on the phone, creasing my eyebrows in all seriousness. 'So you open the camera app, and…' I make a face and then look back at him sheepishly. 'That's all I got,' I grin and shrug my shoulders.

He looks at me with what I hope is some sort of admiration, then tuts, and taps away on my phone, smiling. 'Here,' he hands it back to me. 'I've done it for you. All you need to do is point and click.'

'My kind of camera,' I admit, taking back my phone, and as instructed, I point and click.

'Not at me! The settings for the fireflies!' he exclaims.

'I know,' I smile at him, 'I just wanted a photo to remember this moment.'

'And now you can; over there!' He gestures towards the fireflies.

***

Three hours later, the little man from the bar finally agrees to take us home, at three times the price that it normally costs. At this point, I'm tired, want my bed, and it is completely worth it. The four of us pile into his little longtail, which I honestly doubt could actually take ten people. Sarah is wrapped around Hugo's arms, more for balance than anything; she's had at least four beers, and now is a calm drunk, who doesn't seem to remember that her greatest fear is water.

'Alright, everybody in?' Our captain asks.

'Yes, let's go!' I practically shout.

'It looks like it might be just in time,' Dom says, pointing up at the sky, 'look at those clouds.' He's right. Those black clouds look angry.

'Let's make haste!' Sarah says, slurring every word.

We make our way across, and I've never been so thankful to be on a boat. And then it happens: the heavens open. Sarah squeals then laughs; Hugo holds her even tighter.

The sailor reaches behind him and grabs a bucket.

'What's that for?' I ask with trepidation, not wanting to know the answer.

'Small hole in boat; keep from sinking,' he says with broken English.

'WHAT?' I yell at him.

'Keep from sinking,' he repeats louder.

'No, no. I heard you! But, what the hell? Why would you let us sail in this?'

'You wanted to! You pay good money. Will be fine. You sit, enjoy ride,' he grins at me with three of his front teeth missing.

'Well, that's reassuring,' I say to Dom.

Chapter 13

Thailand
Ao Nang – Phuket

Saturday
Sail 2 hours: Ao Nang – Phuket
Drive 15 minute (cab) to wedding venue (1 night stay)

Couple F
White Orchid Resort, Phuket – Wedding 2 of 2

The next day, thankfully, we were able to get on the earliest boat, from Ao Nang, arriving back in Phuket at 10 a.m. This left us two whole hours to get ourselves together before duties; I've never been so grateful for a late start. Of course Toi, (thank goodness), was none the wiser that we very nearly missed this wedding too.

Sitting in her sizable suite, she's surrounded by purple and white orchids, and family members.

Even with a head of rollers and no makeup, Toi is infuriatingly radiant. Again, I feel a slight pang of jealousy; isn't radiance a prerequisite for any bride? I subconsciously scrunch my nose. *Did I have that? I'm not sure.*

'Is something else wrong?' Toi asks with concern, 'Why are you screwing your face up like that?'

I purse my lips together before speaking. 'I'm sorry.

Nothing is wrong. So, you were talking about your outfits.' I smile, cross my legs, and lean forwards, hoping that I haven't offended her too much.

She gives me a doubtful look then continues, 'Like I was saying, everything was either from Matalan or Monsoon. The whole thing actually only came to £5,000.'

'£5,000? That's insane.' I spent way more than that on my own, "would have been" wedding; shame I couldn't have got the deposit back. Realising my thoughts have drifted once more, I make a conscious effort to focus on the bride, who hasn't seemed to have noticed.

She shrugs. 'That's what it came to; it's just cheaper here. This way, we could spend more on our honeymoon around Cambodia and Vietnam. Come in,' Toi calls to the tap on the door; Hugo enters.

'All good in here?' He grins and steps further into the room.

'Yeah, I've got everything I need,' I go to stand, 'unless there's anything else you want to add?' I aim at Toi, acutely aware that this hasn't been my best work.

She shakes her head and smiles, 'No, I'm good.' She puts her hands on her stomach, '*Ooh*, I'm a little nervous.'

'Natural, natural,' Hugo says, smiling and taking a seat in the adjacent chair, placing a comforting arm around her. 'So, Sarah's finished with all the bridesmaids, if you're ready for her?' Toi nods. 'Great,' he looks around, 'chief bridesmaid, where are you?' She raises her hand. 'Alright, if you come with me, we'll head to the chapel!'

After we've all completed our pre-wedding duties, the bridal party takes a moment, alone. On the other side of the resort, we take our seats in the air-conditioned chapel on the resort's lagoon, and wait for the bridal party. Other guests have now started to arrive: a mixture of sweaty beautiful people, all grateful to step into the cool atmosphere. I sit scribbling away in my notebook, describing each detail from the violet bows around the crisp white chair covers, to the matching colour palate of the bridal party. When all the guests have arrived, the groom takes his place at the front, followed by his best man.

'I know I shouldn't find this funny,' Sarah leans in to me, 'but you've got to love the fact that the best man is wearing those,' she gestures to his bottom half.

I smirk, 'She didn't tell me as much, but I know Toi was pissed. I love that they're not remotely the right colour!' We giggle as I take in the rest of the men in the bridal party: all of them, bar him, are wearing smart, matching, beige Matalan suits with lilac shirts and ties. The best man, however, although he's wearing the lilac on the top, on the bottom, he is rocking a pair of bright blue shorts, covered in pink flamingos; the bottom half of the assigned wardrobe, was the only thing he forgot to pack. Personally, I think that secretly, the rest of the party is looking at him in envy; even at 4 p.m., it's still boiling outside.

Gazing around at the venue, I take in the floor to ceiling windows. Everything is white, crisp and clean here, and the flowers from Toi's bedroom are now all around, in a contrasting explosion of colour. Suddenly, and unexpectedly, I feel my eyes well up. *Man; this is stunning.* I sigh, beating myself up; every time I think I'm over Leo, I get this surge of emotion that pulsates uncontrollably through me. I guess it doesn't help that I'm on a conveyor belt of weddings.

The chief bridesmaid is already in the chapel, stationed at the piano, next to the altar, playing some effortless background music. 'Well, that's nice,' I find I say out loud, but can't help but feel sad. 'I love and hate this at the same time,' I whisper to Sarah. She squeezes my hand before smiling reassuringly.

'I know you do hon. Honestly, me too.' She sighs slightly. 'Our time will come; it's just not now. It's like the sun and the moon, they both shine at different times.'

Dom leans across Sarah, to face me, 'I think a better metaphor, if you're going for one, considering you're a writer, is: "Stop comparing your chapter one, to somebody else's chapter twenty-five."'

'You were eavesdropping?' I say, embarrassed.

He nods, 'One of my strong suits, don't you think?' And smiles at me, kindly. 'I love Einaudi too.'

'Who?' I ask and start looking around. 'Is that a relative I haven't met?'

He sniggers, 'No, it's the music! You said you love it, I love it too; I saw him live once.'

'Oh, yeah?' I decide to distract myself.

'Yeah, we were in London for work, and on our day off, we took a tour of St Martin in the Fields, have you heard of it?'

'In Trafalgar Square; yup.'

'That's the one, so we came out, headed towards the fountains, and heard music. I was wondering if it was Michael Nyman or Einaudi, expecting it to be coming from a couple of speakers, but no, right there, right in the centre of Trafalgar square, he was on stage, with a string quartet.' He shakes his head, 'It's truly one of my favourite moments, ever.' His eyes glisten over as he travels back to the memory in his mind, then he scrunches up his whole face before opening his eyes, almost angry.

'What's wrong?'

‘Nothing,’ he snaps at me before looking sheepish. ‘Sorry.’ He stands up and marches outside.

I go to stand but Sarah grabs my arm, ‘I’ll go check if he’s OK,’ she stands up, and smiles at me. ‘I’ve got to be outside when the bride arrives anyway.’

Staying where I am, and watching her go, I feel a frown form on my face.

‘I really wouldn’t take it personally,’ Hugo says from my side.

I scrunch my nose, ‘It’s hard not to, but I know it’s nothing to do with me.’ *Probably.*

‘Oh look, here she comes,’ Hugo says, sitting up in his seat.

The rest of the bridesmaids, flower girls and father of the bride, arrive with Toi, by speedboat, from across the resort lagoon; her veil, catching the wind, and waving effortlessly behind her.

‘I kind of feel we should have *James Bond* music here or something, don’t you?’ Hugo quips.

The groom turns to watch her approach. Hugo leans into me and quietly hums the *James Bond* theme tune. I bite my lip to stop myself from laughing. Then I see her properly. *Wow. She is a vision in white.*

When they arrive at a dock, they exit the boat, and walk alongside the building, towards the doors at the back of the chapel.

Surrounding the chapel are lots of tall trees, creating nice shady spots. The bride is standing in one of said spots, being patted down by Sarah with a handkerchief, followed by a makeup brush.

The wedding itself is annoyingly beautiful. But I have to say, I loved what happened after: the happy couple released butterflies, which apparently, is a symbol of love, hope and beauty; followed by planting a tree, which is a symbol of providing for their future family. But maybe the most exciting: all the guests gathered around for photos and were surprised by a baby elephant, dressed with a pink draping.

When all this is finished, we climb into a wooden boat to get us to the other side of the lagoon.

'What is it with boats on this trip?' Sarah huffs and grabs Hugo's hand as she shakily hoists one navy vintage Mary Jane heel in, before swinging her other one on deck.

'Maybe you'll be over your fear by the end of the trip?' I suggest. She gives me a very doubtful look. 'Maybe not then,' I conclude.

Standing right at the front of the boat, I breathe in. Even though it's a man-made lagoon, it's so magical. It reminds me of my wedding venue; I'm so dreading Hawaii.

Dom is off with the bridal party, and bride and groom, taking their private shots, while Sarah, Hugo and I are to stay with the guests during cocktail hour, which is fine by me.

We reach the other side of the resort and are greeted by smiley waiters with cocktails, as promised. I've got to say, I do like this part of the job. Cheekily, I reach for one and take a sip. *Umm, I do love a mai tai.*

We take a seat in the lobby area, outside of the main hall. Every table has a variety of small, (admittedly, very English), snacks on it and Sarah dives right in.

'What are these?' she crunches down.

'Pork scratchings,' I say. 'The bride said it's her dad's favourite snack, so it's a nod to him.'

'They're not bad.' She makes a face of approval, then grabs a napkin. 'Good Lord though, it is so hot here,' Sarah dabs her face with it.

'But you still look beautiful,' Hugo says, clearly surprising himself, as he looks down at his cocktail, then takes another sip, and makes excuses about checking on preparations.

'Yeah, right!' Sarah aims at him before emerging from her napkin and frowns. 'I'm a sweaty mess.'

I giggle and pick up another napkin, 'Come here,' I say to her, wiping her smudged eyeliner from her cheeks.

'Thank you.' She smiles at me. 'Is Hawaii cooler than this?'

My smile drops slightly, 'It's a different kind of heat, but, yes, it'll be a bit less humid.' I clear my throat, 'You know, there's something I've been meaning to say to you.'

'What is it?' Sarah says, looking at me kindly.

'Well, I—'

'Ladies and gentlemen!' I glance over my shoulder and see the bridal party has returned.

'I'll tell you later,' I bat away; happy to avoid it for as long as possible.

'Please now head into the main hall. Inside is a real treat: traditional Thai dancers and musicians!' the best man in the flamingo shorts gestures.

It's a full half an hour before Hugo comes to join us at our table, but he returns with a degree of poise and approval.

'All running to plan?' I ask, checking out the cute wedding favours: a purple high-heeled shoe with truffles inside.

'Yup. All English food over there, and all Thai food there.' Hugo takes a seat.

'Why are they having two cuisines?' Sarah asks.

'A couple of the extended family members aren't very adventurous eaters apparently,' he defends.

'Ladies and gentlemen, please be upstanding for the bride and groom,' a loud voice booms from over my shoulder; we follow suit and stand with everybody.

'There is so much food, it's insane!' Dom joins us at the table with a full plate.

'I don't think you're meant to get food yet!' I whisper to him as people are clapping the couple in.

'Oh my God, it's so tasty!' He's taken a mouthful of something on his piled-high plate. 'I love this.'

I can't help but laugh. 'Dude, you're meant to be taking pictures!'

'Which is exactly why I am grabbing a few mouthfuls before shooting!' He puts his plate down, grins at me with just his lips and his mouth full, wipes his hands on a napkin and then swings his camera round and into action. *I suppose he has a point.*

Aside from taking pictures, about every twenty minutes for the next couple of hours, Dom comes over to our table, stuffs his face with food, then disappears to refill his plate.

'Are you leaving anything for the guests?' I snigger after his latest trip to the buffet.

'This is my favourite food — ever — and it's fresh, authentic, and best of all? Free!'

I laugh out loud this time, then watch him walk away. He stops at the head table talking with the happy, now slightly drunken, newly-weds, and they all laugh loudly at whatever he's just said. He's really rather tall with nicely shaped shoulders from the back. I like how his linen shirt hangs loosely, but still frames his perfectly formed broad shoulders. *He must work out. Have I seen him work out here?*

'Hey Liv!' Hugo's voice breaks my examination of

Dom's physique.

'Yes?' I ask and then finally advert my eyes, to see both Sarah and Hugo grinning at me.

'You're gazing at Dom,' Hugo shapes his sentence as fact rather than a question.

'What? Me? *Nooooo.*' I elongate the last word. 'I was, *um.*'

'Admiring him from behind?' Hugo helps to finish my sentence. My mouth opens but no sound comes out. 'You were literally eating him up with your eyes. What was that bet you made in France?' He looks at Sarah and then back to me. 'That you and Dom might sleep together by the end of the trip?' Hugo raises his eyebrows, playfully.

'Now, stop it.' I frown at him. 'There really is nothing going on.'

'Oh, I realise that; it's clearly all in your head right now,' Hugo continues, obviously on a roll. I look imploringly at Sarah to try and help me somehow, but Hugo persists, 'This is exactly what you need: get over your ex, by getting under Dom.'

I feel my cheeks start to redden. 'How do you know, I'm not over my ex?'

'I may have overheard a little of your conversation with Sarah at the first wedding.' He shrugs, guiltily, 'I'm sorry that happened to you, Liv.'

Letting a small smile escape, I appreciate him not asking me about it, 'Thanks.'

'So, what do you think?' he persists.

'Oh, yeah, it's a great idea!' Sarah says sarcastically, 'Sleep with a colleague, and still have to travel around the world with them? No, thanks!'

That seems to have done it, Hugo's expression has fallen.

'So, you've never slept with, or had a relationship with a colleague?'

Sarah turns her face upwards, as if to tap into her memories, 'No, don't think I ever have. Wouldn't want to muddy the waters, you know? Just not worth it.' She reaches across the table to top up her water, and I observe Hugo's completely crushed expression. He decides to turn his face to mine, shrugs, ever so slightly, then shakes his head, and appears back on his mission. 'So, I'm not saying it has to be anything serious, just, you know, bish bash, bosh.'

'Bish bash bosh?' I say, grinning.

'Exactly.' He shuffles in his seat. 'Now, I'm going to make sure the bride is happy, why don't you come with me then you make your move!'

'I will do no such thing,' I say, horrified, sitting back in my chair, arms folded. 'I don't want to make a move!' Looking across the room again, I notice Dom's perfectly formed bottom, then turn back to see Hugo smiling at me, almost like a sibling who knows me a little too well. 'Your heart is still broken; I can see that. I'm not saying fall in love and marry the guy; just think about it. Have a chat, have a walk, have a *snog*,' he grins, taking great pleasure in imitating an English accent. I shut my eyes to gather myself and by the time I open them again, Sarah's at my side, dragging me up from the table.

'Actually, Hugo, *I've* got to go and see if Toi needs a touch up, right now; no point in you bombarding her too. Liv can come with me. Bye!' And with that, she marches me across the dance floor.

'Thank you! Good Lord, he didn't seem like he was going to let that go!'

'I'm here for you, Poppet!' She links my arm with hers,

and grins at me with love, as we approach the top table. 'So, how's my favourite bride?' She focuses all her attention on Toi, now.

The bride looks up at Sarah; upon closer inspection, she is way drunker than I'd realised. 'Thank '*eff* we've done our first dance! I don't *fink* I can *sh-tand uppp*.'

I bite my lip and take a sideways glance at Dom, who's eyeing up the buffet behind the bride.

'I'd say, you're all now *offs th-clock*,' she slurs. 'It's an open bar, go and have *shome funs*.'

Oh, my. Top points for the drunkest bride so far.

'Are you sure you don't want a freshen up or anything?' Sarah says, putting her professional hat on for what I'm sure will be the last time this evening.

The bride throws her arms down, dramatically on the table, '*Ah*, go on then! But Mr photographers,' she wags a finger at Dom, but it points right past him and she sways in a now standing position. 'Absolutely no *s'more* photos; you *understandings*?'

'Absolutely,' he says, grinning from ear to ear.

'Now, go and eat something! *Yous* probably haven't had *anythings* have you?' The bride leans into Dom.

'You know, I am pretty hungry,' he nods.

Sarah whisks the bride away and I'm left with Dom, as the groom starts talking to his best man.

'Liar,' I say.

He shrugs his shoulders, 'Guilty. Let's grab a plate and head outside for some air, shall we?'

I shrug, trying to act casual, ignoring the butterflies that have suddenly appeared in my stomach. 'Sure, I could get some air.'

I grab a plate of melon balls as Dom now chooses a plate

of king prawns.

'How are you going to walk and eat those?'

'With ease and talent,' he says, piling them high.

'Remember Malaga?' I laugh.

Dom pauses, 'Yeah, I couldn't quite get the pink out of that shirt.' He makes a face. 'Alright, I'll be more careful,' he grins.

The night is now pleasantly warm, even in just my little strapless orange number. I've piled my hair on top of my head with the assistance of the doughnut from Singapore, lots of clips and, courtesy of Sarah, a lot of hairspray. Having my hair up allows my silver hoops with feathers to display with ease.

'I like your earrings,' Dom says as we exit the ever-increasingly loud reception hall to the corridor.

'Oh, thanks.' I play with the largest feather that's dangling down on my right ear. 'I got them when I was in Alaska; they're my favourite.'

Dom nods, 'I guessed as much. You've worn them almost every day since we met.'

He's noticed that?

'I noticed them on the plane from LA, first, actually.' We walk a little further, in silence, before he breaks it. 'You know, continuing our chat from yesterday, I've decided: I'm kind of jealous of you,' he says, before stuffing a prawn in his mouth.

'You are? Why?' I ask, before taking a bite of honeydew, as we take a left turn towards the veranda and gaze out over the moon-lit lagoon.

He stops to lean on the barrier and sighs while taking me in. He cocks his head to one side and pauses. I feel heat starting to rise in my face once more. 'You're, I don't know?

Free,' he gestures with a prawn.

'And you're not?'

He thinks about this for a moment, and the sides of his mouth tilt down slightly. 'Well, in one sense, I suppose I am. I mean, I'm not with Heather anymore. But, what I meant was, you are free to travel around the world as you see fit; that's...incredible.'

'Well, it's not exactly as I see fit; I'm told where to go, really.'

'That's not true.' Dom stands up, 'I heard that your boss actually listens to you and respects your opinion.' His beautiful face forms into a frown. 'Mine doesn't respect me. Or want my opinion.'

'Well, maybe you're working for the wrong company,' I say, casually.

'Funny you should say that. They actually want me to transfer to London, to a sister magazine.'

The butterflies in my stomach suddenly flutter in spirals for a moment; I hope my face doesn't reveal that. 'Oh really?' I pop another melon ball in my mouth.

'Yeah. They said that my role is changing.' Dom makes a face.

I swallow, 'London's not so bad you know. Beautiful museums, history, people...' I smile and lean on the barrier.

'I'm *from* London, remember? How can you stand the weather?'

I shrug, 'I'm not there much.'

He points a prawn at me, '*Aha*! See! Free!'

'So that's why you've been extra grumpy, *huh*?'

'Extra grumpy?' He answers with his mouth completely full.

'*Um-hmm*.' I nod. 'Extra,' I confirm. He narrows his

eyes.

What are you doing, Liv? Are you flirting with him? What's wrong with you? Do you like him? No, I don't think so.

'Why's your face doing that?' he interrupts my internal questioning.

'Doing what?'

'You're frowning but have big eyes and they're moving fast from side to side; you OK? Do I need to get someone?'

'I'm fine,' I shake my head, embarrassed, 'I was told by my ex that I used to talk with my face, not my mouth.'

'He sounds like a charmer; why'd you let him go?' he asks, sarcastically.

'I didn't. He let *me* go, remember?' I stare off across the water. *Dammit, are my eyes welling up*? 'So, what's your plan then? Which magazine is it?' I attempt to change the subject, but he doesn't answer. Looking back at him, Dom stops chewing and stares at me with so much sympathy I don't think I can take it. 'Stop looking at me like that.'

'I'm so sorry. It's just horrible,' he finishes his mouthful and swallows. For a time neither of us say anything, we just stare at each other. Finally, he breaks the silence, 'How could anyone leave,' he takes a step closer to me, 'you.'

I have no idea how to respond to that.

'What do you think happened?'

I exhale loudly. 'I think, initially I came up with every scenario possible, but honestly, I've no idea. Of course, I blamed myself at first, assuming I'm not marriage material; then I'd get mad, and I wondered if he'd cheated on me or if there was someone else.' I sigh again. 'But overthinking and ruminating became too much, so, I've been literally running away, from my feelings, and from everything else.' He throws another prawn in his mouth and chomps away; thinking. 'Anyway, I guess I'll never know, so, time to move on *huh*? Maybe from tomorrow, I'll get some kind of closure.' I stab another piece of melon with my fork.

'What do you mean?' he swallows.

'Do you remember I said I was left on a beach in Hawaii?'

'*Ah huh*,' he nods, and then his eyebrows rise so high, they almost join his hairline. 'No!' He says in horror.

I nod, 'Yup.'

Chapter 14

Thailand – Japan – USA
Phuket – Bangkok – Tokyo – Kona

Sunday
Depart Phuket Airport at 09:10
Arrive Bangkok International Airport at 10:30
Duration: 1 hour and 20 minutes (4-hour 20-minute layover)

Depart Bangkok International Airport at 14:50
Arrive Tokyo Haneda Airport at 22:30
Duration: 5 hours 40 minutes (1-hour 25-minute layover)
Time change: Tokyo 2 hours ahead

Depart Tokyo Haneda Airport at 23:55
Arrive Kona International Airport at 11:55
Duration: 5 hours 40 minutes
Time change: Kona 19 hours behind
Drive 15 minutes to hotel (3 nights stay)

Couple G
Hilton Waikoloa, Kona, Hawaii

OK, I can do this. I give myself a little spritz of revitalising spray, close my eyes, and take a deep breath. Having finally confided the truth to my colleagues, Sarah holds my hand as we exit the plane. We've flown into Kona, which is on the west side of the Big Island of Hawaii. We step through one of the tiniest airports you've ever seen; you can see from one side to the other. It's rather like a wooden hut without walls, so the air flows freely through.

We hop on the little bus to the car rental place, and when we arrive there's got to be a total of only twenty cars.

'*Aloha*!' The cheery man in a shirt full of palm trees greets us warmly.

'*Aloha*!' I reply, way cheerier than I actually feel. 'We've made a reservation; *Blush*; party of four.'

He scans his pieces of paper, 'Yup, here you are. So, you've got your choice of cars, your SUV's, compacts…'

'*Ooh*! Let's take that Wrangler!' I exclaim, my mood suddenly lifting, as I point at a particularly jacked up, sunshine yellow Jeep, with huge wheels.

'Can you actually see yourself?' Dom laughs, and towers over me. 'How exactly are you getting in that with those little legs?'

I stand my ground, even if I'm closer to it than he is, 'I will have you know that I drove one around LA on my latest trip — a couple weeks ago,' I add, amazed that it was only a short time ago. 'You can bounce yourself right in via the step up bar. We have to take it; it's SO FUN to drive! Makes you feel like you're seven foot tall!'

Dom snorts, 'Well, you need all the help you can get.'

I walk past and hit him in the stomach, then start attacking the buttons around the removable soft top cover.

'Oh, no, no! What are you doing? It's got like 40,000 poppers!' Dom says, in horror.

'And they've all got to be done back up, before returning,' our rental man smiles.

'No problem at all,' I say smiling. 'Trust me! Have you seen the stars here? You just wait! It would be insane not to have the opportunity to go for a drive, and just look up.'

My colleagues all look at me, smiling affectionately.

'The Jeep it is,' says Hugo.

'Great choice,' the rental man with the palm trees approves. 'Keys are already inside for you.'

Fifteen minutes later we pull up to The Hilton Waikoloa and I take another deep breath. We're welcomed by two doormen, who not only help us out of the car but take our luggage for us. A third member of staff takes the keys from Dom, (his face frowning at the scrunched up soft top and million and one buttons to do back up), then he whisks our lovely little car away. A fourth man, I recognise as Kai, the member of staff who helped coordinate my would-be wedding. He walks up and places a *lei* around each of our necks and a fruity looking cocktail in our hands.

'*Aloha* and welcome to The Waikoloa! The wedding party is very excited for you to be here.'

'Thank you!' We all chorus between sips, and my colleagues exchange looks of glee.

'If you all follow me, we shall get you checked in and settled. Anything I can do to make your stay even more pleasurable, do not hesitate to ask.' He opens his arms and gestures for us all to enter the lobby. I walk in last, and he cocks his head to one side, trying to place me; I'm too embarrassed to say, "Yes, you do know me from somewhere," and walk straight in.

After we've checked in, we're given a map and directed to the building, where our rooms are located. The resort is so large, there's a monorail and a boat to get you about. My colleagues are chattering away, from check in, to boarding the little air-conditioned train that takes us to our side of the resort; all I can think is some lucky woman is going to get married here, and I wasn't fortunate enough to. I take some more deep breaths and try to steady myself. I've got to get it together; I'm interviewing the bride later.

'Liv?' Sarah calls my name.

'*Huh*?' I blink away any sign of sorrow, and slap on a professional smile.

'How are you doing, hon? You're awfully quiet.'

'Oh, I'm fine,' I lie.

'I ain't buying it honey,' Hugo says and reaches across for my hand, from the seat opposite me. 'As soon as you're done with the bride tonight, we're getting *pissed.*' He finishes the sentence in an English accent.

Smiling at them, I can't help but feel protected somehow. 'Thank you, guys. Oh, this is us.' We make our way out of the monorail carriage and walk along a uniquely decorated corridor with various pieces of Oceanic and Asian art; it's basically a museum disguised as a hallway. It's truly awesome, but all I can see are ghosts of moments past: Leo and I walking hand in hand or stopping to kiss. In the present, we make our way to the lifts, around a beautiful fountain in the courtyard, and numbly, I see in my mind's eye where I ran, crying in my wedding dress, back to our suite, alone. The lift door closes around the *Blush* team, but I see Becky holding my hand as Leo's mum was going on and on about all the money that was wasted, and how she couldn't believe it. The lift door pings me into the present, and I feel tears have spilled onto my cheeks, but I just let them roll; we walk to our rooms, and I look behind me, oddly expecting to see him; a place so full of heightened emotional memory, I can almost feel his presence. I feel nervous, as if it's going to happen all over again. Then I realise my colleagues have stopped walking; I guess we're outside our rooms. I look down at the room keycard in my hand: 2657. Looking up at the door we're outside of, it matches that number. All of my colleagues are looking at me with the most sympathetic eyes; I try to smile through my tears.

'Why don't I just come into your room and help you freshen up,' Sarah offers, stroking my arm, gently.

'Oh, no, I'm fine, honestly. I'll just throw some water on my face, a little moisturiser and something from the mini bar, and I'll be ready for anything!' They all look at me, doubtfully. 'OK, obviously this sucks, but I'll be fine,' I repeat. When their faces don't change, I try another tactic, 'I'll suck it up, I promise; I'm nothing, if not professional.' I sigh, 'Look, I think I'm going to hide in here until I have to do the interview; I'll see you tonight in the Twilight Bar when I'm done.'

They reluctantly leave me, and I insert my keycard, and push the door open. Annoyingly, it's exactly the same as the suite Leo and I stayed in; from the luxurious bedding, to the artwork. I frown at a perfectly pleasant frangipani picture as I remove my flip flops. Leaving my luggage at the foot of the bed, I walk over to the piercingly blue view, and draw the curtains. Setting an alarm that allows enough time for a good shower and freshen up before I meet the bride, I decide that I'll be professional when I have to, but for now, I throw the covers back, curl up and just let myself sob silently into the world's fluffiest pillow.

***

When my alarm goes off, I feel extremely disoriented: *Where am I? What time is it? What am I supposed to be doing?* And then it hits me like a brick wall: *Hawaii; six p.m.; interviewing the next bride.*

A swift shower, costume change, and a small makeup and hair effort later, I'm making my way to the restaurant overlooking the ocean. I've decided that every time I get a flashback of Leo, I'm going to give myself a compliment; maybe this will trick my brain into being positive.

Walking up a couple of stone steps that are lined with tiki torches, I take a deep breath. *OK, I can do this*. 'Hi, there's a table under —' Oh, my God, I didn't check the names of the couple with Sarah; they're still, *Couple G*, in my notes. '*Um*.' I falter. 'I'm from *Blush,* I'm meeting the bride-to-be?' I say hopefully. *God, this is embarrassing.*

'Ah, yes, Missy is waiting for you.'

Missy. OK, great, her name is Missy. Missy: I can remember that. 'Thank you,' I say to the happy helper, who guides me in, and leads me to an outside table that's occupied by what can only be described as the most beautiful woman I have ever seen. Her long dark locks cascade effortlessly around her toned shoulders and her smile literally lights up the room, which is impressive to say, as it's sunset.

'You must be Liv!' She stands and I strain my neck to see her face.

God Lord, it's another giraffe.

'Pleasure to meet you! Please sit!'

I do as instructed, and slap on, what I hope is a convincing, "I'm happy to be here," smile. 'Nice to meet you, too, Missy. How are you feeling? Excited?'

'I am. It's a dream, really! Oh, I hope you don't mind, I got us a round of cocktails,' she gestures to the blue concoction in front of me.

'I don't mind at all!' I say, as I pick up my umbrella and cherry clad glass, inspecting it; *I think I like this bride.*

'It's a Blue Hawaiian,' Missy says, then takes a sip of her own. 'Can you believe how beautiful this place is? I'm so happy to be back here,' she takes her glass and holds it to me to cheers, which I oblige.

'Oh, you've been here before?' *Me too*, I say silently, and take a sip; it's a delicious mix of pineapple, coconut and Blue Curaçao.

'Yeah, me and my fiancé came here when we were kids, one Christmas. Our families used to be best friends, you see.'

'Used to?' I can't help but ask.

She takes a sip again, then takes a deep breath, 'Yeah, we've known each other since we were kids; we were neighbours for a while. Anyway,' she pauses, 'please don't put this in the article, but our mums fell out, and haven't spoken since. When we got together as teenagers, neither mum approved, but his mum was, well, off the record?' she asks, insecurely.

'Off the record!' *Maybe*, I think to myself. Perhaps a drama can distract me from my own feelings.

'She was just ghastly to me the whole time we were together, and that's actually what broke us up for a few years.'

'Oh, wow, really?' *This would make for an interesting article.*

'Yeah, it's crazy. She would always go out of her way to

make me feel uncomfortable and unwelcome; I just couldn't take it anymore, so I ended it. We dated other people, but nothing was that serious; I guess we both knew that we were destined to be together, despite our families, you know?' She smiles at me optimistically.

'So, I guess your mums have put all that behind them, now?'

'Oh, no!' she cries, and makes a face, 'I don't know, it's a mess; his mum still hates me, my mum hates the fact that we got back together. In spite of this, we invited them all, of course, but, *erm*,' she shakes her head, 'none of them wanted to come, and so, we got the idea to elope. We saw the competition, entered on the off chance that we'd win, and we did. I still can't believe it if I'm honest; neither of us could have afforded this on our own. With no help from either side, it would have taken us forever to pay back credit cards, and...I'm sorry, that's a little too much information isn't it?' She laughs nervously, takes a sip from her glass, then looks around and smiles, 'But, at least, this way, with only one friend each, I won't have the fear of anyone standing up and saying: "I object."'

I smile, 'I promise I won't put any of that in the article. I mean, on first impressions, I'm thinking the tone will be: the boy next door, childhood sweethearts, overcoming odds to be together...'

She smiles so broadly, I'm pretty sure I've got her approval. 'Thank you.' Her expression falls ever so slightly, 'Between you and me, my fiancé; gosh I like saying that word; anyway, he's really taken it to heart, more than me, so I'm the one who's had all the meetings, and decided everything. And don't get me wrong, I'm hurting too, and I would have loved our families to be here, and to all get along, but, life isn't a fairytale, is it? I'm not sure why I'm telling you this,' she adds, with a slight eyebrow twitch.

'Me neither,' I admit.

She laughs, 'I can actually; I may have had one of these before you arrived,' Missy gestures with her glass, then considers me. 'I have to say, you're a lot nicer than the other girl I was dealing with, Heather, was it? It was as if she had a chip on her shoulder, or something.'

I nod, making a mental note to not take out my heartbreak on this lovely woman. 'Well, can I say, I think you're stronger than you look,' I can't help but admit.

She nods at me, 'I'll take that as a compliment.'

***

Monday

The next day, I wake up with only the mildest hint of a hangover, and enjoy an espresso from my complimentary in-room machine, alongside a room-service breakfast of a couple of pastries. I take it all onto the balcony, overlooking the ocean. God damn it, you can see the beach where my would-be ceremony would have taken place; it's surreal really. *What is the universe trying to tell me? Is there a reason why I'm here again?* I sip, close my eyes, feel the warm breeze upon my face and try to concentrate on my breathing. I hear the song of a couple of morning birds, then open my eyes to watch the tops of the palm trees dance majestically.

After several Blue Hawaiians, neither Missy nor I were really up for an interview, so we've rearranged it. The more we drank, the more I felt inspired by her: deciding to go ahead with her wedding without any family support; *how strong is that?*

I want to be the person who makes her own decisions and chooses to live life by her own rules, not somebody else's. I know I'm not fully living, I'm running. But if I sit still, then my feelings might catch up with me. I can't fully feel it all over again. I just can't do it. *But what if I can?*

OK. I sit a little taller. Just because something truly terrible happened to me here, it doesn't mean I have to hold onto it any longer; after all, we are a result of our thoughts and actions right? I nod at myself. I don't want to feel pain anymore. I'm done. I'm done with all this: feeling sorry for myself; feeling I'm not worthy; feeling I have to change to be good enough. No. I'm done believing those things. Alright, I'm going to embrace this; whatever the reason is that I'm here, I'm going to have fun.

I whip out my phone and message Sarah:

"Fancy a snorkel?"

No sooner have I pressed "send" she replies:

"Sounds fun, Poppet. But I've got my final makeup and hair consultation with Missy, after breakfast. Hugo's with me too. Maybe ask Dom?"

Pausing for a moment, I tentatively type out the same message to Dom. I go to put my phone down and it beeps. He replied with two words:

"Love to."

***

'Unusual to see you without a camera attached.' I walk towards Dom, who's embracing a morning off, from one of the sun loungers, surrounding the saltwater lagoon.

'Good morning to you too! Unlike you to miss breakfast.' He sits up from his reclined position to greet me.

'Oh, I didn't, I just fancied a little room service; some "me time" you know?'

He sighs. 'I do.' He kindly chooses to acknowledge that I don't want to talk about it, and moves on swiftly. 'So, snorkelling! What's the plan? What do we do?'

I place my bag down, behind him, 'Are you telling me you've never snorkelled before?'

'Yup. Virgin.' He grins and bares all his teeth, and I giggle.

'OK, so we head over there,' I point to a little hut, 'grab some flippers, masks, and snorkels. I'd say keep your t-shirt on as it's super easy to get too much sun while in the water. Are you wearing sunscreen?'

'I am, Mum, yes.'

I laugh, 'I'm sorry; just being thorough.'

He shrugs, 'I'm teasing. I live in California, remember? Every day is a sunscreen day.'

'I like that.' I smile. 'Alright, let's go.' I slip out of my flip flops and leave them under Dom's beach lounger, and we pad over the warm sand to the rental place. 'We'll take two sets, please. If you could put them on room 2657, that would be fab,' I say to the young lady inside the rental hut, who turns to oblige.

'Oh, no, just get yours,' he starts but I cut him off.

'It's your first time; I'd be honoured.'

'Thanks.' We take our equipment towards the water and kit up. 'How on earth do you walk in these things?' Dom gestures to the flippers and does an impression of a drunk penguin.

Holding my mask and snorkel, I follow him, 'Lift from the knee, pick your leg up all the way and you kind of flick it out,' I demonstrate with large steps, flipper-first.

'Excuse me?'

'You heard me! Flick it out.' I laugh, pointing to my feet, as we both waddle to the water.

'This is a family hotel,' he says with all seriousness, 'I will be doing no such thing.'

'You're funny! When did you get a sense of humour?' I ask, sarcastically, as we approach the water.

'About the same time you decided to get out of your feelings.'

'*Um hmm.*' I narrow my eyes playfully, and we pause as the waves caress our flippers. Feeling my feet sinking slightly in the sand, I giggle and try to steady myself.

'So, how was the bride last night?' he asks, as he attempts to balance and put his mask on, simultaneously.

'She was nice.' I enjoy the waves crashing against my legs as I wade in a little further. 'I actually felt quite sorry for her; no family is here, on either side, to celebrate, but she loves him so much that that's all that matters.'

He holds his hand to his chest and puts a shocked expression on his face. 'What? Hold on. Are you telling me that a wedding is supposed to be about the *couple*, and not the *family*? Now, *that* is a crazy revelation.'

'Shut up!' I go to bat him and he moves to the side so swiftly he falls into the water with a big splash.

'It's up my nose! It's up my nose!' Dom says when he surfaces, and he sits up in the water.

In between laughing, I try to help him back up, 'You didn't put the mask over your nose, silly; *woah*!' He's too strong for me and pulls me in with him and I enter head first, emerging like a bedraggled mermaid, with my hair completely over my face.

We both sit in the shallows laughing until we can compose ourselves. I clear my throat, and tie up my hair with the band that's on my wrist, then arrange the mask to sit like a pair of sunglasses on the top of my head. 'Like I was saying, the mask goes on like this,' I shift in the water to face him and adjust his, 'So you see, the little nose shape part goes amazingly, over your nose.' I laugh again, examining my work. 'There. Beautiful.' I grin and we just look at each other for a moment. 'So, the next thing I'd say is to practise breathing through the mouthpiece of the snorkel.' I place my mask on, but leave the snorkel dangling, so I can keep talking, 'It can take a little getting used to breathing in and out from only your mouth.' I then place the mouthpiece in my mouth and he copies me, nodding.

We both stand, walk a little further in, then dunk our heads in the water, lift our legs, and float a little. Kicking my flippers gently, I grab his hand to bring him gently even further away from the shallows, then let go. Turning my head I can see he's really concentrating on breathing. I give him a little thumbs up and cock my head to one side. He points up to the surface and I pull my hands back to position my body vertically, and break my face through the lagoon, treading water. He joins me and I take my mouthpiece out of my mouth.

'You alright?' I smile.

He takes his mouthpiece out too, 'Yeah. You weren't kidding; it's weird isn't it? Scary almost.'

'Yeah, you get used to it though. Admittedly, I think I had a little panic attack the first time I did this; my mind was telling me I couldn't breathe. So, every time you find yourself saying that, just say "breathe deep."'

'Thanks, teach,' he smiles. 'Shall we head back in?'

I nod, 'Let's find some fish. The lagoon is actually open to the ocean over there,' I point to my left, 'don't worry,' I smile at his worried expression, 'there's a barrier where fish can get through, but sharks can't.' His face relaxes, so I continue, 'There are signs down there that tell you the names of the fish, which is pretty cool, look out for those.' We both place our mouth pieces back in and dive under.

We swim gently side by side and I gaze around to spot something. I love wearing flippers, you feel weightless and powerful. We swim around a little reef, and our first shoal of fish appears. I grab Dom's hand again and squeeze it; he turns his head and I point to the cool stripy yellow and black fish. We pass a sign in the water that has a matching picture, and below it reads "moorish idol." Dom dances a little and I can see the glee in his eyes through his goggles. The fish glide around, then pass us, majestically. Dom turns his body around to watch them go then I feel a tug on my leg and he spins me around. There are yellow tangs, and these really neat dark ones with an orange teardrop by the tail, again, another sign indicates it's an "achilles tang."

We swim further and, picking up my speed, Dom chases me; I have to remember not to laugh, or water might come through my snorkel. Pointing to Dom's left, there are what I remember from my last trip as parrotfish. They're beautiful, like neon disco fish: bright blue, pink, purple, and green; they are by far, one of the coolest things in here. Then I scream through my snorkel; a long thin fish grazes right past me. *"Trumpet fish"* a sign informs me a few minutes later. I can see Dom's trying not to laugh at me, and then suddenly he points and swims past me. I turn my body to swim in the other direction, and there are turtles. Three of them swimming gracefully together. I catch up with Dom in a few flipper-fueled motions, then watch Dom; he's mesmerised. He turns and faces me, extends his fingers and thumb closely together, then puts the tips of his fingers to his chin, and then gestures towards me as if blowing a kiss, but I recognise it as sign language for "thank you." I do it back to him, remembering that that is also the sign for "you're welcome," then I touch my hand to my heart, and try not to smile too wide with the snorkel in my mouth. He holds his hand out and I take it, we then paddle together, following the turtles around the lagoon.

I've no idea how long we're in the water, but eventually Dom gestures for us to exit, and we swim to shore. When we get to the shallows, we both stand and take our goggles off.

'That was insane!' Dom says with glee, as we wade awkwardly in our flippers towards the sand. 'Thank you so much for this experience.'

I grin from ear to ear, 'You're so welcome! What was your favourite fish?' We reach the sand and both bend down to take our flippers off.

'*Erm*, I liked the blue striped snappers, and the longnose butterfly fish, *ooh*, or the ones that were right in the coral, and we could hear them chopping away; how weird was that?'

'Very weird; it was like bacon sizzling, or something,' I laugh as we walk back to return our equipment.

'What about you?' He looks at me, waiting patiently for my reply.

'Let's see, apart from the parrotfish,' I think, as I enjoy the sand under my feet, 'I loved the raccoon butterflyfish and the one I've no idea how to pronounce; what was it? Hum

hum, something?'

'Yeah, that was amazing! No idea though, it had a lot of "u's" and "n's" in it,' Dom says as we return our flippers.

'The *humuhumunukunukuapua'a.*' The lady in the hut answers for us. 'Snorkels and goggles over there in the buckets please.'

We turn and place the rest of our equipment in the buckets of soapy water, as instructed. 'Dare you to say that five times,' I challenge Dom, who tries, and fails, after several attempts.

'I had a good time with you,' he says after a beat.

'I did too.' I look up at him. 'And you know what the best part is?' I grin at him, cheekily.

'What?' He says softly.

'You've got big goggle marks around your eyes; looks like you're wearing invisible glasses.' I grin and laugh again.

'As do you, my dear! Only, I'm too much of a gentleman to say anything.'

'Yes, that's the first thing I noticed about you when we met: your tact, and delicate way with words.'

He smiles at me affectionately. 'I'm just going to run to the loo; meet you back at the lounger?'

'Sounds good.' I watch him go, and enjoy his wet t-shirt, hanging onto his shoulders. Smiling to myself, I turn and walk back to the lounger. Grabbing my towel from my bag, I dab my face, which is still stretched into a smile.

'Liv?' A voice comes from behind me, and I freeze in my towel. *No. It can't be.*

'It's you, isn't it?' The voice continues. Silently, I stay rooted to the spot. 'Aren't you going to turn around?' I feel a light touch on my right shoulder, it both burns and feels icy. 'Come on, don't be like this. Look at me.'

Hesitantly, I lower the towel that I'm now gripping onto, and turn slowly, not wanting it to be true. But, sure enough, there he is; I take in the man who broke my heart, and left me in this very hotel a year ago.

'I can't believe it's you,' he smiles warmly. 'You look great! Been snorkelling? It's as good as we remember, right?'

I'm having an out of body experience. Has someone stolen my voice box?

'I mean, it's amazing how the water can feel cold after a while, in Hawaii? Still find that strange, you know.'

I shake my head, 'Leo?' Oh, there's my voice. And all I've managed to utter is his name.

'Did you finally move over to *Blush* magazine?' he continues rambling. 'What are you doing here?'

I narrow my eyes at him, 'I'm doing a wedding piece, we're collaborating with *Blush.* How did you know *Blush* is here?' I take a beat and say slowly. 'Wait, what are *you* doing here?' Now he's the one who's silent. For what feels like eternity, we just stare at each other, then I break the silence. 'Oh my God. Are you the *groom*?'

He smiles weakly and laughs uncomfortably. 'Well, *uh*,' he scratches his head awkwardly, 'Yes.'

'And you're getting married where *we* were going to get married?'

'Well,' he kicks a little sand in front of him, 'They do have the best mahi-mahi, and I knew the hotel so well you see. Beautiful spot...' The last part of his sentence fades away as a laugh escapes from my mouth.

'Mahi-mahi? Beautiful spot?! Are you kidding me?' I say darkly. *This is not happening.* I'm asleep, it's a dream, and any moment I'm going to wake up and he'll be gone; just like always.

'There you are honey-kins!' A voice sounds behind me, then suddenly the beautiful, curvaceous Missy, strides past me and drapes her toned arms around my ex-fiancé, giving him an incredibly over-the-top, Hollywood-esque kiss on the lips. His frightened eyes remain open, and focused on me. *I think I'm going to be sick.* I fumble for my bag and flip flops.

'Would you excuse me for a moment, I just need to, *um*, yeah.' I gather my things up in my arms as quickly as possible, and dash off in the opposite direction, as fast as my bare feet will let me with a mixture of disbelief and nausea.

I spot Dom walking towards me; his smile drops to a look of concern when he sees my face, and he rushes over, 'You OK?' He places a concerned hand on my arm. 'You look like you've seen a ghost.'

'I have,' I pant, leaning on a nearby palm tree for stability. I can't catch my breath. Dom looks at me with concern,

'Too much sun? Do we need to get you to a doctor or something? Or maybe just Hugo, he's good with asthma attacks, panic attacks?' he offers through guesses.

'No. The groom,' I pant. 'The groom is,' I can't finish my sentence, it's too surreal. My eyes well up, and I gingerly motion behind me with my thumb. He, not so subtly, stares immediately in the direction of my motion.

'I don't understand,' Dom says, looking over my head, and then back to me. He tries to help me finish my sentence. 'The groom is...?''

'My ex-fiancé.'

Chapter 15

USA
Kona

An hour later, I'm in my suite, sitting on my gorgeous king size bed, still completely speechless. Meanwhile, Sarah is pacing in front of me.

'Leo is *Leon*?! We were told the groom was called Leon! I thought it was funny that we never met him, but each bride is different, right? But, he's *Leo*? *Your Leo*? This is *friggin'* nuts! I mean, when you said you had an ex called Leo, I admit, I thought, "*huh*" but not...like...*woah*.'

'Leo is short for Leon,' I find myself mumbling, but Sarah's on a roll,

'OK, so here are our options, as I see them: 1. We let the whole thing go ahead. You come down with the flu or something, stay here, order room service. I make notes instead of you; I've watched you do it, plus you've got all your notes from the other weddings, so I'll just use them as examples. 2. You punch him in the face, tell the bride what an arsehole he is, break up the wedding. However, we'd then be a wedding short for the article; problematic, I admit. 3. You ask him to explain himself, and if you see fit to forgive him, you get back together, and, now, I'm going to put it out there just to be thorough—' she pauses and meets my eyes, 'you and him become a couple in the article?'

All I can manage is a small scoff.

'I'll take that as a no then. 4. *I* punch him in the face, you tackle the bride—'

'Thanks hon,' I stop her, mid-flow, 'but I think I just need to talk to him. Ask him...' I shrug my shoulders, 'Why? How?' I stand up with some newfound determination, just as there's a knock at the door. My stomach seems to have suddenly housed the entire company of *Cirque du Soleil*, and my knees buckle, landing me back on the bed.

'I'll get it,' Sarah says and then stops. 'Do you want me to get it?'

'Who is it?' I say with a shaky voice.

'It's Dom,' a voice says from the other side of the door.

Sarah looks to me for confirmation and I nod to indicate he can come in. When she opens the door, he's standing with a brown paper bag in each hand. 'I brought dinner, drinks and a proposal. Sorry,' he adds when he catches my eye.

'So,' he settles down next to me. 'First thing: prosecco, Pinot Grigio, or beer.' He looks at me with eager-to-please eyes.

'I hardly think we're celebrating here,' I say, taking out the prosecco.

'I know, I'm sorry; I went back and forth on that, but it goes really well with sushi.'

I smile at him. 'I'll go for a beer. Thank you.'

He whips out a bottle opener, takes off the cap, and effortlessly hands me the ready to go beer.

'Now, I know you're veggie—'

'How observant of you,' Sarah says dryly, but I can't help but be touched by this.

He frowns at her then carries on, 'So, I got you a simple cucumber and avocado *maki*.'

'That's perfect, thank you.' Although, I'm not sure I'm

hungry yet.

'And finally,' he crosses one tanned leg over the other and leans forwards. 'Would you like us to pretend that we are a couple?'

'What?' I say after a sip of my Coors Light.

'Hear me out. I propose that, to make it easier for you while we're here for the next two days, that we pretend to be a couple. It would show him that you've moved on, and I can act as, like, your bodyguard, of sorts.'

I stare at him as Sarah pipes up. 'Are you kidding? What use is that going to be? We want answers,' she makes a fist and hits it with her other hand, 'or at least a couple of bruised eyes! How is that going to help?'

'No, I like it,' I finally say out loud.

'You do?' Sarah says, with surprise.

I smile at Dom, 'I do.' I stand up and take to Sarah's pacing. 'He always hated when guys were around me, I doubt that's changed about him.'

'But what about interviewing him? And the day itself?' Sarah asks, helping herself to a beer.

'I don't know yet, but maybe that's how I'll get my answers; I wonder if he's told her about me?'

'Well, if he hasn't that's a sure way to make him squirm.'

I stop and point at Sarah, 'Exactly. I'm going to be nice, polite, calm, adorable, and hang off your arm? It will drive him nuts, which I *kinda* love.'

'Well, OK!' Dom says, raising his own beer to mine. 'Let's do this!'

***

Tuesday

The others made the most of walking around the resort last night and enjoying the *lū'au*, but I took the time to clear my head, and, admittedly, cloud it with alcohol at the same time. This morning is annoyingly, just as beautiful as yesterday, as I sit on my balcony, sip my espresso, breathe, and remember that I am going to take the high road. God damn it, the weather is perfect, and so is this view. I hate him. *What the hell, universe?! Why are you doing this to me? What can I possibly learn from this?*

My door goes, and I'm dressed in nothing but my complimentary robe. *Oh well.* I pull it tighter and open the door to see my new "lover's" face, dressed in matching attire.

'Care to join me for an angry morning coffee?' I bark at Dom.

He nods, 'I'm liking this energy on you.' He steps into my room, adjusting the belt on his robe, and observes the mess. '*Woah*, what the hell happened in here?' There are reams of paper from my notebook, ripped out, screwed up, and thrown around the room — an attempt at me bullet-pointing the truth about the groom. He looks around taking in my empty sushi container, various discarded wrappers and packets of the entire contents of the snacks from the mini bar, an empty bottle of wine that Sarah only had a glass of and, 'What is that?' Dom's looking at my attempt at a Jackson Pollock on the wall.

'Wasabi and soy sauce. I may have been picturing his face there as I threw them,' I say with venom.

He nods, 'Understandable. So,' he steps over the outfit I was wearing yesterday that's screwed up on the floor, 'I was thinking we should come up with a backstory.' He turns around to helpfully pick my sorrowful outfit up, puts it on the bed, and my bra and pants fall out of it, and land back onto the floor. 'Whoops, I'm so sorry.' He turns away, embarrassed, but at this point, I'm too full of rage to care that he's seen my lacy bright orange Calvin Klein set. '*Um*, as I was saying: backstory. If I've learnt anything from all those girly films I've watched, it's to get your backstory straight.'

'Alright,' I agree, feeling slightly calmer in his presence. I head to the coffee maker, 'What do you want?'

'To come across as believable.' He sits down on my bed, 'Now, I've done a little acting, so I'm comfortable with improv—'

I cut him off, smiling, 'No, I mean, what coffee do you want?' I gesture to the tray of Nespresso pods.

'Oh, I like the espresso.'

'Me too.' I smile. 'We're practically a couple already!'

The machine whirrs into action and I take a look around the room; it is a bit of a mess. I start picking up all the bits of paper and throw them into the recycling side of the bin.

'I'll help you.' Dom stands up and heads for the bathroom, 'I'll grab a wet towel for the wall.'

'Great idea; thank you.'

There's a second knock at the door as I pick up the last of the paper and look at my phone for the time; I did say I'd meet Sarah for breakfast; am I late?

Of course, it's not Sarah.

'We need to talk.' Leo pushes his way into my room and shuts the door with panic. 'I don't have long; Missy thinks I've gone back to the room for my Fitbit for the gym. Look, since we broke up—'

'Excuse me?' I walk towards him slowly, backing him into the room, picking up the empty bottle of wine as I go, to point it at him, 'We did *not* break up. *You* left me at the altar, remember? In this very hotel, no less!' I swing the bottle in the recycling, fold my arms, and look at him properly. *God damn it, he's better looking than I remember.*

'I'm sorry.' He hangs his head. 'I was stupid, and young.'

'Stupid, I agree with, but young? Leo, it was last year!' I say angrily. 'No note; no phone call; no messages; you didn't reply to any of my emails or texts. You completely ghosted me! It was as if I never existed in your eyes!'

'I'm sorry, I just couldn't go through with it, OK, because...' he looks past me and takes in the room. 'Wow, did you have a party in here or something?'

I open my mouth to retaliate but Dom flushes the loo and then steps out from the bathroom. Leo jumps, and whips his head around, in surprise.

Dom walks towards us, picking up my bra on the way, 'We were playing a game and *uh*,' he throws the garment onto the bed, 'kind of got carried away. Hello, I'm Dom,' he holds his hand out for Leo to take, 'photographer of your wedding, and boyfriend of your ex-fiancé.' I try to keep a straight face.

'Leon,' he responds, doubtfully, taking Dom's outheld hand, limply, clearly taken aback. His eyes slide to me, 'I'm sorry, I thought you were here alone.'

'No bother,' Dom answers for me, and puts a casual, yet protective arm around my shoulder. It feels good. And satisfying. Man, he smells nice. 'We were just having our morning espresso before heading down to breakfast.'

Leo appears speechless as he darts his eyes from me to Dom and back again, taking this in. 'I was, *um*...'

'Just going to explain to me why he left me at the altar,' I finish his sentence for him, looking at Dom.

'Excellent.' Dom smiles at me then we both turn to Leo. 'Fire away, mate. We'd all love to hear.'

Leo clears his throat, and attempts to stand his ground by straightening up, despite the fact that Dom is several inches taller. 'Oh, I think this needs to be a private conversation.'

'Between you and my girlfriend? I don't think so,' Dom says, ever-so-threateningly.

I can't help but smirk. *This is perfect.* 'No, it's alright honey.' I look up at my hero, place a hand gently on his fluffy-robed chest, 'I honestly think a little closure would be good.' I keep my hand where it is but return my gaze to my ex-lover, 'How about we talk when I'm supposed to be interviewing you alone tonight, after dinner?'

He looks at me sceptically. 'Aren't you talking to Missy before then?'

'We've got our re-arranged meeting, after you meet with Hugo, yes,' I answer with what I hope is poise and confidence, as opposed to what I actually feel: mild loathing and a need to lash out.

'Are you going to say anything?' Leo widens his eyes ever so slightly; he hates being threatened.

'I haven't decided yet.' *At least that's true.*

'Look, just think about it, OK? You've clearly moved on,' he wafts a hand in our direction before backing away to the door, like a fearful animal, holding my gaze, afraid I'll pounce at any moment. 'Alright, I'll see you later then.'

'Nice to put a face to the name,' Dom calls after him.

Leo smiles weakly, pauses at the door, then narrows his eyes, 'How did you say you two met?'

Dom and I look at each other and both smile before facing

Leo and saying at the exact same time: 'On a plane.'

***

Sitting next to the floor to ceiling windows of the dining area, overlooking the lagoon, Sarah is digging into the largest omelette I've ever seen. Meanwhile, I pour from the huge cafetière on the table, filling my mug then Dom's. 'You were great at *improv-ing* by the way.'

'Why, thank you!' He does a little bow in his seat. 'I did a little am-dram when I was at uni.'

'Oh yeah? Oh God.' I glance up and feel a jolt of ice go through my heart.

'What's wrong?' Dom takes the cafetiere from me, before I spill it everywhere. He and Sarah follow my gaze.

'So *that's* Leo.' Sarah says with spite, but I'm not capable of responding. Missy is even more beautiful in the daylight. She's clearly been taking every advantage of sitting by the pool, and soaking up the Hawaiian sun. She's talking with the hostess, giggling, stroking Leo's arm, affectionately, weaving her fingers through his, and truly beaming. Leo looks a little pale in comparison, but he's also wearing a huge smile; he hasn't spotted me yet.

'Oh, God, now I know who she is, I feel so stupid. I think I'm going to throw up.' I take a sip of Sarah's glass of water.

'The only person who looks like they're going to throw up is Leo,' Sarah says, eyeing him up like she might jump over the table and deck him one, for me. Having the sudden urge to run and hide, I then feel Dom's warm, comforting hand on mine.

'Remember, you're not alone here.'

I take in his soothing smile and bright aqua blue eyes. He

really is handsome. God, I feel sick. And confused. 'Thank you.' I smile, weakly back at him.

'Oh hi!' Our moment is ruined by the presence of both Missy and Leo, standing right by our table. I look up and thankfully Dom hasn't moved his hand from mine. I feel protected, and suddenly, absolutely fearless. 'It's my *Blush* team!!' Missy says excitedly. 'No, Hugo, though?'

'He's on his way down,' Sarah says. 'He wanted to have everything he needed for your meeting with him, so you can get started right after food.'

'Fab! Ah, well, it's so great to finally meet you all in person!' Missy continues, 'Dom, the missing piece in our puzzle.' Missy bends down and gives him a hug. Leo and I catch eyes: his wide and fearful; mine narrowed with repulsion. Missy then straightens up and links arms with Leo. 'I had such fun with you and Hugo last night, Sarah; you're all so fabulous and talented.' Her demeanour changes ever so subtly, 'And Liv, Leo-kins tells me,' she directs at me, 'you guys used to date or something?' she says with an air of disbelief.

'Or something,' I find my mouth saying before my brain stops me. *So, he has told her something.*

'How weird is that? What a small world! You and—'

'Leo-kins,' I finish her sentence with false joy.

'You didn't mention this over our drinks the other night,' she says calmly, but there's a coldness in her gaze.

'I only found out he was the groom yesterday,' I say, honestly.

'How is that possible?' she says with polite incredulousness, looking from me to Leo and back again.

'All the couples on my paper are only letters. Couple G,' I gesture to them both and think to myself: *G for "good grief, how is this happening?"*

'*Hmm.*' She takes that in, and seems to accept it, 'Right, well, there we are then.' There's an uncomfortable silence, but then Missy returns to her pleasant nature, 'OK, so,' she sits in Hugo's empty seat, 'we're going to have a girly chat later,' she smiles at me, 'but I just wanted to say, thank you all for being here.' I suddenly feel enormously sorry for her. 'This is the happiest I've ever been. I feel blessed and I know you're being paid to be here, but I want you all to enjoy this as much as possible too. See it as a holiday for yourselves, anything we can get you, I'll make sure I can, and I am just so excited that this is actually happening.' She laces her delicate fingers together and rests her flawlessly defined chin on them. I want to hate her, I really do, but she's too damn nice. I smile at her and then, I can't help it, my eyes are drawn to her left hand.

'Oh wow,' I say, unintentionally out loud. *How did I not see that the other day?*

She untwists her fingers, and places her left hand in her right, to take in the sizable sapphire, 'I know, it's a bit much isn't it?' Her voice is filled with nothing but love, as she looks up at Leo, who's, quite sensibly, completely quiet.

'It's beautiful,' I can't help but agree, keeping my eyes focused on the ring.

'Thanks. Well, anyway, I'll leave you to your breakfast, and look forward to seeing you later! We've got that cabana facing the ocean,' she points out of the window to where I'll be interviewing her.

'Great; see you,' I say, with a small, but what I hope is a vaguely confident voice. Missy stands up to take her leave, joins hands with Leo, and off they walk to a table across the other side of the room. We watch them go in silence. She has the air of Grace Kelly: elegant, classy, timeless.

'He gave her a sapphire,' I say sadly, still looking in their direction.

Dom scoffs, 'A blue mineral. What's so good about that?'

'It's my birthstone. Leo knew I wanted one.'

'What did he give you?'

I sheepishly hold up my right hand, 'This.' He now takes my right hand in his left and examines the simple, silver band on my right ring finger, that consists of two feathers touching in the middle.

'*That's* your engagement ring? It looks like it came from Accessorize.'

I sigh, 'I think it did,' I say honestly.

'Don't get me wrong, that's a great store; I got presents for my sisters there all the time, when I was in London, but...' he frowns.

'It didn't matter at the time, it was what it meant that mattered.' My small smile falls as I stop myself mid-sentence, 'Turns out, it meant nothing.'

'Then why are you still wearing it?' Dom asks carefully.

I shrug, my eyes now on my ring. 'I don't know. I took it off my left hand, but, if I didn't wear it at all, then it would become real.' I raise my head to see him taking me in.

'Isn't that a good thing? You don't want to be with that guy,' he gestures in their direction. 'You should be with someone who knows how precious you are, and can't wait to plan the rest of his life with you. Not someone who,' he pauses, now looking so intently at me, that my heart flutters, 'doesn't see what he has. You're better than that, Liv.'

I don't know what to say, so I bite my lip.

Sarah coughs, 'Well, I'm just, *um*, going to help myself to some of that papaya up there. I'll be right back.'

Dom is still holding my right hand, and protecting my left. 'Do you want to get some breakfast?'

'Oh, no, I don't think so. Besides, I'm, *um*,' I scrunch my nose, 'not much of a breakfast person.'

'That is the biggest load of bollocks I've ever heard in my entire life,' Dom squeezes my hands slightly.

'What do you mean?'

'You? Not a breakfast person? We've been travelling around the world together and I have never seen you miss a meal. In fact, when I first met you on that flight, you actually jumped out of sleep, to make sure you didn't miss the food trolley.'

A little hoot of laughter comes out of me, involuntarily, 'What can I say? It's like a sixth sense; it's as if the smell of food is an alarm clock.' For a moment we just sit there smiling at each other. *Do I really like this guy? What is happening right now?* 'Well,' I break the silence. 'I suppose I could go for some papaya.'

***

'Earth to Dom? Hello?'

'I love it here. Turtles, *and* dolphins. I love dolphins!'

I can't help but laugh at Dom's utter delight, as we walk from the dining hall, around the resort to the cabanas, past Dolphin Quest.

'They're awesome, aren't they?' He can't hear me, he's gone; hanging over the bridge like a five year old.

'Look there's a calf!' Dom points with glee. I rest my hands on the bridge next to him, and lean over, watching the mum and baby dance together. 'I've always been in two minds about this.'

'About what?' I ask, but he hasn't averted his eyes.

'I love it when you see dolphins in the wild, in their own natural environment, you know, but they're really well looked after here, aren't they?' He gestures towards a member of staff, who's having a cuddle with one of the dolphins. He rolls over onto his back — the dolphin, not the member of staff — and gets a good belly scratch.

'Tomorrow if we come down to breakfast earlier, and grab a seat by the window; we'll see them leaping around the lagoon.'

'Amazing,' Dom's eyes continue to follow the calf as he responds; his mouth lifting into a subconscious smile.

'Can we just stay here?' I say, edging closer to Dom and resting my head on his shoulder.

'Sure.' He puts his head on mine.

'Well, aren't you two just the cutest couple, ever!' Missy pokes her head round to smile at us both. 'Can I steal her away from you?' she tilts her head to one side.

'Of course. See you later, sweetheart,' Dom plants a gentle kiss on my cheek. His lips are soft, I think I want them there for longer.

'OK, great! Let's go!' Missy links her arm through mine and off we go. Glancing over my shoulder, I mouth "thank you" at him.

Missy guides me to the perfectly positioned cabana, and I gaze out at the ocean I'd seen so many times in my dreams over the last year. I take a deep breath and decide to jump right in. 'Alright, so, shall we start from the beginning?' I take my notebook and pen out of my bag. 'You first met when you were neighbours, when—'

'Oh no,' she cuts me off, 'we're not talking about me,' Missy takes me by surprise.

'We're not? But that's the whole point about this article; it's all about the brides in this piece. Sure, I'll talk to Leo too, but our audiences want to know about you.'

She smiles, 'Thanks, but, I want to ask *you* some questions first.'

I feel my eyes widen, and my heart beats a little faster. 'Oh. Me? What do you want to know?'

'Leo said you went out, but he's very fuzzy on the details.'

'Oh, really?' I respond, unsure of what I'm going to say next.

'Yeah,' she shrugs. 'He talked about his past girlfriends, but failed to mention a,' she gestures her open palms at me, 'beautiful, travel writer, until last night.' She scrunches her face up slightly. 'I just feel like there's something he's not telling me. Is there something he's not telling me?'

I swallow, 'Well,' I begin.

'Oh God, I knew it. There's something he's not told me. You're not still together, are you?'

'What?! No! Of course not.' I find my hand reaching for hers to console her. 'Look, it doesn't matter what went on with Leo and I. This is about you, your day and your future happiness, OK?'

She wavers, 'Still, I would feel a whole lot better if you told me why it ended,' she says in a small voice.

'Honestly, I'd like to know that too.'

'So, *he* broke up with *you*?' she says slowly, working it out in her head.

'He left me, yes.' *Oh God, this is awkward.*

'OK.' She takes that in and glances down at her hands. In my awkwardness I fiddle with my fingers and my eyes are drawn to my tan line on my engagement finger; like an invisible ring and glaring reminder of my hideous past. I look up and watch her eyes slide to my hands. She looks closer at my left one, and I feel myself starting to well up.

Stop it Liv, she'll see you. Glancing out to the ocean, I attempt to blink away my tears. 'Gosh, I forgot how beautiful it is here,' I say, trying to distract her and myself.

'You didn't say you'd been here before,' she states to the back of my head.

Whoops. '*Um*, *er*, didn't I?'

'Liv?'

'Yes?' When I'm sure my eyes have swallowed the tears, I turn back.

She looks at me doubtfully. 'When did you and Leo break up?'

I take a deep breath, 'A year ago.'

She falters ever so slightly but remains poised. 'And what happened?'

I bite my lip, then point over to the lookout to our right, 'He left me over there, at the altar, and the first time I'd seen or spoken to him since, was yesterday. When I found out he was the groom.'

'*Woah*. How the hell are you writing about the wedding?'

I shrug, 'I'm filling in for Heather, it was a last minute thing…'

'No, I don't mean literally how, I mean *how* are you going to write about my wedding, which,' she again takes the details in, 'was supposed to be *your* wedding? Are you OK?'

'Am *I* OK?' I feel a rush of affection for her. 'Are *you* OK?'

'At least I know he wasn't cheating on me.' She's relieved and suddenly I feel very sorry and almost responsible for her.

'When did you get back together with Leo?'

'About ten months ago. Leo just turned up on my doorstep and said he wasn't going to live the rest of his life without me.'

'Gosh.'

'I'm sorry,' she sighs. 'OK, look, this is obviously less than ideal; for you and me both. It's not every day your fiancé's ex-fiancé writes about your wedding in the top bridal magazine in the world; I'm sure it's going to be a riveting read!'

'Oh, I've no intention to sabotage you or your wedding,' I say, and find I actually mean it.

She smiles at me gratefully, 'Thank you. However,' her expression changes completely, 'who's to say he's not going to leave *me* standing there, too? The coward.'

'Again, might make for a riveting read!'

She bursts out laughing. 'I like you.'

'I like you too,' I say honestly.

'Leo's going to hate that,' she says, brushing the perfectly ironed white cloth of the cabana bed, in front of her.

'Oh, yeah,' I agree. 'So, I have to ask, when did he propose to you?'

Her cheeks flush, 'The first time?'

Ouch.

'About two weeks into seeing each other again. I actually turned him down and told him not to be so ridiculous.'

I burst out laughing. 'Oh, God, I bet he saw that as a challenge then.'

'You're telling me. He asked me three times. Sorry,' she adds, apparently my face reads more than I want it to.

'It's fine,' I try to brush it off.

'It's not though, is it?'

I shrug.

'No,' she sits up even straighter. 'I mean it; it's not good enough.'

'What are you doing?'

She furiously types into her phone. 'I'm telling him we're all done, and he's to meet me here.'

Without intention, my hands grab her phone, 'No. Please don't. Leo aside, I literally have not done my job here; I have nothing to write about...that you'd want to read anyway,' I add, with a quick smirk.

She waves me away and prizes her phone back with a surprising grip; she's definitely been working out in the lead up to her big day. 'We'll have a chat another time, but right now? We need answers. And if we're going to do this,' she waves over a waiter, 'we both need to do it with a drink in our hands.'

***

I sip nervously on my mimosa. *Alright. This is happening.* I sit here with a woman I should technically hate, but actually really like. *This is so messed up.*

'How's my beautiful *fianc—oh*?' Leo takes us both in and stops in his tracks.

'Now, which "fiancé" are you referring to, exactly?' Missy cocks her head, points to me and then herself, while narrowing her eyes at him.

'Well, *uh*, you of course, honey.' He smiles, frightened.

'*A huh*, don't "honey" me. Me and my new bestie here, have a few questions for you,' she says darkly. 'Why didn't you tell me that you were engaged before?' She narrows her eyes at him, and folds her arms.

'Because it meant nothing!' Leo blurts out before sheepishly looking at me.

'*Woah*!' I put my hands in the air. 'From my memory, we really cared about each other, you arsehole! It was you who proposed to me!'

'Well, yes it was but—' I cut him off.

'But, clearly it meant nothing to you, as you left me, standing right over there!' I point to my right.

Now, it's Missy's turn. 'You told me, there was nothing serious that happened between us breaking up and getting back together.'

'Well, I—' Leo starts but she's on a roll.

'Being, not only engaged, but almost *married* to another person, is a pretty big deal, buddy.'

'Well, yes, it is. But, you see—'

'Which you casually forgot to tell me about?'

Leo is starting to sweat, and it's nothing to do with the heat. 'I was waiting for the right time, and—'

'And why would you bring me to get married in a place where you'd already planned a wedding with another, may I add,' she gestures at me, '*lovely* woman.'

'Is this why your family isn't here?' I ask, just clocking.

'What?' Missy looks hurt. 'Wait, your family was here for *that* wedding?'

'Well, yeah, they approved of Liv,' Leo says and immediately regrets it.

'Excuse me?' Missy sits up even taller and then hands her mimosa to me. I give mine a good gulp and then place them both down on the side table.

'Oh, come on, that relationship truly meant nothing. I want to be with you; I always have!' Leo tries to reason with

Missy.

'Again, thanks,' I say, arms folded.

'How dare you.' Missy shakes her head. 'You know how much it took for me to try and get over the fact that your family would never give us their blessing, but you throw that in my face, after all this secrecy? You are off your '*effing* rocker if you think this marriage is going ahead.' Missy suddenly swings her legs round, off the cabana and onto the stone, standing up to face him. She points at him, opens her mouth to say something and then closes it again in rage and begins to march off, 'And don't even think about following me!' Missy turns her head to yell behind her. Leo stands, paralysed between his old and new love.

'Well that was a shit show,' I say.

Leo sighs loudly and looks out to the ocean. I take in his frame. God, the number of nights I spent dreaming about that frame. For a moment I want to reach out and touch him. What did it feel like to touch him? I can't remember. Do I want to know again? Maybe this is what the universe was trying to do? Get us back together? Do I even want that? This man has plagued my dreams for a year, and clearly, he's spent very little of that concerning himself about me. Why am I wasting my time, to quote Kate Winslet, on someone who "does not and will not love me back." Wait. *Do I still love him? Did I ever?*

'I'm so sorry,' Leo says quietly to the accompaniment of the crashing waves. I stay silent, so he turns around. His eyes are filled with tears. 'I'm *so* sorry,' he repeats before sitting by my side. 'At the time, I thought I wanted to marry you. But, the truth is, you're too good for me.'

'That's the biggest load of bullshit I've ever heard.'

He laughs, then sighs again, 'OK, what do you want me

to say?'

'I don't know; that you're a coward; a compulsive liar, or you have commitment issues? But, clearly that's not the case. It was just me.' Pausing, as this realisation hits me, I then say slowly. 'I just wasn't good enough.'

'Oh, Liv. Please don't be like that.' He looks at me with such sorrow, taking my hands in his, and I let him.

'How am I supposed to be?' I feel myself on the edge of tears. 'You shattered my world,' I say quietly.

'OK, I'll admit, the way I ended things was cowardly.'

'Do you have any idea how humiliating it was to stand there and have to tell all of our friends and family that the wedding was off? Do you know how demoralising it is to have the whole world look at you with that much sympathy? I returned our gifts; I got rid of everything from our life together; I couldn't keep the memory of you anywhere near me. You fell off the planet; no explanation, no closure.' I look at him, and my eyes are filled with tears too. 'You truly are an arsehole!' I almost whisper.

His face crumples, 'I know.'

'Did you even love me?'

'Of course I did.'

'Just not enough to marry me.' He doesn't answer, so I continue. 'And now, only a year on, you're here again, ready to marry someone else?' Rubbing my temples, I take a deep breath. 'I'm done.' I suddenly stand up. 'I need to think; I'll talk to you later.'

'No, Liv, please, hear me out,' he reaches out and grips onto my hand.

'What is there left to say?'

'That, to be honest, it didn't have anything to do with you. Any man would be lucky to spend the rest of his life with you, but—'

'But what?'

'I didn't mean for it to go so far with us.'

'You're not making me feel better.'

'No, I mean, I was trying to break up with you for a while.'

'Again, really, digging yourself a hole here.'

'*Ugh*. This is all coming out wrong.' He lets go of my hand and buries his face in his palms momentarily before resurfacing. 'I cared about you, dammit, but I knew it wasn't how you deserved to be cared about. My family loved you; they really wanted this to happen,' he gestures between us.

'Well, I loved them too; I think that's what made the whole thing even more painful; I lost a family as well as a partner.'

'Exactly; it was about them. I was trying to please *them*, I think, going against my gut. I'm sorry how this is going to come out, but I never got over Missy. Ever.'

Deciding to release my ego for a moment, to hear him out, I sit back down next to him.

'Did Missy tell you she broke up with me?' I nod. 'Well, I made it so easy for her to do that; I never put her first or took her side. It's my mum; she has this power over me, you know?' I sit and just listen. 'Then I met you, and I thought, *OK! Here is a smart, successful, attractive woman; try and make it work.* And I did try, and I did love you Liv, please know that. But I got caught up in the, "what you're supposed to be doing at that moment in your life," phase. Didn't you ever feel that way?'

I think for a moment. 'Maybe.' I sigh, 'To be honest, when you proposed, I don't think I was ready to marry you, but I was willing to.'

'I know you were. But how many weddings did we go to when we were together?'

'Around thirtyish.'

'Exactly; and that wasn't even for work. Don't tell me you didn't feel that peer pressure.' He looks at me and I nod slightly. 'And the jobs we were doing? Man, we were surrounded by weddings, Liv. And then add to that my mum's narcissism? I felt I couldn't go against what she wanted for me; parents know best right?' He says the end of his sentence sarcastically.

'OK, you were truly screwed,' I admit.

'I have been thinking about you, you know.'

'And what have you been thinking?' I can't help but ask.

'That the whole time we were together, I didn't treat you the way you were supposed to be treated. I took you for granted, but at the same time, I couldn't give you my whole heart because I knew it belonged to someone else.' I wipe away a little tear that's escaped. 'Liv, you taught me how to laugh again, and try to love my life.' He grabs my hand again, 'You'll always have a place in my heart, Liv, but, can I ask you something?' I nod. 'Do you think, deep down, that we were destined for each other?'

I think for a moment, then before I know what I'm doing, I shake my head and words are coming out of my mouth. 'I think I loved being adored by your family. And I think, after you left, I had the fear that I'd missed out on my happiness.'

We sit for a moment, hand in hand, watching the waves, before Leo turns back to me. 'Happiness isn't something we can miss out on, it's what we create, Liv.'

'*Hmm.*' I think about this for a second, 'I guess you can never lose it, you just sometimes forget how to tap into it.'

'Although, it seems you've found it again.'

'Dom?' I question and he nods, 'We're not together, we're just friends. We pretended to be together to make me stronger and you crazy.'

He laughs, 'Really? Well, if it's not too inappropriate to say—'

'Inappropriate?' I cut him off. 'I'm sitting in the resort that my ex-fiancé left me in, talking to him about love, life and happiness, before he marries another woman, that I'm going to write about, in one of the world's leading bridal magazine's; I think we've side-stepped and surpassed "inappropriate," Leo.'

'Fine, then. I think you're actually rather perfect for each other. And, from a male perspective, he's either a very good actor, or he truly cares about you.'

I shrug, 'I can't even process that right now, and no offence, but, I'm not taking *any* advice from you.'

'None taken.' He smiles briefly, and we return to silence. Then a thought occurs to me. 'Why here?'

'What do you mean?'

'Why did you choose to marry me here?'

Leo considers his words, and then shrugs. 'I guess I thought if I married you here, it would overwrite a memory, you know?'

'I guess I can understand that.' I play with the ring that Leo gave me, and for the first time ever, it doesn't feel right on hand. Sliding it off my finger, I place it down next to the mimosas, feeling like I've taken off something much heavier. I sigh, contentedly. 'But you've got to admit, bringing Missy here after what you did last year was a bad idea.'

He shakes his head, 'It was Missy. After I'd suggested eloping, she was the one who came up with the idea of coming here again; I couldn't believe it. But, what was I supposed to say?'

'The truth.' I gaze at him. 'Women need the truth.'

He looks down again, heaves a great sigh, then shuts his eyes. 'I'm sorry, Liv. You deserve to be so happy.' He pauses and then decides to continue, 'Even if we did get married a year ago, I don't think I could have ever given you that.'

I look at him and for the first time in a year, feel a sense of acceptance. 'Well, now I know what the universe was thinking, bringing us here, again.'

'What's that then?' he says, defeated.

'Closing a chapter and starting the next. You and Missy deserve to have that.'

'So do you, Liv.'

Chapter 16

USA
Kona

Back on the balcony in my room, overlooking the ocean, once more, I let my feelings wash over me: relief mixed with sadness for finally having my answer, and a side of gratitude, for Dom, Sarah and Hugo, who are sitting inside my room, chatting about everything I said, that went on with Leo and Missy. They're all buzzing from the drama, but I'm sitting still, poised, even, quietly processing everything.

'You know, Dom,' I twist in my seat and aim at him, 'you were completely right.'

He stops and smiles, 'Of course I was,' he says confidently, then he raises an eyebrow. 'When? About what?'

'The more I think, the more I remember how our relationship actually was. I think I was in a state of denial the whole time, you know?' All three sets of eyes are on me, so I continue in my revelation. 'If I'm honest, there were so many moments.'

'Like what?' Hugo asks.

'Well, one minute, he would say all the right things, make me feel like the most important person on the planet, and then the next, drop me like that,' I click my fingers, 'or let me down at the last moment, when something didn't suit him; I always felt it was my fault.'

'When really, he was just in love with another woman,' Sarah chips in.

'Thanks for the reminder.' I smile; I'm not mad at her. 'You know, I remember he went away for a weekend one time, without telling me. He didn't answer his phone, he didn't reply to my texts, then he walked through the door nonchalantly and said he had told me he was going on a lads weekend and I never listened. I always listened! *He* never told me. But, I always felt I couldn't say that.'

'Why not?' Dom asks, now walking towards me, and taking the adjacent seat outside.

'I didn't want to be a nagging, controlling girlfriend, so I pretended that I was OK with it. He was supposed to be my partner; you're meant to compromise and accept them for who they are, not try to change them. I guess I was trying to embrace that.'

'Yeah,' Dom considers his words, 'compromise is one thing, but suppressing your thoughts below the surface, and burying how you feel, is another; it's not healthy, you know?'

'Well, you know what I feel?' Sarah comes out on the balcony too, waving Hugo to join us, 'I feel so much love for you guys!' She pulls Dom and I out of our seats, then as Hugo comes to her side; she envelops us all into one big group hug. 'You are all fabulous and I wouldn't have wanted to be on this adventure with anybody else.'

'You been drinking?' Hugo says, his face inches from hers.

'Just a little gin and tonic from the mini bar.' She grins.

'Sounds good!' I say, moving inside. 'Let's all have one; I'll make them.' The three of them stay on the balcony enjoying the view as I get out two tumblers and two wine glasses, and then dive into the mini bar that has been helpfully restocked.

There's a knock at the door and everyone turns and goes to answer it. 'I'll get it,' I hold my hands up to stop them, walk over to the door, and when I open it, Leo's on the other side. I hear the curtains behind me draw swiftly, and turn to see Sarah's little cheeky face poking out before closing them completely; I don't think Leo has noticed.

'She's gone.' He stands there, numb.

'What do you mean she's gone? Who's gone? Missy?' I frown at him.

He wanders in, slowly. 'She hasn't left a note; she's not answering her phone; what the hell do I do?' I'm silent, but can feel my lips twitching. 'What are you smirking at?!'

'Well,' I shut the door, 'I kind of want to say, karma has come back to bite you in arse.'

He looks desperately at me, 'It has, hasn't it?!' He walks further into the room, and collapses on my bed, facing the ceiling.

I eye the curtains that are blowing ever so slightly in the wind. 'Why are you here, Leo? Why don't you ask your friend to help you; I can't help you,' I say strongly, with folded arms.

He puts his hands over his face, 'I can't, it's just too embarrassing, facing him, and saying she's left me.'

'*A huh,*' I respond dryly. He separates his fingers to look at me, but keeps his hands where they are.

'Sorry,' he mumbles.

I sigh and sit on the bed next to him. 'Look, is her stuff still in your room?'

'Well, yes, but...' he sits up on his elbows, but his body is still reclined.

'Then she's probably just marched herself off to cool down. Leo, you just told the woman you're about to marry, a pretty big secret. She'll just be off somewhere, processing it all.' I take a deep breath and then find myself saying, 'She loves you; she's not going anywhere.'

'How do you know?' His face glares sadly at mine.

I shrug, 'She's a woman in love. Not only did she tell me that, I could see it. I recognise it.'

'Am I the worst person on the planet?' He looks at me with sorrow.

I nod, 'Probably.' Then I take Leo in, and I can't believe I feel a little sorry for him. 'But you're human. Humans aren't perfect; we're all far from perfect.'

We sit in silence. And I glance at the drawn curtains again, wondering what they're playing at, pretending not to be here.

'Do you want a gin?' I decide to ask.

'Always,' is his reply, still in his elbow-reclined position. 'I like it with a slice of—'

'Lime, I know; I remember.'

'Of course you do,' he says kindly. 'You always remembered little details like that.'

I reach for a mug, 'I think it's the little things that matter, at the end of the day.' I pick out a lime from the welcome fruit basket, cut five slices and after placing the first in Leo's mug, put one each into my array of glassware. 'Well, this was a touch we didn't have,' I say, gesturing to the basket, before dividing the contents of a couple of small Gordon's bottles five ways.

'I know; it's a Missy thing.' I turn from my cocktail making, and Leo's face is contorted in pain. Turning back I divide a few bottles of tonic into each, then pick up a glass for me and the mug for him, before walking back over to the bed. ‘Look, you want my honest opinion?’ He nods as I hand him the drink. After taking a sip, he holds the mug in his left hand, rolls onto his right side, leaning up with his right elbow, balancing the drink on his left side.

Again, I put my ego to one side, ‘Let me ask you this: do you love her?’

‘Of course.’

‘And do you want to spend the rest of your life with her?’ I continue, in spite of the dull ache in the pit of my stomach.

‘I do,’ he says with every confidence I wish he had a year ago, with me; what I wouldn’t have done to have heard those words then.

‘Then, there’s nothing else for it. Find her, apologise profusely, and spend the rest of your life making her happy. That’s it. All a woman wants is to feel wanted, needed, and loved; the rest is noise. We want to believe that our partner cares about us so deeply that nothing and no one can come between us, knowing that you can face the world together, through whatever comes onto the path.’ I take in my old love, ‘And you know what, I don’t think we had that in us. You aren’t right for me. You’re completely wrong for me, actually, and I’m completely wrong for you! You hate travelling for one thing!’

‘I do,’ he nods, ‘After a long day working, I just want to sit at home and watch the TV with a—’

‘G and T in your hand; I know. But, me? I want to explore! I want to grow, I want to learn and be immersed in cultures and language and sunshine!’ Suddenly, I can feel myself sparkling from the inside. ‘This is fantastic!’

‘Excuse me? There is nothing about this that is fantastic; my bride is missing,’ he frowns at me.

'Sorry, yes of course, but, what I mean is, I've spent a year obsessing over what it was *I* did wrong to make you leave me, and what was wrong with *me*, but you're just not the right person for me. That's it.' I beam from ear to ear. 'I don't love you, Leo.'

'Charming.'

'No, I mean, we loved a version of each other, but not the true one. You suppressed,' I pause to correct myself, 'no, *I* suppressed *myself* into this person who, quite frankly, isn't even a percentage of who I really am.'

'Yeah!'

'*Whoo*!'

'Couldn't have said that better!'

My colleagues emerge from their hiding place, clapping, cheering and all talking at the same time. I burst out laughing, but Leo has jumped out of his skin, and onto the floor, and is now covered in gin.

'That's my girl!' Sarah puts her arm around me.

'Beautiful!' Hugo is still clapping with gusto.

'What the hell?' Leo says clutching his chest, the gin-filled mug, now empty and lying at his side.

'Nothing like a dramatic entrance. Here,' Dom says, handing Leo a towel from the bathroom. Taking it, Leo pats himself down and looks at us all.

'What is it with you and surprise bedroom guests?' Leo looks at me.

I shrug, 'What can I say? I'm surrounded by love!' I hold out my hand for Leo to grab, 'Come on; let's go find your bride.'

***

'Alright, so let's see, where have you looked?' I ask as we board the air-conditioned tram, and take a seat.

'*Erm*, well, I just rang her and messaged, I didn't actually look around the resort.' He's sheepish now.

'Really? Way to put in an effort, dude! This resort is huge! She could be anywhere, and she's clearly hiding from you. Alright, think: where would you least expect her to be?'

He thinks for a moment, 'Out of the sun; she loves sunbathing, so somewhere shady?'

'Well, the sun's already down, so I don't see how that will help, but we've got nothing else to go on.' I think for a moment. 'OK, the lobby's too obvious; she's not in your room; maybe a restaurant? Sarah and Hugo, why don't you start at the Italian, and then work your way round from there?'

'OK!' Sarah stands and they exit the train at the next stop.

'Alright, where should we look? The spa?' I suggest.

'No, I don't think so,' Leo shakes his head. 'She'll want to be alone, and not have to talk to members of staff.'

'*Ooh*, I know, what about the jacuzzis in the caves?' Dom pipes up excitedly.

Leo shrugs, 'Let's try it.'

We get off at the main entrance near the lobby, walk up and then back down the grand steps, that lead you through the open, columned space, where the ceremony is due to take place tomorrow, then make our way round the lagoon, and into the first cave, where you can see the backside of a waterfall.

Following the path, we weave around now, out of that cave, along a tiki torched lined path, and then up some more stone steps, and over one of the suspension bridges, above a swimming pool. Winding down the next set of steps, and over to a path, with very little light, Dom, who's leading the way, suddenly stops. 'Oh, wow!'

'What? What is it? Do you see her?' Leo says, still on the bridge, looking around, but I notice Dom's gaze is up.

'No, sorry. It's just, wow.'

I join Dom, gazing up at the velvety black sky that's glittered with millions of stars; they look like tiny diamonds. 'I told you!'

'I don't think I've ever seen that many stars. To quote Hugh Grant, "Is that right?"'

'What are you talking about?' I smile, looking up at him, and he turns his face to mine.

'You know, from his film with Sarah Jessica Parker where they're in witness protection and they go out of their cabin in the middle of nowhere and see a sky full of stars. What was it? *Have You Met The Millers*?'

I giggle, 'I think you mean, *Did You Hear About The Morgans*?'

'Oh yeah, that's the one.'

'Yes, yes, the stars are lovely!' Leo says impatiently from my other side. 'Can we please keep looking?'

I snigger, 'Yes, of course. Let's go.' I enjoy the glint in Dom's eye as we head towards the caves, with a covered pool and several hot tubs. My ears are filled with the powerful sound of the waterfall. Scanning the cave with my eyes, I can't spot her but I enjoy the floodlights, creating a mystical, warm blue glow everywhere. We continue around, and sure enough, there she is, alone in a hot tub, in the furthest corner of the cave.

'Missy!' Leo calls over the noise of the cascading of the

falls around us. She looks up, spots us, and folds her arms, turning away.

'Well, what are you waiting for? Go in and get her!' I shout at him, over the soundtrack of water.

'You have to jump in the pool to get there; I'm not wearing swim shorts.'

I point to his shorts, 'Then take those off and swim over there in your pants.'

'I'm not wearing any,' he says embarrassed.

'Oh, for God's sake.' I walk to the side and kick off my flip flops, and remove my sundress to reveal my green and pink, flower Ted Baker bikini. I can feel the eyes of both Dom and Leo on me.

'You didn't have that when we were together.'

'I didn't have *myself* together, when we were together.' I smile at Dom, who I can't help but notice isn't looking at my eyes. I dive in and smile to myself as I swim over to the runaway bride. 'Hi!' I say, as I reach the hot tub, 'Can I join you?'

'*You* absolutely can, but the idiot over there needs to stay clear.'

I sink my body into the warm foamy water, and take a seat, 'He's not wearing any underwear otherwise he would have swum over.'

'*Ugh*, he's so gross. Why am I with him again?'

I play with the bubbles while answering, 'Because you love him. Because you're childhood sweethearts. Because you're in this beautiful place.'

'That was *your* beautiful place,' she fires at me.

I shake my head. 'It was never my place. You know, he said he was trying to rewrite a memory by marrying me here?'

'Is that so?' she says, unconvinced.

'Yeah. But the thing is, he couldn't. He couldn't marry me, because he's always been in love with you. Why he chose not to tell you about me, I have no idea, and it's not my place. In fact, this is rather bizarre, having to convince another woman to marry my ex.' I adjust myself to sit cross-legged in my seat.

'I'm sorry,' she looks at me and sighs. 'God, he's an idiot.'

'I agree.' I look up and you can see a couple of stars, from a tiny gap in the caves over our heads. A small smile forms on my face and I have to concentrate on making my face neutral; I don't think Missy has noticed.

'You know, I felt so smug coming here,' Missy confesses, 'I was like, "I finally get my happily ever after." Sure, it hurt that our families said they wouldn't come, but, now?' She puts her head in her hands, 'I'm just so embarrassed. They must all think I'm a right moron; a naïve, little girl.'

'Can I tell you something?' I say, untying and retying my messy bun.

She nods, wiping her brow and smoothing back her hair that's in a plait.

'I think you bring out the true Leo.'

She shakes her head, 'What does that mean?'

'Well, I think you make him brave. He never stood up to his mum when I was around.'

'Weren't you listening before? He never stood up to her when we were together either.'

'No? Then why did he fly to Hawaii to marry you, without his family? He chose you. He told me: it's always been you. I just didn't know that when I was with him.' I can see she's starting to soften, so I continue. 'Look, you're going to do what you feel is right for you, and I completely respect and understand that. But, I think you know what you want, deep down in your heart; we always know if we let ourselves be truly honest.' I decide to test this. 'What does your gut say right now?'

'That I'd like to punch him,' she says without hesitation.

I laugh. 'Good. Good. Anything else?'

'That,' she shifts so her feet are on her seat, and she can lean her elbows on her knees, with her face in her palms, 'that it took a lot for him to stand up to his mum.'

'OK! There we go. Anything else?'

'I've never wanted to be with anybody else.'

'*Um hmm*,' I gestured for her to carry on.

'I'm probably going to forgive him. But, God, I'm mad at him.' She makes a face and smacks the water with her palms.

'And you're allowed to be! I've been mad at him for a year!'

'But you've got Dom, right? So, everything turned out OK for you, no lying.'

'Actually, we're not really together.'

'Really?'

'Yeah, we made that up to throw Leo off his balance.'

'Well, it worked; you two were very convincing,' she raises her eyebrows, then shakes her head again. 'I can't get over the fact that he felt the need to hide such a big secret from me. Does he not trust me? Did he think I couldn't handle it? Why did he feel he couldn't talk to me?'

'Why don't you ask him?'

We both turn to look at him and Dom, who are watching us.

'I will. But I'm going to let him stew for a while.' She

settles in her seat, with her back to Leo.

‘Good plan,’ I agree, taking in Leo’s worried expression and guiltily enjoying every second of this. I watch as Dom is gesturing to Leo. Missy, noticing where my gaze is, turns again to face them.

‘I wonder what he’s saying?’

‘I think he’s trying to tell him to get in, and come and get you,’ I say.

We watch as they comically gesticulate at each other. Then Leo pushes Dom; Dom pushes back; Leo pushes even harder and then there’s a grand splash, as Dom, with one more almighty shove, pushes Leo in the pool.

Dom looks at us both grinning and gives us a thumbs up, and we both burst out laughing.

Missy catches her breath, ‘You sure you’re not a couple?’ she asks me, right at the moment Leo’s face appears.

‘I’ll leave you two to talk things through.’ I stand to climb out, and Leo grabs my hand.

‘Thank you, Liv.’

I nod and smile, and we take each other in.

‘Thank *you*, Leo.’

‘For what?’

‘For letting me be free.’

‘I think you just set yourself free.’

‘We both did.’

Chapter 17

USA – Canada
Kona – Vancouver – Victoria – Tofino

Wednesday
After wedding ceremony, depart Kona Airport at 23:50

Thursday
Arrive Vancouver International Airport at 07:40
Duration: 5 hours and 40 minutes (2-hour 50-minute layover)
Time change: Vancouver 3 hours ahead

Depart Vancouver Airport at 10:30
Arrive Victoria Airport at 11:04
Duration: 34 minutes
Drive 5 hours: Victoria - Tofino (3 nights stay)

Couple H
MacKenzie Beach, Tofino, Canada

Watching the man you've dreamt about marrying, marry the person he was ultimately meant to be with, has a kind of poetic ending; don't you think? And of all the emotions I thought I'd experience throughout this trip, closure wasn't one of them. I smile, take a deep breath, close my eyes, enjoy the smell of pine trees, and the feeling of wind in my hair from my open window, as we weave along the winding road to Tofino, on Vancouver island.

'Man, it's beautiful here,' Dom says from the driver's seat.

'I know; I love these trees,' I say wistfully. 'They make me smile.' I take in row upon row of green lusciousness.

'It reminds me of Sequoia National Park; have you been there?' He glances over to me in the passenger seat.

'No, it's on my list though,' I say and return to my blissful position of enjoying the now.

'Oh, it's amazing. Although, I have to say, the weather here is not exactly the same as California! Would you mind closing your window?' he shivers.

'Not at all.' I smile and press the button to whizz it back up.

'Well, I for one, am grateful we're in a cooler, slightly moody climate, after all that heat,' Sarah pipes up from Hugo's lap where she's been for the whole five-hour car journey. 'When we landed in Vancouver this morning, it was like I could finally breathe, you know?'

'You realise you live in LA right?' I say, twisting around in my seat.

'Yes, and I'm *from* New York; what's your point?'

I shrug, smiling, 'Well, LA's warm. But,' I consider this too, 'I guess it's a different type of air; a different atmosphere.'

'Exactly,' she says, pointing at me from her horizontal position. 'I spend most of my time inside, with crisp air-conditioning.'

I wiggle back, to face forwards. 'I think I love all types of heat,' I say, thinking out loud more than anything. Smiling, I tap my feet happily to the music on the radio. 'I like this song; who is it?'

'Sarah Bareilles. It's called, "Brave."' Dom glances at me once more, and my stomach flips as something passes between us. *Man, he's got beautiful eyes.* I smile awkwardly at him, then clear my throat.

'Right. *Um.* Well, anyway, the weather right now, kind of reminds me of Monterrey.'

'I love Monterrey!' Dom says. 'When were you there?'

I think for a minute, trying to let the butterflies in my stomach settle, 'Last year in October.'

'Nice! Yeah, weather-wise, it can be like this, say, from like, September through to December in Monterrey,' Dom says from my left. 'I love Carmel too; have you been there?' I shake my head. 'Oh, we should totally go! There are all these amazing galleries everywhere; it's got such a creative vibe,' Dom says, as we weave around another corner of road-lined pines.

'Is there time when we get to California?' I ask, knowing the answer.

'Not really.' He pulls his bottom lip out into a pout. 'Well, I'll just have to take you another time.' He grins, but I smile sadly, knowing that'll never happen.

'Oh, this is it!' I sit up, spotting the sign for "Ocean Village," while simultaneously distracting myself from my thoughts. There are little pod-like, glamping huts everywhere, from the edge of the beach, extending right back, into the trees. We park up and I'm the first to exit the car.

'Oh, yeah! This is more my temperature.' Sarah gets out and stretches.

'I have to admit, it is kind of nice after all the humidity,'

Hugo says, but I'm sure he's just agreeing with her; he loved the heat in Dubai.

It's a pleasant temperature, but definitely cooler; I pull on my light jumper over my vest top.

Looking around, no one is in a rush, no one is panicking, and there are no obvious dramas. There are a couple of families on the beach, laughing and watching their toddlers play in the sand, and a couple of surfers, riding a wave. It's romantically rustic here; I feel like we've stumbled upon a beautiful secret, only a few people know about. A wash of relaxation flows over me, but I can't quite explain why.

'Penny for your thoughts?' Dom appears at my side with his token backpack camera bag he's been carrying all trip.

'I feel...inexplicably relaxed; I don't know why.'

'You don't know why?' He tilts his head at me, and I shake my head. 'You've finally got closure. You can move on with the next chapter of your life, that's...' he looks sad all of a sudden, '...amazing.'

I furrow my brow, 'Your face doesn't match your words. What's wrong?'

He shakes his head, 'You're lucky to have closure, that's all.' He brushes me off. 'Shall we meet the next happy couple! No dramas here, I hope!' He winks at me.

'I've only got one ex-fiancé, so we should be good.' I give him a playful nudge and we make our way to reception to check-in.

***

We're all sharing a pod which is split level, and comprises of two little apartments: Sarah and I upstairs, and Dom and Hugo downstairs. Inside, they've got a cute and cosy cabin feel, and ours has a balcony, that I can sit on and enjoy the ocean. Oh, and work, yes; I have work to do. With all the drama in Hawaii, I haven't written about the last few weddings properly.

'So, there's a welcome dinner, right?' Hugo says after helping me and Sarah up the stairs with our luggage.

'Yeah, at six,' I say, opening my handbag to get my laptop.

'Shall we all go for a little stroll along the beach, after Dom's finished talking to the bride and groom? Think I could do with the fresh air,' Sarah says, still looking car-sick-white.

Shaking my head I gesture at the laptop, 'You go ahead, I'll embrace the free time to settle in and remember why I'm here! I'm three weddings behind.'

'Fine! As I've said before, all work, no play!' Sarah teases.

'Really, it's been all play, no work!' I make a face. 'You guys go ahead,' I repeat, and they head off. Making myself a cup of complimentary herbal tea, to take out with me, I then choose a seat on the balcony, place my mug down, and hug my laptop for a few seconds, smiling at the waves; God, I love the ocean. We're one row back from the front, but everything is on a slight incline, so the pods in front don't block our view. It is uninterrupted, unfiltered beauty, and I love it.

After about an hour and half, I feel I've got a good grasp on each of the last three weddings. I'd love to look at Dom's photos of India and Thailand, though. The sheer beauty of colour and culture was breathtaking. As if on cue, he appears below me.

'How's the writing coming?' he says, from the ground,

like Romeo gazing upon Juliet, but with a beer in his hand.

'Great.' I put my open laptop on the chair next to me, 'I'd love to look at your photos at some point, in case I've missed anything.' A little white lie, as I know I haven't.

'Consider it done, my lady!' He sways slightly as I stand up and lean on the balcony, looking down at him.

'Are you drunk?' I smirk.

'Nope.' He grins.

'High?' I venture, and then he answers in a stage whisper,

'Best wedding so far!' And mimics smoking a *joint* at me. I can't help but laugh out loud. 'Come on down; you can try some.'

'I'll freshen up and be right down.' In truth, I've never touched the stuff; I've never done drugs of any description.

He points to the ground, 'I'll wait here. It's so beautiful, man!' He gazes off into space.

Bending down, I click "ctrl s" then shut my laptop, and bring it inside, along with my mug. The night is starting to draw closer, as we near sunset, and despite being absolutely beautiful, it's a little chilly with the cool ocean breeze. After using the bathroom, I grab my chequered wrap and sunglasses, and I'm good to go. Walking down the wooden steps, and placing my sunglasses on, I acknowledge I have butterflies. *Where the hell did they come from?* I walk around our building and when I see Dom, he's staring at a tree and giggling to himself.

'Having fun?' I wrap my makeshift blanket around me.

'I am.' He smiles at me, as if in slow motion, and strokes my wrap. 'That looks cosy.' He opens it and envelops the two of us in there, like it's our very own cocoon. 'There. Perfect.' His face inches from mine.

'You know we're not in Hawaii anymore; you don't have

to pretend to be my boyfriend now.' He's got a couple of freckles on his nose that I've never noticed.

'Who's pretending to be anything? I am a man enjoying a warm snuggle, from my very good lady friend: Olivia The Brave!'

'Alright then, *Cheech.*' I put my left arm around his waist, and he twists round, so his right arm is draped over both of my shoulders and we walk to the beach, with the wrap still around the two of us. 'Let's join the party.'

'The party,' he points at me, with his left hand 'is wherever we are; we're the cool ones on this trip, you know that? I like Sarah,' he nods, 'but I've got to say,' he faces me again but our noses almost touch this time, 'her makeup scares me a little.'

'Is that so?' I smirk.

'Yup.' He faces the direction of the beach now, as we get closer to the party, 'I think someone like you has it sussed.'

'Oh, yeah? And what do I have sussed exactly?' I play along.

'Your natural beauty,' he shrugs, 'You look great with or without makeup. Like I said: got it sussed.' He smiles at me like a cheeky fifteen year old. I don't know what to say to that, so I just smile. 'You're awesome.' He suddenly leans his head on mine and gives my right arm a squeeze and inhales deeply, 'And you smell so good, like, a piña colada.'

I burst out laughing, 'I smell nothing like rum.'

'No, not rum,' he takes another sniff, 'you're all, coconutty.'

I subconsciously reach my free right hand to my head, 'Oh, must be my shampoo.' He buries his nose in my curls. 'I'm loving the compliments, but not gonna lie, that's a little weird, Dom.'

'I know.' He straightens his head again, 'I haven't smoked *weed* in a long time; I think my senses are on overload, and it's good!'

'You're such a goofball,' I laugh.

'I *am* a goofball!' He declares as we continue our intimate stroll. 'I've forgotten how to be a goofball. I like being a goofball. *Goofball*. Isn't that a good word?'

I laugh, 'So, *goofball*. I read about this beach near here that has some pretty cool starfish. We're not needed in the morning; do you fancy coming with me to check them out?'

'I would like that,' he nods. 'It's a date.'

I furrow my brow, awkwardly, 'Really?'

He squeezes my shoulder, 'Well, no, not a *date*, date. You know a...' he looks around as if that's where he'll find the rest of his words.

'You have no idea how to finish that sentence do you?'

'Nope,' he says laughing. We reach the party, still tangled as though we're in a three-legged race. 'Let me introduce you to the groom; he's awesome.'

'Does that mean he gave you the *weed*?' I ask quietly.

'It does.'

The groom is tall and handsome, and just as *baked* as Dom.

'So, here's the busy little bee! Hi, I'm Devon, welcome to our wild wedding!' He moves his plaid-clad arms out to the side, like he's welcoming an old friend.

I love how relaxed Canadians sound all the time, never mind, *high* Canadians; it's so soothing to listen to.

'Thank you so much; we're really excited to be here.' I extend my hand from the blanket, but Dom's arm remains over my shoulders. Devon takes my hand and uses it to pull me, and Dom into a big hug. 'Oh, OK,' I say in our awkward three-way sandwich. I seem to be the only one who's a little uncomfortable though. Devon finally lets go and stands tall.

'Do you smoke, Liv?' he asks me. While adjusting his Toronto Blue Jays baseball cap slightly.

I shake my head, 'I don't, but thank you.'

'No worries, *eh*. Come over here, and meet my beautiful bride-to-be.' He leads the way around several wedding-goers, all laughing in small groups along the beach, who don't seem to have a care in the world.

'Everyone's so relaxed!' I can't help but say it out loud.

'Yeah! Why wouldn't we be?' The groom smiles at me.

'Well, let's just say you're the first wedding to not have any drama.' I raise my eyebrows to my cocoon partner who gives me a goofy grin in return.

Devon reaches a beautiful redhead. He slips his arm around her waist and kisses her on the cheek, 'No need for drama when you've got love.'

She wraps her arms around his neck, kisses him on the lips then turns to me, 'Hey! You must be Liv; I'm Zoey! Welcome to our little wedding!' She comes over and gives me a big, warm, hug, like we've known each other forever, but since Dom hasn't moved, it's another three-way snuggle. 'You are so welcome here!' She stands back, one hand on my arm, the other on Dom's, but her eyes are on my wild mane, 'I love your hair.'

'Thanks, I'll need to tie it up in a bit, otherwise it just gets bigger and bigger in the ocean air.'

She waves her hand, 'No, let it be; let it flow, man. It's beautiful! Always be wild and free, man. Wild and free.' She nods slowly, as if to answer a voice I can't hear.

Is everyone high here? I feel like I need to catch up somehow.

'You don't have a drink!' Zoey looks at my empty hands, reading my mind. 'Let me get you one.' The bride turns casually away before I've even answered her.

'So, how are all the preparations going?' I ask Devon.

'Groovy. Chilled day tomorrow. Chilled wedding day, the day after. There might be rain, there might not be. We're easy, man.' He pauses to sip his bottle of beer.

'Do you have a backup plan for the ceremony if it does rain?' I ask.

'We get wet.' The bride returns with a beer for me, smiling away.

'Rain is nature's tears of joy; we will dance, we will sing and hear her call.' Devon sways and grabs Zoey and they have a little spontaneous dance moment; I try to hold in a snigger.

'Tell me, are you spiritual Liv?' Zoey steps closer to me, still dancing, waving her arms in my direction in a free movement dance.

'*Erm*, I love a bit of yoga?' I shrug. 'Admittedly I haven't done very much in a while, but I know I always feel balanced after.'

'Right on!' She nods at me, still mid-flow with her arm wafting. 'We're going to have a morning class tomorrow, if you'd like to join us? Around ten?'

'Absolutely! I'd love to; thanks.'

'Yeah!' She grins. 'Now, go and help yourselves to food, guys! We're serving over there in a few minutes!'

***

The food is all vegan, and I've never tasted anything so delicious.

'Everything we're eating is all ethical, sustainable, and locally sourced. And this is all recycled packaging and cutlery. We just really want to do our bit to save the planet, you know? Nothing is ever enough, but something is always better than nothing,' Zoey grins; she's so chilled, she's almost horizontal.

We're all sitting around little campfires and fire pits along the beach, and I can't help but wonder when the guitar is going to come out. *Ooh, there it is.*

The best man comes over, sits cross-legged on the sand, and starts strumming away, to no one in particular, but I can see it's catching Sarah's eye. Hugo pines after Sarah, rather disgruntledly.

'I've always wanted to play,' Sarah says, stroking the bottom of the wood — of the guitar.

'You can, man! Everything I'm playing right now, I taught myself,' he says to her while he continues to strum.

'Wow,' she gorps at him. I can't help but roll my eyes, as I play with the Graham cracker in my hand.

'I saw that,' Dom stage whispers at me, returning with two more beers.

For the last few hours, he hasn't left our cocoon, and I've got to say, I kind of love it. I welcome him back in and he snuggles into the sand.

'I know, since becoming a vegetarian, I do miss marshmallows; who knew you could get vegan ones?' I lay down the cracker on the plate in front of us, place a little vegan chocolate on it, and pop another marshmallow on a stick, and aim it at the fire.

'I think you might be the queen of changing the subject!' He pops the rest of his prepared marshmallow sandwich from the plate in front of us, into his mouth, before talking with his mouth full. 'So, tell me,' he muffles, then munches quickly, but it takes longer than anticipated, and he puts a finger up to me as if to say, "one sec."

'What's that?' I laugh loudly at him as he tries to chew faster and faster with puffed out cheeks, but his mouthful doesn't seem to go away. I twirl my marshmallow then place it on the chocolate. He's chewing rapidly but nothing seems to be happening. I laugh and lick my fingers. 'You're like a little squirrel.' I continue to laugh at him and all he can do is narrow his eyes at me, while chewing.

Finally, he swallows, and then continues, 'Bloody, hell that was hard work. Anyway, as I was going to say,' he softens his voice, so he can't be heard over the crackling of the fire. 'Why aren't you impressed with that?' he nudges his head towards the guitar duo.

I keep my eyes on Sarah, who's now holding the guitar, and the best man has his arms around her, placing her fingers in the correct place. 'I don't know, it just seems a little...fake, that's all.'

'What would impress you then?'

I turn to him, watching the flames dance in his eyes. 'Well, let's see.' I think for a moment. 'I've absolutely no idea.'

He patiently looks at me, 'Humour me.'

I place a second Graham cracker on top of my marshmallow, to complete my s'more, 'Well. My idea of what I wanted was all askew, so, I guess, *erm*,' I take a deep breath, and decide to be vulnerable. 'I would be impressed by someone who is actually kind, honest, loving, supportive, loves adventure, and is creative or artistic.'

Pausing, I realise he's looking at me intently and suddenly I will him to kiss me, but we just continue to gaze at each other. The butterflies from earlier have returned to flutter around my stomach. His eyes move to my lips for a moment and then back to my eyes. He sweeps a lone strand of my hair away, and we continue to stare. *I'm not going to lean in*; I need to know he wants to kiss me too. We inch closer. God, I'm tingling. I blink and then before I'm ready, he cradles my face, brushing my cheek gently with his thumb, and suddenly his lips are pressed against mine. They're as soft as they look and have the delicious taste of vanilla. I let my body relax into it and feel nervous energy rise from my toes to the top of my head. *Wow.* I've never been kissed like this before.

It could be moments or hours, but too soon he pulls away, still cradling my face. I look at him and for a moment, neither of us say anything.

'I'm sorry,' he says softly.

I smile, 'What are you sorry for? That was…'

'Inappropriate,' he inaccurately finishes my sentence, and drops his hand away. Suddenly, he's standing up and walking away.

'Where are you going?' I call after him.

'I'm sorry,' is all he replies, before walking into the darkness.

Chapter 18

Canada
Tofino

Friday

Even after his behaviour, I still knocked for Dom to come and see the starfish with me, at Chesterman Beach. But there was no answer, not even from Hugo. Sarah didn't come back last night, so I couldn't ask her to come with me, either. Not a single one of them is answering their phones, so here I am, pulling up to the beach, by myself. I walk onto the sand. It's not quite warm enough to go barefoot, but I do anyway. I love the feel of sand on my feet. The grey sky matches my mood as I walk along, enjoying the cool ocean breeze in my face.

What the hell is up with Dom? We've been getting along so well! I know it's not me. I suddenly smile at myself. *Wow. I know it's not me!* I'm proud of how far I've come.

I take in the expansive beach. The tide is out, which is perfect for starfish spotting. I've chosen a boho head scarf this morning that allows my messy bun to protrude out the top, little strands blowing gently in the wind. I listen to the crash of the waves as I get closer to the rocks. *Oh wow!* Sure enough, there are dozens of colourful starfish. Moving closer, I crouch down to get an even better look. Gosh, these are amazing! Shame Dom had to miss this. I whip out my phone, take a picture of a particularly awesome bunch of pink, yellow and blue ones, and send it to Dom in a WhatsApp message.

After a beat, the two little blue ticks appear, so I can see he's read it, and is typing something back. I wait, staring at my phone like a teenager, breathless for his response; it now just says he's online. *He doesn't know what to type*. Then the word "typing" materialises again, and I feel my heart skip a beat. I wait once more, eyes glued to the screen, then it returns to say he's online, then "last seen at 9.05am."

Humph. I tuck my phone back in my bag and decide to forget about him, and whatever his problem is. This is truly magical, and I'll be damned if I'm going to let my head ruin this beautiful moment. I've let go of some major demons in my life, I don't need to create new ones. I know that I don't need a man to feel complete, I have everything I need, right here, right now; I try to tell myself, a little unconvincingly.

Losing track of time, I enjoy sitting by myself, taking in the view, when I spot a figure approaching me at a jog. What a lovely idea to jog on the beach. *Ooh, what time is yoga?* I check my phone for the time then a voice makes me look up.

'All by yourself?'

I look at Hugo as I return my phone to my bag. 'Didn't have you down as a jogging man.'

'I needed to let off some steam,' he shakes his head, and comes to join me on the rocks. 'I did the bomber plane trail this morning.'

'Oh, neat! I read about that. It takes you to the World War Two plane crash, right?'

'Yeah.' He's not smiling.

'You didn't enjoy it?'

'I was supposed to go with Sarah, but she is *otherwise engaged.* What the hell is she playing at?' He looks at me with sad eyes and I put a supportive arm around him.

'I have no idea.'

'No,' he says firmly, '*She* has no idea! How much clearer do I need to make it that I'm crazy about her? Turns out I'm just crazy. I'm done, Liv. She doesn't see me that way, and never will.'

'Now, what kind of attitude is that?'

'A realistic one?' he shrugs. 'I hate this. I'm done playing games, you know? I just want to grab her and tell her.'

'What's stopping you? Any girl would love that.'

He shakes his head, 'No, not her. I missed my chance; I'm in the friend-zone. She'll never see me as more than that, ever.'

'You, however,' he smugly smiles at me. 'Now that was one hell of a kiss last night!'

I put my hands to my face, 'You saw that?'

'I did,' he nods. 'Man, that was a kiss! So, that's why I'm a little surprised to see *you* here. Dom didn't come back last night, so I kind of assumed…'

'What? No! Did you miss the part where he stood up and walked into the darkness, leaving me in the sand without an explanation?'

His eyes widen, 'I guess I did. I couldn't take it. You guys were kissing, and Sarah was shimmying up to Mr. "I taught myself to play the guitar, look how smooth I am." I just went to bed.'

'Wait a minute. Dom didn't come back? Where the hell did he go?'

He shrugs, 'Beats me.' He sighs. 'Oh, we're a bloody mess, aren't we?'

'I don't know, maybe it's for the best? I've just got closure with Leo, the last thing I need to do is fall *heart* first into another relationship. And plus, I'm leaving after the next wedding; what am I thinking? A long-distance thing? That's never going to work! No. I'll just put it down to a misplaced amount of affection for a friend who's looked after me, and made me laugh, sees me for who I am, and loves adventure just as much as I do, and...' I let my voice trail off, and blink away some tears. 'Fancy a yoga class with me?'

***

We park outside our little pod, then walk to the beach. I take some deep breaths as we head towards Zoey, and a couple of friends and family, already gathering for the morning yoga. As we get nearer, I see Dom is with them. My heart jumps into my throat.

'Maybe I'll skip it,' I say, going to turn away but Hugo grabs my hand.

'No! You were just telling me in the car how much you were looking forward to it. Come on, you're going to see him at some point; may as well be now!'

I make a face. 'Fine.'

When Hugo and I reach the sand, the bride smiles and waves, 'Morning, guys! You're just in time! Grab a towel, we're just about to start.'

Dom turns his head and sees us both. His face flushes pink, and it has nothing to do with the cool ocean breeze.

'Guys, let's make some space for them in the back row there, so they can go next to Dom.'

'Oh, no!' I find myself yelling over the waves. 'Not

necessary at all, we'll just join in from over here.'

'Nonsense!' Zoey says, casually, 'It's no trouble!'

Her friends obediently make room and wave us over. I nod in pretend gratitude. I take the spot to the left of Dom, but refuse to look at him, despite the feeling of his eyes burning into me.

'*Ooh*, wait up! Have you started yet?' I hear Sarah's voice. I turn to my left and see her running along the beach; she's holding hands with the guitar man, from last night.

'For God's sake,' Hugo mutters under his breath. 'Maybe *I'll* skip it.' He goes to pick up the towel and leave but I grab his arm this time.

'What better time than now, *eh*?' I say in my best Canadian accent. He reciprocates by poking his tongue out at me, and stays put.

'Would you mind?' Sarah and her conquest make their way through the friends, and they move to position themselves right in front of us. 'Hi!' Sarah beams, all post-coital. 'Great day for it, isn't it.' She grins and turns to lay out her towel, oblivious to Hugo's scowling.

'OK, shall we begin?' Zoey says facing us all. 'Let's start in a seated, cross-legged position, and when you're ready, join your hands together at your heart.'

The group takes to the sand and gets comfy. I close my eyes and take a deep breath, but I know it comes out more like a huff.

'We need to talk, Liv,' I hear Dom whisper from next to me.

I keep my eyes shut. 'Forget it,' I whisper back. 'You're sorry, that's that. Let's just do some yoga.'

'And now let's all take a moment to close our eyes, and our mouths…' Zoey says.

Whoops

'...and connect to a little gratitude, or intention you might have for the day,' Zoey speaks from the front.

I take a couple more deep breaths and try to let go of my tension. It's not working. 'You know that was a really shitty thing to do,' I whisper, angrily, still with my eyes shut. I hear an exhale, but he doesn't respond. I peek one eye open, and he's got his eyes closed and is trying to focus on his breath, or trying to find the right words, I'm not sure.

'OK. Let's begin with a little twist, take your right hand, and place on your left knee, move your left hand behind you, and place your fingers down to reach the ground; inhale and lengthen; exhale and twist.'

We all move together and I try to focus on the waves to calm me down, but now that I'm right here next to him, I can feel my anger rising. I twist to my other side, so I'm facing him, and heatedly whisper, 'Who does that? You know what I've just been through.'

He opens his eyes, 'I didn't mean to let it happen,' he whispered loudly. 'You can't say you didn't want it to!'

'And let's swap sides,' Zoey says from the front. Dom turns his head.

'How dare you? You're the one that kissed me, remember?' I whisper loudly.

He turns his head to face me again, 'I believe there were two pairs of lips involved.'

'You guys kissed?' Sarah says from the row in front, 'That's amazing! Why didn't you tell me?'

'Because you were a little busy, weren't you?!' Hugo chips in, in a very angry whisper.

'What the hell's your problem?' Sarah snaps back.

'You're so blind!' he replies.

'What? What the hell is that supposed to mean?'

'Guys! What's happening back there?' Zoey says from the front. 'Shall we focus on our breath?'

'Sorry.'

'Yes, of course.'

'Absolutely.'

'Yup.'

We all chorus together and everyone shushes.

'And now, let's head onto all fours for a little cat-cow, to loosen up the spine,' Zoey says, as everyone transitions.

'Did I loosen up your spine yesterday?' the best man winks at Sarah.

'*Ugh*,' Hugo says out loud.

'And now, when you're ready, head into a downward facing dog. Peddle the feet...' Zoey continues.

'What's up with you?' I bring my head to look forwards, and see Sarah angrily looking through her legs at Hugo. I turn to my left.

'How can you have such little respect for yourself?' Hugo says, facing Sarah, but still in a downward dog, clearly not able to hold his feelings any longer; now was indeed the time.

'Excuse me for having a little fun! Who put a stick up your arse?' Even upside down, Sarah looks angry.

'And now, let's raise the right leg, bring it forwards, and move into warrior one,' Zoey instructs.

'And I suppose after last night, you're an expert on sticks up arses?' Hugo says with spite.

'*Woah*, man, don't talk to my lady like that,' the guitar playing best man decides it's time to get involved.

'Do I need to separate the group back there?' Zoey says and a few people laugh.

'No, no, we're fine!' I answer for everyone.

We're all silent for a moment, and then I can't help it. 'And so what if I did want you to kiss me. You wanted to kiss me, and then you just buggered off!'

'And into warrior two,' Zoey leads. My face is forward, and I can feel his eyes on me.

'Liv. Let's talk about this somewhere else, shall we?' Dom says quietly.

'Sure. I'll talk later. Unless you're going to run away again?' I say turning my head to face him.

'I didn't run away,' he says quietly.

'Oh, so heading off into the darkness is something that you always do after a mind-blowing kiss?'

'Mind-blowing?' Sarah says, turning her head to face us. 'Why didn't you tell me this?'

'You didn't come home last night!' Hugo and I say together.

'Alright!' Sarah says facing the ocean again.

Hugo gathers his towel, 'I can't do this; I'm leaving.'

'And reverse your warrior!' Zoey says, raising her voice slightly, and I watch him go.

We return to silence.

'Mind-blowing?' Dom questions.

I sigh. 'Yeah.' I stick with my choice of word. 'Didn't you think so?'

'And now windmill into a low lunge, transitioning into a plank or half plank, and an upward facing dog,' Zoey flows so gracefully.

'I would. But—'

'But what? What's the problem?'

'And into child's pose,' Zoey says, and we all shift back. I rest my head on my towel.

I hear him sigh, 'I'm embarrassed.'

Turning my head, I see he's facing me, 'More embarrassed than me? You left me sitting alone in the sand, after that magical moment.' My turn to sigh. 'Was it just me?'

'Come on.' He straightens up, and grabs my hand. Taking me away from the group. His beautiful aqua eyes look sadly into mine. 'I'm sorry.' He puts a hand through his messy beach hair, 'It wasn't just you.'

Of all the things I said to Hugo earlier, I'm not sure I mean a single one of them, as he takes both my hands in his. *Please kiss me again. Please.*

'I really loved last night, but,' he pauses, and shrugs, 'I'm just not ready.'

'Not ready for what?' I feel myself soften. 'It was just a kiss.' *A damn powerful one, but just a kiss*, I say in my head.

'For a relationship. I need closure with Heather,' he says, honestly, and simply.

I can't help but feel an enormous rush of affection for him. 'Of everything you could have said, believe me when I say, I truly know what you mean.' I smile at him, albeit a little sadly.

'We haven't got much left of this trip and I don't want to lead you on. I'm not sure I'm ready to fully be there mentally or emotionally, for anyone, right now. Does that make sense? Oh God.' He puts his head in his hands. 'I'm so sorry. I really didn't mean to do that last night.' He reappears and looks pained; torn, even.

He's so different from the ghastly man I met on the plane. We just simply look at each other. *Gosh his eyes are beautiful*. I nod, 'Of course that makes sense. Let's just be friends,' *for the moment*. I finish my sentence in my head, once more.

'Oh really? Thank you.' He's visibly relieved and comes over and gives me a big hug. 'Thank you.' He gently kisses my cheek and I feel him linger there for a moment, making my insides ache.

'Want to finish the yoga class?'

'Absolutely, we only did the one side,' he says, putting his arm around me.

'Well, I'm nothing if not a little unbalanced.'

He chuckles, as we make our way back to the group.

'So what do you think of the starfish?' I pull away from him slightly, and focus on the scenery, instead of wanting to be in his arms.

'I love the galaxy you sent me.'

I scrunch my face up at him, 'I didn't send you any pictures of stars.'

'Yes, you did.'

I pause for a moment, 'A group of starfish is called a galaxy? You're making that up.'

'Honestly! I remember that from a guide at Monterey Aquarium.'

I shake my head, 'Sounds awesome.'

'Oh, I have to take you, sometime.'

'I'm not here forever you know,' I smile at him. *If only we had more time.*

***

'We were friends before, for years, and on a group trip, here,' Zoey shrugs, 'it just happened.' She looks at Devon, adoringly and I scribble away in my notebook. 'I saw him in a different light. I know it's a cliché, but, that's why they're clichés: they're true. There was something about the waves, the moonlight…'

'The hot tub,' Devon interrupts, and they both burst out laughing. I like this couple; they're so relaxed in each other's company, it's inspiring to see. I sit there, peel a satsuma, and watch them just read each other without words. *God damn it.* Just over one man, now I need to get over another. Oh, to be looked at like that. I know that's what I deserve.

The bride turns to me, as I throw the first segment in my mouth. 'It's funny how things don't turn out the way you thought they would. Life has a sense of humour, you know? Like, you're pointing in one direction, and then you're brought to a crossroad; the universe makes it very clear which way you're meant to go.'

'I like that,' I scribble away, as Zoey continues.

'And you can see it in other people so much more easily than within yourself. Take you for example.'

'Me?' I glance up and smile, 'What do you see about me?'

She flicks her eyes over to where Dom is standing, chatting to a wedding guest, then back to me. 'You're soulmates.'

I smile politely, 'With Dom?' Feeling uncomfortable, I scratch my nose, even though it doesn't need itching, 'We've decided to just be friends.'

She cocks her head to one side, like a persistent puppy. 'Oh no. That's not over. The way he kissed you last night. Wow! Talk about a connection!'

'It was like fireworks,' Devon confirms. I feel my cheeks blushing madly.

'Oh, she's all embarrassed,' Zoey beams and places her hand on Devon's, 'Look, we don't want to step on any toes, but just to say, we know love when we see it.'

I almost choke on my satsuma. 'Love?' I scoff. 'Oh, no. *No*. Definitely not. Love?' I look at Dom, laughing away with the guest, and feel my stomach do a flip. 'Oh, good Lord, I'm in love with him.' I quickly fly my hands up to my face, as if I can push the words back in.

Zoey smiles at me, 'Don't worry, we won't say anything!'

'I'm so sorry, this is supposed to be about you,' I clear my throat, 'Right, where were we?'

***

Saturday

Several hours after the most beautiful wedding: simple, unfiltered, and emotional, I take a walk along the beach by myself to clear my head, with a bottle of beer in hand. I love that it was a barefoot wedding, where shoes were optional. I love the way the bride and groom not only talked to each other, but the way they spoke to each other without having to say a single word. I gaze out at the night's sky; it's a little overcast, but a few stars are starting to appear. I stop and breathe. Isn't it crazy how we can forget to do that? I almost feel like I've been holding my breath for an entire year, just waiting for someone to come and take away another part of my happiness. But none of that was real. There wasn't a problem for an entire year; I *held on to a problem* for an entire year. And when we don't acknowledge something, it just festers, like a huge gaping wound, that we put a plaster over and try to pretend isn't there. Seeing Leo, that was my healing; letting go of Leo has left a scar, but it's no longer a wound. It's a part of me, and that's OK, and I feel stronger for it. Am I going to hold on to this Dom attraction and rejection for a year now, too? *No.* I sigh. Definitely not. I'm done putting others before myself; I'm going to take care of myself; I deserve that. Everybody does.

The sound of the party in full swing is a nice accompaniment to the crashing waves. I sit on the sand to take a moment, and hug my arms around my knees. Moving my eyes up, I gaze at the stars once more, and tap my feet along to the drum and bass that's started up, behind me.

'Hey! What are you doing by yourself?' I turn to see Dom dancing his way over to me. He sings as he approaches, 'I'm wishing on a starfish!'

I giggle. 'Those aren't the words. I believe it's: "wishing on a *star.*"'

He shrugs, 'Poetic licence and circumstance,' and he holds his beer up to cheer with mine. The bottles clink happily, and he takes a seat next to me.

'Enjoying yourself?' I ask, taking a sip.

'Absolutely! This vibe is exactly how I'd like my wedding to be, if I ever have one.'

My stomach dances, 'Oh yeah? You think about that?'

'Well, can't help but do that when you take a lot of wedding pictures. If I'm honest, I think it's just a piece of paper,' he whispers, even though we're the only ones on the beach. 'At the end of the day, I think the quality of the relationship is way more important than the status. But, if I do happen to get married?' He gazes off for a moment, 'Obviously, no bloody flowers.' He laughs, and shakes his head, 'I don't know, I think so many weddings are a cardboard cutout of one and the same: too much tulle, crazy expensive detailing, and the formality of rules, like having all your guests sit on one side at the ceremony—'

I point at him, cutting him off, 'I don't like that either! If I get married, I want a sign that says, "Choose a seat, not a side, you're loved by both the groom and bride."'

'Cheesy,' he nods, 'but I like it!' He grins at me, and his whole face is beaming.

God, I want him to kiss me again. *Stop it.* 'Have you seen Sarah?' I decide to change the subject, and my line of thought. I still haven't talked to her, she's been touching up the bride and bridesmaid's makeup and hair all day, and now she's nowhere to be seen. Turning to my bag behind me to whip out my phone, I start typing her a message, but then see her. She's not happy. Understatement of the year. Sarah furiously stomps her way over to us, and on closer inspection, I can see she's been crying.

'Maybe this is just a girl moment,' Dom stands to leave, but it's too late.

'That arsehole is playing the same game with a bridesmaid!'

'What do you mean hon?' I stand too and offer her my beer; she takes a long swig.

'He's over there,' she points down the beach, 'with bridesmaid number two, teaching her how to play the bloody guitar!' She takes another glug, finishes the bottle, and passes it back to me. 'And, to top it all off, he's now denying anything happened last night! I WOKE UP IN HIS ARMS THIS MORNING!' she yells the last part of the sentence with us.

'Jesus,' Dom says under his breath.

'Anyway, 'e*ff* it. I've decided to get obscenely drunk on the job. The only person and thing that needs topping up now, is me, and my alcohol level!' She stomps off, back towards the party.

'Yikes. See, this is why I've never had a one-night stand!'

'You haven't?' Dom asks.

'No. I haven't. I'm just not that kind of girl.'

He smiles at me, like I'm his little sister, full of affection, but definitely not love. *Dammit.*

Chapter 19

Canada – USA
Tofino – Nanaimo – Vancouver – Los Angeles – Malibu

Sunday
Drive 3 hours: Tofino – Nanaimo
Depart Nanaimo Airport at 13:20
Arrive Vancouver Airport at 13:53
Duration: 33 minutes (2-hour 22-minute layover)

Depart Vancouver Airport at 16:15
Arrive Los Angeles International Airport at 19:01
Duration: 2 hours 46 minutes
Drive 1 hour to hotel (3 nights stay)

Couple I
Calamigos Ranch, Malibu, California

If someone had told me that a month after my last assignment in California, I'd be heading back there, with a healed heart that's full of hope, I wouldn't have believed them. I love that the final wedding of this world trip, martial extravaganza, is in California; Malibu, to be exact. It's almost like I've come full circle: I have my answers and I'm finally determined to move on with my life. Looking over at Dom, however, he's hardly looking serene; he's practically pulling out his hair. 'Are you OK?' I ask softly as the plane descends into LAX. I pick up my bag and pull out the little bottle, and I wave it at him, 'Want to use my revitalising spray? I swear it'll make you feel better. It...'

'Please put that bloody thing away,' he says angrily.

'OK. Sorry.' I return it to my bag and frown at him.

He looks at me, filled with absolute dread, and shakes his head. 'I'm sorry. I just can't face her. I can't!'

Softening again, I place a gentle hand on his arm. 'Look, I said I'll go with you for support; if you want?'

He shakes his head. 'It'll spur Heather on; you're here because she isn't,' he says, not for the first time.

'But you said she probably won't be there,' I remind him.

'I know she'll want to get one last argument in, somehow. Plus, like I said, maybe that will be a good thing; I need closure.'

'Yeah, but you don't need to be unjustly yelled at.'

'Unjustly?' he mimics me.

'Yes. Unjustly,' I confirm my word choice.

He grins at me and places his hand on mine, that's still placed upon his strong, tanned, forearm. He nods his head, and breathes out heavily. 'You know what? Yes. Please come with me. I was there for you, now you can be here for me. It has a nice symmetry to it.'

'Ladies and gentlemen, welcome to LAX. The local time is seven o' two in the evening, and it's a comfortable 63 degrees…'

I sit a little taller, ignoring the rest of the arrival announcement. 'Great!' He's still smiling at me. 'What?'

'Your wash bag is rather accurate, isn't it?'

'My wash bag?'

'Yeah. Little Miss Sunshine; you really are a little ray of

sunshine, you know?'

I feel my cheeks start to pinken slightly, 'Why, thank you! So, getting back on track, let's talk this through; you live in Hermosa right? But, Malibu is very much the other way.'

'Don't worry about it. We'll all drive together tonight to Malibu, that way we get a...' he falters, 'good night's sleep, and Hugo and Sarah can do their thing with the bride tomorrow.' He leans in slightly and lowers his voice, 'That is, if they manage not to kill each other in the process.'

I make a face. Sarah's sat with her gaze fixed out the window, and arms folded. Hugo's matching her body posture, complete with a frown, that hasn't left his face since we left Tofino.

I turn back to Dom, 'So, yeah, so we head off early tomorrow I guess?' I continue.

'Exactly, it's kind of perfect not being needed there until the day after tomorrow, so we can head off to my apartment nice and early, grab the remainder of my stuff if she hasn't burnt it, and then continue to drive down to stay with my mum in Laguna, before driving back the day after.' He sighs then smiles weakly, 'It'll be fine.'

***

The hotel is about an hour's drive north of LAX, and I've got to say, I forgot just how crazy the driving is here. The roads are huge: seven lanes, and no matter what time of day or night, you get the same experience; it's like London but on steroids. We zip along in the carpool lane in our newest rental: a red Mustang.

'I feel ridiculous in this,' Dom says, sulking; he wanted to get the BMW 4 series.

'Oh come on!' I say with glee from the seat behind him.

'It's so tacky! I feel like a tourist in my own hometown.'

'Plus, we've got to hold our luggage in our laps,' Sarah chips in, grumpily.

Feeling slightly guilty that I insisted on the convertible, despite several, "this is not going to happen" and "I told you so's," after about half an hour, we and our luggage all fitted in. 'Well, I'm very grateful to you all,' I say, but neither Sarah nor Hugo give more than a huff of response. 'All of these were rented out last time I was here, and you can't not have this experience! Oh, we're not taking "The 1?"' I sit up, holding Dom's driver seat, and looking back at the exit for the Pacific Coast Highway, disappointed.

'No, the 405 and the 101.' He glances at me in the rearview mirror, in between keeping an eye out for erratic drivers. 'There's no point in taking the "PCH;" you won't be able to see anything now; we'll save that for tomorrow.' Dom smiles at me then his eyes fix on the road once more.

Despite the pleasant climate outside, it's a frosty hour-long drive. Sarah in the back seat with me and Hugo in the passenger seat, neither of whom have really said a word since we left the last wedding. Not even Dom's appalling singing along to some 90's classics on the radio, can crack a smile out of either of them.

Finally, we wind our way to the wedding location: a ranch in the Malibu Canyons.

'IT'S SO PRETTY!' I gasp, pawing at the window, as we make our way to the car park. Every tree is lined with fairy lights. 'I love it, I love it, I love it!' I squeal and tap the back of Dom's seat as we head to the valet.

'After your reaction at the Essex wedding, I thought you

might,' Dom laughs, as we come to a stop and he pulls the handbrake on.

'You've been here before? This is so beautiful. It feels like Christmas!' I'm giddy.

'I have indeed been here before,' Dom smiles and moves on a little too quickly. 'So, you love Christmas, *huh*?' He looks at me in the rearview mirror, as we wait in a queue for valet parking.

'Oh, yeah, best time of the year, hands down. Well, that, and Thanksgiving; whenever I've been travelling, I like to be in America or Canada around then; a day to focus on the gratitude in your life? How lovely is that?'

'I'm grateful I can get out of this car soon,' Sarah mumbles from next to me, Hugo huffs in response, so Dom takes that as a signal to keep talking.

'I have to say, Thanksgiving is my favourite too.' We move forward and then break again, next in line. 'Kind of a novelty really, knowing that it's an extra holiday Brits don't celebrate.' We shuffle forwards once more, then come to a stop. A young man opens the driver's door, and after Dom exits, the valet folds the seat, reaching in to take my suitcase from my lap, and gives me a hand out; I feel my mouth is still hanging open.

'Welcome to Calamigos Ranch,' the valet laughs at my face, but I don't care; this is a natural, honest reaction and I'm going with it. Practically skipping, I thank him with a tip, and he heads to the other side, to help Sarah.

Eyes still wide with wonder, I turn to Dom, who's fishing out his bag from the boot, 'Why didn't you tell us it was so beautiful?'

'I'm a man of surprises!' Dom wheels his case round to meet me, once more.

'So, when was the last time you were here?' I ask as we walk towards the entrance, leaving the grumpy twins to sort themselves out.

He moves uncomfortably, 'It was actually just before I left, at the beginning of this trip; I came with Savannah and Jackson.'

'Who?'

'Couple I,' he looks at me sideways.

'Wait. You *know* the next bride and groom?' I look at him in surprise as we wheel our way past the entrance.

'Well, if I'm being totally honest, I'm a part of the wedding party.'

'What?!' I stop in my tracks; standing now below an archway of icicle fairy lights between the lined path of impressive redwoods. 'Why didn't you say anything until now?'

'I was kind of dreading it if I'm honest; Heather's a guest too; hence me wanting to get my stuff first.'

'Oh,' I make a face. And then we continue walking.

'And I thought if I didn't talk about it, maybe it would go away. Daft right.' He smiles sheepishly.

'No, I get that.'

'Thanks. A few of the guests are a bit two-faced, if I'm honest, but Jackson is one of my best friends. I actually told him and Savannah about the article, and may have convinced the powers that be, that this would be a great end to the piece. They're super nice, they deserve it.'

'How do you know them?' I ask as we walk further into the magical setting.

'School. We used to come here all the time.' He shakes his head. 'Man, this place is full of memories.' He looks around and stops for a moment, clearly seeing, just as I had, the ghosts of his past.

'Well, maybe it's time to make some new memories, *huh?*'

He smiles at me, 'Absolutely.'

***

Sarah and I are sharing a two-bedroom bungalow, and it is gorgeous: warm wood, rustic features and earth tones fill the entire place. Setting down my bags, I walk out onto what I thought was just a balcony, but it's a full on, private, outdoor space.

'Oh, wow, Sarah, come out here!' There are pots of eucalyptus, olive and lemon trees everywhere on the wooden deck, and consistent with their theme: twinkling fairy lights strung above my head. Little blankets rest gently over two chairs, either side of a small round table, set for two, with candles, a complimentary bottle of wine and two glasses. I pick up the bottle of wine and read the label; it's a local Sauvignon. I love that we're in the middle of wine country. Placing it back down, I pull out a chair and take a seat, wrap the blanket around my bare legs, and gaze up at the stars. 'Man, this place is lovely,' I say, not for the first time, as Sarah comes out, and looks around.

'I don't know,' she munches on a cookie, and hands me one. 'It's a little too outdoorsy for me,' Sarah scrunches her nose and takes the adjacent seat.

'Thanks! Oh, wow, they're warm!' I take a bite and gaze around. I love it.' I smile into the darkness. 'Cookies and wine? It shouldn't make sense, but it does!' I nibble away happily. 'So, I've got to ask,' I start, and pour us both a small glass. 'What are you really mad about?'

'Thanks,' she takes the glass I offer her, then pauses before taking a sip. 'What do you mean?'

I take a sip, and close my eyes for a moment, before opening them again, 'It's as if I can taste the sunshine.'

'You're hilarious, you know that?' she shakes her head, then sighs. I don't respond, I just give her space to answer my question. 'Well, of course I'm mad at that ass-hat of a guitarist.' I give her a doubtful look but remain silent. 'And,' she falters, 'what the hell is Hugo's problem? It's like he's suddenly trying to be a protective big brother? I don't need that for '*effs* sake! I'm a grown-ass woman!' She takes a large sip of her wine, and I still remain silent. 'He's been acting so weird recently, I have no idea what it is, and it's just really started to piss me off. What the hell does he have to be mad at? What? It's like he's upset I didn't ask his permission or something. What's up with that?' I sip away then swirl my glass around. 'You're really going to say nothing?' I shake my head and give her a small smile. 'Well,' she huffs, 'I don't think I want to talk about it anymore.' And a cheeky smile spreads over her face, 'However, I would be *very* interested to talk about this "mind-blowing" kiss.' Air quotes weren't needed with the amount of emphasis on those words.

I shake my head and sigh, 'Well, *I* thought it was "mind blowing,"' I repeat the air quotes that she did, 'but, he just wants to be friends.'

'Ouch.'

'He needs closure from his ex. And I mean, come on, if anyone can understand that, it's me. Plus, what was I expecting to happen? This is the last wedding, Sarah. I'm going home after this.' I shrug sadly, 'I'm not going to see him again, so.' I gaze off into the distance. 'It was over before it began, I guess.'

'Well, that's just sad.' She puts down her glass but still holds onto the stem, swirling the golden liquid around.

'Yeah, honestly, I don't think he was sad about it, he—.'

'No,' she interrupts me, 'not sad for him, sad for me!' She sits up tall, 'I've got so used to you being around, I'd forgotten that when this was all over, you'd be leaving; stupid I know. Oh, I'm sad now.'

'You were sad before,' I say smiling.

'Oh, no.' She shakes her head, 'I was *mad* before. Now, I'm *sad*.'

'Look at you, so good at feelings,' I mock lovingly. A rush of sadness waves over me too, as Sarah regards me, and pushes her cat-eye rimmed glasses a little further up her nose,

'Poppet, you've become like a sister to me,' she says in a softer tone. 'Promise me we'll keep in touch after this.'

'Of course.' I lean forward.

'And you better come and bloody visit!' She barks at me.

'Absolutely; likewise. London's nice and cold for you.'

'Perfect.' She clinks my glass with hers.

***

Monday

'Some moron at the door thinks this is a suitable time to wake people up,' Sarah shuffles out of my room and back towards hers.

Fresh from the shower, I'm only in my complimentary robe, but walk out anyway, into the lounge and kitchen area.

'Morning,' I yawn.

'That is some impressive morning hair!' Dom laughs at my mane, and I take the liberty of shaking it up even more, curls bouncing around in every direction.

'Why thank you!' I rub my eyes and head for the coffee machine.

'I'll do that,' Dom stops me, grabbing the pot, and points with his other hand back to my bedroom. 'You go get dressed; the pre-glow has almost started.'

I turn on my heel, and head back to my bedroom, shutting the door behind me. De-robing, I whip on the clothes I've already laid out. I'm quite excited about viewing a sunrise in California. I'd said to Dom I thought Southern California is best known for its sunsets, but he assured me, you just have to know where to look.

About ten minutes later, with my overnight bag in the boot and hair safely piled up in my signature messy bun, Dom winds the rental down the canyon with ease. He grins, lightly turning the convertible at every corner like a delicate racecar driver; it's as if the two are connected. I sip my take away coffee, tilt my face up, feeling the early morning breeze brush my cheeks, and soak up every second of this.

'I'm not driving too rough for you, am I?' he asks, kindly.

'Are you kidding? This is amazing. It's like you know every turn before it happens; I'm assuming you've driven this road a fair few times?'

'Oh, yeah, countless,' he grins, 'as soon as I got my licence, I was away! This was always a favourite spot for lunch with my school friends, and then when we all turned twenty one, I was always the chauffeur.'

'That's nice of you.'

He shrugs, 'I always preferred driving to drinking.'

'Me too.' I smile. We continue down, smooth twists and turns and after the next corner, suddenly, there it is: the Pacific Ocean. 'Yey!' I scream and tap the top of the convertible like a drum. 'To quote Kate Winslet, "This is amazing, this is amazing!"'

Dom laughs as we turn onto, "The 1."

'You're quoting, *The Holiday*, now?' He grins.

'Told you, it's my favourite! Man,' I gaze out at the water, sparkling away, reflecting the morning's sky of deep purple, raspberry and peach. 'This is so beautiful!'

'It is,' he agrees, giving me a sideways glance.

I sigh contentedly, 'It must be so nice to live here, with all this clean air and space.'

'Honestly,' his tone is reflective all of a sudden, 'if you don't have that clarity and space in your mind, it doesn't matter where you live; you will always feel claustrophobic, caught, or down, and it doesn't matter where you are in the world, or however many times you move, or even how spectacular the view is,' he gestures to the glittering water, 'there will come a time when you realise, the peace that you're searching for is within you, but you've got to practice tuning in, and listening to your own heartsong. You're not going to find it on the outside.'

'When did you get so spiritual?' I smile at him.

'I don't know. My mum talks like that all the time. Maybe being away has given me a chance to reflect, you know?' He glances at me and I can't quite read his expression.

'I do. I'm a completely different person from the one that you met on the plane from LA.'

'Me too, I think.' He shakes his head as we park up and walk towards the beach.

'Oh my God, this is beautiful!' I can't help but say again,

as we step onto the sand. I sip my coffee and take it all in. If it's possible, the colours of the sky have gotten even more vivid. Automatically, I take my flip flops off and feel the cool sand between my toes. Turning to Dom, he's just standing there, gazing out, lost in thought with his hands in his pockets, as I resist the urge to skip on the spot. 'I love it here,' I declare then turn back to the ocean.

I spot the sun peeking up above the horizon, below the Malibu pier. 'This is stunning!' Dom reaches my side, and we stand in comfortable silence for a moment, taking it in. 'Thank you so much for bringing me here!' I place my coffee cup in the sand, get out my phone, and take a few snaps. 'Come here,' I spin around, turning my back to the sunrise, 'we have to have a selfie!' I switch my phone to selfie mode; our mirror image shows his amused face towards me, not the camera. I turn to him, 'The camera's that way,' I cock my head.

'You realise, we'll just be silhouettes right?' he laughs.

'Whatever, loser, can you stop being a professional photographer for one second? This is a moment, and I'm capturing it!' I stand on tiptoes, put my arm around his lower back, then try to take the picture, but my phone falls in the sand. 'Whoops, never been very good at photography.'

'Good thing you have me then.' He bends down to pick it up, then crouches, so his head is in line with mine, puts an arm around me, and positions the camera. I smile at the camera, then he moves his face to kiss my cheek, and takes the picture at the same time.

He straightens up and I touch my hand to my face, 'What was that for?'

'For reminding me what's important in life: sun, sea, sand and friendship.' He hands me my phone and I feel my face fall.

Friendship. Fantastic.

We sit in the sand until the sun has completely come up, by which point my coffee is cold, but the surrounding temperature is starting to rise, so it doesn't matter.

'Do you know a good place for breakfast?' I ask, sipping what feels like ice coffee.

'I do,' he points at the end of the pier, 'Malibu Farm Cafe has delicious food.'

'Great!'

'But it's not open yet,' he says simply. 'Don't worry, we'll stop for something on the way, but in the meantime,' he fishes into the side of his backpack, 'how about a cookie?'

He hands me one of the complimentary cookies from the hotel, and gobbles up the other, in two bites.

'Hey, do we have time to walk along Carbon Beach? It's not that far from here, right?'

His face twitches, but he covers up whatever thought that was, with a tight grin, 'Sure. It would be like a twenty-five minute walk from here, though, so why don't we head back to the car for a few minutes, drive a little further along, and then get back onto the beach.'

'Great! Let's do that then!' I excitedly scramble to my feet.

He wasn't kidding, he drove for two minutes then we exited the car and walked towards the beach entrance.

'It always amazes me.' I'm shaking my head as we walk past what looks like a very unappealing property.

'What does?' He presses the key to lock the car.

'That these houses look so understated, dull even, and yet, you walk on to the beach and look up, and they are the most astounding properties you've ever seen.'

'They're alright, I suppose,' he says, looking at his shoes.

'Alright, you suppose?' I say, as we walk onto the sand. 'Come on, these are amazing!' I gesture to the mansion in front of us, while removing my flip flops once more. 'And the sunshine! It's not too hot, and there's a light breeze! I run to the water with glee, pull up my harem trousers to my knees, revealing my sun kissed legs, letting my toes get wet with an incoming wave. 'And these houses have the ocean on their doorstep; the ocean!'

'You really are a small child aren't you?' He stands on the sand with folded arms.

I respond with a poke of my tongue. 'There's nothing quite like walking along a beautiful beach, is there?' I grin so wide, I'm not really asking for his opinion. I breathe in the salty ocean air. 'God, this is amazing. You're so lucky to live here! Doesn't it just make you feel alive!' I spread my arms out.

'You're not going to burst into song, are you?' he asks, but he's not embarrassed.

I start singing "Another Day of Sun" from *La La Land* with my arms out wide, twirling around. Getting to the chorus I stop abruptly as I notice a man watching me from the adjacent property.

'Don't stop, I was enjoying that,' the man smiles, leaning on his beautiful glass balcony, amusingly looking down at me.

'I'm so sorry; I couldn't help it. Enjoy your morning.' I go to walk further along but notice Dom has stopped moving.

The man's eyes move to Dom, 'You brought a girl to see me?'

I'm confused. 'You know him?' I ask Dom quietly.

'I do,' he says cautiously. 'Morning, Dad.'

'Have you come to tell me you're here to change your mind?' Dom's dad says in a calm tone.

Dom stands taller, 'Absolutely not.'

His dad nods, 'Suit yourself,' he says casually. 'Are you coming in?' The man turns into his house as Dom types a code into a keypad, which opens the door to the property. He steps in, holds the door for me, and I follow Dom up the wooden steps from the beach.

'Oh my God; you're rich?' I whisper to him.

He turns abruptly, stopping on the steps and nearly knocking me backwards, 'No. My *family* is rich.'

Hmm. 'What did he mean: change your mind? About what?'

He sighs. 'You'll see.'

***

I wipe my feet excitedly on the mat at the top of the stairs on the deck and pull my trousers back down. *Good Lord, I'm standing in one of these houses!*

Dom's dad returns with two empty mugs, 'As a Brit, I'm guessing you'd like a cup of tea?' he says to me with a smile, exactly like Dom's.

'Oh, no,' I wave at him, 'black coffee for me please; I'm actually, I think, the only Brit on the planet who doesn't like tea.'

He cocks his head to one side, '*Hmm.* You and my wife.' Then disappears into the house again.

'He's nice,' I say to Dom, who's looking out at the ocean.

'*Um hmm.*'

I go to join him, enjoying the crash of a wave, 'Man, this view. You are so lucky to have woken up every day looking at this. Did you grow up here?' I ask.

'I did indeed; when we weren't in Laguna. This was my grandad's house, then we moved in when I was about eight or nine, and grandad bought that one,' he points down the beach.

'Wow.' I take this in. 'Why didn't you tell me you lived here?'

'My proud son here doesn't wish to be associated with his heritage.' His dad appears again with a tray of three full cups of coffee, and two bowls: one empty and the other full of strawberries. He places everything down on the glass table and sits down on one of the surrounding plush cream chairs.

Dom turns, stone-face to him. 'Not when it has terms and conditions attached to it; I'm fine as I am, thank you,' he says strongly.

'You'll always be my son,' Dom's dad says warmly. 'Come, sit,' he gestures to the chairs around him, and we both take a seat.

'So, my son has no manners, I'm Raymond Barton-Reynolds,' he leans forwards and holds his hand out to me.

'Liv Bennett.' A wave of familiarity washes over me. 'Wait, Barton-Reynolds? As in, Barton-Reynolds cosmetics?'

'One and the same,' he says proudly.

'Oh wow! I love your revitalising spray!'

'Thank you; Dom's eldest sister came up with the idea after a flight to New Zealand.'

I throw my arms down in excitement. 'It's my go-to product when I'm travelling! I use it every time I go on a flight! And...' I dig in my bag, 'I have it here!' I whip out the little colourful sprayer and wave it around.

Raymond smiles at me with amusement before turning to his son. 'You see what you're missing out on here? You are seeing the joy that our family's products give to others!'

Dom's expression hasn't changed. 'We're done talking about this Dad.' His crossed arms remain firm and I look awkwardly from one generation to the next.

'Fine. Have it your way,' Raymond says softly, and I can't help but feel his sentence is full of love. 'You know where it is when you come around, but in the meantime, like I said, you are always my son.'

I lean forward, go to grab a strawberry, and pause, 'May I?'

'Help yourself,' Raymond smiles at me.

I take a little bite, and it is absolutely perfect: juicy and sweet. I swallow and then cock my head to one side, 'Hang on.' I look at Dom, 'your last name is Russell.'

'No,' Raymond says firmly, with a hint of impatience in his voice, while leaning forwards and selecting a strawberry. 'My father's *first* name was Russell. Dominic here decided to take it and create an alias for his...' Raymond pauses to search for the right word, and it seems he can't keep the disdain out of his voice, '*business*; like I said, he doesn't want to be associated with his heritage.' He swiftly picks the head of the strawberry off and pops the rest into his mouth, gazing pointedly at his son.

Dom sighs; clearly this isn't the first time they've had this conversation.

'I'm sorry, I didn't mean to cause any tension.' I place the head of my strawberry in the empty bowl.

He throws the head of his strawberry in the bowl with mine, 'There's nothing you're saying that's out of turn,'

Raymond says, crossing one hairy tanned leg over the other.

‘I’m proud of my family, you know that Dad. Just, please don’t start,’ Dom says in a very small voice.

‘Fine, fine,’ Raymond holds his hands up. ‘Tell me all about your adventures, then.’

***

As we whizz down the Pacific Coast Highway, I gaze out at the ocean and desperately want to ask Dom a million questions, but due to the look on his face, I haven’t said a thing since we left.

‘Go on,’ he says finally.

‘Go on what?’ I try to reply nonchalantly.

‘Ask me what you’re dying to ask me.’ He sighs, and moves a strand of hair out of his eyes, as it blows in the wind.

I shuffle in my seat to face him, ‘What’s waiting for you when you come around?’

He makes a face and then briefly turns to me, ‘My inheritance.’

‘OK,’ I say, taking that in. ‘And what does he want you to come around on?’

‘He wants me to be like my sisters, to follow in the footsteps of the family, just like he did, and his father before him, and join the company. Until then, I don’t get a single cent.’

‘Wow. But, wait, I don’t understand. Your dad’s still alive.’

‘Yeah, but when my grandad died seven years ago, he left every grandchild...’ he pauses and glances at me, ‘let’s just say, a substantial amount of money.’ He returns to face the road, 'But my dad is holding mine hostage.'

'What the hell does that mean?' I kick my flip flops off and pull my legs up to sit cross-legged on my seat.

'According to him, it means, I don't deserve it because I have turned my back on the family, and therefore, I don't deserve the money.'

I sit with a frown on my face. 'But I don't get it, he seemed to have so much love for you.'

'Oh, don't get me wrong, my dad loves me immensely, but has never understood why I would want to, I don't know, make a name for myself? Decide my own future? Live a life that I've chosen, not one that's been planned out for me? You should have seen his face when I first told him that's what I wanted to do. And, man, what he said when I showed him my website?' Dom shakes his head and sighs, 'All he could do was find fault with it. He doesn't think I'm good enough to do anything by myself; he doesn't think…'

I reach across without thinking and put my hand on his leg. He smiles softly and then continues, '...he doesn't think I'm talented or smart enough without the family name behind me. How is it so hard to comprehend that I might have my own dreams, you know? It's so narrow-minded for God's sake.'

'So, all of your sisters work for the company?' He nods. 'And what about your mum?'

His whole demeanour changes. 'Honestly, she dips in and out of it, but mum's a creative soul; I think that's where I get it from.' He smiles at the road ahead of him.

'What does she do?'

'Socialise.' He laughs. 'But, when she's not doing that, she volunteers for a couple of charities, and she's an artist. She actually designed the labels for *your favourite product there,*' he says the last part of his sentence overenthusiastically, while gesturing to my bag in the passenger footwell.

'I'm so sorry,' I say, still embarrassed that I did that. 'I just got super excited! How often do you meet someone who's invented something you use practically every day?'

He doesn't answer, he just takes a deep breath. 'It's like my whole life was designed and laid out for me, even before I was born. I'm the only male in my generation so naturally I should *want* to have this *honour* to carry on the family legacy.' He slaps the steering wheel, 'I want to be free, I don't want to work in a job that I know I won't love, in a suit no less! Can you imagine me in a suit every day?' He glances my way and I shake my head. 'I want to be excited to wake up every day, wear whatever the hell I want, perhaps jetting around and waking up in different places around the world, experiencing and immersing myself in culture, art, history, nature, I want to document it all; I want my office to be where I feel like working that day.'

'I couldn't agree with you more.' I suppress the sudden overwhelming urge to reach out and kiss him.

'You know, even before dad told me he wouldn't support me financially unless I joined the company, I made the decision that I wanted to stand on my own two feet, make my own way in this world, make a name for myself, not ride along on the tailcoats of my ancestors.' He shakes his head, 'Money isn't everything people think it is, but freedom? That is priceless.'

'That's good. You should be a writer!'

He scrunches his nose affectionately, 'I think I'll leave that to the expert. Alright, from one shit-show, to the next!'

Chapter 20

USA
Malibu – Hermosa – Laguna

Upon first glance, I like Hermosa Beach very much; it's a sleepy, but hip town, and you can just sense it's brimming with young talent. We pull up at a two story beach house; Dom's apartment is the top one, two rows back from the beach itself. As we exit the car and walk towards the building, I take in the row of surfboards lined up, a faint carpet of sand, and a classic car in the driveway.

'You've got a 560 SL? What year is it?' I walk around examining it. It's clearly seen better days, but it's still an impressive collectible.

'1985,' he says simply, leaning up against the rental car, observing me, impressed. 'It was a gift from my grandad for my 21st birthday; it's the only car I've had since.'

'Amazing.' I bend down and look inside; for a two-seater, it's got a surprising amount of stuff in there: several dog-eared *National Geographic* magazines, an assortment of flip flops, a tripod, a crumpled-up jumper, and a pair of sunglasses sitting nicely on the dash. 'Man, it's nice to see a car with a CD player.'

He laughs at me, 'I'm sorry?'

I giggle, 'I remember one time, I rented a car, I brought all my favourite CDs with me and then felt completely stupid when I looked at the dash and there wasn't a CD player.' He laughs even harder.

'You're seriously old school, aren't you?'

'Sweetie! You're home!' A shrill voice comes from the first floor of the building.

In an instant my body ducks down. I don't know whether to stay crouched, hiding, or to pop back up. Suddenly I have the urge to crawl back to the safety of the rental, or under the SL, I'm not sure, so I stay put.

'Sweetie?' Dom says, laced with doubt. 'Heather, after the last time we spoke, I didn't think I'd ever hear you call me that again.'

I glance through the windows and spot her; she's annoyingly breathtaking.

'Oh, don't be silly,' Heather bats her hand, and starts, barefoot, down the wooden stairs. Her long, toned and tanned legs are exaggerated with her tiny white jean shorts and her slightly see-through fluorescent orange strappy top, showing off her impressive physique. 'Sweetie, I think we needed a little cooling off after we both said things we didn't mean, right?'

'Right,' Dom says slowly. 'But I haven't heard from you. You haven't answered your phone or replied to any of my texts or emails. A month is a long cooling off period, Heather.'

'Why are you calling me Heather?' She flicks her perfectly straight, and shiny raven locks over her shoulder. 'You know my name is bunny!' She places one hand on her hip, cocks her head flirtatiously to one side, as if she was posing for a magazine shoot.

She's at the bottom of the stairs now, and I'm still crouched down awkwardly; I don't think she's spotted me, and I think I've gotten away with staying invisible.

'Heather this is Liv,' Dom gestures to my hiding spot. *Dammit.* I poke my head over the car.

'Hello!' I say with an embarrassed wave, but a cheery tone.

Heather's body literally retreats backwards as if I'm poisonous. 'Oh,' she stares me down, the only way another woman can. Moments later, she rearranges her face into a dazzling smile. 'Hey there! And why are you here?' Her expression is pleasant, but the tone is threatening.

'No reason at all,' I find my mouth saying. 'I'll just wait in the car, shall I?' I go to walk back over to the rental.

'Liv replaced you on the article,' Dom says dryly; I stop in my tracks.

Heather's mismatched expression and tone continue, 'Is that so?' Her eyes scan me up and down, I feel like I'm being body-searched. 'Well, thank you, I hope the article is very successful.' Again, her words are nice, but the tone is scary. 'But, come on, with a photographer like you,' she slowly glides over to Dom like a python, slithering a toned arm through his, before snapping her head back at me, 'any writer in the world would do.'

'Don't be rude to the woman who saved not only the article, but most likely my job and everyone else's.'

Heather's face twitches for a mere second but I caught it. 'Well, sweetie, I—'

'Stop calling me that!' Dom interrupts her. 'Look, Heather, I'm here for closure. I'm here to get my things, move out and move on. You gave me no indication that you wanted anything other than that.' He removes her arm gently and folds his back up.

She wavers for a mere second, then she jabbers away, hands in the air, as if they're play fighting, 'OK, I admit, I was angry about getting fired; I was angry that you wouldn't take my side—'

'You didn't tell me what your side was, Heather! All you did was say you'd been sacked, you didn't know why, that I couldn't ask any questions, and that if I went on the trip, we were over. I went, therefore it's over! Right?'

'Why don't we talk about this inside; alone.' Heather adds, looking at me.

'No. Liv is with me, and anything you have to say to me, you can say in front of her.'

'What do you mean "*with you*?"' she says cautiously, then points and scoffs, 'You're not together are you? Because, come on, I really don't see that.'

'No, we're not together, we're friends, but—'

'Didn't think so,' she interrupts Dom. 'You'd never be with someone like *her*; she's just not your type.'

My mouth involuntarily hangs open and I quickly shut it, while trying to stand a little taller.

'What? Beautiful isn't my type? Smart? Talented? Funny?'

He called me beautiful. I can feel myself blushing. 'Thanks Dom, but I feel you're getting a little off-piste here!'

'You're right.' Dom moves his hand through his hair and says "alright" to a passing group going to the beach. 'Let's all go inside.'

'Fine.' Heather slaps on a fake smile and gestures with her hand, 'After you.'

'Thanks.' I meet her expression, narrow my eyes to the size of slits, and make my way up the stairs. Not only can I feel her close behind me, but her strong bitter-sweet perfume wafts up my nose; I briefly scrunch my face in distaste.

'Well, I guess it's a good thing I didn't go on the trip; by the looks of it, they fed you too well!'

I look back and she's looking at my arse. 'Excuse me?'

Her eyes lift to meet mine, 'Oh, no offence! I just watch my diet; you understand.'

Narrowing my eyes at her again, I try to remember I'm here for Dom, not to start a cat fight. I get to the top of the stairs and wait for them both to pass me. She goes ahead into the apartment, but Dom grabs my arm,

'I'm so sorry. She's being hideous to you; it's only because she's threatened.' I smile at him, grateful that he stuck up for me, and flattered me. 'Look, I don't want to do this, but I think the longer you're here, the more horrible she'll be. Maybe it would be best if you didn't come in.' He looks embarrassed.

'Honestly, whatever you want or need me to do, I'm here, or not here,' thinking that there's no way I want to spend another two seconds with that woman.

He sighs, thinks for a moment, then nods. 'I think I need to do this alone. I want to hear what she has to say; I owe that to our relationship, you know?'

I feel my stomach flitter. 'Of course, I get it. I'll take a stroll along the beach or something. It's *allllll* good.' I extend the "all" too much, attempting to be casual. 'You know me and sand.' I feel my voice falter. I don't want to leave him here by himself; I have an awful feeling about it. 'I'll be fine!' I smile at him. 'Good luck.' He kisses me on the cheek and then heads into the apartment.

***

Walking to the high street first, I have a feeling that this may take some time. I get a green smoothie and sip nervously as I wander along, looking in all the windows. I hope Dom's OK. I wander past a theatre; *huh, Jay Leno does stand up here on selected Sundays? That's cool.* I take a picture and send it to my dad. Continuing on, I pass a spiritual shop; the incense draws me in. As soon as I step over the threshold, I instantly feel my shoulders relax.

'Welcome! Come on in,' the shop owner smiles kindly at me before going back to meditating behind the counter.

Thanking her, I wander around. I love these shops. With thanks to my mum, I've definitely got an inner hippy side to me. I smile at some familiar books on chakras and the law of attraction, angel cards and an array of Himalayan salt and Moroccan lamps. Then I stop at the crystals, reading the descriptions of each, before picking up Black Tourmaline, and reading the little card: *"The best all-round protection, especially against harmful spirits and energies. Tourmaline is also good for joy, emotional healing and love."*

I'll get that for Dom, I decide; sounds perfect. I move along the selection, and stop as my eye is drawn to one that is almost iridescent. I read its card: *"Rainbow Moonstone: New beginnings. Thought to bring balance, harmony, hope, enhance creativity, compassion and inner confidence." Hmm,* I'll get this for myself. I'd love it in a necklace though.

'We also have those in the jewellery section if you'd like,' the owner says to me still from her seated position.

I smile at her, 'Are you psychic or something?'

She just smiles at me, 'They're over here, if you would like to have a look.'

I get a closer look and sure enough, there is a simple, raw, jaggedly shaped but smooth to touch, rainbow moonstone, attached to a delicate silver chain; it's perfect.

Buying them both, I exit the store, my new power crystal around my neck, and head to the beach. Looking at my phone, I don't see any update from Dom, and I sigh as I reach yet another endless stretch of sand. Taking in my surroundings, I love the pier and decide to stroll along it; I have a funny feeling that I've been here before. Silly as I know I haven't, but still, there's something I can't quite put my finger on.

I walk the length of the pier and on my way back, I see a familiar figure walking towards me; he's smiling.

Dom grabs me and starts dancing and singing, 'City of Stars' from *La La Land.*

'You're happy! Does that mean it's over?' I ask tentatively.

'No, it's just starting.' He continues to dance and sing.

My stomach flips, 'What do you mean?'

'We're going to give it another try.'

'Who is?' I say slowly, wanting to make sure I'm not making assumptions.

He stops dancing for a moment, but is still holding me. 'What's up with you? Me and Heather, of course! She explained everything to me, and we're going to give it another shot!'

My stomach plummets as he spins me around and starts singing again. I don't know what to say; he's obviously oblivious of my inner trauma. 'Why are you singing that?' I ask instead of sharing my thoughts.

'Because! This is the pier!'

Momentarily, my inner movie geek takes over my emotions, 'This is the *La La Land* pier?! I *knew* I knew it!' Then my expression falls. 'Dom, are you sure you're making the right decision?'

He nods, 'I think so. I think this feels right. We'll see how things go. She even started talking about marriage…'

'What?!'

'I mean, for me it wouldn't be right away of course, we'll basically be starting from scratch again, but she told me that's what she wants some day, and asked me to think about it.'

'But you said to me…' I feel like I'm on a sinking ship, '...you said, what was it? That you'd rather have a quality relationship than a piece of paper!'

'Well, sure, but maybe this is right. Maybe it can be quality *and* a piece of paper.' He shrugs, 'Plus, isn't this what people are supposed to do at some point in their lives?'

'For "some people" maybe,' I can feel hopelessness rising inside me, 'but you're not just "some people" you're...' I can't finish the sentence out loud. I wiggle out of his arms, turn, and gaze out at the ocean in frustration. *Who is this guy?* It's certainly not the man I've got to know; he feels different, somehow.

'I want to say thank you,' he says from behind me.

'Oh yeah? For what? I haven't done anything,' I say simply, still facing out to the ocean.

'Oh, you have! More than you know.' Dom bends down next to me and leans his arms on the pier railing.

I finally turn to face him and smile weakly. 'Well, you're welcome then. Look, I got you something,' I go to get it out of my bag but then stop, it seems pointless now, 'but never mind. I don't think you'd like it; maybe I'll just keep it.'

'What is it?' he grins and looks at my bag.

'Oh, nothing, forget it,' I try to brush him off.

'No, what?' He stands tall, over me, smiling away, 'I'm

not going to leave you alone until you tell me.' His expression is so playful.

'Fine.' I swing my bag round, reach in, then open my palm for him to see the simple stone.

He examines it for a moment, 'You think I need protection?'

'You know what it's for?' I pose a question instead of answering him.

He shrugs, 'My mum loves this kind of thing.'

'So does mine.' I smile sadly; another thing we have in common.

He takes it from me gently and examines it, before lifting his eyes to mine, 'Thank you, Liv. You're truly amazing, you know that? I'm so glad I met you, and I wouldn't be here without you.'

'Nonsense, this is where you live,' I try to joke. He draws me in for a big hug, and I breathe him in. I scrunch my nose as he smells of Heather's perfume; it feels wrong. I pull away. 'So, what's the plan now?'

'She's just packing and then we're headed to Laguna to see my mum.'

'Wait, Heather's coming with us? Why?'

'She's a guest at the wedding tomorrow, remember, so it only makes sense for her to drive with us.'

I pause and then a thought occurs to me, 'Not that I don't want to meet your mum, but, if you're back together, why don't we just stay here, there's no need to drive to Laguna. I'll get a hotel or something,' I add, as I reckon, Heather is likely to poison me in my sleep.

He goes to say something, then changes his mind, and says, 'I've already told mum we're coming and she's putting a dinner together, so.'

'OK.' I take this in and try to think of another excuse not to spend any more time in a car with Heather than I have to. 'Couldn't we get Heather on the way back from your mums?' I say this out loud without thinking it through.

He frowns slightly, getting irritated, 'We could, but Heather loves my mum, and insisted on coming.'

I bet she did. She doesn't want me alone with her man for one more second.

'Anyway, it will be fun! Road trip with my girls!' he puts an arm around me, and I don't want him to let me go. 'And I can't wait for you to meet my mum. She's volunteering today, so we'll meet her there.'

'Volunteering where?'

***

'*Ugh*, I have ALWAYS hated this place; it just stinks of fish!' Heather, now dressed in a skintight, black and white Hugo Boss number, and high Jimmy Choos, I can't help but feel underdressed in my harem trousers, simple vest top and trusty, well-worn flip flops.

'Would you keep your voice down,' Dom says to Heather as we head towards the entrance. 'They do amazing work here.'

'Of course, of course! I think they do too!' She links arms with him and walks ahead. I feel like the lone, lost puppy of Laguna, following them obediently. I sniff the air, and have to disagree, it doesn't smell here.

We walk through the gate, and I read the sign: "Pacific Marine Mammal Centre."

'Hi Dom, how are you?'

'Fantastic, Hope, thanks. Great to see you!' A lady in a

blue t-shirt gives him a hearty hug; it's slightly awkward as Heather hasn't let go of his arm. 'And Heather, nice to see you! It's been a while.' I can't help but notice the welcome isn't as warm for her and I sneak a little smile.

'I was just saying to Dom, what *tremendous* work you do here: rescue, rehabilitate and release mammals in need!' Heather says, as if she's memorised their slogan. 'We're *so proud* to contribute to such a fine organisation!' Heather dazzles her pearly whites again, but I don't think she's fooling anyone.

Dom clears his throat, 'Hope, this is my great friend, Liv; we've just travelled the world together, on a project.'

I hold out my hand and she shakes it with glee. 'Wonderful. Terrific to meet you, Liv! Alright, your mum's nearly done, but do you want to see who we've been working with recently?'

'Absolutely! How's Sammy?' We walk towards what I'm guessing is the main part of the rescue centre. There are several sheltered enclosures, each with a little outdoor pool and a door for the animals to head inside.

'We released him last week! Definitely the toughest sealion we've come across yet!'

'He had that fight in him, you could tell.' Dom is beaming, clearly in his element. 'Oh, you've got some elephant seal pups in?'

I take in the small, strange looking animals, that are quite accurately named; seals that have little trunks.

'Yes!' Hope gets closer to their enclosure, 'This fast one is Ziggy,' I take in his tiny frame, 'and that's his sister Miggy. She's not quite as energetic yet, but she will be.' Miggy is sitting in a corner, timidly watching Ziggy dive in and out of the little pool in front of them and slip around like the floor's covered in butter. 'So, if you're happy here, I'll tell your mum you've arrived?' Hope asks kindly.

'Absolutely.' Dom whips out his camera and takes a couple snaps. He turns to me, 'They're never the best pictures with the wire mesh, but I can't help but take a few photos whenever I'm here.'

'Of course you can't.' I smile at him, and I notice Heather staring me down again. I eye her up too.

'Always with his camera!' I completely forgot Dom said his mum is English, and I'm somewhat comforted by her accent. I look to see a vision of a woman walking towards Dom. He lowers the camera and smiles wide; I don't think I've seen him smile like that at anybody else.

'Hi Mum!' He stands and they have the biggest hug; I'm so touched by it, I don't realise I'm grinning from ear to ear.

Heather pushes past me with her arms open, 'Madeline! So, *gorgeous* to see you! You really are inspiring, working, when you don't have to, in a place like this!'

Letting go of Dom, Madeline's body stiffens, but you can tell she's polite, so she opens her arms to receive Heather's hug. When she's hugging Heather, I spot her eyes roll, and then land on me. Madeline's eyes widen ever so slightly; she knows I saw that, and she smiles at me. 'You must be Liv,' she says, mid-hug, much, I'm sure, to Heather's annoyance. 'I've heard lots about you,' Madeline says over Heather's shoulder.

'You have?' I say to her face only, as Heather still hasn't released her grip. Madeline gives Heather a little pat on the back to indicate to let go, and reluctantly she does.

'Yes. The English writer! So nice to have another Brit on this side of the pond.' Madeline glides over to me with grace; if this is what she looks like after a day volunteering in the sun around mammals, I wonder what she looks like when she makes an effort.

I extend my hand, 'Mrs Burton-Reynolds, I'm so pleased to meet you.'

She smiles at me with such warmth, I feel like I've known her forever. 'Oh, please call me Maddie.'

'Maddie, then.' I nod.

'So, *Maddie*,' Heather says from behind us; I wonder if that's the first time she's called her that. 'Dominic and I were just saying how much we miss having you over! It's been a long time since you came to *our* house.'

I'm pretty sure that's for my benefit, not Maddie's.

'Oh, well, I'm sure we'll find time,' she says politely. 'I'll just grab my bag and we'll all head home, shall we?'

'Actually, I've got a surprise!' Dom says excitedly.

'You have?' Heather squeals, with all her hopes clearly up, 'I know I asked you to think about it, but I didn't expect it *here*,' she says with mild disgust, 'but, at least it's finally happening! Oh, Dom I—'

'No, no,' he cuts Heather off, with slightly widened eyes. 'I've arranged for us to have a sunset whale watching trip in Newport!'

Heather frowns at him, 'Really? We literally just drove past there, half an hour ago!' she whines.

'Well, it wasn't sunset then,' he says simply. 'And we had to meet mum first, so…'

'*Ugh*, I don't want to go on that boat,' Heather pouts. 'We've been on it a million times! And my hair's all done.'

Maddie looks from me, to Dom, to Heather, and back to Dom, clearly calculating a plan. 'I tell you what, why don't you come back with me, Heather. We'll have a catch up, a nice glass of wine and prep dinner. Then Dom and Liv can go on the boat, and meet us in what? Two, three hours? That's the time I'd planned for dinner, so it's all working out rather beautifully!'

'Fab! Yeah, it's an hour of travel time, and then a two hour boat ride,' Dom says.

'Perfect! Sounds like a plan!' Maddie says and Heather opens her mouth to say something and decides against it; stuck between wanting to impress her prospective mother-in-law, and keeping me from being alone with Dom.

'Great!' Heather smiles tightly, then narrows her eyes at me, but I think I'm the only one to see it.

***

We pull up at an underground car park. '*Um*, Dom, that says: "Staff only,"' I point to the rather obvious sign.

He smiles at me, 'Yeah, I know.' He whips out a card and the barrier in front of us lifts up. 'I didn't tell you what I did before joining the magazine, did I?' He grins like a small child.

After we've parked up, we walk our way back into the sunshine. 'Heather wanted me to join her at *Blush*,' he explains. 'A pay raise, good benefits, more of a serious career, so,' he shrugs, 'that's what I did, but, I have to tell you, nothing has compared to this job.' He grabs me by the hand, and we walk onto the dockside.

'Well, look who it is!' A woman, I'm guessing in her late forties, comes out from behind the counter, 'You are a sight for sore eyes, mister.' She hugs him warmly. 'They told me you were coming tonight; you changed your plans a couple times, though: party of two, then four?'

'And back to two. This is my friend, Liv; she's never

been on a whale watching trip before.'

'Well, you are in for a treat!' she says with so much excitement, you'd think it was her first time as well. 'And the sunset sailing? For goodness sakes! It's going to be beautiful! I can feel it!'

'Thanks; I'm excited!' I say, catching her wave of enthusiasm.

'Oh, and she's from the UK, too! I *love* the accent!' I smile at her, ever the Brit, unable to take a compliment. 'Now, I just need you to jot down your information for health and safety: name, address, phone and email, and then we're ready to go! Oh no,' she's looking at my flip flops. 'Do you have any other shoes? Flip flops aren't allowed on board.'

'You know, I do happen to have ballet pumps in my bag.' I look at Dom. 'This is why you asked me to bring them?'

Dom shrugs, 'I wanted it to be a surprise.'

'Well, it was, and I love it,' I say as I finish scribbling my details.

'So, which boat are we taking today?'

'The catamaran!'

'I love the catamaran!' Dom squeals, dancing slightly from side to side, then looks at me. 'The dolphins love to play with the boat; you get the best pictures!'

'Oh, you used to be a photographer here?' I ask, as we walk to the dock.

'Of course, what did you think?'

'That you just sailed around, larking about all day?' I say, feeling silly. Of course he was the photographer.

'He wasn't just *a* photographer,' the woman says in a low voice, 'he was the *best* photographer we've ever had.'

'Every time I say I want to come and visit, they let me

take pictures; I share them and donate all the money I get back to Newport Whales.'

'But, that's not the only reason why we love him,' she beams, 'Dom's so talented with wildlife and marine photography; that magazine is missing a trick not using you to do that.'

'It's not that kind of magazine,' Dom says sadly, as we step aboard.

'I know.' She taps him on the arm. 'Anyway, here we are.' She guides us to the front of the catamaran where there's a couple of sellotaped signs on seats saying "reserved."

'Thank you, lovely!' Dom gives her a hug.

'Not that you'll be sitting in those seats for long, but still, we wanted to make it special, as always. Have fun!'

'Thank you,' I call after her, then turn to Dom, 'This is so exciting! Thank you for bringing me here!'

'You are more than welcome,' he breathes in the sea air. 'God, I love it here. You know when you just feel at home, or something just feels right? That's how this boat feels to me.'

'How often do you get to come back?' I ask sadly, knowing exactly that feeling and realising that I'll never be able to have that with him.

'Nowhere near as much as I'd like.' He pauses, then says, 'But way more than Heather likes.' He looks at me, and I don't respond. 'What?'

'Nothing.' I look out at the harbour.

'No, tell me; I want to know what you're thinking.'

I pause, considering my words for a second, then look directly in his beautiful aqua eyes, 'You should be allowed to do what you want to do, whenever you want to do it. If this fills you with joy, then do this,' I say firmly.

'Heather said it was time for me to grow up. She wanted me to be around people who are moving on with their lives.'

'But, if you were happy where you were, why did you need to move on from it? Do you even like working for *Blush*?'

He thinks for a moment. 'I don't know. I like the people there.'

'That's not what I asked.'

He ponders, tilting his head, 'I find it a little boring if I'm honest.'

'Well, why don't you consider getting your old job back? Clearly, they would take you on full time in a *splash*.'

'A *splash*?' He laughs at me. 'You mean a flash?'

'Flash, splash, they'd take you back immediately!'

He smiles sadly at me. 'Yeah, they would take me back, but that's not what Heather wants.'

'Screw Heather!' I say a little louder than intended. 'Sorry,' I add, 'I just mean, you're allowed to pick your future, and it doesn't have to sound good to anybody else. Be selfish in planning your life and be really clear about what will fill you with joy; it's as simple as that. Although,' I look at him with all seriousness, 'some people say that it's not very mature to be a *30-something wannabe wanderluster*.'

'Who said that?' he says, shocked.

'You did,' I grin cheekily, 'when we first met.'

'Well, I was a moron.'

'Agreed.'

He playfully pushes me, as we hear the tannoy sound. 'Alright, good evening, everybody! Who is ready for a ride?' I turn to see the lovely lady from earlier now in the captain's quarters, speaking into a mic. I turn back and smile at Dom.

'We have the following crew on board…' She continues to list everybody, and gives some safety announcements, but nothing is clear, only the fact that Dom and I are just staring at each other. '...and of course we have our gorgeous photographer Clare on board with us this evening, *and* I am very excited to announce that we also have a crew alumni, Dom! Why don't you stand up for the crowd and give them a wave!' He does as she asks and, although he's a little embarrassed, I feel he's loving every single second of this. He sits back down and the announcement continues. She then goes on to ask if there are certain nationalities on board. 'And do we have any Brits here today?'

Both Dom and I throw our arms up in the air and woo. I laughed at him. 'You're only half a Brit.'

'Still counts!' He grins.

'So, you are in for a treat today! Our two amazing photographers will be capturing moments throughout the whole trip, for you to check out, at the end, and we have the option for you to purchase any pictures of your memories created this evening. We are in for a beautiful ride, smooth sailing is predicted, with a gorgeous sunset due. Earlier today we had a humpback sighting, both mama and calf, so we're hoping they'll appear again, for you all this evening! You'll see Dom and Clare climbing over the ropes, but for your safety, we ask that you remain behind the barriers, with two feet on the deck at all times. Thank you so much, sit back, and enjoy the ride, folks!'

We cast off, and I can immediately feel the cool ocean breeze. 'You're allowed to climb over the ropes?' I say excitedly. 'Does that mean I can too?'

'No, weren't you listening?' he says with all seriousness. 'Two feet on the deck at all times!' He smiles at me. 'You'll get a great view, wherever you are.'

We sail away into the silky-smooth open ocean, and the movement of the boat is hypnotic. I love it. The sky is transforming into the pre-glow, and I smile at the fact that, regardless of what happens next, I'm here, right now, with this awesome man.

'What are you smiling at?' Dom says from behind his lens.

'Are you taking my picture?' I say, just realising, but I'm not offended; I even pose.

'No,' he says, then snaps away. 'Just testing the light and the composition.'

'And how is the subject of the composition? Pleasing?'

He lowers his camera slightly, and smiles sweetly, 'Very...I'll be right back, just going to chat with Clare; you OK for a minute?'

'Absolutely! I've got the ocean; what more could I want?' He turns to walk away, then spins and takes one more shot of me. 'Would you stop that!' I tease.

'Stop what?' He grins like a child, takes one more photo of me, and then he's gone. A moment later, he's back with a glass of bubbles.

'You're going to drink and sit on the front of a moving boat? I don't think that's a good idea,' I point to the glass.

'It's for you. You said, what more could you want? I thought bubbles, so I got bubbles.' I take it, thank him and enjoy a sip before giggling out loud. 'Drunk on one sip? Deary me, maybe I'll take that back,' he reaches for it, but I bat him away.

'No, I was just thinking, I bet Heather is hating this.'

'I don't know, she's always wanted to be close to my mum, but they've never really clicked, you know; it's actually kind of awkward to watch,' he makes a face.

'No, I meant us, being here. Without her,' I add, pointedly.

'Oh. Yeah,' he suddenly looks very guilty. 'I'd planned this for just the two of us, when you'd said you'd never been on a whale trip, then after I'd spoken to Heather, and knew mum would love it, I thought it would be a nice surprise for us all to go on a boat trip.'

'It *is* a nice surprise! Who wouldn't love this? It's almost sunset, wind in your hair, salty sea breeze, possible dolphin and whale sightings, and now bubbles!' I raise my glass. 'This is amazing. Thank you for bringing me here,' I say, for a second time, and truly mean it. 'Although,' I add, 'a part of me wishes you had told me; I'm a little cold,' I say honestly, moving my shoulders up and down in the cool ocean breeze.

'Oh, I've got that covered.' He puts down his backpack, which I've known as his lens bag, and he fishes around. 'I couldn't tell you to bring more layers, because then it wouldn't have been a surprise! Here.' He whips out a hoodie with "Pepperdine University" emblazoned on the front.

'Thank you!' I hand him the bubbles to hold for a moment and wiggle into the oversized jumper. 'Oh my God, this is perfect. Perfect! Thank you!'

We sail around for about half an hour, and Dom points, 'Look, right over there!'

'What am I looking at? It just looks like strong waves in the distance, to me.'

'Nope,' Dom says, definitely, 'It's a pod of dolphins. I'd guess there's a couple hundred of them there.'

'What? Really? Wow!' I excitedly grab the side of the boat as we sail nearer, and sure enough, there they are: hundreds of them. It's as if they're giving us a private display. Couples, then groups of them jump out of the water together, diving back down, as though they're synchronised swimmers performing a routine. I watch as they weave around the boat.

'Told you they like to play with the boat!' Dom says to me, while taking shot after shot.

'They're literally dancing with the boat!' I practically shout with joy and watch with glee as a few of them dart between the two hulls of the catamaran. Under the boat they go, several are trying to out-race us, up ahead, all around, everywhere you look. 'They're everywhere!' I giggle. I feel like a small child, wooing and cheering, as the dolphins jump out of the water, and back in again, over and over.

Dom lowers his camera for a moment and takes in the joy on my face.

'This is incredible! Thank you for sharing this with me!' The boat suddenly jolts me forwards as we go over a large wave, and I bump right into him. We both laugh, and he puts an arm around me, to steady me. He points to the water.

'Did you know this is a tuxedo dolphin?'

'You're kidding?'

'Nope.' He grins. 'You can see they're mainly black, but the stomach and up between the fins is white, which looks like a tuxedo.'

'I love that! How fancy!'

A voice sounds over the tannoy, continuing the trivia, 'Did you know that all dolphins are whales, but not all whales are dolphins?'

'Fascinating!' I grin at Dom, who's just taking in my joy. 'You know, if we don't see anything else, it doesn't matter, this has truly made my day!'

'I'm glad.' He keeps his arm around me, and our eyes

haven't left each other's.

And I'm glad that it's just the two of us. But, I don't have the nerve to say that out loud.

After the pod has wished us goodbye, we continue to sail around on our search for sealife. Despite the temperature dropping, I feel warm, grateful, and lucky to be alive. I notice our speed decreases, and then the engine whirrs to a stop. The tannoy sounds once more. 'Folks, the Queen Ann ahead of us, has reported mama and baby humpback, in this area, so we're just going to hang out, and see if they'll come and say hello.'

'So, what are we looking for, exactly?' I ask Dom, excitedly, as we head to the front of the boat. He swings his leg over the barrier, and sits on the bow.

'You're looking for what's called: the blow.' He smiles at me, waiting for a joke, but I'm intent on learning what to look for. 'It's when the whale surfaces; they expel air, and it looks like white spray that shoots up. If we're lucky, they'll breach for us.'

'Amazing.' I excitedly scan the horizon. 'I'm happy to wait for that possibility,' I say to the back of Dom's head.

'Yeah, it's definitely a game of patience; I think that's why Heather's always hated it, she's so—'

'Dom!' I point and see my first ever "blow."

He turns with lightning speed, his camera up to his eye, and he snaps without hesitation; *God he's good.* He pauses, camera poised and scanning like I am, but with his lens. The feeling in my stomach is a little like being a kid at Christmas.

Suddenly, I see something. 'Is that a fin?' I say out loud.

'Yup, it's her dorsal fin.'

'How do you know it's a "her?"'

'Juveniles and females have smaller curved dorsal fins,' Dom says without moving a muscle.

'Yup, everybody, we can see the calf ahead at 12 o'clock. That means that mama isn't too far away,' the tannoy announces.

I feel the boat move forward with purpose. *That's strange.* Dom's suddenly up from his pose and swings his leg over the barrier. He grabs my hand, 'Come with me.' We run to the back of the boat, and sure enough there's a reason why.

'Ladies and gentlemen, 6 o'clock, 6 o'clock! We have mama, she is pushing the boat along!'

Dom snaps away and I feel like I have a front row seat with the most incredible creature I've ever seen.

'Oh my God! This is amazing!' I squeal with delight.

The rest of the crowd is behind us, and everyone is just as impressed as I am. Then the whale swims to the port side and the whole boat runs to follow, and just like that, she's gone.

'That was insane!' I cry.

'I don't think she's done yet,' Dom says, eyeing the velvety waves. And we wait, we watch and suddenly see one "blow" followed by another. Dom's camera is poised and ready, then the baby leaps into the air, twisting her body, followed by mama, who towers above; my mouth flies open. They both seem to fall backwards in slow motion and land on their backs with an almighty splash. I squeal and clap my hands excitedly to a chorus of cheering around me.

The sunset is now in full swing, enveloping the waves in deep reds, pinks and purples. 'How perfect was that?' I say to a complete stranger next to me, who grabs my hands with glee, and practically jumps up and down with joy too.

'OK, folks,' the tannoy crackles, 'we hope you loved that as much as we did! What a real treat today! We're going to head back now towards the dock. Remember you can grab a drink and enjoy the sunset and afterglow, on the way.'

'It's not over yet,' Dom smiles at me.

'It's not?' I'm grinning so hard, my cheeks are starting to hurt.

'We go past a buoy, and there's a surprise on there,' he says quietly to me.

'How many times have you been on this trip?'

He thinks, then shrugs, 'I don't know, maybe in the high hundreds?'

'And I'm going to guess that you're just as excited every time?' I smile at him.

'It's different every time! How can you *not* get excited?' He throws his arms out to the side. 'This is life! This is living! This is enjoying every unpredictable moment!' He looks at me, observing that despite his hoodie, I'm shivering slightly. 'Get in here,' he opens his arms for me, and gives me a squeeze. 'Hey, you want to learn something neat?'

'Always.' I smile up at him, still cradled in his arms. He removes one hand from my back, and I follow it over my shoulder, not wanting to let him go just yet. Dom takes his hand, and outstretching his fingers together, he turns them, so they're horizontal to the waves, with his palm to the sun. 'What are you doing?' I smile as he tucks back one finger after the other.

'Every finger is worth five minutes.'

'OK,' I say, slightly unsure.

'Here. Let me show you.' He turns me gently, so my back is now nestled into his chest. With his arms either side of my frame, he softly takes my left hand and holds it up, and turns my hand to mimic how his was. 'Clench your fist.' I do as instructed. 'Now, hold out your index finger, so it's resting on the horizon.'

'Alright.'

'OK, now, place your middle finger on top of that.' Again, I follow instructions. 'You see now the sun looks as though it's on top of your middle finger?'

'Yeah,' I smile at the horizon.

'Like I said, each finger is worth five minutes, so we've got ten minutes until sunset.'

'Wow. I love that.' He steps from behind, to my left side, and I manoeuvre my body to hug him once more. Dom places his arms around me, and holds me, as together, we gaze out at the ocean.

'I'm so glad I met you, Liv.' He sighs, contentedly, as I snuggle my left cheek into his chest. The sky displays the most beautiful sight I've ever seen.

'This is perfect.' I don't realise I've said it out loud until he chuckles gently.

'It is, isn't it? Promise me, you'll keep in touch when you go back to England.'

A part of my stomach falls. *Of course, he's with someone else, silly.* I squeeze him a little tighter. 'Of course.' We silently stay wrapped in each other's arms, I don't know how long; it's both sad and beautiful in equal measure.

'Look, there they are!' He points at a tall, red buoy and on it are about ten sealions, all piled on top of each other. 'We do this last in case we don't see anything,' Dom says to me. 'These guys are always here.'

I let him go, 'I'll let you get back to work,' I smile at him. He kisses me on the top of my head, like an affectionate older brother, and walks off to get the best shot. Pulling up the hood of his hoodie, over my head, I then trace the edge with my hands, and pull the material from the neck up around the bottom of my face. Eyes closed and inhaling, I breathe in his aftershave. Suddenly, I pause, fly my eyes open, catching myself; *what are you doing Liv*? I straighten up, fold my arms, take a deep breath, and vow to myself, that *I* am my top priority now. I don't need to get into a relationship or get attached to another man; particularly a man who is involved with someone else. He lives here, I live in London. It's as simple as that. But then I look at him. He turns and waves me over. *Dammit. I do have feelings for this man.*

'Oh my God, they stink!' I say as I get closer.

'Yup, but you can't deny that they're cool.'

'Very cool,' I confirm. I don't want this journey to end.

'OK, so, I've just got to pop inside and put the photos on my laptop; want to see my shots?'

'Absolutely!'

Both he and Clare set up their laptops next to each other. There's no competition, just a pure and utter undeniable love for what they do. They're both very talented, although I'm biased and think Dom's are better. Dom is talking animatedly, to someone about the pictures he took, and I look from one computer to another. Clare took some photos of the passengers too, either pointing at the dolphins, or with the sunset or afterglow behind them. Suddenly, I see a picture of Dom and I, in our snuggle moment.

'Sorry, couldn't resist,' Clare says, grinning. 'You two are super cute together; you make a beautiful couple.'

'Oh, we're not together!' I say, a little too loud. 'He's still with Heather.'

She nods, folds down the corners of her mouth, 'Oh, OK.

Well, I stand by that statement.' She smiles, then turns to take details of a fellow customer to send photos to, and I hit the spacebar to pause the slideshow.

We do make a beautiful couple.

Chapter 21

USA
Newport – Laguna

We drive back to Laguna Beach in the darkness and I'm a confusing mix of blissfully happy, with a side-helping of foreboding loss. I glance over at Dom, and just stare at the side of his beautifully chiselled profile.

'Do I have something on my face?' he subconsciously touches his chin.

Whoops. I shake my head, 'No. I was just thinking, I can't believe that the day after tomorrow, this will all be over.' Glancing away and then back again, I pause, not quite sure how I'd like him to respond. When he doesn't, I clear my throat and decide to continue my internal monologue out loud. 'When this whole journey started, I was absolutely dreading it. But,' I sigh, 'it's the only reason I'm ready to move on with my life. And, I've got to know some of the most awesome people.'

'I know, I'll miss being with Sarah and Hugo twenty-four-seven, too,' he lowers his bottom lip. I smack him on his toned bicep. 'Hey!'

'You've changed my life,' I say, honestly.

He smiles, and gives me a little glance, 'You've changed mine too.'

As we drive into Laguna, I shake my head, looking at the dark ocean on my right. 'I can't believe you grew up between Malibu and Laguna.'

'OK,' he wiggles slightly in his seat, 'so, I know why you loved Malibu, but Laguna? *Hmm*, let me guess, you liked the show, *Laguna Beach*?'

'Oh, Bex did, but, no; have you seen, *Dead to Me*?'

He nods his head, 'Funny you should say that.'

'Why?' I pull the sleeves of his hoodie down to cover my hands and snuggle into it a little more.

'Do you remember the episode where Christina Applegate's character...what was her name?'

'Jen,' I reply firmly.

'That's right, so where Jen was trying to sell Steve the house with an amazing view?'

'Yes,' I say slowly; my eyes widen.

'Well, that's my mum's house.'

I shift in my seat and slap his arm again. 'Shut up! Oh my God! How exciting!!'

'It's actually the house I grew up in, here.'

'Stop it!' I say sitting up with excitement.

He chuckles, 'You are so easily pleased.'

We drive along passing a lifeguard tower, and then turn into what I'm assuming is the main high street, 'Gosh, this is cute.'

'Cute?' he smirks.

'Yes, it's adorable; beachy, laid-back, charming. Tell me: where's your favourite place to go, here?' I take in the quaint shops and galleries, all teasing me to explore.

He thinks for a moment, as the car starts to climb and wind its way up a mountain road. 'It depends, if I want to get away from it all, there's a pirate tower that has a stone tide pool; that's kind of cool. Although, it's recently become a bit of a trendy *Instagrammable* spot. There's a couple of gorgeous wine bars, rooftop bars, but probably The Cliff restaurant; the view is insane, and they put flowers in the salads.'

'Fancy! If only we had more time.' I make a face, as, again, I realise too late, that I've said that out loud.

He pulls up outside the house and then turns to me, with a small smile, 'I know.' We exit the car and climb up the drive; I can feel the anticipation building in my stomach. 'Here we are!'

'It's so beautiful! Oh, man,' I look down.

'What's up?'

'I suddenly feel very underdressed for this building.'

He chuckles, 'You're dressed just fine; beach casual like me.' He smiles and puts an arm around me as we head to the front door. Dom takes out a key, hidden in a large rock out the front of the house and opens the door; it's all dark inside.

'*Hmm*, I guess they're on the patio?'

'SURPRISE!!!' The lights suddenly flick on and we're met by the smiling faces of about one hundred people, clapping and whooping. I jump out of my skin, and I'm really glad I haven't sworn in front of a room full of strangers.

'Welcome home, sweetie!' Heather makes a point of cat-walking herself over, from one side of the room to the other, arms out-stretched, 'We're so glad to have you back darling!' She's transformed from her perfectly more than acceptable day outfit, to a floor-length, strapless gown of deep purple and black. I'm not embarrassed to say, it reminds me of a painfully thin Ursula from *The Little Mermaid,* as she slithers closer, and plants a huge kiss on his lips. I can't help but notice him getting red in the cheeks, as he puts a hand on each of her arms, to gently pull her away.

'Wow. Thank you!' he takes this in, and looks at the smiling faces around us. 'Man, it's good to see everybody. Everybody this is Liv, she—'

'Sweetie,' Heather interrupts him and makes an effort to stand in front of me, as if I weren't there, 'everyone is just *dying* to catch up with you; you've been away for so long!!' Heather marches him away from my side and into the room. He glances over his shoulder, meets my eyes and mouths, "I'm sorry."

I shrug, and stand there in the doorway, sheepishly smiling at some friendly faces, then, thankfully, I spot Maddie walking towards me; she truly is a vision of a woman. Her loose wavy blonde hair glistens in the light, and has an elegant bounce as she walks.

'I'm sorry I didn't warn you when we met earlier; I couldn't think of a way to tell you without Dom hearing.'

'Oh, don't be silly!' I say, and scramble for something nice to say, 'What a lovely idea!'

'Well,' she lowers her voice, 'to be completely honest, it wasn't my idea. I had a quiet evening planned where a few close friends were going to pop by for drinks after our dinner, but Heather orchestrated the whole thing into a bit of a party.' She frowns and says even more quietly, 'I wasn't even sure she was still on the scene, but, anyway,' she smiles again, and returns to a normal volume, 'let's get you a drink.'

'Oh, thank you, but maybe I should get changed, I feel rather scrappy and underdressed,' I gesture to my windswept ensemble.

'Nonsense, you look perfect. I'd be a little more casual too, but Heather encouraged me to change into something more formal!' She smiles at me kindly with playful eyes, saying something her mouth doesn't. 'Now, how about that drink? What's your favourite tipple?'

'What do you have?'

She smiles at me. 'Everything, dear. The cocktail of choice though is Dom's favourite, an—'

'*Ooh*, yes, please, I'll take an espresso martini then.' She doesn't respond with words, but you can almost see the cogs in her brain moving. 'What is it?'

'Nothing, dear, nothing.' She looks around and waves over a caterer carrying a tray. We each take an espresso martini. She holds her glass to mine, 'Wonderful to meet you, Liv.'

'You too, Maddie. Cheers.'

We each take a sip. It's the most perfectly balanced one I've ever had, but something is slightly different about it.

'Rum.' Maddie reads my face.

'*Ah*, of course. He said rum over vodka; I'd forgotten.' Again, Maddie looks at me with amusement. 'You have such a beautiful home,' I say, glancing around at the open space, hoping to move the conversation away from my ponderings.

'Thank you. I love it.' She places an arm around me, and introduces me to a few family members and friends as we pass; they are all charming and polite.

Eventually, we step outside. 'Oh wow.' I take in the still, crystal blue, lit swimming pool; the warm light of lanterns; a perfectly placed fire pit; the skyline, and the black ocean in the distance. 'This is out of this world.'

'Here, let's sit by the fire,' Maddie gestures to me and we both take a seat.

I play with my new necklace and take a deep breath, soaking in the beautiful night. 'You are so lucky to have this view.'

'I am.' She smiles, then casually leans back, 'So, tell me, what is it like to travel the world, for a living?' Maddie takes a napkin and a piece of passing watermelon from a caterer's tray, and takes a bite with her perfectly lipsticked mouth.

I shrug, 'It's wonderful.'

'I'm so envious. I really wish I'd travelled more when I was younger. Where's the best place you've ever visited?'

'Honestly, everywhere I've been has a hidden gem, it's so hard to choose, but, I tell you,' I look out at the town's lights below, twinkling like stars in the darkness, 'there is something about here that is so special; I can't quite describe it.'

She smiles and raises an eyebrow. 'Maybe it's not just the setting?'

'What do you mean?'

'There you both are! We were looking *everywhere* for you!' I hear Heather's voice before I see her face. She's holding Dom's hand, almost dragging him along. They sit in two of the empty seats around the fire. Heather is smiling smugly, then her eyes settle on me and her face falls, 'Why are you wearing that?'

'Oh,' I'm still holding my necklace, 'I bought it in Hermosa; it represents new beginnings, and apparently—''

'No, no!' She waves her hands, 'Not the silly cheap glass around your neck. Why are you wearing *Dom's* sweatshirt?'

I go to open my mouth, but Dom speaks for me, 'You know how cold it gets on the boats; I brought it along for her.'

Ha. She can't really say anything to that.

'Oh, how was it? Did you have a good time?' Maddie asks excitedly,

'It was amazing. Honestly, one of the highlights of the

trip.' I look at Dom, who's smiling back at me.

Another caterer passes with a tray of espresso martinis, and we all take one, apart from Heather.

'You're not having one?' I say with surprise. 'They're so delicious!' I take another sip, and smile at Dom. 'And who knew, rum instead of vodka is in fact, just as good.' Dom opens his mouth to say something but Heather interrupts.

'Oh, no, they're *so* bad for you: an upper and a downer? Plus, it's calories I just simply can't afford to be having; I care about my figure.' Raising my eyebrows, I nod and feign interest then take another sip to stop myself from saying anything back at her. 'So, Liv, there is someone who I've been *dying* to introduce you to,' Heather's evil eyes gleam at me.

'Since this morning?' I say doubtfully.

I hear Maddie snigger quietly from my side and try to pass it off as a cough.

'Yes! You know, as soon as I saw you, I just thought: this is the perfect person for Liv.'

Dom looks at her, 'Who are you talking about?'

'Kevin, silly!' she pats his arm.

'Kevin?' Dom makes a disapproving face and shakes his head. 'I don't think so.'

'Honestly,' I lean forward, 'not to be rude, but I'm very happy here. I'm not interested in getting involved with anyone. And anyway, I'm leaving the day after tomorrow so—'

'Which is exactly why it's perfect!' Heather winks at me, 'Who doesn't love a holiday fling!'

'Oh, no, really,' I protest, but it feels like a runaway train, I can't catch up with.

Heather stands up and waves someone over. 'Come on!

Live a little! I've already told him *all* about you.'

You don't know anything about me. I say in my head, narrowing my eyes at her.

'Liv, this is Kevin! Kevin, this is Liv! The one I was telling you about!'

Kevin is definitely a pretty boy, but not a patch on Dom. I smile politely, and hold out my hand, 'Nice to meet you.'

His blonde wavy, Ralph Lauren model hair cut is styled to within an inch of its life, and he has a cardigan draped over his shoulders. 'Heather didn't tell me how beautiful you are!'

I bet she didn't. I look over at Heather and she's got her arms folded in triumph, like she's just solved a huge problem.

'I love your accent; I've always loved the British,' he says kindly, whilst taking a seat.

'Why thank you Kevin!' Maddie says, and I can't help but laugh.

'I guess that's why you're friends with Dom then, liking the British, and all.' I smile.

'Him? No, no. He's neither English nor American; he's a confused mutt,' Kevin jests.

'Excuse me, that's my son there,' Maddie warns, but sips her drink happily.

'You know, I kid,' he winks at Maddie. 'But,' Kevin turns to me, 'I bet you'll be glad to finally get away from this one,' he jabs Dom playfully on the arm. Dom's expression is unimpressed; I have a feeling he can't stand this guy.

I take a deep breath and decide to be honest, 'Actually, I'm really going to miss him.'

Dom turns to smile at me, and for a moment there is nothing but me and him, staring into each other's eyes. *I don't want to leave you.* I wonder if he can sense my thoughts.

'Ah, isn't that cute,' Heather says, without a trace of kindness in her voice.

'Around the world in a month, *huh*? What was that like?' Kevin smiles.

Man, his teeth are white. 'Incredible. I got to write about some amazing places.'

'Oh, she didn't just write,' Dom says.

'What d'you mean?' Surely, he's not going to share what happened in Hawaii with everyone?

'She did some modelling in Singapore!' he grins at me. I'd forgotten all about that.

'Oh, that's fabulous! I didn't know they did modelling for *plus* sizes; good for you!'

'Plus sizes? I'm like a 10,' I say, frowning.

'Exactly, that's what I mean! Good for you!'

'Heather,' Dom warns, and she closes her mouth and grins at me.

'So, just the one wedding left to write about then?' Kevin says, determined to get to know me.

Gathering myself and sweeping away her comment, I answer him, 'Yeah, the final one! I can't believe it; it's actually gone really quickly.'

'It has,' Dom says, still looking at me quite intently.

'So, how do you know Dom and Heather?' I ask Kevin, determined not to look at her; I can almost feel the burn of her stare.

'We all went to school together!' Kevin replies kindly.

'So, we've all known each other for a *very long time*!' Heather chips in.

'In Laguna or Malibu?' I ask, ignoring her.

'Malibu. That's how we know the bride and groom

actually,' Kevin says, and I furrow my brow.

'Oh, you're going too?'

He grins widely, 'I am indeed, and I was wondering: how are you getting to the wedding?'

'*Um*,' I look from him to Dom and back again, 'we drove in a rental, so, we'll head back in that.'

Kevin shakes his head, 'Oh, no, I've got a much more fun way to get there.'

'You do?' I take a sip of my cocktail.

'Don't listen to him. We're fine with the car, mate,' Dom says.

'At least hear him out, sweetie,' Heather says, and I don't know whether it's the fact that she's now manoeuvred herself onto Dom's lap, or the fact that she's giving me the most smug look, but I really want to smack her square in the face.

'So,' Kevin turns excitedly to me, 'I flew myself over here to Laguna, so I'm flying back to Malibu; I need to keep my hours up you see. So, why don't you come with me? It will be nice to have such beautiful company.'

'Your hours? Wait a minute,' I shift towards him slightly. 'You have your own plane?' I ask incredulously.

'I do indeed.' He sits up a little taller with pride. 'Dom here, used to as well, but he sold his.'

I look at Dom wide-eyed, 'You can fly planes?'

'Yes, he can,' Heather says with one hand caressing his hair. 'Do you remember our trip to Napa, sweetie?' She then whispers something in his ear, but he shakes his head then replies.

'It wasn't really my plane; it was my grandad's. I sold it for grandma when he died. He taught me to fly, but I'm more of a car man really, so it didn't make sense to keep it.'

I smile at Dom, then a thought occurs to me. 'How many seats are there?'

'Four,' Kevin says, smiling.

'Oh, well, we could all go together then? Drop the rental off at the airport?' I suggest.

'No, I don't fly,' Heather says sharply.

'Plus, Sarah and Hugo would need a car to get back.'

'Right.' My plan, firmly squished.

'So, is that a, yes? Will you accompany me to Malibu?'

'Well, I'm *working*, I'm not part of the wedding party,' I feel my eyebrows knit together.

'Of course, of course!' he plays with his silly, arm-tied sweater. 'I mean, you know, can I transport you there through the air? And, you never know, maybe when you've finished working, we could have a dance or something?'

'We'll see,' I shrug, non-committedly. 'I don't know how much work is involved yet.'

'But, you'll come with me in my plane?' he presses.

I can't see why not. 'Sure. Thank you.'

'Fantastic!' Heather taps her legs, 'So it's settled, Liv will go with Kevin, and I'll go with *my boyfriend*, Dom.'

Was it really necessary to say that out loud?

***

I'm staying in the most sophisticated guest room I've ever been in. Everything is crisp and white, with soft lagoon blue detailings, from a feature wall, to pillows, and the curtains. I even have my very own balcony! Marvelling at the view, I whip out my phone, and take a picture. There's a soft tap at the door; it comes ajar, and Dom's beautiful face peers through the gap, 'Do you have everything you need?'

'Absolutely.' I smile at him. 'This room is insane, by the way.'

'It used to be mine, you know.' He steps in and closes the door.

'It did? Gosh. Having this view must have been a real attraction for the ladies.'

'What ladies?' he says, innocently. 'Heather's the only person I've been with since school.'

'Wow. That is a long time.'

'I'm not that old,' he winks at me.

'Speaking of Heather, won't she mind you being in my bedroom?'

'I just told you, you're in *my* bedroom.' He laughs. 'She's taking a bath.' His expression drops and he looks at me, conflicted with something. 'You know, it's funny.' He walks over and sits on the edge of the bed. 'I feel,' he pauses and looks at his hands. 'I feel…' he tries again, but something is stopping him.

'Why are you here Dom?' I stay rooted to my spot by the window, despite wanting to dash across the room, kiss him passionately and push him onto the bed.

'I don't know what I want.' He looks at me, pained. 'I've been with Heather for over ten years. Now that I know we're back together, I'm not stupid. Even if she hadn't said earlier, I know what women want; I know what I'm supposed to do; I know what the next step is, but I can't help but think...'

'Think what?'

'That I'm missing something.'

'Well, how are you supposed to feel OK after hours of being back with someone who, for the past month, you hadn't seen or spoken to? You thought today was about closure, not a reunion; no wonder you're confused.'

'I'm not talking about missing something from Heather. Well, I guess, I sort of am. I'm talking about, missing,' he gestures with his hands, 'something.'

For a moment, neither of us say anything, we just look at each other. Finally, I can't help myself. 'What do you want me to say Dom?' I feel my arms fold in, to try and protect my feelings. 'That you should leave the woman that broke your heart and then so effortlessly picked it back up again today?' I take a deep breath, 'Or that I haven't been able to stop thinking about our kiss in Tofino, and that you should run away with me, back to England?' I shake my head. 'No, I'm not going to be the reason why a couple breaks up.'

'So, I'm not mad, am I? We have...*something,* don't we?'

I shrug, 'Well, yeah, but, you're the one who told me you wanted to be friends. What? You've just changed your mind now?'

'Like I said, I don't know what I want.' He combs a hand through his hair, and it falls effortlessly back into place. 'What am I supposed to do? Heather's always encouraged me to get more serious about life, and, I don't know, be a grown up, I guess. But, when I'm with you? I feel like I can do anything, be anything, go anywhere; I can be myself, you know?'

I nod and find my eyes have filled with tears. There's another gentle knock at the door, and I turn to the balcony to wipe my eyes. 'Come in,' I say with a little wobble in my voice, and turn back around. The door cracks open and Maddie steps slightly in the room.

'I just wanted to say goodnight and that I'll serve breakfast at six thirty for you tomorrow, so you can head off as soon as possible.' Maddie meets my eyes and smiles softly, then turns to Dom. 'Oh, and Dom, Heather has requested you bring her a "tepid water."' She manages to say this without a snigger, which I don't manage to suppress. As soon as I start laughing, so do they. Maddie wipes her eyes, 'OK, kids, I'll see you in the morning.'

Dom then stands, 'We'll continue talking tomorrow, yeah?' he says softly, and I nod, knowing there'll be no time or place, after he leaves this room.

'Dom, wait.'

He turns, 'Yes?'

'I, *um...*' *What? What is it you want to say, Liv?* I shake my head, 'Just,' please *don't go.* '*Um*...sleep well.'

He reaches his hand forwards and brushes my cheek. 'You too.' With a click of the door, he's gone.

Chapter 22

USA
Laguna – Malibu

Tuesday

I don't really sleep. I seem to stay in a perpetual state of hypnagogia: drifting in and out of consciousness, replaying the scene with Dom in my head over and over, with various versions; from Heather walking in and shooting us all, to my favourite: me running to the bed, Dom kissing me wildly, before giving me the best night I've ever had.

When I roll over and read 5 o'clock on my phone, I get up, repack what little I brought with me, throw my hair up into a messy bun, grab my yoga leggings, a little workout top that conveniently says, "The path to inner peace begins with four simple words: Not my F***ing problem," and head outside to do some yoga; I need to get out of my head.

I pad downstairs, and it occurs to me that the door might be locked, or worse, maybe there's an alarm? I creep even quieter, as if that will make a difference if there is an alarm, but thankfully, the kitchen spotlights are on, and I see everything is already open. Walking through the floor to ceiling, wall to wall, glass doors, and past the fire pit, I look around the lantern-lit garden. I guess someone must be up somewhere? I can't see anyone, so I pick a spot on the grass, to the left of the swimming pool, overlooking the sleepy city and beach below. The sun is yet to wake, and even though it's cool, it's absolutely perfect for my state of mind: it's fresh, and feels like a new beginning. My bare feet wiggle on the grass. Standing tall, I close my eyes, purposely place my arms down by my side, palms facing forwards, and stand in mountain pose, taking a deep breath in.

Boy, I've missed this. It's ironic really. Whenever I'm particularly stressed, I avoid yoga. I know that it will make me feel better, but for the last year, I've really struggled to be consistent. But, I know, whenever I step on the mat — physical or metaphorical — yoga's got an unbelievably calming effect on me; whatever I've been doing, whatever I've been thinking, it has a way to unwind my body and mind, no matter how tangled I've become.

Heading into a sun salutation, I immediately feel a sense of relief. I repeat the sequence several more times, then continue on to a *vinyasa* flow. Concentrating on my breath, I can smell coffee, clear air, and the roses that are flowering next to me. Thoughts of Dom float through my head the whole time. I attempt to push them out but I can't. He's there. Heather comes next. *Ugh*. What is it about her? Why is she so irritating? *I'm sure it has nothing to do with the fact that she's sleeping with the guy that you'd like to be with*, my subconscious points out. She's probably wrapped up in his arms right now. Shaking my head, I transition into a downward dog and my necklace swings into my face, as if my subconscious is telling my thoughts to *shush*. I take it off, place it on the grass, tuck the front of my t-shirt into my trousers, and move into a headstand, facing the house; maybe I can drain some of these thoughts out.

Upside down, I suddenly see Maddie in the kitchen,

filling up a glass of water; she's dressed in something not too dis-similar to me. She glances out and spots me; all I can do is smile; I can't wave from here. After she's filled her glass, she walks over.

'God it's been years since I've done a headstand; I'm so jealous.'

'To be honest, I haven't done this the whole time we've been away; I sort of forgot who I was. Feels nice to try and remember.'

She puts the glass down. Then standing with space between us, takes some deep breaths, does a couple of moves before turning, and transitioning into a headstand; her face towards mine.

'Impressive!'

'No, your resilience yesterday was impressive, my dear. This is just an old gal trying to keep up with the delightful young woman in front of me.'

I laugh and nearly lose my balance, but manage to stay upright.

'So, are you always an early riser?' I ask, ever the English woman who doesn't know how to accept a compliment.

'Oh yes, I love this time of day. Just me, my thoughts: I like a meditation first thing, then a little workout, followed by a breakfast out here; only then do I feel ready for my day.'

'When I was a kid, my mum tried to encourage me to meditate with her, but I struggled with it; unless it's a guided thing, I find my thoughts drift too much.'

'And? That's the whole point. You sit *with* the thoughts; you allow them to come and go. It's about separating yourself from those thoughts, rather than allowing them to take over, and you becoming them, so, you then become the observer of your thoughts; they aren't happening *to* you, you are just looking at them.'

'That's so profound, Maddie. I'll try to remember that.' For a moment we both just look at each other in silence. 'Dom has your eyes.'

'And his father's stubborn attitude,' she adds. 'I never said how much I like your rainbow moonstone, by the way.' Her eyes lower to my necklace on the ground.

'Oh, thanks! It's new; I got it in Hermosa.'

'It's perfect for you,' she says, like a wise sage.

'Really? Why do you say that?'

'Well, it's said to protect travellers; you're a world traveller.'

I smile, 'I am.'

'It is also said to protect those who are left behind by a traveller.'

Hmm, I was left behind by Leo, I guess. Or does she mean Dom?

She continues, 'But you're also wanting to connect to your higher power? Good for you!'

'I am?'

'Yeah, it's connected to the crown chakra. It's a stone that represents a need for spiritual guidance. It's also a good stone for getting in touch with your emotions, and as a necklace, you wear it close to your heart, so it will fend off negative energies.'

'It will?'

She smiles at me, 'It's also a traditional ancient totem of undying love; it can remove anger and allow you to accept the love of others. It's got nurturing powers that encourage you to believe in your own worth.'

'Wow. That wasn't all written on the description card; I

got it for new beginnings.'

'Well, here's to your new beginnings.' She wiggles slightly, then gently lowers her legs, turns around, and moves to a child's pose with her arms stretched towards me, 'OK, that's it for me.' I follow her lead, then sit cross-legged, facing her.

'I know it's none of my business, but for what it's worth, it is clear there's something between you and Dom.'

'You heard us talking yesterday?' I'm embarrassed, but it feels effortless to talk to her.

'I did.'

Am I really going to confide in his mother about this? What the hell, I'm probably never going to see this woman again. 'Even if we do get another chance to talk, I have no idea what it is that I want to say.'

She sits in front of me, and places her hand on mine. 'My son doesn't talk about his feelings; ever. The fact that he tried last night is a big deal.'

'But, he's with Heather. I'm not going to be the person who breaks up a childhood love; I'm not that person.' I pick up the necklace and play with it.

'Between you and me,' she nods, 'it's been such a long time, I've learnt to tolerate Heather. She comes across tough but underneath it all, I think she's insecure.' She frowns, 'In spite of that, there's something that I just don't trust about her. But you? And, admittedly, it helps that you're a Brit, I'm sure,' she smiles at me, 'anyone can see what a pure soul you have. And you know, the connection that you clearly have with my son, is wonderful to watch, and, honestly, rather rare.' I don't know what to say, so I stay silent. 'If you do feel the way I think you feel about him, you know you're allowed to say. And if my son is too stupid to realise what's in front of him, well, it is truly his loss.' She smiles at me sadly, 'But, like I said, it's none of my business. Would you like some coffee?'

'I'd love some.'

We walk into the house together just as the pre-glow is happening. I take a seat at the kitchen bar, and my eye immediately goes to a canvas of a seal across the room; its huge black eyes stare at me.

'Oh my God, that's the picture Dom was talking about. He said his favourite picture was of a seal in Newport Beach.'

Maddie brings over two black coffees, 'Yeah, that's my favourite too.'

'I didn't see it last night,' I say, staring at it.

'Well, there was a lot happening last night. Do you take milk or sugar?'

'No, just black, thank you.'

'Girl after my own heart.' She sits next to me and sips her coffee.

I'm still staring at the canvas. '*Man,* he's good. It's like the picture's telling you a story.'

I can hear Maddie's smile in her voice, 'I'd like to say he gets it from me, but I paint; I wouldn't know the first thing about cameras. My late father-in-law gave Dom his first camera when he was about five or six, and even then, he had a better eye than the photographer we used for the company!'

I turn to face her now, and bite my lip, considering whether I should say anything. 'Now, I know this is none of *my* business, but, since you were kind enough to share your wisdom with me,' I pause.

'Go on.' Maddie looks at me with intrigue.

'Have you talked to your husband about supporting Dom to pursue his dreams, and allowing him to rightly have his inheritance? I bet he could put it towards investing in his own company.'

She sits and takes me in for a moment, 'He told you about all that?'

I nod, 'And I know, I've overstepped a line here, but I'm leaving tomorrow, and I don't think he'll ever say this to either you, your husband or Heather. He has a passion and a love, and he wants to explore and create. Personally, I think he's wasted merely taking pictures of centrepieces, and young models in tulle and lace. He gets so excited and inspired by his environment, and the world around him...' I giggle, 'You should have seen him when we were in Thailand with the fireflies, and yesterday? God Lord, he just came alive on that boat.' I look at her, smiling at how passionately I'm talking, 'Maddie, we've spent most waking moments of every day, for the last month together, and when we were working, he's bored. He needs someone to stand up and support him to do what he wants to do.'

She considers me for a moment, 'I suppose it's obvious from his website. The wedding section is unquestionably beautiful, but the nature and particularly the marine life pictures?' she sighs. 'They've definitely got this sparkle to them.' She sips her coffee. 'You know, he's never told me he doesn't like his job at the magazine.'

'He told me that Heather wanted him to get a serious job. But really, I think he's trying to prove to you and your husband that he can stand on his own two feet, wherever his career takes him. And, again, I know I'm overstepping, but from what Dom's told me, your husband is rather resistant to supporting such an unpredictable career like freelance photography, isn't he?'

'Indeed,' she says, shortly. 'But, without that bravery of a seemingly unreachable dream, we wouldn't be living the way we do, with the abundance that we have.'

'Oh,' I say suddenly, 'complete side note, but I have to tell you, I love your revitalising spray; the design makes me smile every time I use it; thank you for designing such a beautiful product. I use it every time I travel, and sometimes when I'm home, and miss travelling.'

She laughs, 'You're very welcome.'

I smile back at her. *Gosh, I like this woman.* 'I'm sad I'm leaving.'

She taps me on the hand. 'I know dear. Me too, actually.'

'*Ugh*, I have always hated that picture, it freaks me out!' We turn to see Heather at the bottom of the stairs, looking at the seal, before turning to us. 'Where's the coffee?'

***

After a delicious breakfast, I hug Maddie goodbye, and Dom and Heather drop me off at John Wayne Airport.

'I'm guessing we'll get there before you?' I ask as I shift my overnight bag from one shoulder to another.

Dom takes his sunglasses off and looks at me, 'It's only about half an hour in the air, but Kevin has to do flight and safety checks, and then you've got the drive the other side, and I'd imagine he'll give you more of a tour than you'd expect, so,' he shrugs, 'we'll probably beat you,' he says this sadly, not with any of his usual playful banter.

'Am I insane for going on a plane, as the only passenger, with a complete stranger?' I whisper to Dom. Heather adjusts her lipstick in the passenger mirror and couldn't be less interested in what I'm saying.

'Oh, well, if we don't hear from you, we'll send out a search party,' she sniggers.

I think she'd more likely wear slippers, a unicorn onesie and zero makeup to the wedding, than she would give me a second thought.

'OK, well, great. You can head off; I'm sure he'll be here in a minute,' I fluster, not wanting to be in Heather's presence a moment longer than I have to. Thankfully, sure enough, a cab pulls up and out Kevin pops. He honestly looks like a model, wearing sunglasses that somehow emphasise his chiselled cheekbones, and I take in, what I'm now guessing is his standard look: a cardigan draped over his shoulders.

'Morning, everybody!' He strides over, carrying nothing but a small overnight bag and buckets of charm. Reaching my side, he puts a casual arm around me; I don't know if I like it. 'So, are you ready for the ride of your life?'

'Sure. We'll see you there?' I smile, unsure at Dom.

He, in turn, smiles at me, as Kevin spins me off in the other direction. 'You take care of her, OK?' Dom calls after Kevin, who's now walking me to the airport entrance. He either ignores him or doesn't hear Dom, as I give a small wave.

'*Sooooo*,' Kevin drawls over each word. 'My plane is just over this way.'

'This is like something out of a film.'

'Oh, I don't really watch films; far too busy with my business you see.'

'What do you do?'

'This,' he smiles proudly.

'What do you mean?'

'I'm a pilot.'

'Really? Wow.' That would be kind of convenient to marry a pilot; enabling me to travel all over the world for the rest of my life. I shake my head and wonder where those thoughts have come from.

'Yeah. I got my private licence as soon as I could; I was sixteen. So was Dom by the way; we did it together.'

'*Huh.*' I wonder why he didn't tell me that after all the time we spent together; is he embarrassed by his wealth?

'Then I got my commercial licence at eighteen; flew with a couple of smaller airlines first, then made my way into Emirates, but decided to come back home full time and teach.'

'What prompted that? I'd love to fly myself around the world forever,' I say wistfully.

'Honestly, I'm ready to settle down. I just need to find the right girl, I guess.' He winks at me. 'One can't travel the world forever.'

Well, this one intends to! I don't answer him out loud, but that's exactly what I intend to do for the rest of my life. All I need to do is find someone who's willing to do that with me. 'So, what got you into flying, then?' I decide to put the focus back on him.

'It's something all the men in my family have done for generations. Although, I'm the only one to have it as my actual job; I wanted to turn a family hobby into a career.'

'Sounds like me.' I've said the words before I thought about them. *I don't want to lead this man on.* 'What does your family do?'

'They're all doctors.'

'Do you think they wanted you to follow in their footsteps?'

He shrugs, ‘Maybe. But then, they wouldn’t all get perks of being related to an *actual* pilot.’ He grins again, ‘Plus, I don’t think I could ever have done what my dad does. Too messy.’

‘What does your dad do?’

‘He’s a cosmetic and reconstructive surgeon.’

I can’t help but laugh out loud. When he looks offended, I add, ‘I’m so sorry. I’ve just never met a plastic surgeon before. I bet he’s got a million stories.’

‘Oh, he does,’ he says as we walk towards his hanger. Suddenly he stops, and poses while glancing left to right, as if someone’s taking his picture, ‘But, he refuses to tell us a single one.’

‘I’m guessing he’s done celebrities then?’ I can’t help but ask, while attempting to ignore his weird behaviour.

He nods, ‘Definitely. But, like I said, I’ve no idea who, however,’ Kevin dramatically pulls open a wide-spanning metal door, and reveals a little prop plane, ‘he did say that the plane was named after the very first celebrity he worked on; he bought it for me,’ he adds simply, as if buying your child a plane was a perfectly normal thing to do.

‘Wow.’ I walk in and check out the shiny, four-seater, blue and white prop plane. Looking at the front, there’s a single letter there: “J.”

I furrow my brow, ‘Well that’s frustratingly cryptic. But, at least you know it’s probably a “her.”’

‘How do you know it’s a “her?”’

‘Oh,’ I’m embarrassed after his comment about no time for films, ‘I may have watched a film on Netflix that said it’s good luck to name a plane after women.’

He nods, ‘Yup, that’s right. So, I know you’re a world traveller, but have you ever been on a plane like this before?’

'No, first time,' I smile at him, slightly uneasily. I wish Dom were here; this doesn't feel right.

'Fantastic!' He continues to run through safety checks with me. When he's done, he pushes the plane out of the hanger, locks the doors, then opens the passenger door for me. I step up, standing in the instructed designated place, not on the wing, as warned, then take a seat. He shuts my door for me, then walks around. I'm suddenly terrified. And I'm not afraid of flying. Is this a good idea? Why are there two steering wheels? Oh, yeah, it's a teaching plane. I'm suddenly afraid of breaking something.

He hops in, and hands me a set of headphones equipped with a built-in mic.

'What are these for?'

'Think of it like a helicopter; it'll be too noisy to talk without them.'

Accepting them, I put them on and try to remember to breathe.

'Alright,' I hear him talk through his mic, and into my ears; it's surprisingly clear. 'Can you hear me OK?'

'Yup, loud and clear.'

'Perfect, I can hear you too. You look cute in those; not everyone can pull them off.'

'Thanks.'

'OK,' he moves his attention onto the plane, making some adjustments on the knobs in front of him. 'Control tower, this is 4532, awaiting permission for take-off.'

I can't help but be impressed. I'm with a pilot, who's a descendant of doctors; my family would be so proud.

'OK. Roger, thank you. We'll await our next instruction.' He turns his face to mine, 'We've got just one plane ahead of us, then we can take off.'

When it's our turn, the roar of the engine is intensely loud, even with the headphones on.

'Here we go!' He grins from ear to ear.

We're in the air quicker than I thought. 'That didn't take long to get up.'

'Never does.' He winks. 'No, it's because we're much lighter than a commercial plane.'

Sooner still, we're climbing higher and higher, and I love it. 'Gosh, I love flying!' I don't realise I've said this out loud, until I can hear him chuckling.

'Do you want to fly?'

'Me? Fly the plane? You're kidding?'

'Nope, it's very easy; I'll show you, so what you'll notice is, it's like a car, but, not only can you go side to side.' I giggle as he wobbles the plane from left to right, dipping the wings as we go. 'But you can also go dramatically up and down.'

'*Aghhh*!!' I scream as he drops the height of the plane then climbs back up within seconds. He laughs this time. 'Don't do that again!' I won't tell him that that was actually fun.

'So, just hold your hands at ten and two, like a car.'

I tentatively place my hands as instructed, 'OK, great; what next?' I stare straight ahead and prepare him to tell me the next step before I take over.

'That's it; you're doing it.'

'What!? Oh my God, I'm not ready!' I yell, wide-eyed.

'You are adorable; you're flying it.' He sits back and places his arms behind his head.

'I'm flying a plane,' I say to kind of calm myself down. 'I'm flying a plane!' I repeat, but excitedly. 'I'm freaking out a little, but I love it. You can feel the wind in the steering wheel, *huh*?'

'Yup. There's quite a bit more movement than a car, but you're doing great though,' he smiles at me.

'Will you take a picture of me, please? My phone's in my bag.'

'What's your password, *oh*.' I know my phone just unlocks.

'You really should have a password; any old weirdo could take your phone.'

Ah huh.

He snaps a few photos of me. 'There. Something to remember, *huh*?'

'Absolutely.' My phone starts ringing to indicate Facetime. 'Wow, who would have thought there's reception up here!' I say smiling.

Kevin answers it, 'Hi! Where are you?'

'What are you doing?' I say, not wanting to take my eyes off the sky, for fear of a suicidal seagull or something.

'Say hi to Dom!' Kevin points the screen towards me.

'That's Dom?' I glance briefly to see his disgruntled face before returning to the clouds. 'Dom! Look! I'm flying a plane!'

'Amazing.' I can't see his face, but his tone is deadpan. 'We're just stopping at Ralphs; do you want anything?'

'I think we're OK.' Kevin answers for the both of us, which makes me frown. 'Don't you miss this view, buddy? It's glorious.'

'It is,' he replies. I hope he's talking about me, not the clouds. 'OK, well, we'll see you soon,' Dom says, with a sad tone.

Kevin hangs up, 'Do you make a habit of answering people's phones?' I can't help but ask.

'Only when I know they'll wind up my buddy there.'

I fly for a little longer before Kevin takes the wheel again.

We descend into Santa Monica Airport, just like Dom said, about half an hour later, and land on a similar looking runway to John Wayne.

We slowly head to a hanger, and Kevin does a little three-point-turn kind of manoeuvre, then stops and gets out. He opens the doors to reveal another impressive space, with one difference: a rather shiny sports car; the make is unmistakable.

Unbuckling my seatbelt, I hop out. Kevin walks to the front of the plane and begins to push it into the hangar.

'You have a McLaren?' I ask incredulously. I keep forgetting that I'm probably with a millionaire.

'It's one of my cars, yes,' he says simply.

'Now *that's* something I'd love to drive!'

He laughs, 'Really? You're a car girl?'

I nod, 'Yeah, I used to go to all kinds of car shows and museums with my dad, all around the world.'

'*Huh.*'

I know this impresses a man; it's admittedly a line that I've used many times, but I don't want to encourage him.

'Have you ever driven something like this before?'

'Nope. But I'm a fast learner,' I tilt my head.

He winks at me. 'Alright then.'

'Really? You're going to let me drive your half a million-pound car?'

'Dollar,' he corrects, 'But, yeah, why not? Give the lady what she wants, I say.'

***

'HOLY '*EFF*!' I haven't even put my foot down, and we're zooming along the Pacific Coast Highway.

'Exciting car, *huh*?'

'This is the most thrilling car I've ever driven!'

'You know, you can go above thirty miles an hour.'

'Is that all I'm doing?' I laugh. 'It feels so much faster!' I giggle with glee the whole way.

When we arrive at Calamigos, I practically skip out of the car, handing the valet the keys, before turning to Kevin. 'Thank you so much, that was amazing!'

Kevin beams, clearly proud of himself, and tips the valet before answering. 'You're welcome, beautiful.'

My stomach turns; that felt wrong. I give him a tight smile, as we walk through the entrance, and it's just as charming during the day as it was at night.

'Gosh, I love it here,' I say, out loud, but not particularly to Kevin; I don't need a response, I'm stating it as a fact.

'Really? I've always found it a little cheesy.'

I stop walking, 'Are you kidding? This is so charming! I love it! It's a BBQ ranch, woodland retreat in the Malibu Mountains, wrapped top to toe in fairy lights. Seriously, what's not to like?' He pulls a face and doesn't respond. 'I think it's gorgeous,' I continue.

'They do a lot of filming here,' he says as we continue our walk towards the entrance.

'They do?'

'Oh yeah, I think an episode or two of *90210; The Biggest Loser, Wayne's World 2, Grey's Anatomy, The Bachelorette,* and *The Bachelor.*'

'That is so cool.'

'Tourist,' he winks at me.

'Hey! I am allowed to think that's exciting; even if I haven't heard of half of those,' I add.

'Well, hi there!' Sarah walks casually around the corner, in uncharacteristic flip flops.

'Hi! You look relaxed.'

She smiles, 'I am. Last wedding: I'm pumped!'

'But, you're not wearing heels?'

She looks at her feet. 'No. Decided to let my feet breathe for a minute.'

I laugh at her and give her a hug. 'Sarah, this is Kevin; he's a friend of Dom's from school, would you believe?'

'I would believe; Dom told me where you were when he arrived with Heather.' She's smiling but it's more of a grimace. She holds out her hand for Kevin, 'Lovely to meet you.'

'You too, Sarah.'

'Well,' I turn to Kevin, 'thank you again for the flight and the ride! I guess I'll see you later.'

'Looking forward to it.' He steps in, places a hand on my side, and kisses me on the cheek. It's not unpleasant, but, seriously, I've just met this man; I don't want his lips anywhere on me.

'OK.' I give him another tight smile, 'Bye, then.' I grab Sarah's hand and walk off.

'I'll be waiting for that dance!' He calls after me. I pretend not to hear him.

'He's a bit keen, isn't he?'

'Indeed.' I make sure there's enough distance between him and us, then turn to Sarah, 'I have a problem.'

'What's up?' She looks so relaxed, I have to take a beat.

'Hang on, I have to ask: why are you so relaxed? Did I

miss something?'

She grins. 'You did.'

'What?'

'Well, when you and Dom left, Hugo and I were doing our thing: last minute plans with the bride, *yarda yarda*. Anyway, after dinner yesterday, Hugo came over for a little glass of wine, we started talking, and basically didn't stop until the morning.'

I smile at my friend, 'You talked. That's your big news?'

She nods, 'Yup. He told me how he feels about me. And you know what, Liv?

'What?'

'I'm pretty sure I like him too.'

'That's wonderful! You guys would make a super cute couple!'

'Oh,' she flusters, 'that's far too much pressure, for right now. I think I need a little time to clear my head, so, I'm flying out to New York to see my parents for a few days, and, after that,' she shrugs, 'I'm willing to go with the flow!' I giggle with her, and give her a huge hug. 'So,' she regards me with all seriousness, 'tell me, what your problem is: that you flew in a private plane here or that you got to drive a supercar around the Malibu Mountains?'

'No,' I say, smiling, 'Although, both of those things were awesome,' I can't deny.

Sarah continues her serious tone, 'Is it that you're so beautiful that a man you just met has literally taken you for a joy ride?'

I laugh at that one. 'No, listen!'

'I know,' she says smiling sympathetically this time, 'it's the fact that the guy you're in love with is here with his horrid ex-girlfriend, turned girlfriend, instead of you.' I go to open my mouth but she speaks instead, 'That's right; I know you're in love with Dom, and it's very clear that he's in love with you too.'

I decide not to challenge her. 'Have you met her?'

'I have indeed had the displeasure; who would have thought that much toxicity could be packaged in such a tiny frame.' She pops an arm around me and we start walking again. 'Now, I know you're here to work, but, this is the last wedding, and you're leaving tomorrow, so, it is literally now or never; girlfriend or no girlfriend; you've got to tell him how you feel.'

'Well, I sort of already did. He came to my room last night.'

'What?! Tell me everything!'

'Well, there isn't really anything to tell. He said he doesn't know what to do.'

'Well, take away any confusion and plant one on him!'

'It's not as simple as that, Sarah; he's been with Heather for over ten years.'

'And?'

'And?! That's a long time! They're childhood sweethearts. I'm not about to break that up, no matter how much I want to.'

She considers me and what I'm saying, 'You're a much more decent person than I am. OK, fine, well, if you're not going to make a move, you're going to show him exactly what he's missing out on.'

I shake my head, 'What do you mean?'

'You are in America darling, and we are the queens of the traditional makeover!'

'What? Oh *no*, I don't need a makeover; I'm fine just as I am.'

'Of course you are, Poppet, and I don't really mean a makeover; just let me do your hair and makeup tonight, OK?'

I smile at her, 'You sure you want to take this on?' I point to my classic large messy bun.'

'Absolutely! Just hand me the chainsaw,' she plays. 'I'm kidding! I'm an expert, and you are my friend and I've been dying to play with it since we met!'

'Alright then. But first, where's the bride? I need to actually do some work.'

Chapter 23

USA
Malibu

Savannah is everything you'd hope to be on your own wedding day: calm, poised, beautiful, excited to start the next chapter of her life, and so in love with Jackson. Her bridesmaids are off, putting last minute touches around the venue, so it's just her and me sitting in her suite. Just like every bride, she's grateful, honoured and humbled to be involved in the article, but she's being extremely open. Of course, that could have something to do with the bottle of champagne that we're working our way through; her idea, not mine.

'I just can't believe we won if I'm honest; I think Dom rigged it.'

'He may have told me he had a say in it,' I admit, smiling at her from my seat opposite hers; trying to remember that I still have a job to do, and mustn't get, to quote Jude Law, "inordinately pissed," before absolutely necessary. But man, this is good champagne.

Savannah gestures to me with her glass, 'I knew it. He's such a great guy; you know? He encouraged us to enter, and a few weeks later, we were contacted!' She makes a face. 'Let's leave that out of the article; I don't want to be the reason anyone else gets fired.' She takes a sip of her bubbles.

'What do you mean? Who did you get fired?' I stop

scribbling in my trusty notebook.

She throws her hand over her mouth, then lowers her voice, not that anyone can hear us, 'Heather doesn't know this, but I'm the one who got her in trouble.' She winces. 'I feel awful that she lost her job.'

'Hang on, rewind and back up a second; what happened? How could you have got her fired?' She looks at my notebook, and I make an effort to put my pen down. 'Off the record.'

'Well, I was in the office for a meeting with Sarah and Hugo for my initial ideas about the feel of the wedding, and I noticed Heather wasn't there.'

'OK,' I say, leaning forward, 'Was she supposed to be?'

'Yeah. Which I thought was strange, since we've known each other for ages. I thought she'd want to be there anyway, regardless of the fact that it's her job, but, when I was leaving the building, I went to use the washroom, and I walked in on them about to get busy.'

'OK, well, why didn't Dom get fired then? Surely, an office couple canoodling isn't a fireable offence is it?'

'Apparently it is if it's your boss,' she says bluntly.

'Wait.' I take a beat. 'What? Heather wasn't with Dom?' I say slowly, piecing together an awkwardly shaped puzzle.

'Not in the bathroom I walked into, no.'

'Oh my God. Does Dom know?'

She shakes her head, 'I don't think so.'

'So what? She got let go, because a client witnessed that?'

'I guess so? All I know is that the day after I met with Sarah and Hugo, Heather was no longer working there, and I got an email saying that you were taking over.'

I let this sink in, then can't help myself. 'I'm sorry, but I have to ask, why are you telling *me* this?'

‘I don’t know.’ She thinks for a moment, ‘We’ve made pretty good work of that bottle of bubbles,’ she reasons, ‘it’s my wedding day, and you have a kind face; I feel I can trust you.’

‘Thanks,’ I smile at the compliments. ‘Have you talked to Heather about this?’ I dare to ask.

‘No, she refuses to.’ Savannah goes to say something, then thinks twice.

‘What were you going to say?’

‘I love Dom. Not like that,’ she responds to the expression I guess I’ve morphed my face into. ‘I love Dom like a brother, he’s a great friend, and I want him to be happy.’

‘You don’t think he’s happy with Heather?’ I can’t help but ask, and hope.

‘I don’t know. She was always one of the sneaky, two-faced girls at school; I’m not sure she’s grown out of that.’

Maybe I should say something to him about how I feel?

‘Anyway, thank you for listening to me blab away.’ She takes a sip of bubbles. ‘Would you like another glass?’ she offers.

‘Oh, no, thank you,’ I wave her away. ‘I’m supposed to be working.’

She puts a delicate hand on her hip, ‘Excuse me, I am the bride, this is my wedding, and you will absolutely have a top up, if that’s what the bride demands. You’ve been around the world! This is your last wedding, you’ve interviewed us, just take a mental note of the surroundings; I hereby give you permission to have a little fun.’

I grin at her, ‘Well, if I have to.’ She twists my arm with very little pressure.

‘There we go!’ She grabs the bottle and starts pouring.

***

It's a sunset wedding, so at four p.m., after I've done everything I'm supposed to, there's plenty of time to head back to my room to get "Sarah-ified." I decide to tell my roommate what the bride told me, which fully backs up Sarah's argument that I should talk with Dom.

'I'll think about it,' I say. My stomach churns nervously. *Am I actually going to say something? No. I can't. But I want to.* I take a deep breath to stop my own dizzying thoughts. 'I'm just going to focus on finishing this job and then, if and when the time presents itself, I might.'

'You know,' Sarah pauses from applying some eyeshadow to my eyelids. 'Moments don't always present themselves. Sometimes you've got to create them; it's up to you to design your own future.'

'That's deep, have you thought about putting that on a fridge magnet?' I say sarcastically, and then grin at her.

Completely unphased by my attempt to divert the conversation away from my feelings, she continues lightly brushing my face, 'I'm just saying. This may be the only moment you have.'

'As Captain Jack Sparrow would say, "Wait for the opportune moment."'

'I literally have no idea what you're talking about,' she looks at me with a blank expression.

'Dom would,' I say simply.

She smiles at me, 'Isn't that the point? You two get each other. All these little weird moments you share together.'

'Weird moments?' I enquire.

'Excuse me, *cute moments*: laughing like you have this little secret language between you; it's adorable. I just don't want you to miss out on taking your shot.'

About an hour later, we're ready. I've opted for my floor-length, burgundy, off the shoulder dress with a large slit at the front left hand side, and I feel a million dollars. I only own one pair of fancy heels: they're satin, close-toed, that strap around my ankles, with a little line of silver glitter to detail the edge; they were my maid of honour shoes for Bex's wedding. They're comfy, and I love them, but I haven't worn them in about three years.

'Feels strange being this tall,' I remark.

'*Ah*, you're cute, thinking that's tall.' Sarah pats me on the head; even in her flip flops she's towering above me. 'You look beautiful. Are you ready to see?' She hasn't let me look in the mirror yet.

'Yup, let's do it.' She takes a step to her right and I take in my reflection, in the mirror behind her. 'Oh Sarah, thank you.' I touch my hair, she's got it up in an old Hollywood glamour style with finger waves, and a low bun. My makeup is so subtle, but makes my eyes pop and she's applied lipstick to match my dress; a little bold, but it works.

'Am I good, or am I good?' She appears behind my shoulder in the mirror.

'You are amazing. Thank you so much,' I say to her reflection. 'You look very beautiful too.'

She's gone all out in another beautiful 1950s black and white, Audrey Hepburn style dress, that nips in at the waist and then goes out to exaggerate her perfect hourglass figure. 'Thanks chick.' She steps into her high black and white vintage Mary Jane heels.

'Oh, great.' I turn to face her, tilting my head backwards and my eyes up to see her face, 'Now I look like a child going to the prom with her mum.'

She laughs hard at this. 'I'm going to miss you so much.' She reaches out and scoops me up in her arms.

'I'm going to miss you too.' I can feel myself almost tearing up.

'Alright, stop it, get away!' She pushes me back. 'You're going to ruin your makeup!'

'Alright,' I agree, blinking away any sign of tears. 'We'll have a proper goodbye tomorrow at breakfast. Now, let's go and have a great time.'

'That,' she points at me, 'I think we can do!' She puts her arm around me and we walk out of our room.

The wedding is in the most idyllic spot. The "altar" is underneath a five story Californian Oak tree, with droplets of fairy lights, that appear to be dripping off the branches.

'It's so magical!' I can't help but exclaim as we walk our way to our designated seats. 'And, who would have thought, I'm finally walking down the aisle!' I joke to Sarah.

She links arms with me, 'I'm honoured to walk with you, Poppet.' She bumps me affectionately with her hip.

Looking around, I can't help filling my heart with joy and hope; there has to be a happy ending doesn't there? My eyes glance to the right side of the rows of seats for guests. I spot Dom, camera in hand, standing at the front, looking rather delicious in a sharp black suit, crisp white shirt and black bowtie; he's looking right at me with wide eyes. I smile at him as Sarah and I continue our walk down the aisle. He takes a picture of us both, then lowers his camera, meets my eyes again, and suddenly everything disappears; there is only him and me. Our eyes are locked until we reach him; then I spot Heather sitting with her back to us, talking to another girl.

Sarah unlinks her arm from mine, 'I'm just going to check

on the bride; I'll see you in a bit,' and she walks off to my left.

Neither Dom nor I say anything, we're still just staring at each other.

'Hi,' I finally break the silence, and give a small smile.

'Hi.' He shakes his head, 'You look…' he searches for the right word.

'Oh my God, is that you Liv? You're unrecognisable!' Heather's voice breaks our eye contact, and it's clear that her comment is not a compliment.

'Thank you. You look very beautiful Heather,' I say kindly, and actually mean it. She's a vision, in *white*. Her low cut, plunging neckline dress, has sparkles like the lights on the tree, but somehow, it's no way as charming.

'Oh, this old thing. It's just something I threw together.'

I highly doubt that. She folds one tanned leg over the other, revealing yet again, another pair of spectacular shoes: high and pointy sparkling silver and dusk blue, fireball glitter, Jimmy Choos.

'So how was your trip?' She grins at me, and I can't help but notice it's a little like having The Joker smile at you: it looks happy but is in fact, rather terrifying.

'It was fun! I got to fly the plane and drive his McClaren!'

'You did?' she says doubtfully.

'I did.' *Where is she going with this*? 'Why?'

'Oh, nothing, it's just that, he must *really* like you; he doesn't let just any old stranger from England handle such precious things.'

'I'm sure that's not true. Anyway, let's take a seat, shall we?' I gesture to Dom and look at the four chairs closest to the aisle. There are delicate signs taped to each, they read,

"Dom" "Sarah" "Hugo" and finally, next to Heather, "Liv". *Perfect.* I walk slowly over to sit next to her.

'Oh, I wish I was wearing a dress like yours,' she says, ever so patronisingly.

'You do?' I say, doubtfully.

'Oh, yeah, you can hide all manner of sins underneath them.'

'Excuse me?' This dress compliments every curve, and if ever I knew someone was talking absolute bollocks, it's right now. I look awesome; that is a fact.

'Oh, no offence, it's just that, *my* dress,' she stands up and twirls around in her impossibly high shoes, showcasing her athletic body, 'doesn't leave anything to the imagination, so—'

'Heather, that's enough,' Dom snaps.

'What sweetie?' she tilts her head innocently.

'You're being very rude.' He frowns at her.

'No, I'm not.' She smiles at him sweetly, trying to wrap him around her little finger.

He lowers his voice, 'I'm going to have to go back to work any second now, I don't have time to deal with this. Liv is my friend, she's no threat to you, so knock it off, sit down and play nice.'

It's all I can do to not stand up and start clapping and whooping. She falters for a moment before dazzling her pearly whites at everybody, and parking her arse next to me. 'Fine.'

Other guests begin taking their seats, and Dom starts snapping away. It's not until he moves away from us that Heather leans in. 'Alright, missy, listen up.'

'You're a little in my space here, Heather.' Her nose is almost touching mine.

'Yeah, well you are in *my* space, *capiche*?'

'*Non capisco!*' I answer in Italian.

'What? Whatever. You are,' she waves her arms about, '*literally* in my space, here in California. You don't belong here, so stop trying to fit in,' she says threateningly.

'I'm not trying to fit in!' I justify. 'If you didn't notice, I'm here, *working*, when you could have been, but *you* got fired.' I can feel myself getting increasingly angry. 'I hadn't met you before, I didn't take this away from you, I was *asked* to do this, OK? So why don't *you* just back off, and let me do my job.'

She sits, arms crossed, with a huge frown on her face. 'No,' she mutters quietly. Her fury is clearly about to boil over. 'No, I don't know what you think you're doing and I don't know what game you're playing, but you're *not* going to win.'

'I'm not playing any game!' *God, I want to slap her.*

'Savannah looks beautiful,' Hugo says, walking over with Sarah, just in time. He takes his seat, completely oblivious to the tension, but Sarah observes the scene and clocks an upcoming catfight; I bet our expressions are a right picture.

'Everybody good here?' she says doubtfully with highly raised eyebrows. 'Heather, why don't you take my seat, then you'll be nearer to the action, and next to Dom.' *And away from my friend*, reads all over her face, but she doesn't say it out loud.

'Oh, no, thank you. I'm fine here. He'll be working anyway, so may as well sit here.' Heather glances at her friend who smirks at us both and folds her arms.

Sarah looks from Heather to me, awkwardly, 'OK, then.' And she takes a seat.

Heather leans in from my right and whispers in my ear,

'I'm watching you.'

Not a moment too soon, we're all told to stand, and the bride makes her entrance. There's a groomsman to our left, who's been playing the guitar softly, he now picks up the pace and starts strumming the opening bars of Bruno Mars' 'I Think I Wanna Marry You.' As he begins, in his mellow tone, the bride bops her way down the aisle with her dad, to meet her groom; *now that's my kind of entrance.* The musician is now tapping the side of his guitar like a drum, singing acapella. It's gorgeous, and every single person is smiling, clapping and bopping too; apart from Heather.

When Savannah reaches the front, untraditionally, she and Jackson kiss, and everyone around cheers, again, apart from Heather. As the friend on the guitar finishes and blows a kiss to them both, we're gestured to all take our seats by the officiant, and the ceremony begins.

'Friends and family! Welcome to the ceremony of Savannah and Jackson. Today they will start the first day of the rest of their lives together. I know that each and every one of you means something to them, and they want to thank you all for being here. First, I'd like to invite a man who is working three roles this evening: friend, photographer and now, reader. Dom, please come on up.'

Huh, he didn't say he was speaking.

The crowd claps and Dom stops by his seat, leaning over, 'Will you snap a picture of me?' I think he directs at me,

'Of course.'

'Absolutely, sweetie.'

Heather and I answer together. I turn to look at her, and there's practically flames coming out of her ears.

Dom's now at the front, and he stands in front of the mic. At the risk of getting my hand slapped, I don't take my phone out, but Heather makes a point of taking several pictures, while loudly whispering to the friend next to her, 'doesn't *my boyfriend* look so handsome; I love *my* other half.'

I take a deep breath, and focus my eyes on Dom. He smiles at Savannah and Jackson, then takes a folded piece of paper out of his suit jacket pocket. *God, he looks handsome.*

'Hey everybody, I'd like to read you a poem by Mary Carolyn Davies, entitled, "Love."' He clears his throat and then begins:

> 'I love you. Not only for who you
> are, but for what I am when I am
> with you.
> I love you. Not only for what you
> have made of yourself, but for what
> you are
> making of me.
> I love you for the part of me that you
> bring out...'

He pauses and then looks up and without a shadow of a doubt is looking straight at me, not Heather, me. And he then continues reading while looking at me.

> '...I love you for putting your hand
> into my heaped-up heart, and passing
> over all the foolish, weak things that
> you can't help dimly seeing there.
> And for drawing out into the light, all

> the beautiful belongings that no one
> else had looked quite far enough to
> find.'

I dare to smile at him as he finishes the poem, before he turns to the happy couple. 'Congrats guys; I love you both.' He hugs them in turn, and then walks back up the aisle to continue taking pictures of the rest of the ceremony.

Oh my God, did he just announce to everyone that he loves me?! No. Don't be so silly. He must have been looking at Heather. Must have. I don't dare look to my right.

During the rest of the ceremony, I have to keep reminding myself that I am being paid to be here; forcing my attention back to the present moment, and ticking off things to remember to write about: another friend reads a poem; the officiant says something funny, what was that? *Bugger.* Wedding; I am writing about a wedding. Traditional vows with a personal update; exchange of rings; big kiss; applause. *OK.* I stand with the rest of the crowd to greet the new Mr and Mrs, and cheer as Savannah and Jackson head off for photos. I can't wait to leave this seat. As soon as it is appropriate, Sarah grabs me by the hand and pulls me into the moving congregation to lose Heather.

'Holy '*eff*,' is Sarah's opening line, when we've safely rounded the corner. 'I *knew* he loved you, too!'

'So, it's not just me, he was looking right at me, right?'

'Good Lord, you could have cut the sexual tension in the air with Heather's Jimmy Choo heels.'

'I've got to go and speak to him,' I nod, determinedly. 'I'm going to do it.'

'Yes!' Sarah cheers in the air, throwing her arms up and

nearly knocking out a grandma. 'So sorry,' she aims at her. 'Love! Woo!' she justifies, then pulls me a little further along, away from anybody. 'OK, I've got to be on duty for the next half hour or so. Oh shit, so does Dom. '*Eff.*' She pauses, creating a new plan. 'Alright, come with me, take notes, whatever, and then when he's finished snapping, you can declare your undying love, move here and we can go for cocktails every Friday!' She holds out her tattooed and *hennaed* arms in triumph.

I laugh, but hold my palms up, 'Hang on, I've got to figure out what I'm going to say first, and more importantly, I really need the loo. Where will you be? I'll meet you in five.'

'By the entrance, then the waterfall, then the Ferris wheel,' she says quickly.

'There's a Ferris wheel here?' I say, impressed.

'You really didn't do your homework, did you?' she fakes annoyance at me. 'Never mind. Try each of those spaces until you find us. I'm so excited!' She grabs my hands, squeezes, then let's go, and runs off in the other direction.

Alright, freshen up, then declare undying love. Christ. I walk toward the loos and spot the most awesome thing: a large chalkboard. "*Hopes and Dreams*" it reads at the top, and the board is covered in different handwritten aspirations. Despite my need to pee, I grab some chalk, resting just below the board and make a little scribble. I smile at it then head into the ladies.

Pushing the barn-style doors open I make my way into a free cubicle. I hover and relieve myself, while simultaneously trying to calm myself down. *OK; I'm actually going to do this*! When I've done all the necessary bits, I flush, pull my dress back down, and reach to open the lock, when I hear Heather's voice. I freeze on the spot and stay exactly where I am, in the secrecy behind my cubicle door.

'The '*eff-ing* nerve of her!' she yells.

'I know, she is *so* rude!' a voice replies, which I assume belongs to Heather's friend.

'Did you see the way they were looking at each other when he read the poem?'

'I'm sure he was looking at you!' the friend says with false sincerity.

'No!' Heather responds sharply. 'No, he wasn't. He was looking at *her*! That sun-washed, wannabe hippy! No,' she says with force. 'No. I can't have this! I'm so close!'

Close to what? What does she mean?

'Just hang in there,' the friend reassures. 'You convinced him the other day to think about marriage, right?'

'Yeah, I did,' she whines, 'but, I don't know, I'm not convinced. He told me from the beginning that he cared,' she pauses and then lowers the tone of her voice to imitate him, 'more about the quality of the relationship than the status.'

'Well, that's nice,' the friend says.

'Nice? Nice!' She's practically hysterical. '*Nice* isn't going to get me hitched. *Nice*, isn't going to legally bind me into his family once and for all.'

'Trust me, once this silly bitch is out of the way, he'll realise you're the only one he wants to be with.'

'I just want him to hurry up, propose so I can get my hands on that money!' I feel my mouth fall open. 'For '*eff's* sake,' I jump to the sound of a bang, as Heather has clearly hit the adjacent cubicle door to mine. She continues, 'I've worked long and hard on him for years to join his dad's company. When I knew that had really gone south, the only thing I could think to do to stay with him was pretend to support his stupid idea that he could be a photographer for a living. A photographer? Please. He's not even that good!' Involuntarily I inhale sharply, then cover my mouth. Luckily, the noise of the party outside, I think, covers me up. 'That money *deserves* to be mine!' I can hear her clicky-clacky heels clearly pacing back and forth. 'The sooner we get married, the sooner we can get divorced, and the sooner Dom will be transferred to London, then Matt and I can celebrate in the Maldives or something.'

'You are so bad!' the friend jokes.

Bad is the biggest understatement of the century. And who the '*eff* is Matt?

'Alright let's go and congratulate the stupid bride. Didn't you think the dress made her look fat?'

'Definitely,' the friend obediently agrees.

'Oh, maybe she's pregnant! That must be it. Can't believe Matt had to fire me in the hope she wouldn't say anything.'

'Kind of serves you right for having sex in the office.'

'True,' Heather agrees. 'OK, let's go. How's my "Oh my God, you look beautiful, I'm so happy for you" face?!' she says with false over-enthusiasm.

'Perfect!' They both burst out laughing, then the room fills with the sound of the clicking of their heels leaving; the barn doors swing wildly; and finally, silence. Even so, I give it a few seconds, either that, or I'm actually frozen to the spot in shock.

I can't believe it. Well, I mean, I can, she's horrible, but poor Dom. What the hell am I going to do? Staying glued to the spot, seems the only thing possible; what if she's just outside? I can't hide here forever! Taking a deep breath I unlock and open the door, then poke my head around the cubicle; nobody. *OK*. Stepping out, I wash and dry my hands, take in my reflection and nod at myself. Yup, this is happening; I'm doing it, I'm going to talk to him. I shake my hands, to get rid of tension, roll my shoulders and move my head from side to side, before taking another deep breath and marching out.

The party is in full swing: cocktails on trays, canapes being passed around, everyone is joyful, laughing, and the night is twinkling away. Alright, where did Sarah say they'd be first? The waterfall? No, the entrance I think, or was it the Ferris wheel? Oh bugger. I stop in my tracks to mentally gather. OK, think, Liv. Where first? Think. Entrance. It was definitely the entrance. I head off in that direction, past jolly guests, smiling politely and pretending I'm not a girl on a mission about to break some catastrophic, and hopefully, at the same time life-changingly awesome news, to my potential new love. I reach the entrance and they're not there. I look around just in case.

'Can I get you a car?' A young, pristine looking valet gestures with an open palm to the line of vehicles, ready to assist.

'Oh, no, thank you,' I smile and wave my hand at him, 'I'm looking for the wedding party?'

'Back inside, I'm afraid,' the smart valet smiles at me.

'Great. Thank you.'

Back I head. OK, where was the waterfall? This way, I think? Why am I wearing heels? I can go literally half the speed in these things. *Ah*, perfect: a sign. There's a wooden post pointing towards the right, with the words "waterfall" carved into them. I can hear it, I'm nearly there. I march down a wooden pathway with delicate white fencing on each side, wrapped, of course, in fairy lights. Charming lamp posts line and light the way too, as the night has drawn in.

'There you are! What's the rush, beautiful?' I hear Kevin's voice behind me.

Ugh. Turning, I see he's doing a light jog to catch me up. Coming to a halt, I frown, 'Are you following me?'

'Maybe.' He winks, 'Kind of adorable, isn't it?'

It's kind of creepy actually. I'm not quite brave enough to say out loud.

'So, like I said, where are you headed?' He's now right in front of me and smells like he's had several of the complimentary cocktails.

'Just, *um*, need to speak to Dom about something; work related,' I add, trying to sound nonchalant and failing miserably.

'*Uh huh.* So serious!' He makes a face then moves around me in a sort of mating dance, before blocking my path and putting a hand on the small of my back.

'*Erm*,' I look over my shoulder, taking in the placement of his unwanted palm, then turn my face to his, 'not to be rude or anything, but I really do have to get going, so, if you wouldn't mind.' I jolt my head slightly and smile politely before going to move. He jolts to the side, blocking me once more, his hand stays firmly on my back, and then he uses it to push me into him. 'What are you doing?'

'Let's be honest here Livvy.'

'My name is Liv,' I say, frowning.

'Exactly what I said, *Liv*,' he drunkenly emphasises my name. 'We're both young, free, single, gorgeous; let's just see where tonight goes, shall we?'

I put my hands up to his chest to push him away. 'You and I are going absolutely nowhere, Kevin; this, or any evening.'

'Oh, come on! You're so uptight! Loosen up a bit, English, and have a bit of fun!' He pulls me in closer; he's so strong.

'Kevin, let go of me,' I warn.

'Just one little kiss, come on! I promise you, once you've had a taste of *this*, you won't want anything else!'

'*Ugh*. Get off me!' I say, louder this time.

'You got a glimpse earlier, but now, let me give you a proper ride!' He tightens his grip even more.

'You're hurting me! Let me go!' I try to wriggle free, but I can't.

'Come on!' he whines, and I can feel his hands all over me.

'No!' I shout even louder, 'Get—'

Before I can stop him, he's planting a big sloppy, alcoholic kiss on me, breathing heavily and pulling me even closer. He's trapped my arms in place; I can't move. He presses his face harder and harder into mine. Tears start rolling down my face.

'GET OFF OF HER!!!' I hear Dom's voice roar, and then suddenly, Kevin is off me and in Dom's strong hands, grabbing each of his shoulders, then spinning him around. 'What the '*eff*, mate?! She said no! What the hell are you doing?!' Dom pushes Kevin forcefully away; he stumbles and nearly falls over, but stays upright, swaying slightly.

'Are you OK?' Dom asks me, concerned. I nod and wipe my wet cheeks as Dom strides over and puts a protective arm over me.

'Wow! Why is everyone so serious!' Kevin holds his hands drunkenly up like he's about to be arrested. 'I thought this was a wedding!' He sways and looks at Dom, 'You've already got a girl man, and here you are trying to meddle with my little bit of wedding sex that Heather flew in.'

'Excuse me?' I manage to muster and wipe away another tear that's escaped. I try to stand a little taller, and catch my breath; Dom holds me even closer.

Kevin narrows his eyes and looks from me to Dom, exaggeratingly, like he's watching a tennis match. 'Oh my God,' Kevin finally says.

'What?' Dom snaps angrily, 'What could you possibly have to say now? And aren't you going to apologise here?!'

'No.' He points from me to Dom. 'I didn't clock before. You two...'

'Us two what? Dude, apologise to Liv, *right now*!' His voice is furious.

'You're in love with her!' Kevin says this as fact, not a question.

I move my eyes from the floor to Kevin, who's now wavering his accusatory pointed finger at me, 'And you're in love with him; there's no other reason as to why you wouldn't want to be with *this,*' he gestures to himself.

I dare to look up at Dom, and he's looking at me sadly, and my stomach flips. *Oh God, maybe he doesn't feel the same.*

Kevin blows a raspberry, 'Well, screw you both. I'm going to have a drink.' And with that, he stumbles off in the other direction.

I hug Dom and burst out crying again. *Dammit. I hate being a damsel in distress.*

'Hey, hey. It's alright, he's gone now.' He holds me close then lightly strokes my hair.

'Thank you for saving me,' I manage to say in between sobs. 'I don't know what I would have done if you hadn't.' I take a few deep breaths and compose myself. Then loosening my hold ever so slightly. I glance up; *it's now or never.* 'Look, I've got to say something.' I take another deep breath.

He looks at me with gentle eyes and a soft smile, still with his arms wrapped around me. 'What is it?'

I sigh and go for it, 'I overheard Heather in the bathroom.'

'That's normal, you can hear what people are doing in bathrooms; they're actually not very private.'

I laugh and shake my head, 'No, not that. I overheard her saying something; I was hiding in a cubicle; she has no idea I heard.'

'Heard what?' he asks gently while brushing away the remnants of another tear.

'I, *um*, don't really know how to say this, but here we go...she's cheating on you. And using you.'

'What?' His expression completely changes as he shakes his head slightly. 'No. That can't be right. And what do you mean, "using me?"'

'I'm so sorry, but she said the only reason she wants to be with you is for your family's money.'

'What? No. She's...no.'

'I'm afraid you're going to get hurt. Dom, I care about you, I...' Faltering, I will myself to continue. 'I...' *Oh my God, I can't say it. Oh, come on Liv!!* 'I love you!' I blurt out, unattractively. For a moment we just stare at each other, 'And I have to know Dom: how do you feel? Do...do you feel the same about me?'

'Yes, Dom, how *do* you feel about her?' We both jump apart and turn sharply, to see Heather slowly walking towards us.

'I...*um*.' Dom is overwhelmed, I can tell; he puts a hand

through his hair. Heather takes this moment to gaze at me.

'That's quite the elaborate story you've made up there; I'm impressed! Clearly you are a *great* writer.' She draws closer and closer to me, venom bursting out of her narrowed eyes. 'I said nothing of the sort. How delusional, desperate,' she tilts her head, 'and rather sad, to invent such a ridiculous tale, to steal *my* boyfriend; *my* high school sweetheart; *my* true love, not *yours*.' She's now only a few inches from me. I open my mouth, but nothing comes out; I'm truly speechless. She takes this opportunity to continue. 'You are small, insignificant and nothing but a jealous little bitch, and, how convenient,' she looks at her naked wrist, and pretends to read the time, 'I believe your work is finished now, isn't it? So, I think you better go, you're beginning to overstay your welcome.'

I look at her incredulously, 'Heather, I heard every word you said in the loos. I'm not about to stand here and let you do this to Dom for a moment more! He is the kindest man I have ever met, but you can't see that through your gold digging eyes.' I suddenly find my courage and stand up tall, despite not even coming close to her height. 'You don't deserve someone like him. So, why don't *you* back off!'

She cackles. 'Oh, I'm not going anywhere! Dom and I have a history and a future. *You* have nothing but the fantasy you've created in your head.'

Dom stands there, saying nothing, looking hopelessly from Heather to me.

'Aren't you going to say anything?' I ask Dom with desperation.

'This is...a lot to take in. I can't...' He weaves another hand through his hair.

'Look, you've got him all upset,' Heather steps in and

takes his hand. He numbly stands there. I take in her fingers entwined with his, and suddenly feel very sick. 'See? Like I said earlier: you don't belong here.'

My eyes fill with tears. I'm emotionally exhausted and all I know is that I want to get out of here; I'm done, and this isn't a fight I'm going to win. I turn and hurry away.

'Liv, wait!' I hear Dom's voice behind me, but I don't stop, I pick up my pace even more, heading towards my room. Tears are now cascading down my face as I race past the party, now in full swing as a live band has everybody on the dancefloor for an unconventional, pre-dinner boogie. When I'm finally there, I burst the door open and thank my lucky stars that I began to pack this morning. I hear my phone singing in my bag, which stirs me to move even faster. Running first to the bathroom, I sweep all my toiletries into my vanity bag; then back into the bedroom, I throw in my PJs and the clothes I'd lined up for tomorrow morning in my open suitcase, then zip it up. Scanning my eyes quickly around the room, I think that's everything. *Bollocks, my laptop*! I locate it from the lounge, throw it into my handbag and then head out the door.

The lights from the fairy-lit trees blur as my eyes continue to leak, yet I don't stop running. A barbecue buffet is now being brought out, I think I see the bride to my right, I'm pretty sure that was Kevin to my left, and then I practically bump into Sarah and Hugo, at the entrance.

'Liv!' Sarah's happy expression drops at the sight of me. 'What the hell happened? Where are you going?'

I shake my head, 'I've got to get out of here.' Tears continue to stream down my face.

'No, you can't!' Her eyes fill with tears now.

'I'll ring you when I'm back in England, OK?'

She looks at me with so much sadness that it makes me cry harder, 'OK.' She grabs me and gives me a hug.

'You look after yourself, alright?' Hugo hugs me quickly and smiles sadly.

'Let's get you a cab.' Sarah takes my hand and we run into the parking lot together.

We head towards the smiley valet from earlier, whose pleasant face wavers as he takes my suitcase before swiftly opening a cab door for me; I dive in, 'LAX please,' I tell the driver, while silently urging the valet to quickly throw my case in the boot. Turning, I see Sarah's face pressed against the window.

'I love you,' she shouts, tears now streaming down her face too. 'You're the best friend I never knew I needed.'

'And you're mine.' We both sob for a moment, then I look past Sarah and see Dom running towards the car. 'Go, please go!!' I practically shout.

The driver starts up the engine, and with the crunching sound of gravel, we pull away at speed. Out of the back of the window, I see him halting next to Sarah, he yells my name and I wave sadly as the cab turns and speeds away, and just like that, my heart is broken.

Chapter 24

USA
Malibu –Los Angeles

As we wind our way down the mountain, the cab driver knows better than to ask questions. Unapologetically allowing my tears to flow, I whip out my phone and see if I can transfer my flight to tonight. I've got a missed call from Dom and a voice message notification, but ignore it. Going into my emails, suddenly "Dom" is flashing up on my phone; I cancel the call. OK, I tap away. I've got up my flight details. Dom rings again, I press cancel once more; all the while my tears are getting stronger. I search to see what my options are; there's a flight leaving at ten fifty-five, that's still got a few seats left, so I transfer my ticket, making a note of the new booking reference in my little notebook. Dom rings again, and pressing cancel for a third time, I turn my phone off.

It's not until I've stepped out of the cab that it occurs to me how silly I must appear: dolled up to the nines, but at the same time, I must look like I've been hit by a bus. Even so, I rush my way towards Departures, and print my boarding pass from one of the machines, to avoid turning my phone back on. A part of me is desperately wanting to hear Dom call my name just before I go through security, but equally, and just as strongly, wanting to place some armed guards between him and me. All documents in hand, I join the fast moving queue for security and when it's my turn to show my passport, the immigration officer looks up and transforms her bored expression into one of wide-eyed intrigue. 'I'm guessing business, not pleasure?'

I smile politely. 'Wouldn't it be nice to be both?'

'Ain't no such thing, honey.' She looks at my passport and boarding pass, then meets my eyes again. 'You look cute though; he's clearly a moron.' She hands everything back to me and ushers me to move on. 'Next please.'

Shuffling along the security line, I take a quick daring glance backwards. He's not there. Of course he's not. That only happens in movies, right? Why didn't I answer my phone? I'm so bloody stubborn. It's too late now anyway, Little Miss Runaway; you've made your choice.

Heading to the ladies as soon as I'm through security, I lock myself in a cubicle. Closing the lid of the loo, I take a seat and some deep breaths, then finally remove my heels. What was he going to say in the car park? Should I have stayed? Was that my romantic moment and I missed it? Oh God, I'm so stupid. Picking up my phone again, I tentatively hover my thumb over the on button but something stops me, and I throw it back in my handbag.

Instead of facing reality, I open my case and take out the outfit I was planning on wearing on my flight: my trusty harem trousers, a yoga t-shirt, and my cosy "...be kind" jumper, with flip flops; fluffy socks at the ready too for when we've taken off. Then I take my vanity bag out. I'm definitely taking all this makeup off; I don't want a single reminder of this evening, for a moment longer. It's not until then that I spot it. I reach down, shimmy some other clothes out of the way; I've still got Dom's hoodie from the boat ride. I pull it out slowly and look at it. I'd forgotten it was in there. I was going to give it back at breakfast. Putting it back down, I slip out of my dress, neatly fold it and get my comfy clothes on. I then pick his hoodie back up and smell it; it smells of sea salt, espresso martinis and his aftershave, or maybe I'm just imagining that. Throwing it over my handbag, I decide to wear it on the plane.

Zipping my case back up, and unlocking the door, I head to the mirror and look at my reflection; a sad woman looks back at me. I meet my own eyes and involuntarily shake my head. *I'm such a stubborn idiot*. My hair and makeup look so silly now in my casual clothes. Beginning my *de-Cinderella-ing*, I take out all the pins in my hair, shake my hair loose, then find a hairband. Running my fingers through the front of my hair a couple times, so it's all going backwards, I then swoop it all up into my normal messy bun. Now, opening my vanity case, I locate makeup remover pads and get to work. After a blurry Ozzy Osbourne moment, I'm fresh-faced and it's as if it never happened; I hope the evening can be erased just as quickly in my mind. Going to close my makeup bag, I spot my rainbow moonstone necklace, and slowly take it out, placing it around my neck; maybe it will protect my heart from the traveller I've left behind.

When my flight is called, it feels so very strange to be by myself. Even though I've travelled alone a million times, I sadly board the plane, solo, after my month-long adventure with the three of them; no one to joke with, no one to fight with. Smiling politely to the crew, I find my seat and then chuck my pull along bag in the overhead locker, put Dom's hoodie on, take out my eye mask, headphones, then put my handbag under the seat in front of me. Adjusting the pillow, and unwrapping the blanket, I curl up, and don't wake until we land in Heathrow.

***

USA – UK
Los Angeles – London

Tuesday
Depart Los Angeles International Airport at 22:55

Wednesday
Arrive at London Heathrow 16:10
Duration: 10 hours 15 minutes
Time change: London 8 hours ahead (BST)

Of course what greets me when I exit Heathrow is rain. Cold, wet, miserable rain. Admittedly, I've always liked the weather reflecting my mood, but right now, it just makes everything a little bit sadder.

I walk numbly towards the Tube and board. I'm just like anyone else on this carriage: avoiding eye contact, silent on the outside, but inside, dealing quietly with issues and demons.

When I arrive home, a strange feeling consumes me: I'm filled with nothing but cold stillness; it doesn't feel like home at all. Unlocking my door, I push gently to move the pile of letters that grace my carpet. Stepping inside and shutting the door, I feel sad and alone; even turning on my fairy lights doesn't make a difference, it just reminds me of Calamigos, and the man I left standing there. I swiftly turn them off, dump my handbag on the couch, and drag my suitcase in, walking mindlessly to the washing machine, unzip my case and start throwing everything in.

I should have stayed and heard Dom out, but, I just had to get out of there: somewhere between Kevin forcing himself on me, Heather's hurtful words, and Dom's silence, I just couldn't take it; at least, that's what I've been arguing with myself about, since I left Malibu. Pressing "go" on the machine, I stand up and aimlessly start walking around my apartment.

I wonder if I should just call him, be the frigging grown up for once. Man, I feel bad about how I left Sarah and Hugo. After all we've experienced together, I didn't even say goodbye properly. Closing my eyes, I stand still in an attempt to gather myself, and sigh for the millionth time, knowing that I can't rewrite history. I made the split-second decision, to get the hell out of there. Now, I've got to live with the consequences. My eyes dart open. Unless I handle it right now. I pick up my phone once more, then freeze. *No. I can't.* I place it back down on the couch and walk away from it.

So, what now, Liv? Even though it's nearly May, I suddenly realise my apartment is absolutely freezing, or maybe that's just a reaction to my sorrow? I turn the heat on and realise I'm ferociously hungry. Heading to the kitchen I begin opening and closing cupboards, but of course, after being away for a month, and with my trip before that, there's nothing apart from some mixed herbs and spices, a couple of cans of bean salad, a bottle of Sauvignon Blanc, and a packet of Bourbons. Ignoring the bottles of vanilla vodka and Kahlúa, that will now forever remind me of Dom, I decide to get Chinese delivered. But, in the meantime, I open the Bourbons and the bottle of Sauvignon Blanc.

Heading to the house phone to avoid turning my mobile on, I dial my usual Chinese place; yeah, I know, it's a little sad to know the number off by heart. It starts ringing and I cradle the phone between my ear and shoulder while simultaneously pouring the white wine into a glass. I look around at my empty flat. So here I am: a large glass of vino in hand, biscuit crumbs on Dom's top; a sad, lonely woman about to order Chinese for one. Cue *Bridget Jones*' intro, 'All by myself!' If it wasn't so sad it would be funny. I even used to own those PJs that Renee Zellweger wore, you know the red ones, with the penguins?

'Oh, hi.' They answer and stop my train of thought, 'I'd like to make an order for delivery please?'

***

An hour later I'm thoroughly marinated in both bubble bath and wine. Having brought my dinner into the bathroom, I throw the last veggie spring roll into my mouth before emptying the bottle of Sauvignon into my glass. And this is when I decide that now is the perfect time to turn my phone on.

I reach over and grab my phone from on top of my towel, narrowly avoiding dropping it in the bubbles. Taking a deep breath, I go for it. My phone immediately pings dramatically into life with every notification bell, chime and jingle. It takes my phone, and brain, a few minutes to catch up. Twenty-one missed calls, the voicemail notification is up, eight text messages, fifteen WhatsApp messages, five new emails and two messages from Facebook. I decide to dive into the voice messages first.

'You have eight new messages. First message: sent

yesterday at 8:15 p.m.' Beep. 'Liv.' Dom's voice pants through the phone, as if he's running at the same time. 'Where have you gone? We need to talk. Call me back, OK?'

I press save. *'Next message: sent yesterday at 8:25 p.m.' Beep.* 'I can't believe you just got in a cab! Pick up! I've got to talk to you!'

Pressing save once more, the next message sounds, 'Liv! Please pick up, come on, you can't leave like this. Call me back,' Dom sounded even more panicked.

The fourth is also from Dom, and even shorter, 'Are you going to the airport?'

My stomach flips and after saving the message, Sarah's voice blasts through the speaker of my phone. 'DUDE! It's all kicking off here!' I sit up in the bath. 'Seriously, you need to turn the '*eff* around!'

WHAT?

The message continues, and she's hyped up, 'Oh, you've turned your phone off, haven't you? *Ugh*! How am I going to reach her?' I hear Hugo's voice in the background.

'If she's gone, there's nothing you can do, honey.' *He called her honey, aw.*

''*Eff* that. Look.' Her voice is louder now, 'Your happiness could just be waiting for you here; you've totally got it all wrong. Alright, I'm going to message and email you, and whatever else I can think of, in case you check those somehow. OK.'

It beeps off. *'Next message...'*

'OK, not that I want to ruin this for you,' Sarah says reasonably, 'but just in case you have the sense to turn your phone back on, Dom and Heather are fighting; out loud, in the middle of the wedding! It's bloody brilliant! *Ugh*. I am willing you to turn your phone on!'

'Next message...'

'TURN YOUR PHONE ON!' Sarah yells. 'He's confronting her about everything. EVERYTHING. The job, the affair, the relationship, the money.' Sarah is giddy. 'Shame this isn't going into the article!'

'What happened? What happened?' I yell at the phone.

'Next message...'

'OK, Little Miss Stubborn,' My stomach gives another lurch at the sound of Dom's voice, once more, 'I'm guessing you've turned your phone off and have irrationally gone to the airport, so I'm heading that way now.'

'WHAT?!' I actually yell at the phone out loud. Did he come? Did I miss him?

'You have no new messages; first saved message...'

'NOOOOOOOO!!!' I yell, and my voice reverberates around the bathroom as I hang up from voicemail, then scramble to dry my hands properly on a nearby towel and look at my messages. Several from Sarah and Hugo, merely saying varying, blasphemous varieties of, 'Pick up, pick up, pick up, pick up!!!'

And only one from Dom, 'OK, you're not answering, I get it. I'm sorry.'

And that's it. He's sorry? What happened? I have to call Sarah. I dial and it goes straight to voicemail. Oh, what time is it now? I quickly do some time zone scanning in my drunken head: OK it's what, eight now? That's one there. Oh, no, bollocks, she's on her way back to New York to see her family. I try Hugo. Voicemail too. *Damn. Oh, maybe he's going with her? That's awesome.*

Holding my fingers over the phone, I go to call Dom, then pause and realise a bottle of wine in, is probably not the best way to have a conversation with the potential new love of your life. *OK.* I place the phone down on the side once more, dunk my body then dry off, I place my hair in a towel turban, and wrap up in my bathrobe. Marching myself to the kitchen, I drink an entire pint of water, slap my cheeks a couple times, then take several deep breaths, nervously calling Dom's number. *Voicemail.*

My heart plummets. *Serves me right.*

Chapter 25

UK
London

Thursday

As far as my company knows, I travelled home on my planned flight, sans drama-queen exit, and thank the Lord, I don't have to show my face in the office until Monday. Since my bubble bath revelation, I've tried calling Sarah several more times, but it just keeps going to voicemail. And after Dom didn't answer the first time, I haven't plucked up the courage to call him again. So, what does one do when there seems to be a big hole in your life? Dive into work. I pour myself into the article, reminding myself that the sooner I wrap this up, the sooner it will be over. After several more packets of biscuits and numerous cries later, I hit send on my article, ready for editorial approval. And just like that, it's over.

Closing my laptop and that chapter of my life, with finality, I pick up my phone, hesitate and put it back down again. I want to ring or message Dom, but something stops me. Where would I even begin? What would I say? What would *he* say? Would I ask him if he actually came to the airport? Or, if he's come to his senses and left Heather? And does he want to move to London and be with me? I desperately want to ask him: Are you really in love with me and have you thought what our babies would look like? Clearly, it's all just a little too much. So, I've done the mature, English thing: powered through by pretending everything's OK, while simultaneously burying, and running away, from my feelings.

Picking up my phone again, I scan through the pictures from the last month: a selfie of Hugo and I on the dancefloor at the Essex wedding; Sarah and I, in front of the castle in Scotland; Sarah pretending to lick the large bottle in Bordeaux airport; all of us at the top of the AC Palacio; the view from the wedding reception in Malaga. I shut my eyes for a second; that's where Dom and I tangoed. Shaking my head, I continue: me weighed down by jewellery in Dubai; Sarah and I in our *saris* in Goa; all of us with Bex in front of the Merlion in Singapore. I smile and think of the picture she sent me earlier; she's really starting to show.

Then my smile drops again as I see the fleet of sand cars Dom and I made in Thailand, followed by Dom's, ever-so-slightly blurry face by the fireflies; my sadness grows as I look at the picture of Sarah and Hugo resting their heads together, asleep in Tokyo airport; then all four of us laughing with the sunset behind us, in Hawaii, after Leo's wedding; the galaxy of starfish in Tofino; Dom kissing my cheek on Malibu pier; the dolphins in Newport Beach; the view from Dom's childhood bedroom in Laguna; me flying Kevin's plane; and then the final one: Sarah and I all dressed up before we left our room in Malibu. I swipe back through until I land, once more, on the picture from Malibu pier. Even though I'm smiling, the photo has captured my complete shock of Dom kissing my cheek. His hair falls effortlessly over his forehead. I close my eyes and pretend to feel his lips on me then my whole body jumps as my phone rings in my hands. Opening them briefly, I shut my eyes again; I can't look. What if it's him? What the hell am I going to say? I dare to open one eye and sigh loudly as I see it's my boss, not Dom. *Bollocks.*

'Hi! How are you?' I say brightly, in spite of my bitter disappointment.

'How are you, Miss World Traveller?' Janice responds, matching my cheery tone. 'I've just received your article, and at first glance, it's perfect! Did you have the most fabulous time? I bet you did. Now,'

No need to answer, then.

'I know your first official day back in the office is Monday, but, if you could bring along a hard copy tonight, to the party, that would be great!'

'Party? What party?' I say with what I hope is, as little distaste as possible.

'The Annual Spring Bash?' she says slowly. Janice hates when people forget important dates in the office calendar.

I rub my eyes, 'Oh, I'd completely forgotten, must be the jetlag. Sorry.' *I'm definitely not going.* I snuggle further down in my blanket cocoon.

'No need to apologise, but I do need you there.'

Bugger off! 'Oh, really?' I say with as much doubt as I can muster, 'I'm sure you won't miss me! You know me, I'd just be in a corner somewhere trying to stay awake. Better give it a miss, rest up and be fresh for work on Monday!' My plan is to curl up with Netflix and switch off the world, bucko. 'You don't mind, do you?'

'It's not an invite, Liv,' her tone has changed from friendly colleague, to increasingly stern boss. 'Attendance is mandatory. There's going to be a big announcement, and some special guests, and they want to hear all about the article from you,' Janice adds, with force.

Ugh. I slap on a smile, even though she can't see me, 'Of course!' Fake enthusiasm coming from somewhere. 'I'll print out a copy and see you there then, but, *um*, just a swift reminder,' I try and say casually, 'you know, jetlag of course, where, *um*, exactly am I going and at what time?' I say the end of the sentence quickly and then hold my breath for an answer, casually reaching for a pen and paper and hoping she doesn't yell at me.

'Skyloft at Altitude,' she says, clearly annoyed that I've forgotten, but I guess, grateful that I'm now coming. 'Meet and greet cocktails at seven, dinner at eight, dancing and frivolity planned for ten.'

'Nothing like a bit of planned frivolity!' I jest.

We hang up and after setting my article to print, I drag my unenthusiastic arse to the shower.

***

Just before 7 p.m. I step out of a cab, my freshly-printed article enclosed in an envelope, determined to get in and out as quickly as humanly possible. Every year, the company invitation always says, "smart *casual*" but what they really mean is, "smart *smart*." One year I turned up in my trusty harem trousers, paired with what I thought was a nice top, and a neat headscarf, but was sent home to change; which, admittedly did cross my mind to do again, but this time, not come back. But, I figure, get in there, show my face, eat the food, drink the drink and go home; frivolity will have to be done by someone else.

Adjusting my outfit, I stare up at, and walk towards the

large glass building. Deciding to indeed look as though I've made an effort, I've gone for my simple, yet elegant, black and white, short Chevron dress with long, slightly flared sleeves, a silver belt to nip my waist in, complete with my little heels that I wore at the Malibu wedding; at least I know I can run out of there quickly if needed. Accessory-wise, I'm wearing my rainbow moonstone necklace, and I've straightened and loosely curled my hair, so it's flowing down my shoulders.

Joining a couple of people from the fashion department in the lift, we make our way up. I smile politely, at the gaggle of barely twenty-somethings, feeling desperately old all of a sudden. After Bex left, I've never really had that same connection with anybody else I've worked with. That is, until I met Sarah, Hugo...and Dom. The thought makes my heart sink, so I shake my head ever so slightly and force myself to stop. *Just get tonight over with and then you can think about what the hell you're going to do with the rest of your life.* I could leave my job and run away to...I don't know, where was it that Julia Roberts went, after Italy and India, in *Eat Pray Love*? Indonesia? Yup, that was it. Maybe I'll do that. There's nothing here for me anymore, or anywhere else for that matter. Suddenly, I feel very lost.

The lift pings me out of my potential future plans and self-deprecation, and I step out, following the giggling gaggle to the Skyloft. We use the building for Press work, so I have been here a number of times, but, that's usually in Altitude 360; I've never been in the Skyloft.

Apparently, it's a really cool room: reclaimed brick and wood flooring, so stupidly, I imagine it's a little rough around the edges, but as I walk in, it reminds me of a cool New York loft. The view is nuts: The Eye, The Shard, Big

Ben and the Parliament Buildings; God, it's beautiful, all lit up. I smile and remember why I love London so much. *OK, maybe not Indonesia.* Maybe I'll ask Sarah to move back to New York, and we could be roommates there? New York's kind of busy and bustling like London, so I won't be able to hear my thoughts; that sounds perfect. *But she's with Hugo now, isn't she?* My subconscious reminds me.

Stepping in further, there's a photo op area to my right, with a fake green wall and our *Wonder Magazine* company logo everywhere. The beauty team gaggle is already there, posing and pouting for the photographer, who is loving every moment. *Photographer. Dom. Dammit. Where's the booze?*

The room is already alive and bursting at the seams; lots of people have clearly arrived early to take full advantage of the company's party budget. Again, I smile politely as I walk past several colleagues, including Judy, ironically from the "Health and Fitness" department, who's enjoying a bucket-sized glass of some colourful concoction, to herself.

I take in the rectangular space, with the bar to my left, and to my right, a couple of little alcoves. Each is filled with comfy seats and brightly coloured pillows, next to the floor to ceiling windows, revealing London in all its glory. At the far side of the room there's one extensive table, decorated and ready to go for dining. There's little name tags in each place setting; *oh bugger, I'm going to be sat next to some chatty-Cathy, aren't I*? I sigh and feel completely detached and despondent.

'Well, here she is! The star of the moment!!' I turn and see Janice walking over, from the photo op area, with a couple of well-dressed individuals I've never met. My boss takes the envelope from my hands, then plants an unusual and inappropriate kiss on my right cheek; clearly she's indulging as much as Judy. Janice tells me they are our new sponsors and introduces me, with a slight slur, to each of them; I struggle to take in their names.

'Lovely to meet you all,' I smile, and hope that my sadness isn't as obvious as it feels.

'We would love to hear all about the trip from you, Liv! We were just hearing about it from the photographer's perspective, and we—'

'I'm sorry,' I interrupted her, 'from *Dom's* point of view? How...' I swallow, '...how is that possible?'

She looks at me as though I'm rather dim, 'Well, we were introduced to him and we had a conversation, over there,' she points behind me, towards the dining table. My heart flips and I don't dare turn around. 'Are you OK dear?'

'Wait,' I smile, 'Dom's *here*?' I say and can feel myself either about to burst out laughing or crying, I'm not sure which.

'Excuse me,' a soothing voice comes from behind me, 'I was wondering if you could help me with something?'

Turning slowly, sure enough, there he is, only a few feet away, walking towards me. I look into those aqua eyes, hopefully. 'Oh really? What's that then?'

'Well, you see, I'm looking for this girl; we met on a plane,' Dom adds, and stops in front of me. 'And after a rather long journey, I've come to realise that I don't want to spend another moment without her.'

I think my heart's going to burst out of my chest, but I try to play it cool. 'Is that so? You, *um,* don't have a girlfriend already then?' I check.

'Oh, no.' He shakes his head and smiles at me, 'Well, I did, up until very recently in fact. But, I realised there's just someone else that makes my heart sing.'

I giggle, 'Your heart sing?'

'Hey! Go with me! I've watched a lot of movies and I had a long flight to practise.'

'I'm sorry.' I smile, but try to return to a serious face, 'She sounds very special.'

'Oh, you have no idea. Despite her bad habit of stealing other people's clothing...'

'I'm sorry about that, I—' he holds his hand up gently to *shush* me, and continues,

'...and a tendency to completely overreact, she has this way of making the people around her feel alive, special and seen. And to top it off, she's beautiful,' he takes my hand, 'funny, talented,' he leans in slightly and lowers his voice, 'and an *incredibly* fast runner.' I can't help but burst out laughing. He looks down, 'But in her trusty running shoes, I'm afraid she's ready to run away, again.' He meets my eyes again, and his thumb strokes the top of my hand.

I shake my head. 'I'm not going anywhere,' I manage to say.

'Good.' He smiles, 'I was all ready to do a nice little speech like this, in the car park of a fairy-lit wedding venue...' He stops and gently places both of his hands now, on my arms, 'and you didn't stay long enough to hear it.' I can't help it, a tear falls down my cheek. He gently brushes it away then cups my cheek in his left palm. 'So, here it is: Thank you for saving me from myself, and actually believing in me when I didn't. For showing me the light with Heather; it turns out you did protect me from evil.' He puts his right hand in his pocket and takes out the stone I gave him in Hermosa. He pops it back in his pocket, then he takes both my hands in his; they're warm and I never want him to let go. 'And thank you for seeing the real me. Not the me who

I'm *supposed* to be, but the me that I *want* to be; the me that doesn't even exist yet.' He shakes his head, 'You have such an appetite for food,'

'Hey!' I say, lightly.

'...and for life,' he grins, 'for everything, and I want to experience that with you.' He stops and looks at me, 'Too cheesy?' he checks.

I smile and shake my head, 'Keep going.'

'You know, when I was reading that poem at the wedding, it wasn't Heather who came into my head, it was you. I haven't been able to get you out of my head since we met, actually.' He looks at me so intently, I feel my knees weaken.

'I'm so in love with you, Liv,' he says softly.

'I'm in love with you, too.'

He grins wide, with a mixture of relief and excitement, and then draws me in, and kisses me in front of the crowd. The room disappears.

I think I hear clapping and whooping, but nothing else matters, nothing else exists. I think my heart may explode with joy. When we finally break away, I hear a familiar voice.

'Told you you'd have your wicked way with him by the end of the trip.'

'And it's about bloody time!' I look to my right and Sarah and Hugo are standing right there, holding hands.

I squeeze Dom's hands, then rush over and give them both a hug. 'What are you doing in London? This is crazy!' I squeal.

'We couldn't *not* see this happen!' Sarah responds, grinning almost as wide as me.

'Well, that,' Hugo agrees, nodding, 'but, also, we were

invited at the last minute,' Hugo says, shrugging and smiling.

'You were? Why? Not that I'm not thrilled you're here!' I hug them both again, then turn and take Dom's hand. 'I'm so happy!'

'Your company is officially joining our umbrella! We got a phone call this morning, or rather, yesterday morning? Today in California?' Sarah looks at Hugo, who looks just as bemused. 'Well, no idea, but they said that our trip was so successful, it's an example of things to come. They want to do more and more cross-over collaborations. It's attracted a whole bunch of different advertisers across the board. We've done that.'

'This is too much.' I look around. Dom kisses me on the cheek, and I can't help it, I throw my arms around him once more for a kiss. When I finally pull away, a thought comes to me, 'Isn't it going to be awkward working for Matt?' I ask Dom and scrunch my nose.

'I don't work there anymore,' he says simply.

'What? You don't? What do you mean?'

He smiles at me, 'On my way to the airport, I rang Matt, and left him an, admittedly very colourful, voice message, to tell him I quit. I may have also added, he was welcome to Heather. He rang me back straight away; he no longer works for the company!'

'What?' That response came from Sarah and Hugo, simultaneously.

'We had a whole ten-hour flight together, and you're just telling us now?' Sarah widens her cat-eyes, 'Who's our boss, then?'

'No idea, but, get this, Matt said he had no interest in dating Heather, and if I see her to tell her, to collect her crap from his.'

For a mere moment I feel sorry for Heather. Then I look up at this amazing man, and the feeling passes.

Chapter 26

UK
London

The rest of the night, I'm floating on a cloud of love and friendship. It's as if we could all finally relax, focusing on ourselves rather than everyone around us. The food is sublime, and, unsurprisingly, I've finished every last bite.

Sarah finishes telling her story of the version of what happened after I'd left Malibu, with a final bite of her brownie. 'He looked like a lost little puppy in that car park,' she says with her mouth full.

'I did not!' Dom says, smiling at Sarah, and then he winks at me.

'I've got to say dude, you totally did.' Hugo says pointing his fork at Dom, 'pretty sure I saw you cry a little too.'

Grinning, I put down my own fork, after licking off the last remnants of the brownie's gooey centre. 'Wait, hang on, go back. After I'd run away from you and Heather—'

'Dramatically and without reason,' Dom finishes my sentence, teasingly.

'Without reason?' I playfully hit him, 'You didn't say anything!'

'I know.' He smiles. 'So, after, you'd run off, with every reason to want to get away,' he corrects himself, and I nod in agreement, 'I asked Heather if what you'd said was true. She denied everything and tried to spin it on your jealousy, and me being stupid, not being able to see that. I said I needed to clear my head, and that's when I went to find you; I just left Heather, screaming on the spot. When I couldn't see you at the party, and you weren't in your room, I assumed you'd run off to leave. Then there you were: a pretty little thing in the back of a cab. When you wouldn't answer your phone, I hailed a cab to follow you to the airport.'

'I can't believe you did that,' I kiss him on the cheek.

'Of course! I didn't want to let you go!'

'You're casually missing a pretty dramatic part out,' Sarah interrupts, then turns to me. 'Heather ran into the car park after him, stopped him from getting in the cab, and started screaming, like, bloody murder.'

'That's when it all came out,' Dom says, now holding my hand. 'About her and Matt, how she'd worked so hard on me, and now she wasn't going to get any money.'

Hugo leans forward excitedly and takes over the story, 'The bride came over, closely followed by the entire wedding party, and she asked Heather to leave.'

Sarah's turn to take over, 'That totally got Heather more hysterical, and anyway, when she wouldn't lower her voice, Heather swung for Savannah; apparently she'd forgotten the bride is a blackbelt in taekwondo though, and I guess instinct kicked in; Savannah ducked, and then threw Heather onto the floor, like: *kaboom*!' She demonstrates with her arms, 'It was bloody marvellous.'

'So, after I'd checked she was OK,' Dom took over again.

'Ever the gentleman,' Hugo interjects, and Dom nods, appreciatively.

'And when I realised she wasn't hurt, just unhinged, I flew into a cab, but it was too late. By the time I got to the airport, I couldn't see you, you wouldn't answer your phone, and they said all the seats were taken on the last flight out of LAX. The next available flight was at ten fifty-five the next night, so I booked it, went back to the hotel, grabbed my stuff, got a cab to my place, repacked, met these two,' he glanced up at Sarah and Hugo, 'and here we are.'

I take his hands and kiss him, for what is probably the millionth time. 'I'm so glad you watched all those movies with your sisters.'

'Me too.' He smiles at me, then we hear his phone buzz on the table. He picks it up and reads a message. I watch as his eyes widen.

'What? Who is it?'

'It's my dad,' he says slowly, still looking at the screen. 'He said he had a talk with my mum.'

'OK,' I smile, encouraging him to continue.

'He's sorry and says that the money's mine whenever I want it. He hopes it can help to build my career.' Dom stares at his phone with disbelief, 'And he said to thank…' he looks up at me, '...you.' He looks at me, and shakes his head, 'I don't understand.'

'Well, I might have said something to your mum,' I say tentatively. 'I was leaving, and I wanted to encourage them to think about supporting you in something that you're actually passionate about, instead of punishing you for living your own dream, and depriving you of what's rightfully yours.'

He shakes his head once more, 'I don't know what to say. You really are a woman full of surprises.' The sound of someone clinking a glass three times, pauses our conversation.

'Ladies and gentleman,' Janice slurs, leaning slightly to the left at her position at the head of the table. 'If I could direct your attention this way, please?' She's managed to find a balance between clearly drunk, but still professional.

The room hushes.

'Here at *Wonder,* this has been — honestly — a bit of a shitshow of a year.' I join a few others and giggle at her choice of words. 'But, this latest crossover piece with *Blush* has enabled us to fully merge under the Von Helm umbrella, and has well and truly saved us. And that's all thanks to our very own, wonderful Liv.' I nod and smile bashfully. 'I'm so pleased that the whole team from *Blush* who worked on this piece could join us this evening to celebrate. Would you mind standing please, all of you?'

The four of us stand up, a sense of pride visibly washing over each of us, as the whole room gives us a round of applause.

'And now, if you could all keep the applause going for the woman who's made this evening and the future of the magazine possible: Chrissy Von Helm.'

***

It turns out frivolity was on the menu. The DJ started up shortly after Chrissy's speech and she's been standing at the bar, talking to Sarah and Hugo ever since. Sarah runs over to me, 'You're not going to believe this. She's going to be standing in, as editor in chief for *Blush,* until someone more suitable comes along. Isn't that insane? I get to work with her?!' Sarah is giddy. 'Oh, hi honey!' Sarah turns to Hugo who's just joined us.

'Honey?' I enquire.

'Yes. I'm honey,' Hugo grins from ear to ear.

'So, tell me more about Chrissy,' I look back at Sarah,

who's still smiling.

'She's got a ridiculous amount of contacts and said she wants me and Hugo to continue working for *Blush,* but also, as many other of her magazines as possible. And, not only that, she's got connections with celebrities, so, you never know, soon I might be working at red carpet events!'

'I'm so happy for you guys!' I give them both a squeeze.

'She also said that she wants to talk to you and Dom,' Hugo gestures to Chrissy.

I look up at Dom, make an excited face, and together, hand in hand, we walk across the room to meet her.

Chrissy is thin, sophisticated, and completely ageless; her Wikipedia page says she's seventy, but her face could pass for forty. She looks up at us both and smiles. 'That was quite the entrance, young man.' She then turns to me, 'Perhaps you could edit the end of your article?' She waves an effortless hand at me.

'Oh! Really?'

'Absolutely! Our readers want to not only read about existing love, but new love, and finding it in the most unexpected of places. But that's not really why I asked you over here. After you've finished your final edit,' she aims at me, 'I'd like to offer you something.'

'OK,' I say, ever so tentatively. Based on what Sarah said, I almost hold my breath; *what could it be?*

'It's actually for both of you,' she looks from me to Dom.

'Oh, thank you so much,' Dom says graciously, 'but I no longer work for your company, so I couldn't—'

'I know that,' she cuts him off straight-faced, as if that's an insignificant detail in her plan. 'I do *do* my research, and I know that, as good as your photos of people and wedding accessories are, that's not where you shine. Your website does need a little work, but, in spite of that, your talent for wildlife photography, in particular, shines through. So, I'd like to introduce you to Nick; he works for *National Geographic*.'

Dom's jaw hits the floor. 'Oh! Nick Kallo!' He shakes this man's hand so aggressively; it looks as though it might fall off. 'Pleasure, absolute pleasure! I just loved your photos from the tiger expedition, from January last year; stunning work! And the pandas from the latest issue? Sublime. Oh, and the—'

'Thank you,' Nick cuts him off, smiling, and takes the compliments graciously.

'Now,' Chrissy brings our attention back to her. 'As I said, I've been doing my homework. I've been following your writing for a while too, Liv; you have a real talent for storytelling, reading between the lines, and taking your audience with you on your journey.'

'Which is exactly what we're looking for,' Nick says. 'Our head expedition writer has just found out she's pregnant, so we've been looking for a fresh, new voice, and after reading everything you've written, thanks to Chrissy here; I'm excited.' I notice for the first time that he's holding the brown envelope that I came in with.

'And combining that with your pictures, Dom, I think we could really have something spectacular, for both *Wonder* magazine and *National Geographic*.'

'For both? What is the job exactly?' My heart is in my throat.

Nick smiles excitedly, 'We're going on a year-long environmental, marine and wildlife expedition, cruising down the west coast of America from Alaska, picking up on a coastal road trip from Mexico, down the Pan-American

Highway, then from Chile, catching our final vessel to venture around the Chilean Fjords, and finishing in Antarctica, then of course, returning to Argentina, to fly everybody back to their homes. We'd like you to join the research team, vessels, and convoy, as one of our team of photographers,' he nods at Dom before turning to me, 'and you, Liv, as head writer, to tell our story.'

I'm speechless, so Chrissy takes over, looking at me. 'Your main job of course, would be as their writer for the *National Geographic* feature, but, at the same time, for *Wonder,* I'd like a column about your journey; more of a diary, blog, if you will.'

'We'll also be wanting to release our feature monthly,' Nick says, 'and, I know what you're thinking, when we're not on land, although sporadic, Wi-Fi is available on all vessels, and there are satellite phones for emergencies, so it's absolutely possible to send your work in for editorial approval.' Both Dom and I stand there, our mouths hanging open in stunned silence. 'Obviously, there's a lot more to be confirmed, but are you interested?' Nick asks, since neither of us have said anything.

I look wide-eyed at Dom and he looks at me as if the world has just given us the greatest gift ever.

'Yes! Absolutely!'

'Yes! Thank you so much,' we both speak at once, then burst out laughing.

'Perfect. I'll be in touch with details, we leave at the end of May; will that give you enough time to get everything in order?' Nick enquires.

'I would leave tomorrow if need be,' Dom replies, immediately this time.

'Fantastic, well. Lovely to meet you both; look forward to

working with you,' Nick shakes our hands.

'Now, go and celebrate.' Chrissy walks off arm in arm with Nick, leaving Dom and I screaming and bouncing up and down.

'*National Geographic*? Are you kidding me?' Dom yells at me.

'This is insane! You'll get to take pictures of seals, whales, and walruses!'

'And Narwhals!' he shouts and I can't help but laugh.

'Polar bears?' I question.

'Hopefully in Alaska!'

'And God knows what other wildlife along the way!'

'And you'll be by my side, writing the whole journey.' He scoops me up in his arms and kisses me again.

'This calls for champagne!' I say, when I come up for air, waving the bartender over.

Just like he did on the pier in Hermosa, Dom effortlessly takes me in his arms and starts dancing. 'Oh, it's our song!' he exclaims.

'We have a song?' I say, laughing, as he spins me around, then pulls me close again.

'We do now.' Sarah Bareilles' 'Brave' is playing.

'I would have thought our song was "City of Stars," since we danced on the *La La Land* bridge, and you sang that to me.'

He shakes his head, 'No, too melancholy.' He thinks for a moment, 'But there is a line from the film that definitely sums us up.'

'And what's that?' I smile and gaze back up at him.

'"Here's to the fools who dream."' He kisses me once more, then pulls gently away, 'So, from one dreaming fool to another: will you join me?' he asks softly.

'Join you, where?'
'Everywhere the world dares to take us.'

Epilogue

Thirteen months later

Antarctica – Argentina – Chile – USA
Ushuaia – Buenos Aires – Santiago – Los Angeles

Wednesday
Vessel docks Muelle Puerto de Ushuaia at 17.00
Drive 10 minutes (cab) to hotel (1 night stay)

Thursday
Depart Ushuaia Malvinas Argentinas International Airport at 10.35
Arrive Buenos Aires Ministro Pistarini Airport at 14.05
Duration: 3 hours and 30 minutes (1-hour 50-minute layover)

Depart Buenos Aires Ministro Pistarini at 15.55
Arrive Santiago Airport at 17.15
Duration: 1 hour 20 minutes (6-hour 30-minute layover)
Depart Santiago Airport at 23.45

Friday
Arrive Los Angeles International Airport at 08.15
Duration 6 hours and 56 minutes
Time difference: Los Angeles 3 hours behind

The sand caresses my toes and I watch as the waves hypnotically build and crash in front of me. The sun feels warm and comforting on my face, as I close my eyes and tilt my head towards the sky. I listen to the soundtrack of the ocean, and breathe in the fresh, salty air. *This is bliss.* Gratitude fills every inch of my body. And suddenly I hear you call my name. *I hear you, where are you?*

'Hello?' Feeling a gentle tap on my arm, I stir and drift into consciousness. 'Hey, Brave?'

I smile and lift my eye mask, opening my eyes to see Dom smiling back at me. 'Yes, Flynn Rider?' I reply, lovingly, taking off my noise cancelling headphones.

'We're nearly home,' he says softly, brushing a strand of my hair away. Shifting in my seat, I wiggle back into his warm arms, as he kisses my forehead.

'No,' I smile.

'No?' he laughs.

'No,' I repeat and shrug happily. 'We're already home. Home is wherever we make it; it's wherever I am with you.'

Dom holds me tighter and kisses me on the forehead once more, as we land and begin our next adventure.

Acknowledgements

A huge thank you, first and foremost, to you, beautiful person, for buying this book; you have truly made my day.

I remember reading a Miranda Dickinson novel that in her acknowledgements said something like, "Dreams really do come true; you're holding one in your hands right now." That sentence made me want to create something for myself, and helped me believe that that was possible, so, thank you, Miranda Dickinson.

I owe so much to my editors; fact and language checkers; and overall cheerleaders: Helen Foley, Emma Webb, Ann Jones, Mina Chivite, Khrish Preston, Suzie Bird and Sarah Chanchai.

Next, a big cwtch to my Rockies. Thank you for your support, love, and kind words; I hope to see this book on the big screen too.

To the Canadians, thank you for the summer; it meant more than you know.

And lastly, to my James. To paraphrase Nancy Meyers: "You are the man I always write." Thank you for being my person. I love you.

Victoria Mae was born in London and moved to the beautiful Welsh Valleys for love. When she's not writing she's a musician, world traveller, and mindfulness enthusiast. She loves country music, salsa dancing, and espresso martinis - not necessarily in that order. Victoria is the author of two Chick-Lit novels: Behind The Clouds and Between The Lines.

Victoria Mae loves hearing from her readers, and you can follow her on:

Facebook and Instagram: @victoriamaeauthor
Twitter: @VictoriaMAuthor

Also available from Victoria Mae

Behind The Clouds

The lost love; the best friend; the blast from the past; the perfect man.

Teacher, baker, and romantic dreamer Melanie Butler is about to receive the icing on the cake of her life: her long term boyfriend Evan is finally ready to propose...only thing is, it's to another woman.

Publicly humiliated and broken-hearted, Melanie's slightly unhinged sisters and eclectic group of friends help her find her feet as a newly-found singleton - from a spot of mountain-range meditation to a surprise flight.

Grateful to have best friend Dave encouraging her to move on with her life, she starts dating the handsome and perfect fireman Julian. But when childhood nemesis Craig re-surfaces a little too close to home, his obnoxious words begin to reflect thoughts she's been trying to bury.

And when tragedy strikes, Melanie takes on a huge challenge, beginning to see not only what, but who is important in her life.

Can love defeat betrayals, and can you truly find happiness Behind The Clouds?

Printed in Great Britain
by Amazon

19984466R00274